Praise for Donald James Lawn's
The Memoirs of John F. Kennedy: A Novel

"With a bullet turned non-fatal, suddenly America becomes a different place. Told in the style of memoirs, Donald James Lawn explores how ...America would be a different place had Kennedy remained at the helm. *The Memoirs of John F. Kennedy* is a fascinating and original work, very highly recommended."

—*Midwest Book Review*

"What if the real story, as told by Walter Cronkite, Dan Rather, and other talking heads of the day, was not that John F. Kennedy perished in the November 22, 1963 assassination attempt but instead survived? Imagine a modern American history written from that alternative outcome. If you can't get enough of the Kennedys (Robert plays a prominent role), if you like a good read that gets your 'what if?' juices roiling, this is the book for you!"

—Norm Stamper (former Seattle Police Chief)
Author of *Breaking Rank*

"If you have ever pondered the question about what direction the country would have taken if Kennedy had remained president ...then you will find Lawn's work to be highly interesting. ...It is entirely plausible that most of the events and conversations in the book could have taken place. I appreciated this intellectual work and found it to be a thought-provoking novel. ...I recommend *The Memoirs of John F. Kennedy* to history buffs, Kennedy enthusiasts, and anyone who just wants to take a look at an alternate version of history and ponder 'what if?'"

— Kam Aures, *Rebecca's Reads*

First Place Winner
The Written Arts Awards
General Fiction, 2010/2011

Finalist
International Book Awards
General Fiction, 2011

Bronze Award
Independent Publisher Book Awards
Popular Fiction, 2011

Disclaimer

The Memoirs of John F. Kennedy: A Novel is a work of fiction. It is liberally inhabited with real historical figures whose actions and activities in this creative work originate purely in the imagination of the author. The resemblance to real historical figures is intentional by the author to add realism to the historical context of the story and the mythology surrounding the killing of President Kennedy. History took a far more sinister turn November 22, 1963, than the events portrayed in this book, and the reality of that period and the real actions of its participants, is not reflected in this alternate historical narrative.

Castlefin
Press

Castlefin Press
PO Box 46205
Seattle, WA 98146

Copyright © 2010 by Donald James Lawn
www.memoirsofjfk.com

First edition November 2010.
Second edition November 2011.

Cover design by Kate Thompson
Cover illustration ©1963 Bernard Fuchs
Printed in the United States of America

The Library of Congress has cataloged the softcover edition as follows:
Lawn, Donald James
The Memoirs of John F. Kennedy: A Novel
LCCN: 2010911551

ISBN 978-0-9829064-0-8 [Softcover]
ISBN 978-0-9829064-1-5 [eBook]

The Memoirs
of
John F. Kennedy

A NOVEL

BY DONALD JAMES LAWN

Castlefin Press
Seattle, WA

Driving down the wrong road and knowing it,
The fork years behind, how many have thought
To pull up on the shoulder and leave the car
Empty, strike out across the fields; and how many
Are still mazed among dock and thistle,
Seeking the road they should have taken?

—*Damon Knight, The Man in the Tree*

Prologue

The basic problems facing the world today are not susceptible to a military solution.
                                                                    —*John F. Kennedy*

Richard Paul Pavlick had been relentlessly pursuing his quarry: at a campaign stop in San Diego; then at a street speech in St. Louis; on a tour of the rich man's compound in Hyannisport, Massachusetts, where he had passed within ten feet of his intended victim; and finally at a family gathering in Palm Beach, Florida. He had been stalking the papist pretender to the throne for months. The pretender's wealthy father had bought him the presidential nomination, and he had proceeded to wiggle past Mr. Nixon in the 1960 election by a mere handful of votes that were surely purchased. No one remained to stop him; everyone had given in, but Pavlick was no quitter.

With the engine of his 1950 Buick idling, he watched from only a block and a half away as the president-elect emerged from the stucco-walled gate of his father's Mediterranean-style waterfront home and climbed into the back seat of a waiting limousine. Observing only a few Secret Service agents about, Pavlick shifted into first, releasing the clutch as he slowly eased onto Ocean Boulevard. The moment had finally come. He'd sent postcards back to his doubters in Belmont over the previous months, cryptically informing them of his upcoming fame. His right hand went to the small switch lying on the seat beside him. It had not been difficult to obtain the dynamite now boxed in his trunk. He had carefully packed it along, all these months on the road from his abandoned home in New Hampshire. It would finally be put to good use. From what he'd seen in the quarries of his rocky state, he knew he had sufficient explosive power to destroy anything within fifty feet. Pulling away from the curb, he kept a close watch on the line of vehicles along the side of the road in front of him. How fitting. The man, a Catholic, was going to Sunday morning Mass. He would die in a smoldering crater right in front of his rich father's home. His money and religion would be of no use to him now.

Pavlick was half a block away when he saw her. Mrs. Kennedy, holding the hand of their little girl and carrying their little boy in her arm, had emerged from the gate and was being helped toward the limousine. Damn it! He wanted the man, not the wife and children. He was a patriot, not a murderer. Grappling with his conflicting emotions, he loosened his grip on the tiny switch he had been fingering and drifted ineffectually past the line of parked cars. Looking over briefly, he saw the wife smiling at her husband, who was already in the back seat. She didn't even look up. He had saved her life, and she hadn't even glanced at him to acknowledge her good fortune.

* * *

The presence of Kennedy's wife and children touched a sympathetic chord in the cold heart of a man who would have killed the president-elect on the morning of December 11, 1960, six weeks before he was to have assumed the presidency of the United States. Mr. Pavlick was captured only four days later cruising the byways of Palm Beach, looking for a second chance. His momentary reluctance to flick a small switch altered history.

But the president did not escape that fate on November 22, 1963. There were a thousand choices, large and small, that culminated in the events of that dreadful day—whereas but a few tiny differences might have directed history onto an entirely different path.

What if President John F. Kennedy had survived his fated rendezvous in Dallas?

Chapter 1

I have here in my hand a list of 205...a list of names that were known
to the Secretary of State as being members of the Communist Party and who nevertheless are still working and shaping the policy of the State Department.
—*Joseph McCarthy*

A lie can travel halfway around the world while the truth is putting on its shoes.
—*Mark Twain*

Tuesday, Sept. 3, 1968
Washington, D.C.

Patrick woke with the immediate feeling he had overslept. A glance toward the clock on the nightstand confirmed his suspicion. It was already
8:30 a.m. His gaze first lingered on the clock face, then drifted to the telephone base beside it, and then followed the coiled cord down. Leaning
over the edge of the bed, he saw the handset silently resting on the carpet.
It must have been there a while, as the annoying chirping, intended to
indicate an off-hook condition, had stopped. He stared hard at it for a moment, willing it to reveal its reason for being down there, but it remained
silent—its accusation was its location. Lying back on his pillow, he had a
vague recollection of a half-conscious conversation in which he'd embarrassed himself to the caller's delight, babbling something incoherent from
an interrupted dream. Had it been Devona? Or had he just dreamt it all
and knocked the phone off the nightstand in his drowsy flailings?

He had always been a morning person, enjoying the quality of the early
light and quiet. It just felt right to get up with the sun, to get a sense of
being in rhythm with the day. But last night he'd not gotten to bed until
almost two o'clock due to another late night "driveabout" with his Uncle
Duncan. He got up, replaced the receiver in its cradle, and quickly show-
ered. While drying off, he sneaked out to grab the newspaper delivered to
the apartment stoop. He could usually do this without being observed,
although once last month, with a towel wrapped around his waist and hair
dripping, he was caught by Mrs. Langthorpe from the apartment below
as she walked by. She had surely gotten an eyeful. Patrick wanted to think

she enjoyed the view, although that was not reflected in her scowling gaze. Today the coast was clear.

Patrick could spend a large portion of a morning dawdling over the paper. He loved to read the *Washington Post* over breakfast, front page to back. It was a pleasure of which he never tired. He wondered at times why it was so engrossing to read about the world's turmoil. He was a reporter at the *Post*, had been for almost eight years, and liked to think professional curiosity kept him so engaged. But really, at heart, it was a desire for gossip. Who was doing what to whom, and why? A never-ending novel giving an overview of the human condition, although you would have to be able to read between the lines to get the real truth of nearly any matter.

The Republican National Convention, held in Miami one month earlier, had selected Richard Nixon as the party's presidential candidate. During his acceptance speech, Nixon claimed he was "a new man with a new vision," attributing his change to the revelations surrounding the sedition tribulations of the '64 and '65 Trials. Scientists say that the entire cellular structure of the human body is regenerated about every seven years. With no remaining cells from the previous period, we have an entirely new body. So, biologically speaking, Nixon was almost 4/7ths correct, since it had been about four years since the Trials had begun. Even if he had waited three more years to be fully regenerated cellularly, Patrick thought it was improbable that there was anything remotely fresh regarding Nixon's political ambition, and that he simply wanted the power and prestige of elected office and would do or say anything necessary to acquire it. In that sense, he was still very much the old Nixon, just dragging around a few trillion newer cells that were quickly being schooled in his habitual ways.

Alabama's Governor George Wallace and his running mate, former Air Force General Curtis LeMay, were running on the American Independent Party ticket and were often referred to as the "Bombsey Twins." Wallace, knee-deep in the slime of racial hatred, was predicting an ethnic uprising to purify the white population, while his running mate openly hinted at the nuclear option as a quick inducement for a recalcitrant North Vietnam. Their followers who opposed integration of Negroes into the American mainstream were outraged at the advances in the civil rights arena and the continuing popularity and effectiveness of Martin Luther King, Jr. Wallace didn't really have any chance of winning but hoped to garner enough electoral votes to split the ticket so thoroughly as to require the election to be thrown to the U.S. Congress to decide. In such a situation, he hoped to play kingmaker and salvage some vestige of white supremacy for the South.

There was the usual mudslinging and bickering between presidential candidates. Nixon accused Lyndon Johnson of unpatriotic weakness against communism, a theme he had zealously pounded away at for months in hopes of dislodging some of Lyndon's poll advantage. It was a classically American way of undermining your opponents—accuse them of being feeble in the face of a presumed external threat. Of course, it was always a guilty pleasure to read almost any quote by Nixon's running mate, Spiro Agnew. Today in Michigan, while deriding the current Kennedy administration and the liberal press, he lamented that "those effete, intellectual ergots of errorism have eviscerated the moral vitality of America." This alliterative tirade was prompted by JFK's initiation of drawn-out negotiations with Vietnam, years in their unfolding, that avoided a war against the communists in the North—as if, after the lessons of Korea, there was some grand benefit to be derived from another Asian war. Robert Kennedy, Johnson's vice presidential running mate, had laughingly responded, "Agnew Alliterates, Alienates America." This was turning into a side campaign of malapropism and literary inanity, not politics. *The New York Times*, referring to the previous months' loose usage of word and verse in competing barrages from both sides, pegged it the "doggerel days of summer."

Even with the heated political rhetoric, there didn't seem to be much of an election here. Johnson and Kennedy were comfortable. Their confidence was evident in the tone of their campaign, the unfeigned pleasure in their press-photo smiles, and most of all, in the healthy outlook of the country. Wallace had a small but intense following and was carrying the far-right Southern conservatives, depriving Nixon of the demographic clique he needed to make a serious challenge. He couldn't out-racist Wallace, so he was boxed within a narrow territory of issues that had lost emotional purchase with the voting public. Nixon wore a tangible air of desperation. He had run for president against JFK in '60 and lost. He had run for governor of California in '62, losing again and claiming to the press, "You won't have Nixon to kick around anymore because, gentlemen, this is my last press conference." It was now six years and innumerable press conferences later. He knew that if he didn't hit a homer this time he wouldn't be up to bat again, and Agnew, his running mate, was about as much help as Barney Fife.

Patrick wondered whether God read the paper. That presumed a caricature of divinity with a human figure—a bearded old man in a white robe, sitting on a wafting white cloud with a big mug of coffee in one hand and, of course, the *Washington Post* in the other. Would he be chuckling, roiling, or weeping at the human condition? Or maybe he was just an indifferent observer, like an out-of-towner reading about a local sports team in a city he was passing through. Patrick knew the framing of the question was wrongheaded. God most surely was something else entirely.

* * *

Thinking of all-knowing figures, he remembered again the vague impression of an early morning phone call. Devona? The receiver was on the floor when he woke up. He must have used it. He would give her a call and pretend to be checking with her about his current manuscript. Patrick dialed her number from memory.

Devona had been Patrick's editor for almost six years. He had just turned twenty-eight when he had vainly tried to publish his first book, *Acquainted with the Night*. It had begun as a bombastic diatribe aimed at exposing the foulness of Senator Joseph McCarthy and the House Un-American Activities Committee (HUAC). It detailed the damages done to twelve victims of the HUAC's witch hunts, his Uncle Duncan among them. As a journalist, he should have known rage was neither a palatable nor an effective way of getting his point across. He mailed the manuscript off to over seventy agents and print houses and was turned down again and again. With the still-strong current of anticommunist feeling in the country, the inflammatory nature of Patrick's manuscript discouraged interest in most quarters. He had a full desk drawer devoted solely to letters of rejection.

One evening years ago, in the midst of depression over his failure, Patrick decided to widen his perspective, to follow the path of the great writers, at least those personified as the classical hard-living types who plunged periodically into the darker realms of consciousness. It was a tool, it seemed, that enabled them to extract the pithy, real-life experiences necessary for their craft. He decided to resort to drink. Unfortunately, he had a delicate gastronomic constitution. So, taking a fateful stab at attaining his new perspective, he downed a few shots from an unopened bottle of Jameson his uncle had given him with great fanfare two years earlier. The bottle sat biding its time in the upper kitchen cabinet behind the pancake mix, hardly attracting any attention at all until Patrick deemed its medicinal and mind-altering properties essential to purge him of his publishing failure. After a quick third shot, Patrick's stomach erupted as his throat constricted in protest. A substantial portion of the blistering liquid sprayed from his nose, burning the fine nasal linings with twelve-year-old 80 proof. It felt like he was snorting turpentine, and after that excruciating evening, his singed sinuses smoldered for a week. He was an inept inebriate, a shame to his Irish ancestors, and obviously a failure at failing in the time-honored manner of the hard-living writers. At least he hadn't been standing near the gas stovetop during the event, showing, he reminded himself, there is room for gratitude even in the most humbling of circumstances.

On a dreary winter day, after more months of dismissals and long after his sinuses had healed, he was surprised to find a letter from Brown and Martin in his mailbox. It arrived in a standard white envelope with his address typewritten. There was a printed company logo for the return. He prepared himself for another terse rejection, though this one appeared to be a couple of pages long. *Someone's really going to lay into me,* he thought. He scanned the page quickly for the "We are sorry to inform you..." sentence, but it wasn't there. His manuscript had been read in its entirety and was thought to have "serious potential" as a crossover political documentary and human-interest story.

The letter went on to say the presentation needed work, as it was too caustic to read. It was articulate, but lacked the restraint necessary to reach a wider audience, and "might have been effective as a personal, psychological release, but was ineffective as a piece of literature." The letter then expressed the potential for a better piece of work to be developed from this starting point, stating that "Detached and heartfelt observation is more powerful than vituperation." It was signed "Mrs. D. Williams, Assistant Editor, Brown and Martin Publishing."

He was stunned at the somewhat positive response and wondered if this Mrs. D. wasn't just a sub-editor in the basement Office of Lost Causes at Brown and Martin. *Vituperation?* He balled up the letter and threw it in the trash, then retrieved and reread it. His reaction persisted in varying forms for a few days, until his internal arguments wore down and Patrick grudgingly accepted that the mysterious Mrs. Williams might have a point. One evening he began rereading his work, and for the next three days revisited what he had spent three years of his life creating. Nine months had passed since he had read it, and the passage of time had given him a measure of distance.

"Brown and Martin Publishing," answered the receptionist.
"Devona Williams, please." He waited while he was connected.

During the 1950s, the Red Scare had run like a political conflagra-
tion across America, burning up personal liberties in a quest to purge the
populace of an ephemeral but sinister threat. Senator McCarthy and his
committee leaked accusations of communist sympathies through accom-
modating newspapers to smear political opponents and public figures. Mc-
Carthy made outrageous claims, supported by the flimsiest of conjectured
evidence, without fear of retribution. As a member of Congress, he was
afforded complete legal immunity from slander and libel while speaking
on the record. An accused individual had no recourse other than to fight
the charge in the court of public opinion. Of course, it required further
media attention to report their innocence, but dramatic accusations of
guilt made bolder headlines than long, drawn-out hearings showing such
charges to be false. Most of the accused never received the satisfaction of
having their names publicly cleared, even though they often unequivocally
proved their innocence. And for all their furious hysteria, the McCarthy
hearings never found or convicted any communists. Not one.

To write his book, Patrick had spent years tracking twelve individuals accused in one form or another of being communist sympathizers and
thus un-American. He included his Uncle Duncan among the twelve, as
he was the original, painful inspiration for Patrick's book. Duncan, like
Patrick's father Brandon, had returned from the war in 1945 to a changed
America. Brandon had served in the U.S. Army Air Force in England as
the pilot of a lumbering B-24 bomber, making hair-raising runs over the
German mainland. After his plane was shot down, he spent a year in a German prisoner of war camp before being liberated by Allied ground forces.
Duncan served in the Pacific theater in the U.S. Navy on a tender boat to
Admiral Halsey's carrier group. Both brothers had returned whole, which
was more than could be said of many of their friends.

Brandon obtained his Engineering degree on the GI Bill, while Duncan started a furniture business and gravitated toward small town politics,
aided greatly by his effervescent personality. He was elected town council-
man. Patrick's father was a realist in his view of the world, whereas Uncle
Duncan harbored an idealism undaunted by the ravages of his wartime
experience. He dabbled in all sorts of political explorations, including at-

tending a few American Communist Party meetings, which included a subscription to the *Daily Worker*, its newspaper. And that's where the Mc-Carthy forces pounced.

Duncan Hennessey, since he had a bit of standing in the community, received a heightened degree of scrutiny from the FBI. Had he simply caved in to their demands for names of other attendees, he would have been humbled but not eviscerated. Instead, he stood his ground and refused to cooperate. He could not, in good conscience, fink on friends and neighbors to avoid being steamrollered by McCarthyism. He felt his political interests revealed his curious nature but posed no harm. Besides, he was a returning veteran and thought it obvious he held no sympathies with anti-American activities. But because of his resistance, the FBI leaned on him harder.

Patrick was a teenager at the time and remembered federal agents' visits to their homes, both Duncan's and his own. They interviewed Duncan's family, friends, and furniture store workers. Agents would park their cars in front of the store, intercepting patrons, flashing their badges and asking pointed questions about Duncan's "suspicious" activities. Skating on the edge of the law, these actions cast a malevolent pall meant to grind his uncle down to do their bidding.

Uncle Duncan and Aunt Mary came often to Sunday dinner at Brandon's home in Freehold, New Jersey. Patrick would always listen in on his parents' conversations to get clues to what adult life was about. He found growing up worrisome.

"I'd be glad to turn any commies over to those McCarthy thugs, if only I knew one," said his uncle in his usual self-deprecating Irish brogue. "Maybe I could sic the shinies on me neighbor, George Swindon. He may not be a commie, but he surely deserves a go-round with those boys." Uncle Duncan called FBI agents "shinies" because of their mirror-buffed black shoes. "I could tell them he's a Red. Then he'd have no time for piling all that garbage against me fence in the back. He'd be over with that once and for all, he would."

"I can certainly see the benefits of such a wise move, Duncan," replied his brother Brandon. "Two birds with one stone and all. The feds would be off your back, and George would be on his." Brandon would encourage Duncan, listing the benefits of such a scheme, then give a solemn sideways wink to young Patrick, knowing full well his brother would do nothing of the sort.

But for all the composure in the men's hearts, the pressure took its toll. Duncan's business faltered, then folded. He was not re-elected council-man, and still the FBI persisted in their harassment.

And then Duncan and Mary disappeared.

Patrick's parents were mum but showed little worry. Two months later, the first of many letters arrived, with a postcard bearing a poem inserted inside.

> The seas, sweet Jesus, were frightening
> The soft hills are, Lord, so inviting
> But the kin you've not seen
> Has found solace in 'tween
> So please excuse the enigmatic writing.

Mary had kept in touch with their Irish cousins, and at the height of their McCarthy tribulations she and Duncan escaped to family on the outskirts of Limerick, resulting in the embedded hint and poetic license he took with his first communications. Duncan used to refer to his home-land as "'tween"—the land in between heaven and earth—having more than ample portions of both the beauty and the misery. The first letter was postmarked from Paris, showing that Duncan had gone to great lengths to obscure its origin. However, even if the shinies had been opening and reading his mail, as it was rumored they did on a regular basis, the discov-ery of Duncan's location would have made little difference. They weren't about to chase him to the Emerald Isle. More poems, and then letters, ar-rived over the years, easing the family's worries. Brandon had given Patrick his uncle's original poetic post. The card was framed and was now hanging on his living room wall.

During their time away, the televised Army hearings defanged McCa-rthy and the more ardent national zeal toward anti-communism. A little over five years after their departure, Duncan and Mary moved back to the same New Jersey town and slowly reintegrated themselves into its social fabric. Patrick was attending college in DC at the time and got reacquaint-ed with Duncan by evening drives through the countryside. These became a regular staple of their relationship, and seemed to start later and later as Duncan aged. They would get together in this manner every few months, on the spur of the moment. That's where Patrick had been the previous night. His uncle had called earlier in the day.

"I'd be wondering if my nephew has a bit of time for just a short driveabout in the Dublin Express?"

Patrick could never refuse him, so off they had gone prowling the country roads of Northern Virginia in Duncan's old green Buick till two in the morning. As usual he had a mug of coffee and some sandwiches when he arrived, and they drove for hours. The road map of their conversation was far more prone to zigs and zags than their actual driving: Ireland and how Duncan had spent his time there, the "youngster" generation and its music and dancing, the best car for touring, his Aunt Mary, what Patrick was doing and thinking, and of course politics involving those "Johnnies and Bobbies," as he called the Kennedys—as if there were a whole clan of them holding office.

"Excuse me, who are you holding for?" asked the voice on the line.
"Devona Williams," said Patrick.
"Just one more minute, please. She's not in her office."

Even though his uncle had returned to the United States without too much pain, Patrick's book, *Acquainted with the Night*, was not a happy read. Many lives were deeply damaged. In rereading his manuscript, it became painfully obvious to Patrick that Devona's comments had been accurate—these were the rantings of a man caught up in his own anger and selfishly inflicting it upon the reader. He had made a classic writer's mistake, even knowing at the time the nature of the pitfall and thinking that he had avoided it.

Patrick spent the next month rewriting the first section of the book, taking a more even tone. He sent off a copy of his revisions to Mrs. Williams at Brown and Martin with a cover letter thanking her for having read his submission and taken the time to respond so thoughtfully. He described some of the adjustments he was making and asked for feedback on the first rewritten chapter. Mrs. Williams wrote back within a few days praising his new form, saying she found it "enticingly sympathetic, without angry or maudlin leanings. Just the right balance." She shared a few other comments and ideas and encouraged him to follow through in the same vein with the rest of his subjects. Patrick became engrossed in his rewriting, and over the next six months he and Mrs. Williams carried on a lively conversation via phone and mail until the book's completion.

Acquainted with the Night was published by Brown and Martin in the spring of 1963, and received a positive response as well as brisk sales. It was encouragingly appraised in numerous national magazines and newspapers and even managed to receive a kindly review in *The New York Times'* political section as "a humane and unpretentious exposé of the brooding national excesses of McCarthyism." Of course not everyone agreed. Patrick also received angry letters accusing him of "coddling communists and their Godless ilk," and of being a traitor himself by bedding down in a nest of "scummy pinko Stalinists."

For Patrick it was a watershed. He'd felt impotent against such an overwhelming adversary as the U.S. government and its agents, and ashamed at having been unable to help defend his family and deflect the pain they had experienced. The writing of the book was an emotional catharsis. The public's reaction to his book was a vindication. He had struck back in his own way and was now free of the emotional load he'd carried for much of his early adult life. He was also aware of how much care and support he had received from Mrs. Williams through her intellectual clarity and ruthless editing.

"Devona Williams," came the distinctive voice over the handset. It was a voice whose precise inflections and unfailing grammatical correctness had always impressed and slightly intimidated Patrick.

"Devona, this is Patrick. And how are we today?" he asked, testing the waters. Over the years they had become good friends as well as business associates.

There was a silent moment. "We? Well I, for one, am awake. I am also lucid. Neither trait, I might add, was present on your end in our earlier conversation."

"Ohh. So...," he started, wondering how best to proceed, "did I say anything terribly embarrassing?"

"Nothing that would be useful for blackmail, unless incoherence is worthy of some small remuneration. You did refer, though, to airborne planks. Is there something you need to divulge to me?" She was obviously enjoying herself this morning. "You *really* shouldn't answer your phone in that manner. What if I were a reviewer and recording the conversation? I can see the headlines now—*Notable Author Speaks Gibberish - Previous Books Investigated as Ghost Written!* Maybe you should put that phone of yours in the other room. Or out in the hallway. Let your neighbors answer it. They could do a more workmanlike job than you did this morning."

"I don't know, that seems a bit selfish on my part. You know, denying others, such as yourself, so much entertainment. So why *did* you call this morning? If it's about those footnote additions for the election book, I sent those out last week. They should have arrived by now." He wanted to change the subject and get some distance from his earlier lapse.

"No, I received those already. This regards a different subject entirely. I received a call—from Mrs. Lincoln." She said the last as if it were a trophy she was presenting for approval.

"And how did *she* enjoy the play?" asked Patrick tentatively after a short pause. Did he know a Mrs. Lincoln?

"Oh, my my," responded Devona morosely. "*Evelyn* Lincoln?"

"Evelyn, as in *Kennedy*, Lincoln?"

"Evelyn, as in secretary to JFK, *personal* secretary to JFK, Lincoln," she paused. "You have heard of John F. Kennedy, haven't you?"

Patrick sat up straighter. "Sure, vaguely."

"Mrs. Lincoln called first thing this morning, at 8:00 a.m. sharp, as if she were waiting for me to sit down at my desk. So I called you right away—but of course *you* were asleep. That's not like you. You're such an early riser. Surely your budding fame is not causing you to degenerate into a listless hulk who sleeps till noon, abandoning still-undeveloped talents to beverage and fast women?"

"Undeveloped?" said Patrick chuckling. *Though I wouldn't mind some fast women,* he thought. Devona's thrashing was especially enthusiastic this morning. She was usually so circuitous he didn't realize he'd been humbled until after he'd hung up. But not today. "Besides, I was doing a little midnight rambling around the Virginia countryside."

"With that leprechaun uncle of yours?"

"Yes, himself it was."

"And what did we talk about this time?"

"Well, he is currently proposing mental health exams for anyone thinking of running for elected office. I believe he was referring, in particular, to Mr. Nixon. He seems to think there might be a fundamental deficiency there that could be exposed through psychological testing. He suggested the candidates be told a series of jokes—of which he told me quite a few. He wants to check to see if the 'smile on their lips goes all the way to their eyes.'"

"Hmm. I think that bill would never leave committee."

"True, true. So, did Mrs. Lincoln want you to edit her memoirs?" asked Patrick, getting back to Devona's message.

"No, she requested that you call her."

"Me? I've never even met her."

"So painfully obvious from your earlier comments."

Patrick knew that, had they been facing each other, Devona would be shaking her head sadly with an expression of exaggerated seriousness. "Did she at least say what the call was about?"

"She didn't. She said very little. She identified herself and then asked if I were the editor for Patrick Hennessey. I said yes, *unfortunately* I was. She then asked if I would convey a message to Mr. Hennessey, asking him to call her at her office. I said that I surely would. I asked if there was anything else she would like me to convey. She said, 'Yes, tell him to get to sleep earlier, put the phone in the other room, and, oh yes, have Mr. Hennessey call as soon as possible.' She gave me her number, thanked me and hung up. It lasted approximately a minute. I pondered calling the number to determine if it truly was *the* Evelyn Lincoln but thought better of it. It *is* a Massachusetts phone prefix, so that lends credibility."

"And she didn't say anything about why I am to call?"

"Nothing," said Devona. "Maybe she wants *you* to edit her memoirs."

He could almost see her smiling on the other end of the line. "I wonder if I might be getting invited to one of those Kennedy parties," mused Patrick. "Recognizing talent as they do, maybe they'd like me to make a short speech filled with pithy, ingenious literary devices. You know, where I shine."

"Maybe looking for a different Patrick Hennessey would be my thought. Probably called the wrong number."

Devona gave him the number. He promised to call her back with details.

Feeling unsettled by Mrs. Lincoln's request, Patrick wasn't prepared just yet to give her a call and instead sat back down to finish reading the *Post*. Scanning through to the end of the first section, he spotted an article about a train wreck in Ohio last night. Some confusion with the switching of parallel tracks on the outskirts of Cleveland along the Cuyahoga River resulted in a pair of double locomotives with a following of twenty-four freight cars jumping the rails and piling up like Tinkertoys along the riverside. Lumber and coal were scattered for almost a mile. From the accompanying photo, it appeared that a few of the cars were lodged in the backyards of nearby houses. Imagine waking up to the screeching crash of several hundred tons of train plowing through your patio in the middle of the night.

With that, the floodgates of Patrick's memory opened. Images of last night's dream crowded his mind. He was waiting on a railway platform for the arrival of a train. As it approached, he became aware of its gargantuan scale and realized it wouldn't fit into the station, yet it unrelentingly came ahead. Slowly docking, it destroyed the travel-worn planks on which he stood. Splintering timbers erupted every which way, sending Patrick running. But most memorable was the engineer. He was smartly dressed in suit and tie and watched unperturbed from the cab as the hulking locomotive deliberately demolished the entry to the archaic, undersized station. With an engineer's cap pushed back on his head, he looked up and gave Patrick a jaunty smile—and there was the shock. He bore an uncanny resemblance to the president, John Fitzgerald Kennedy.

The tiny hairs on the back of Patrick's neck seemed to climb up his scalp.

Chapter 2

In America any boy may become president
and I suppose it's just one of the risks he takes.
—*Adlai E. Stevenson Jr.*

The men who create power make an indispensable contribution to the
nation's greatness, but the men who question power make a contribution
just as indispensable, especially when the question is disinterested,
for they determine whether we use the power or the power uses us.
—*John F. Kennedy*

Tuesday, Sept. 3, 1968
Washington, D.C.

"Evelyn Lincoln."

"Hello, Mrs. Lincoln, this is Patrick Hennessey. I'm returning your call to my editor, Devona Williams at Brown and Martin." Patrick was sitting on the sofa in the living room of his Falls Church apartment. He had been eager yet apprehensive about returning Evelyn Lincoln's call. He'd sat wondering about it while staring out at the trees in his courtyard, their green leaves of summer quickly approaching an autumn transformation. He had started dialing the number once, but hung up. Was he nervous? Damn right he was. He was reminded of his difficult high school years and the torture of asking girls for dates. He had dialed again and waited for an answer. The number had a Massachusetts prefix, so he assumed Mrs. Lincoln was with the president at his home in Hyannisport. From what Patrick knew about her, she had been Kennedy's personal secretary since his time in Congress and had stayed with him over the years, traveling to conventions and summits both here and abroad.

"Oh yes, Mr. Hennessey. Thank you for returning my call." There was a slight rustling of paper on her end of the line. "I am contacting you at the request of the president. He'll be returning to Washington tomorrow and has asked that I get in touch with you to request an appointment. Would it be possible for you to meet him at the White House next Thursday morning at eleven o'clock? That would be the twelfth of September."

"With the president?" he asked, trying unsuccessfully to keep the surprise out of his voice.

"Yes, he asked to meet with you for a short discussion. It would probably take only a quarter of an hour."

"Well yes, yes, I can do that. Is this referring to anything specific?" Why would JFK want to meet with him? Visions of being dragged over the coals for having crossed some undefined boundary in his upcoming book came guiltily to mind. But how would JFK know about his second book? It wasn't released yet. It was no secret in the newspaper and publishing world that Kennedy would call an unsuspecting editor or author anytime, day or night, and pointedly commend or criticize an article or book he had come across. Patrick had heard a few such tales, one regarding fellow reporter Mark Waufust, who had angered the president with a piece slanted against the administration's policies. Patrick had overheard Waufust in the newsroom at the *Post* recounting the scolding, and his shock at receiving a personal call from Jack Kennedy at one o'clock in the morning. But, as Patrick understood it, the president usually made calls of that nature on his own, not with Mrs. Lincoln as an intermediary asking for an interview.

"He didn't tell me the reason for the request. He just asked me to set up a meeting. Now, you will need to follow a short procedure to get in. Will you be driving?"

"Uh, yes, from just outside Falls Church. I usually take Route 50 past Arlington and right on in."

"At the White House, come in the side entrance off Pennsylvania Avenue, at the corner of East Executive Avenue. Parking is ticklish, so you might want to walk to the gate."

Patrick thought for a moment. "The visitors' tour entrance? I should come in the East Entrance?"

"Yes, that is correct. You are already scheduled for a tour commencing at 10:30 a.m. You'll be with a group of students from Kansas City, Missouri, who are on a Washington field trip. The sergeant at arms will be prepared with your arrival information. Bring identification, and please arrive about a half hour early. Sometimes these groups can be a little disorganized."

Feeble-minded, more like, thought Patrick, remembering his high school tour of many years ago.

"Linger toward the back of the tour, and you will be further directed by a staff member." Evelyn Lincoln was meticulous even when instructing a visitor on sneaking in the back door of the White House. She had probably repeated similar clandestine directions to other visitors to the White House over the years. "Is that clear?"

"Yes, I'll be there."

"The president has asked that you keep this meeting private at this time. Also, could I have a direct contact number for you? As you might be aware, the president's schedule is hectic and unpredictable, and there may be a need for a last minute change. We don't expect this to happen, but we need some way to contact you, just in case."

"Certainly. My home number is ME3-3449. Or you may be able to contact me at the *Washington Post* during the day, at MD7-9900." *Keep it private?*

"Very good. The president thanks you and looks forward to seeing you on Thursday, September twelfth, at 11:00 a.m." The line went dead.

The president of the United States wanted to see him, Patrick Hennessey! Secretly! He had personally come in contact with JFK years ago, but never since, which left him very surprised at being contacted so long afterwards by the White House.

Thinking about it, he wondered if it might have something to do with permissions around the new book he had recently finished. Five years after the release of his first book, Patrick's second, *Returning to a New Home,* interwove coverage of the 1964 election with the darkly secretive nature of Hoover's FBI and its cover-up of the investigation into the presidential assassination attempt. They had occurred almost simultaneously.

At the time, JFK, still recovering from his wounds, was prone to make fewer personal appearances. His health, and the U.S. Marshals' beefed-up security, limited his ability to mingle with the electorate in his previous free-wheeling manner. Interviews with reporters and informal gatherings followed by the press had become the norm.

By any standard, though, it was a very unusual American electoral contest. Nine months after the shooting in Dallas, Kennedy was campaigning *with* Republican Senator Barry Goldwater. Both the president and his challenger traveled aboard Air Force One debating national issues at each stop. These debates during September and October, staged at ten cities across the country, became the election focal point. Each was scheduled for prime-time, mid-week viewing. Theirs was a refreshingly civilized method of competing—one that could only have happened in the curious period of American politics following the attempted assassination of the president. In earlier campaigns for congressman, senator, and then president, Kennedy's frenetic pace often ran his staff ragged. The U.S. Congressional Presidential Assassination and Sedition Investigation Commission (USCPASIC), or simply "the Trials," as they had come to be known, were unfolding in the background. They mesmerized the nation and rendered the election, which was a foregone conclusion anyway, an almost secondary event.

Because of the Dallas shooting and the emerging revelations of internal governmental involvement, JFK rose to a transcendent position in the national psyche—a condition that could not last in such a diverse and fractious country as America. This electoral shift was mostly in the moderate central portion of the populace. But since this was by far the largest group, political support for Kennedy was more than sufficient to eliminate any suspense as to his re-election. The American people wanted him to survive, and they wanted the country to emerge from the traumatic events with clear leadership.

Returning to a New Home interwove these dramatic events. But the permissions for this new book could easily be handled by a low-level staffer at the State Department and did not require intervention by Kennedy's personal secretary. They did not require direct contact with the president, nor a back-door entry to the White House. Patrick grew concerned. Did the president, somehow apprised of his upcoming work, have so strong a reaction that he wanted Patrick at the White House, in person, for a proper dressing down?

* * *

Patrick reflected on his first personal meeting with Kennedy. As a member of the press corps, Patrick had been following the presidential campaign through the western states in late July and early August of 1964. It was just before the Democratic National Convention was held in Madison Square Garden, and well in advance of the Goldwater/Kennedy debate schedule. Even with little need to campaign, the president still felt it imperative that a normal succession of power be respected and normal election procedures be followed. He wanted to be sure the nation, and the entire world for that matter, realized that even under such dramatic circumstances, the Constitution, the rule of law, and the familiar American electoral process would prevail.

During Patrick's attachment to JFK's press entourage, he would occasionally fly in the "Following Zoo," to which the press corps plane was indelicately but accurately referred. It flew in tandem with Air Force One from city to city. This shadow plane was chartered to allow reporters, writers, and overflow advisors to fly along with the president in the same airspace and at the same altitude, if not in the same plane. It transported reporters not permitted access to the small, rarified press section on Air Force One. Their corporate news sponsors were required to foot the bill for the flights, and the accountants fought as much over reimbursement tallies as the reporters fought over seating arrangements. Access to the twenty-four seats set aside for the press section on Air Force One were highly coveted and very difficult to obtain. But even Zoo flights were over-crowded, and reporters who did not attain—or maintain—pre-eminence on the hierarchical lists as the campaign progressed would be bumped.

At that time, Patrick, in comparison to the veteran political reporters from the major news outlets, was a nonentity. This was despite the fact that he had been working at the *Washington Post* for almost four years and had quickly risen in prominence due in large part to the success of his book on McCarthy. As a published author, he had newfound cachet at the *Post*, especially since he had written and published his book while he was a reporter there. He was recognized as an insightful writer and an up-and-coming player in the current generation of new professionals. This rec-ognition, however, had limited purchase in the specialized environment of political coverage, and he seldom made the cut to get aboard even the ⨍ Zoo. For that reason he found himself stranded at Seattle-Tacoma Air-port after the president's campaign stop in Seattle. He had missed the Zoo cut—again—and had also missed the day's last commercial flight from Seattle to Sacramento.

"There's no flight leaving tonight? How about one connecting through San Francisco or Redding? Even LA would do." Patrick had his overnight bag leaning against his leg while he pleaded with the reservationist. He was tired from the long day of taxis, speeches, and jostling, impersonal crowds. He just wanted to board a flight and settle into some quiet time with a beer and a view out a window. He felt his composure slipping away.

"I'm very sorry, sir," said the middle-aged woman behind the counter, with no apology intended and no vestige of enthusiasm, "but the United 8:15 a.m. flight tomorrow morning is the earliest connection. Of course, that is connecting through Denver, with a two-and-a-half-hour layover, and would arrive in Sacramento at 3:45 p.m. The only direct flight to Sac-ramento does not leave until 4:20 tomorrow afternoon."

"Nothing else?" he implored.

"Well, there is the Greyhound station, sir," she said, staring directly at him with her head tilted slightly to one side. Patrick already knew the Greyhound was an eighteen-hour overnight trip, not an appealing thought.

"Couldn't you bump someone? I mean, I've gotten bumped numerous times. I think it's my turn to get a break here."

"Most of the passengers on this flight are your fellow reporters. Surely you wouldn't want me to release one of their seats, would you?" she asked.

Patrick leaned in conspiratorially, grateful he had finally made a connection with the reservationist, "Really, I don't think they would mind that much. In fact, if you'd like to show me the roster I could make a suggestion." He would love to leave Piper Reston from the *Sacramento Bee* stranded in the lobby.

The woman leaned toward Patrick, "There is something I could do," she hinted.

"What's that?" responded Patrick hopefully.

Without taking her eyes off Patrick, she announced slowly in a loud voice, "Next please," looking pleasantly at Patrick during the "next" and then beyond him toward the waiting man in line during the "please."

Crestfallen, Patrick lingered at the counter. "Shoo," ordered the reservationist, smiling wanly as she flicked her fingernails toward the open aisle.

Patrick was desperate to be in Sacramento this evening so that he could get some rest at the hotel before the campaign chaos began again tomorrow. At this rate he wouldn't even get into town until *after* the Sacramento speech had started at 2:00 tomorrow afternoon, making it a hectic and pointless trip. If this was a relaxed version of Kennedy campaigning, he was glad to have missed the early years.

He was leaning against a counter, staring off across the terminal, contemplating a taxi to the Greyhound station, when he saw a familiar face— familiar to Patrick, but probably not so much the other way around. It was Pierre Salinger, the president's intense, jocular press secretary, who was immediately recognizable to anyone associated with the Kennedy White House. But here in the middle of the airport, the disheveled, overcoat-clad Salinger, carrying too many bags and folders, appeared more a confused Kansas City businessman than a political power broker. Patrick watched him for a moment, surprised to see him here and so perplexed. A close confidant of the president, Salinger always flew on Air Force One. What was he doing here? Their eyes met in a moment of recognition, and Patrick leaned off the counter and walked over with his bag to say hello. Salinger, watching his approach, spoke first.

"You're Hennessey. The McCarthy book guy, right?"

"Yeah, guilty, in person," replied Patrick, smiling a bit at being recognized. "Mr. Salinger," he nodded just to verify their introduction. "What are you doing here? One is over at Boeing Field."

At that, Pierre's face cleared of confusion but flashed in frustration. "Damn, why the hell didn't they tell me?" He looked around with exasperation, and paused. "Oh, maybe they did."

Patrick had heard about it in the press pool. Air Force One had flown into Seattle-Tacoma airport, but after the debarkation of all aboard, the Marshals Service had gotten jittery and moved the plane to Boeing Field. A semi-commercial airport, and one of the test locations for Boeing aircraft, it was only about three miles away. Moving the plane to the new location required Air Force One to take off and re-land after barely gaining a thousand feet in altitude. It was done as a precaution by the marshals, who were extremely protective regarding any perceived threat. No one said what the specific reasons were for the move, but then they rarely did. So Salinger found himself stranded at Seattle-Tacoma, while the president was at Boeing Field. And Patrick found himself stranded at Seattle-Tacoma while everyone else of importance was boarding the Zoo.

"So what are you doing here?" asked Salinger.

"I missed the last flight to Sacramento," sighed Patrick, glancing back at the counter he had just left. "Nothing till tomorrow afternoon. The Zoo's full. I was thinking of chartering my own jet and charging it to the *Post*. That would, of course, be my last act as a reporter."

Time was of the essence, yet Pierre looked at him intently for a moment, even though his thoughts seemed elsewhere. "Okay, let's go," he said, grabbing his bags. He wheeled around and headed out the terminal door he had just come in, flagging a taxi as he approached the curb. Patrick had nothing to lose at this point, so after a moment of frozen indecision, he grabbed his bag and followed.

Pierre piled into a taxi with all his folders and bags, leaving the door open. Patrick was unsure he was invited this far. Maybe Pierre had said, "Okay, I'll go," or "Okay, it's a go," or "Okay, Hennessey, get lost, I've wasted enough precious government re-election time jawboning with you and need to get my ass on that plane with the president." Patrick might have foolishly imagined an invitation. Noticing Patrick's hesitation, Pierre urgently waved him in, saying, "Come on, *come on!*"

Patrick piled in. Pierre was already waving his arms, telling the driver they needed to get to the North Access gate at Boeing Field with all possible speed, before Patrick had even closed the door. The press secretary loudly informed the driver that he was a member of the president's entourage and was an all-around-important person. As he sat back in his seat, he rolled his eyes toward Patrick, indicating that the effort may not have been completely successful. The driver, however, had taken the information at least partly to heart, and, figuring there might be a decent tip involved, tore away from the curb.

"You know Zeke Tackman?" said Pierre as they were flattened against their seat from the taxi's acceleration.

"Yeah, big guy, the *Journal*. Head political analyst."

"Well, his wife went into labor this afternoon. It was premature or something, and he had to get back to New York. I just found out while they were breaking down the hall. Took a flight right after the speech. I was going to reassign his seat to one of the press pool sharks, but just never got around to it. It's unassigned. So when you see him next, wish him and his wife well and thank him for the seat."

"On Air Force One?" said Patrick, surprised. " Don't I need some kind of clearance? A lie detector test or something? Blood samples?"

Pierre stared at him with raised eyebrows. "Don't you think your honest face and good intentions will be sufficient?"

"No."

"Well, you're right, they aren't. I have a little sway here though. Normally we have to vet anyone who gets on the plane, but it's all done ahead of time for the press crew. Not as in-depth as the marshals would like these days, but just to get into the press plane you've got to have passed muster. So, in actuality, without your knowing it, somebody already knows too much about you. It leans to your benefit today." Pierre talked nonstop as he looked around to get his bearings. It was a short trip to Boeing Field. "Besides, I know for a fact that this time it's okay. And, hey, don't embarrass me. Don't pilfer all the little trinkets on the flight."

Patrick wondered how he would know that it was "okay" this time. And what did they already know about him?

"Won't the president be upset that his flight is delayed?"

"Don't worry, Hennessey. I'll find some way to blame it on you," Pierre smiled conspiratorially.

"Oh, thanks," said Patrick. He couldn't promise anything about the pilfering.

"What did you think of his speech today?" asked Salinger.

"I think he looked better than he did in New York, or Atlanta. Not that I have any access, you know, but—"

"I know."

Patrick smiled humbly, being fully reminded of his very junior status in the press corps, but continued, "...he had more fire. In Atlanta especially, he seemed like he was just going through the motions. A lot of people wonder about his health, and I think they really pull for him. This afternoon, though, he had some juice." Patrick was surprised to be chatting so comfortably with Pierre Salinger, the direct buffer between the press corps and the president, as well as the president's friend and advisor. Despite Pierre's renowned amiability, talking with him was a game of chess, and he was particularly adept at not giving away anything that wasn't intended for public consumption. Patrick was not interested in the parry and thrust of that sort of calculated relationship at the moment, since he reluctantly dealt with it during a large part of his day. He was content at this point to be pleasantly surprised at the end of a difficult workday, to be sharing a taxi with a surprising benefactor and enjoying the ride.

"Hear you're writing another book, Hennessey. About the election."

"And how did you hear that?" asked Patrick, not really surprised.

Pierre smiled and shook his head. "Ah, my friend, like a sheep to the slaughter you are."

Both men laughed. Patrick was well aware of the general mocking he received because of his youthfulness. The hard-nosed arena of press and politics was a ruthlessly competitive field that left Patrick a little short sometimes, as he lacked the killer instinct. He partly made up for it with intelligent and well-written articles, but knew he held himself apart from the fray. His editor was exasperated at times when Patrick failed to go for the jugular. Try as he might, he simply didn't have a hardened nature. Only when his ire was aroused could he mix it up.

Pierre cranked down the taxi window as they rolled toward the entry gate, beyond which Air Force One sat idling on the tarmac, engines warmed up and ready to depart. He showed his press and security clearances and was waved through. With Pierre's urging and pointing, the taxi raced to the line of black limousines near the jet, getting as close to the front stairs as possible. It appeared everyone else was already on board. They both got out as a few marshals ran over.

"Mr. Salinger, you just made it. The president gave us five more minutes to wait, and that was four minutes ago."

Pierre paid the driver, who was wide-eyed to be parked within a stone's throw of the gleaming blue, white, and gold body of the presidential jet with "United States of America" in bold lettering on the fuselage. The driver didn't even count the bills stuffed in his hand. It was obvious he had finally figured out that these guys really *were* prominent somebodies.

Patrick grabbed his bag to follow Pierre, when the marshal stepped between them with his hand up. Pierre interceded. "Sharskey, this is Patrick Hennessey. He's a reporter with the *Washington Post*. He's been cleared on the AF One register, and I'll personally vouch that he has a seat and clearance."

Patrick held up his press pass. The marshal looked it over, then reluctantly backed away and waved him through. Both Pierre and Patrick raced with bags flopping between the limos and toward the steps at the front of the aircraft. It had been raining lightly, and the plane gleamed with an extra sparkle due to the thin watery film on its metallic outer skin. It was a lovely sight—the twilight semidarkness descending, the interior lights glowing from the open entry, the line of identical luminous side windows, and the flashing forward, aft, and wingtip beacons of green and red. Patrick would have liked to stop and savor the image, but his legs never stopped pumping. He ran up the steps, following close behind Pierre, and was just clearing the entry when the ground crew started pulling away the moveable stairs. They swung the door closed as soon as Patrick passed through it. JFK didn't like to wait around. The pilots would idle up, ready to depart within a moment's notice as soon as they knew the presidential motorcade was within range of arrival. It was common for Kennedy's pilots to throttle up the engines and be taxiing away from the terminal as the door was still being fastened.

The aircraft's confined, heavily-insulated quiet contrasted starkly with the outside sounds of the racing taxi, screeching traffic, and whine of the turbines. Breathing heavily, Patrick and Pierre piled into the fuselage with bags clanking and water dripping, only to be met with the disconcertingly silent stares of the seated occupants. This didn't seem to bother Pierre. They moved clumsily down the center aisle, passing the open stateroom door of the president's suite.

"That's twenty bucks, Pierre!" Patrick heard the president's familiar Boston-accented voice ring through the open door. "You're last."

"Yes, Mr. President," acknowledged Pierre contritely.

Patrick couldn't help but glance in as he followed Salinger past the door. He saw the president seated, working at his desk in shirt and loosened tie, his dark suit coat resting on the back of the chair. One hand placed to the side of his temple, he was reading a sheaf of papers. A pencil in the other hand, he looked up, barely removing his hand from his shock of brown hair as Patrick passed—and glowered.

As he hurried on, Patrick felt a stab of deflation. His first face-to-face encounter with the President of the United States, and he was dismissed with a disapproving grimace. Oh, that was just great.

"Janie, would you show Mr. Hennessey here to Tackman's seat? That's a dear," said Pierre to a pretty aide as he stowed his bundles in an upper compartment. "Enjoy," he said to Patrick, who squeezed by to follow the aide to the rear press section.

Patrick had long heard rumors of what went on in the confined world of Air Force One while it traveled around the globe. They suggested an intense mix of political brinkmanship and bawdy partying. He never knew what to believe, since there were always five different versions of any story he heard. He was sure the storytellers often embellished facts to inflate the near-celebrity status of their closeness to the president. Because, make no mistake about it, flying on Air Force One was a status-amplifying activity. Sure, a meeting with the president at the White House was a sign of having arrived in the power structure of Washington. However, in the Oval Office one would compete for the president's time with interrupting aides, telephone calls, fluid schedules, and a host of disruptions that would diminish the quality of time spent. Air Force One, on the other hand, was a confined and personal space. It automatically engendered an intimate feeling. Everyone was enclosed in the same small airborne vehicle for a one-hour hop to a nearby city, or for up to ten hours if it was an overseas trip. It was a place where protective public personas were lowered and face time was extended.

Since the shadow plane of reporters and aides that followed the president's plane was called the Following Zoo, the four rows of six seats in the back press section of Air Force One might well be dubbed the "Animal

Cage." It was a generally understood rule that no passengers should migrate further forward than their assigned seat, thereby creating a self-imposed hierarchy resembling the Hindu caste system. And while the Brahmins were in the front of the plane smoking cigars and sipping Dewars or Bloody Marys, in the last four rows were the Untouchables, that lower breed of humans who labored behind typewriters and over pay phones after landing, trying to report on what the forward occupants had done, even though they had not been permitted to view it. That is probably why a lot of the information coming back as Air Force One stories were probably just that—stories completely fabricated by the lower caste members who dearly wished they were more essential than they really were.

There was one small leveling influence though, a reminder that all were created equal, even if some had better seats. There were only two lavatories on the Boeing 707 SAM 26000 that was used as the presidential jet. One was far forward and was reserved for the private use of the president and his family—in this case JFK, Jackie when she would fly along, and occasionally the kids, John-John and Caroline. Everyone else was required to use the lavatory at the far rear of the aircraft. This small, overlooked design feature was a great equalizer, as it required personal assistants, press secretaries, aides, cabinet members, secretaries of state, and all manner of highfalutin' dignitaries to ignobly run the gauntlet of hungry correspondents to empty their bladders. This indignity did not escape the sly humor and rapt attention of the residents of these seats, and any attempt to pretend that the political landscape of the period was a lofty expression of the wisdom of its leaders and the discretion of its press was quickly put to rest over these twenty paces. Pointed questions and catcalls often peppered the resentful visitors to this chaotic domain, and it was often a sense of relief that flushed the faces of those who returned to the safety of the forward sections.

Of course, this might be making the press section out to be less dignified than it really was. As a rule, anyone on Air Force One was at the top of his or her game. However, the speed with which this level of individual development could degenerate into a cerebral mobocracy could be astounding. It did not happen often, and for the most part a certain veneer of professionalism and civility predominated in the press section. But if scratched at the wrong moment, it proved frighteningly thin.

Patrick entered this area with trepidation. Although familiar with the jaded character of journalists, members of his chosen profession, this was a rarefied group traveling at a rarefied altitude, and the interactions were a bit more intense. These were professional reporters adept at peeling away the facade of whatever information they were presented with, and probing the underlying facts for lurking secrets. As he followed the aide to his assigned seat—the starboard-side window seat—Patrick was aware of the interest in him shown by the other passengers. Of course they had little else to do but sit, watch, and wait for takeoff. He could feel quite a few pairs of eyes follow him silently as he walked down the aisle and stowed his bag in the overhead compartment. The aide seemed to recoil after she had shown him his seat, and quickly returned to the comfortable sanctuary at the front of the plane.

After stowing his bag, Patrick had to squeeze by two well-padded correspondents who were already comfortably seated in order to get to his window berth. Fortunately Air Force One was configured with wider seat spacing than commercial flights, but he still felt uncooperative resistance from his two seatmates as well as a bit of embarrassment at being the last on the plane. He sat down and buckled himself in while rubbing shoulders with the man to his left who, even with the larger seats, overflowed into Patrick's.

"Where's Tackman?" Dark gray suit coat, wrinkled white shirt, thin dark tie loosened at the neck, bristly crew cut with a facial shadow beginning to match—his typical colleague in the press was staring at him.

"He's probably on his way to New York by now."

"Why isn't he here?"

"He's having a baby."

"He didn't look pregnant," the colleague said, smiling at his own humor to his friend seated next to him.

"Well, I guess it just didn't show. Patrick Hennessey, *Washington Post*," offered Patrick, shaking his neighbor's meaty hand.

"Did they hold this plane for you?" he asked, not introducing himself.

"No, I was with Mr. Salinger—who was a bit late."

"What were you doing with Salinger?"

"Just hitching a ride, I guess," said Patrick.

"Uh-huh." It was obvious from the hard look on his face that he didn't believe a word of it. Patrick didn't try to explain.

The flight, which had been taxiing to the runway even as Patrick was finding his seat, began accelerating for takeoff. He could feel the plane quickly gaining momentum as he was pressed back into his cushion. The remnants of the sunset were still visible through the water-streaked window, and as the plane gained altitude and slowly banked south, the twinkling lights of downtown Seattle appeared. He marveled at finding himself flying aboard Air Force One.

Patrick often used flight time to write articles. He pulled out his notebook and started to lay down ideas about the Seattle stop. He would call it in to his editor when the flight arrived in Sacramento. He wanted this piece to reflect the president's more upbeat energy level when he spoke earlier today at Seattle's Eagles Auditorium. He had punctuated his comments with his characteristic wit, so evident in past campaigns and so evidently missing thus far in this one. He had even taken a few delicate swipes at Barry Goldwater, who, though an opponent, was a friend from the Senate.

Kennedy was campaigning on a New Frontier platform of social reform and significant extensions of civil rights legislation. This campaign was being conducted in the midst of a de-escalation of American forces in Vietnam while Kennedy re-evaluated the reasons for a military commitment in Southeast Asia. He had already issued a National Security Memorandum initiating a decrease in the number of "advisory" forces, pulling out almost a third of the sixteen thousand troops stationed there. He was rumored to be rethinking the entire venture. Many of his recent campaign speeches reverberated with a questioning look at America's views on the nature of communism and a more creative method of stanching its aggression. There was even talk that Kennedy pondered a rapprochement with Castro, although no one believed such a suggestion could possibly be serious.

Goldwater, a rugged conservative Republican senator from Arizona, delicately derided JFK as weak and capitulating. He called for the reinstitution of harsh anticommunist policies in Vietnam, suggesting massive bombing of North Vietnam to force them to bow to American pressure. He implied that the Social Security system should be dismantled. He also resisted federal civil rights laws, insisting that integration was the prerogative of individual states. It was a stark election choice for the American electorate, as these two men represented widely divergent paths.

Issues aside, the main thrust of this campaign was reassurance. Kennedy had nearly died in the assassination attempt. His survival had been a huge question in the minds of the entire country, and it was a great relief

to see him healed and capable of leading again. His showing up and projecting presidential authority conveyed a much-needed air of confidence.

There was also another drama, still unfolding. The Assassination Trials were uncovering a web of sedition and corruption that reached into
the centers of American government. Complaining about corruption and
ineptitude were common living room, water cooler, and barstool activities, but seeing their vague accusations bloom into national scandal was a
shock even to the most cynical of observers. There was....

"Mr. Hennessey?"

A half-hour into the flight, intently scribbling in his notebook, Patrick
was interrupted by an aide standing in the aisle.

"Yes?"

"Would you mind coming forward, sir? Your presence has been requested up front."

"Ahh, well—sure." Patrick was surprised to be summoned, and got
up. He received suspicious looks and little assistance as he again squeezed
past the two journalists seated beside him. He followed the aide forward,
past the small conference room and toward the front section of the plane.
As they proceeded, Patrick reached out to tap the aide on the shoulder,
"Who asked for me?"

"The president, sir."

Oh God! thought Patrick in alarm. He felt as if he was intruding on
someone's party and had misunderstood an invitation for the second time
today. A flush of panic sent his pulse racing. Even though he had followed
Kennedy for weeks and seen him from afar on the campaign and up close
a few times during rallies, he had never spoken to the man. It was nearly
impossible to get personal time with the president. He hadn't prepared
himself for this at all.

The forward section of Air Force One was arranged to accommodate
a number of configurations. Near the entrance to the plane, past the forward galley and just off the pilot's cockpit, was a small set of rooms on the
starboard side that comprised the presidential suite. One was being used
as a small office, with a pair of leather-upholstered swivel chairs, an adjustable desk, and a sofa that could double as a bed. Patrick had passed this
room and gotten the scowl from the president just thirty minutes earlier.
Across from this room was the senior staff area, an open meeting space
with four more leather-upholstered swivel chairs, two on either side of
an adjustable central table. It acted as a congregation point for the princi-

pal passengers on the flight. Beyond this, further aft, was the galley, then the staff and aide seating area, followed by the press corps seating further back. The plush carpeted interior was much finer than on a commercial flight. The craft had also been soundproofed to an extra degree, which quieted the overriding roar of jet engines more noticeable on commercial flights. This allowed an easier exchange of conversation.

Patrick heard a burst of laughter from up ahead, and a swarm of voices talking all at once. This subsided for a moment to the level of a murmur, and then there was another loud eruption of laughter. The smell of cigar smoke hung in the air. As he entered the open senior staff area, he saw that the four high-backed leather chairs were occupied. Patrick squeezed through a few aides crowded in the aisle. The president sat to his left near the window, his legs crossed, a cigar in one hand and the other draped over the armrest with a drink resting on the nearby table. He was smiling broadly at Pierre Salinger, who sat diagonally across from him. At the president's side was Dave Powers, one of his closest friends and election advisors. He was a man with a photographic memory for places, faces and dates, as well as a charming Irish quality that invited immediate camaraderie. An aide stood in the door of the presidential suite, also listening and laughing. Someone occupied the aisle seat right in front of Patrick, but he couldn't tell who it was, as only the top back of his head was visible.

Pierre was telling a story of a French senator caught in flagrante delicto with a woman during the run up to the recent elections in Paris. Pierre swung his arms wildly, mimicking the senator's shocked confusion when he found out he had mistaken the woman's husband for a reporter. He mimed the senator's perverse relief to find he would not be in the news as a philanderer, but as an assault victim instead. Patrick didn't quite understand the punch line, but everyone else seemed to, or at least they enjoyed Pierre's retelling of the story enough to laugh at it either way. As the laughter subsided, Pierre used the moment to excuse himself to join some of his aides in the next compartment. He needed to work up the press release for the upcoming stop in Sacramento. As he stood to go, he noticed Patrick being ushered in by the aide sent to fetch him.

"Ah, Mr. President, this is our hitchhiker, Mr. Hennessey," he said, looking at Patrick and then, nodding to the president, "Thank you, sir." He edged by Patrick toward the staff area, trailed by an escorting aide, and Patrick was left standing near the end of the small table separating the two chairs, feeling exposed.

"Mr. Hennessey, please have a seat," said the president, smiling as he motioned with his cigar toward Patrick and then to the now-empty seat diagonally across from where he sat. Kennedy picked up his drink and took a sip. The president's mood had obviously changed since Patrick had passed by his open door a little earlier. Sitting in the comfortable seat, Patrick looked across the table and recognized the slicked-back hair and wire-rim glasses of Robert McNamara, Kennedy's Secretary of Defense.

"So, Mr. Hennessey, Pierre tells me you were responsible for his tardy arrival," said the president, staring soberly at Patrick. A quick change of mood.

Patrick's eyes darted in the direction of Pierre's departure toward the staff section. "Uh, yes sir, that was me. I...misdirected him to the wrong airport." Patrick paused and said sincerely, "I'm sorry about that, sir."

"Er, for an Irishman, you're a mighty poor liar. That's not what he said happened," laughed Kennedy, shaking his head. "He said it was because of you that he just managed to get back here. Bad way to start off a conversation with the president of the United States, Mr. Hennessey. Hopefully you can do better in the future."

Patrick smiled sheepishly, flummoxed at being caught in attempted nobility.

"So, how do like my airplane?" asked the president in a friendlier manner.

"A lot. I like it a lot, sir. I never thought I'd see the inside of it. Thank you," he smiled.

"Well, lightning strikes, does it not, Mr. Hennessey? I've noticed that you're a fan of Robert Frost," he said, smiling. He was obviously having a good time with Patrick's discomfort, but it seemed that joshing him through it was Kennedy's way of soothing his nerves.

At first Patrick was unsure of the reference, but in a moment he saw it. *"I have been one acquainted with the night,"* he responded tentatively. *"I have walked out in rain—and back in rain..."*

"...And further still at an unearthly height, O luminary clock against the sky, proclaimed the time was neither wrong nor right." The president completed the stanza with the lilt of a poet and the characteristic intonations of his sharp Boston accent, all the while looking directly at Patrick.

As the president recited the lines of the poem, Patrick was able to get a better measure of the Kennedy he had seen so often from afar. He had no previous personal observations for comparison, but John Kennedy looked like a man who had been to the bottom of things and come back up. He had always had a steely firmness under his charming demeanor, but now he emanated a more forceful gravitas. Nothing specific created this impression. It related more to the sum total of his parts: the gestures, facial expressions, and timing created a sense of something very firm housed in a battered exterior. For he was battered. He had taken months to recover from the shooting. He was noticeably older and a bit thinner, with a slightly hollow look to his face and eyes. His suit hung loosely when observed up close. But the intelligence and situational command shone through even with his reduced vigor. There was no doubt that he had wholly recovered mentally and was significantly improved physically. His sophistication and magnetism were unmistakable, possibly even more magnified given the historical events swirling around him. Patrick felt no lessening of fascination with the man and his destiny.

Patrick couldn't help smiling, since Robert Frost's poem was the source of the title of his book about Joe McCarthy. He was surprised to find the president knew of it and, in fact, knew the poem by heart. He knew Kennedy was well educated in the classics and through his own interest, the current poets, but there was also a history there that might impart an undercurrent. Patrick realized this recitation of verse might not have been the friendly opener it seemed. McCarthy had been a close family friend and confidant of Joseph Kennedy, Sr. and was rumored to have been the godfather of Robert Kennedy's first child. He had dated JFK's sisters, Eunice and Patricia, when he was still a junior congressman. As a fellow Irish Catholic, he had been a surrogate member of the Kennedy household for many years. There had been conjecture and argument at many levels regarding the relationship between JFK and McCarthy. JFK was blamed for not openly censuring McCarthy during the years when both were senators and the freewheeling excesses of the McCarthy hearings were crushing innocent Americans. He refrained from formally censuring McCarthy during the Senate hearings that effectively destroyed McCarthy's stature and led to his degeneration and death from alcoholism. It was a common refrain from JFK's detractors that if he wanted to live up to the ideals of his Pulitzer Prize-winning book *Profiles in Courage*, he should have openly censured McCarthy for his abuses.

Patrick, on the other hand, had done his level best to dismember McCarthy and everything he stooped to, and *Acquainted with the Night* was the tool he used to do it. So at the moment, he didn't know where that left him with the president of the United States, who was looking at him with a serious face after reciting a few lines of poetry while flying thirty thousand feet above Oregon.

It was said that Harry Truman would ask to be informed when Air Force One was flying over Ohio, the state of his arch political enemy, Republican Senator Robert A. Taft. Truman would walk aft, use the toilet, and then ask the pilot to jettison the contents overboard. Patrick momentarily wondered if it were possible for him to be jettisoned off this flight for disparaging one of the president's former family intimates. He could imagine himself flushed into the rarefied, frigid air.

The president, however, did not seem angry, just intent. "So I was wondering how you got permission to use the title of his poem for your book. Knowing Robert as I do, that would have been like prying a tumbler of Jameson out of the old man's hands."

"Well, we didn't actually get a firm approval," remarked Patrick a little nervously. "We wrote to him numerous times with no response, so my editor called him. In fact it was quite an effort to track him down, and when she did finally get him on the line...."

"Let me guess, he talked her into the ground and never did answer the question. Am I right?" The president was enjoying this and obviously had an inside connection with Mr. Frost.

"Yes, sir, that's about it. How did you know?"

"Well, that's Robert. He nearly walked away with my inauguration in '60. I was thinking we'd need to drag him off the stage so I'd get a turn. Figured it wouldn't look so good to manhandle the old guy away from the podium, so we let him just ramble on. Isn't that right, Dave?" asked JFK as he drew on his cigar and exhaled toward the ceiling. It was often suggested that the hardest part of the recent Cuban embargo for the president personally was the diminished trade in cigars, especially the thin Upmann Petit Coronas of which he was particularly fond. Even with the restrictions, he seemed to have plenty on hand.

"Ah, true," replied Dave. "The man never saw a space he didn't feel obliged to fill, rather ceremoniously I might add, with his own presence. Mighty good with the words though." Dave's tone showed his admiration of the man even with his faults so clearly acknowledged. "Really, the greatest poet laureate I've ever met."

"Kind of like 'the greatest White House you were ever in'?" smiled Kennedy. Dave was always referring to events and personages he met in his travels as "the greatest."

"Exactly so," he responded sincerely. This appeared to be an ongoing conversation between the two.

After a pause, Patrick said, "I also called him to try to get a more firm understanding, but he did the same thing with me. Just talked all around everything. We figured since he didn't disapprove the request, it was a tacit assent. We made sure to credit him though, to avoid any trouble down the road."

Kennedy sat back a little, flicking his cigar into the ashtray by the armrest. It was the kind of motion that was so practiced and repetitive, it was nearly unconscious. He looked at Patrick for a quiet moment.

"So you're the Patrick Hennessey who dismantled my Uncle Joe."

Kennedy said this without any noticeable bitterness. It was more a statement than a question, as if he were just putting a face to the name. Patrick had a hard time reading Kennedy, not the least of which was the shock of talking with him at all. He seemed to be a guarded individual, deliberate and watchful. He didn't indicate, either with movement or words, the position he might hold behind the questions he was asking. Good at poker probably. Probing, without obvious rancor, but unrevealing.

Here it comes though, thought Patrick.

"Well...yes, sir. That was me," he answered cautiously but directly. "I was somewhat personally motivated."

Patrick and his family had lived too close to the bedevilment of Joe McCarthy for him to be coy about trying to discredit the senator. He only wished he could have done it sooner and better. He could neither make apologies nor hedge his position, even if it brought the disapproval of a president. It wasn't that Patrick was such a brave soul. It was just a passion at his core that he could not mask, even under such conditions. In fact, he was a little surprised at how easily firm acknowledgment of authorship came off his tongue. He hadn't had time to prepare a more circumspect answer, and he didn't feel this man across from him wanted anything but a direct response. He was aware of the transgression he might be making and sat waiting for a possible career-altering reprimand from the president of the United States.

"So you think the McCarthy investigations were merely a witch hunt serving no national purpose?" Kennedy had become quite serious.

"No sir. I think the *method* the hearings used served no national purpose. It flaunted the power of the Senate and abused its position. True, there were some spies in the U.S. body politic. There probably always will be. And they need to be pried loose from their hiding places. But using the overwhelming power of the government to harass and intimidate innocents, so many of them so flimsily accused, is clearly, in my opinion, an abuse of power." Patrick wondered if he had gone too far but couldn't stop. "McCarthy showed contempt for the law while pretending to be patriotically supporting it. I find his cure worse than the illness."

Both men sat looking at each other quietly with the steady muffled hum of the jet engines in the background, the only movement another flick of ash from Kennedy's cigar.

Behind Patrick an aide poked his head out the door of the presidential suite and said, "Mr. President? We've located the vice president. He's in New York and is on the line now."

The president, still staring thoughtfully at Patrick, exhaled another puff. He grimaced while slowly standing up. The others stood also so he could pass in the tight quarters. Sitting again, Patrick caught the eye of McNamara who had been quietly observing the exchange between the two men. He looked casually at Patrick, then raised his eyebrows and said, "Saved by Lyndon Johnson, heh?"

Patrick closed his eyes. He was in trouble. It was a big mistake to have gotten on this plane.

"Mr. Hennessey." It was the president speaking from behind him.

"Yes, sir," responded Patrick, rising somberly.

The president had returned to the door and was looking at Patrick. "To say I enjoyed your book would be inaccurate. The House Un-American Committee, in my opinion, was an ironic title for that body of investigation. It was un-American in its cruelly excessive pursuit of un-American activities. As you well know, my relationship with Senator McCarthy was complicated by family connections. Nevertheless, that book of yours was well written and, I'd say, needed to be written." He reached out to shake Patrick's hand, a quick and efficient gesture with a penetrating look that was over almost before it registered. The president turned and entered his suite, taking the outstretched phone. The aide closed the door.

Which left Patrick standing in the aisle. There was a sense of being in a darkened room because the person with the only lamp had departed, taking it with him. The intrigue, the intensity, the magnetism had just up and left. Patrick looked around uncertainly. He looked down at McNamara, who after a glance at Patrick, pushed his reading glasses up off his nose and went back to reading a brief he was holding. He decided against re-seating himself and instead excused himself with a nodded thank you to Dave Powers. He walked back to his seat in the press section.

Squeezing over the now-sleeping fellow journalists, he wedged himself into his window space and thought back on what had just occurred. Such a short exchange, such a roller coaster of feelings, but now a sense of guarded satisfaction. Today he had flown on Air Force One, met the president, and not made a fool of himself—at least not completely. That wasn't too bad considering what might have happened.

Taking a deep breath and feeling more at ease, he looked around and saw his surroundings come more into focus. He took a good look at his seat mates. Both were fast asleep, heads sagging, mouths partially opened, looking like anything but members of the intimidating press corps.

The seating area was cluttered with books, bags, and magazines, but not much else. Memorabilia stamped with Air Force One and the presidential seal were a hot commodity, as they were the only real proof that one had been aboard. "As if swarmed by locusts" was how the flight attendants referred to the cabin, cleanly picked of napkins, coasters, glasses, and plasticware when it was tidied up after landing. Even the swizzle sticks with the embossed presidential seal were pilfered. Patrick looked around and pondered what he could nick that might be proof of his attendance aboard, but having missed the served snack, there was nothing left for him to snatch.

Eyeing his sleeping neighbor, Patrick stealthily eased the small package of Air Force One peanuts out from under his pudgy fingers, being careful not to arouse him from his sweaty sleep. He took his neighbor's "official" napkin and fork as well, both with the Air Force One logo. He checked around his space for more booty. In the seat pocket in front of him was the barf bag. No seal. *I'll leave that for a more needy individual*, he thought, and settled back into his comfortable seat for the remainder of the flight.

Chapter 3

Dallas is a very dangerous place, sir. I wouldn't go there.
—*Arkansas Senator **William Fulbright**, to JFK*

I suppose really the only two dates that most people remember where they were,
were Pearl Harbor and the death of President Franklin Roosevelt.
—*John Fitzgerald Kennedy, Dec. 7, 1961*

Friday, November 22, 1963
Dallas, Texas

The crowds for the president's visit were larger and more enthusiastic than anticipated. This was a welcome change, because just a few weeks ago Adlai Stevenson, the U.S. Ambassador to the United Nations, was attacked and injured by placard-wielding protesters while on a United Nations Day visit. Three years ago in 1960, Lyndon and Lady Bird Johnson were chased back into the security of the Adolphus Hotel elevator by an angry, chanting, spitting mob.

* * *

Dallas was an odd city, a harbinger of the "New Texas," with a dynamic financial district dripping in oil money and sky-scraping insurance centers, while still steeped in Jim Crow politics and the sensibilities of an older, harsher era.

Texas had always been a bit apart, strongly independent and resentful of any meddling in its self-sufficient ways. Even from its early days during the forming of the republic, Texas had been guided by a strong aversion to imposed authority. It joined the Union in 1846 to avoid being swallowed by Mexico, only to opt out later in opposition to the North's requirements to forego slavery. Texans were not joiners by choice, but by necessity. As the nation grew up around them, it began to impose precepts of its own on this fiercely self-reliant—or what many would call "cussedly ornery"—segment of the population.

Texans deeply resented racial integration, and in the 1920s Dallas became known as the City of Hate for its key role in the white supremacists' Ku Klux Klan movement. Texas remained a focal point and breeding ground for ultraconservative groups for many years to come. Even during the '60s, getting a job on the Dallas Police Force was easier if one had been a member of the Klan, or at least the regressive John Birch Society.

Over the last twenty years, an influx of fundamentalist Christian immigrants from neighboring Louisiana, Alabama and Arkansas strengthened the shadow side of conservatism. This subgroup was even more hostile and regressive in their political and social stance. Stir them together with the booming oil economy, the strident Texas swagger of entitlement, and the obvious animosity of the local wealthy right-wing patrons of business, manufacturing, and media—and these reactionary themes acquired the punch of a Texas jalapeño chili.

* * *

For the impending visit of the president, many feared there was little chance Dallas would behave itself. Senator William Fulbright, a Democrat from Arkansas, had friends in the city but refused to visit for fear of physical injury. He met with JFK the month before and strongly advised him not to go to Dallas. Byron Skelton, the Democratic National Committeeman from Texas, wrote a few weeks earlier to Robert Kennedy and to Walter Jennings, LBJ's direct aide, warning "Dallas wasn't safe" and should be avoided.

The previous evening, at the Washington, D.C., Shoreham Hotel, Senator Hubert Humphrey had given a sadly prescient but poorly attended talk entitled *Mental Health and World Peace* . He remarked, "...emotional instability afflicts a significant but small minority in our midst that some call the extreme right, some the Birchers. They still see the world in total black and white. They are looking for immediate and final answers. They are still substituting dogma for creative thought. They are still angry, fearful, deeply and fundamentally disturbed by the world around them." He warned that "...the act of an emotionally unstable person or irresponsible citizen can strike down a great leader."

Not all of Dallas was of this intolerant nature. A large and vocal section of the establishment was truly stunned by the venomous outpouring during the recent attack on Stevenson. The *Dallas Times Herald* soberly editorialized that Dallas needed to rein in its angry outbursts and bring itself into the more moderate stance of the United States as a whole. Stanley Marcus of the Neiman Marcus department stores, a member of the Dallas Citizen's Council, focused attention on the affair for fear that it might actually be dangerous to have the rich, Irish-Catholic, United Nations-supporting, liberal northern president drive right through downtown. It was decided, however, that uninviting the president would be an even worse admission of narrow-minded civic failure.

Preparations went ahead, punctuated by warnings from Dallas Police Chief Jesse Curry. In a morning television announcement, he said the police department would brook no interference from extremist groups during the president's visit. He asked locals to report suspicious characters making threatening comments regarding the president. He even went so far as to encourage residents to make citizen's arrests if any riotous conditions were to develop—not the most reassuring of public remarks.

This was not a trip that Kennedy relished making, either. Lyndon Johnson, the vice president, hailing from Texas as a native son, delivered the state for the president's ticket in the 1960 presidential election. It was assumed that if Kennedy were to accept him on the presidential dance card in 1964, Johnson would use his influence to carry the state and the southern Dixiecrat block of conservative democrats. Johnson, a savvy backroom arm twister, was astute and tenacious in the power corridors of politics. But the vice presidency is a thankless political cul-de-sac quite often leading to obscurity. And while JFK had risen from the Senate to the Presidency, LBJ was seen as having fallen from the powerful kingmaker position of Senate Majority Leader to the ceremonial but powerless role of second-in-command. Many people wondered why he had accepted in the first place, when he was so steeped in the brawling conservative politics of the deep south, and nearly antithetical to the liberal sophistication of the Kennedy clan. It was even rumored that Kennedy, flush with victory after the 1960 Democratic National Convention, offered the position as a face-saving gesture, assuming Johnson's self-respect would require him to decline. But to the shock of most party members he quickly accepted, and spent the next three years shining his cowboy boots in his office across the street from the White House.

Kennedy, reaching for accommodation, had adjusted some of his own activities to provide his vice president a more meaningful role. However, what JFK had wanted was someone with the muscle to move the Senate on strategic legislation. Ironically, in hindsight he had emasculated Johnson's power in order to incorporate him into the ticket, thereby losing a cranky but powerful Senate ally and gaining a crusty, frustrated vice president.

Johnson, for three long years on the edges of power in Washington, was losing clout in his home state of Texas. Kennedy assumed Johnson would be able to keep his own state in line, but it was becoming obvious this was not the case. The Texas Democratic Party was at war with itself. Internal squabbles between the archconservative wing led by Governor John Connally and the progressive liberal wing led by Senator Ralph Yarborough threatened to break out in open warfare. JFK was well aware that this could cost him the twenty-five Texas electoral votes in the upcoming 1964 election, and was convinced of the need to personally tour the region to present a show of smiling party unity, even if there were shivs hidden behind the public poses.

Dallas was primed for Kennedy's visit. Five thousand *Wanted for Treason* leaflets were deposited on windshields and storefronts in the Dallas downtown area on the days preceding JFK's arrival. They were paid for by retired Major General Edwin A. Walker, who had been cashiered by Kennedy from his command of the 24th Infantry Division in West Germany in 1961 for indoctrinating his troops with right-wing propaganda. Walker became a focal point for the far right-leaning citizens of Dallas, living in a house within the city limits and flying the American flag upside down on a flagpole in his front yard. The flyers showed front and side mug shots of the president with a list of perceived treasonous offenses such as coddling communists and supporting racial integration.

There was also a full-page ad with a funereal black border headlined "Welcome Mr. Kennedy to Dallas" in the *Dallas Morning News*. It was funded by the John Birch Society and detailed grievances with the president from the viewpoint of the oil-rich business community.

* * *

In Fort Worth, Kennedy had been reading the day's newspaper while waiting for Jackie, and bristled at its confrontational flavor. "We're really headed into nut country today," he commented over breakfast at the Hotel Texas.

It was a quick hop from Fort Worth to Dallas's Love Field for Air Force One, carrying the president, Air Force Two with the vice president and his entourage, and the Zoo with the press corps. The planes gained only seven thousand feet in altitude before dropping back down for a quick landing. It was a lot of machinery to throw from one side of a twin city to the other, when a motorcade would have been only a thirty-minute drive. But driving to Dallas would have meant a motorcade back to Fort Worth after the Trade Mart luncheon.

During the short flight, Kennedy worked on the speech he was to deliver at the Trade Mart. It was his practice to pick away, rewrite until the last minute, and then lay aside a large portion to extemporize once he got on the podium. This usually surprised anyone who had received an advance copy, and many a frustrated reporter had learned the hard way never to pre-submit a Kennedy discourse.

"I'd be careful about what you say in Dallas," said Congressman Albert Thomas, a 30-year Texas political veteran hitchhiking on Air Force One. As a friend of JFK, he sat near the president in the forward cabin. "It's a tough town."

Kennedy intended otherwise, knowing he would get no better chance to speak directly to the heart of the right-wing conservative establishment. He was especially encouraged by the vast crowds that had come out to greet them in Fort Worth, and would use the motorcade through Dallas to gauge the mood of Texas at the heart of his opposition. The oil money—the Hunts, the Murchisons, the Richardsons, and the forces that Governor Connally represented—were dead set against his presidency. Kennedy had no illusions about the hatred that would be hurled at him and his ambitions for social reform and the elimination of the oil-depletion allowance, a traditional free ride for the oil barons. But he also sensed an opportunity to really speak his mind. Dallas might be a tough town, but he was a tough president and planned to launch a withering broadside at the extremist bigots, right in their own back yard.

"Okay, Albert, what do you think of this?" asked the president, calling Congressman Thomas to his side. Speaking in his cadenced speech-giving mode, he began, "There will always be dissident voices heard in the land, expressing opposition without alternatives, finding fault but never favor, perceiving gloom on every side and seeking influence without responsibility. Those voices are inevitable. But today other voices are heard in the land—voices preaching doctrines wholly unrelated to reality, wholly unsuited to the sixties, doctrines which apparently assume that words will suffice without weapons, that vituperation is as good as victory and that peace is a sign of weakness." Kennedy paused and looked at the congressman.

"Ouch. You might get away with that since no one will know what vituperation means," joked Thomas.

"Well, they can look it up. And in the meantime, they might reflect on how much of it I withheld," said the president, continuing after a quick scribble with further changes, "...we can hope that fewer people will listen to nonsense. And the notion that this Nation is headed for defeat through deficit, social decay through equality for all races, economic bankruptcy through Medicare and Social Security, a weakened populace through public education open to all, or that strength is but a matter of slogans, is nothing but just plain nonsense."

"Well, obviously not hoping for the keys to the city," smiled the congressman. "But really, Jack," he emphasized more seriously, "be careful out there. Dallas can be nasty."

They touched down at Love Field just a few minutes behind schedule, at 11:40 a.m. The three planes parked in a row on the tarmac. The welcome was thunderous, and after a lengthy "fence parade," the Secret Service pulled the president and first lady away from the gathered crowds and shepherded them into a waiting limousine for the ten-mile procession toward and through downtown Dallas.

* * *

John Kennedy had been president for almost three years. He had weathered the early Bay of Pigs fiasco in Cuba and the trying Vienna summit with Khrushchev. There had been civil rights upheavals, the Berlin Wall crisis, communist advances in Southeast Asia and the race for space with the Russians. He rebounded strongly two years after his inauguration to confront the crisis of Soviet insertion of nuclear offensive missiles in Cuba. Through a series of intense domestic and international crises, he had grown into a successful and respected leader.

But on a personal level, he was in upheaval. Though sensitive and caring in many ways, he was a philandering husband to a wife who adored him. He had been raised by a dynamic, immensely successful, doting father who molded his family in his own image—one that radiated accomplishment and power, but left moral considerations sorely wanting. Joseph Kennedy, Sr. had taught his boys to take what they wanted from the world without guilt, and sexual conquests were high on that list. A sign of virility and an expression of manliness, they were a natural perk of power: "A day without a lay is a day wasted," according to the family's patriarch. And during Jack's childhood, his father led by example, even bringing his paramours home. Occasionally, the Kennedy children had to endure an evening meal shared with a starlet or mistress sitting beside their father at the table, to the humiliation of their mother, Rose. Theirs was an upbringing like no other. But the father's influence waned over the years, both personally and politically, as the son grew into himself. And then, in 1961, a severe stroke rendered Joseph Kennedy mute and wheelchair-bound. His diminished presence was an ironic reminder of the enormous influence he had wielded and lost.

For Jack Kennedy, flagrant womanizing was a lesson well learned but poorly examined. Now though, it was a question he was being forced to ponder. His and Jackie's son, Patrick Bouvier Kennedy, born prematurely, had died only three months earlier. Suffering from hyaline membrane disease, his life ended a short 48 hours after birth. Jack had held Patrick's tiny fingers while his son labored to breathe through slowly constricting lung tissue. He perished from exhaustion as his tiny overworked heart gave out. And for all the powers of his office, none could save the president's son. Jack was distraught at telling Jackie what had happened. She had previously lost two children during pregnancy, yet it was Jack himself who was inconsolable. He fell apart, sobbing on his knees at his wife's hospital bedside. Later he was overcome with grief at the funeral, and after the service, Cardinal Cushing had to pry him from the tiny casket. He had been shaken to his core with a mix of despairing grief and personal guilt. In the days before Patrick's birth, he had been with another woman, and grief drove home the awareness that his personal actions were unforgivable. They could not be excused by any amount of paternal instruction. No longer oblivious to the pain his philandering caused, he could not escape his remorse.

And on a political level, the Profumo affair had recently brought down the government of his close friend and political ally, British Prime Minister Harold Macmillan. Kennedy saw firsthand what a sexual exposé could do to an administration. The tragedy of his son's death, the toxic effect of philandering on his marriage, and the political implications of a revealed scandal all brought home the dangerous ground he was treading.

* * *

"Jackie," said the president as he leaned toward her, "take off your sunglasses. They want to see your eyes."

"Alright," she said reluctantly, removing the last shred of security behind which she could hide.

It was such a brilliant day that without them she squinted into the Texas sun. But if Jack wanted them off, they would come off. He was better at all this campaigning than she. In fact, she had never gone on any of his domestic politicking trips during all his years as president.

She abhorred the false enthusiasms and the endless smiles, waving to throngs of people she didn't know and would never see again. But she had loved the excursions they had made to Europe over the last three years and knew that she had helped sway many of the world leaders to Jack's side. She enjoyed this immensely. The crusty and pompous Charles deGaulle had a grandfatherly quality she found completely endearing. With her mastery of the French language and her extensive knowledge of French history, they quickly became fast friends. Theirs was a friendship that riveted the world press, as few had ever penetrated the French president's aloof demeanor. And Jack, instead of feeling threatened by her unexpectedly central role in his travels, reveled in her newfound popularity. "I am the man who accompanied Jacqueline Kennedy to Paris," he announced to delighted journalists at the Palais de Chaillot, leaving Jackie, at his side, both slightly embarrassed and immensely proud.

Even Khrushchev, with his barely suppressed brutality, had been swayed by Jackie's charms early in Kennedy's first term. In Vienna, after a particularly grueling and unsuccessful round of discussions between the president and the Soviet ruler, Jackie and Jack attended the requisite state dinner. During the course of the evening, Khrushchev's aloof curiosity slowly gave way to fascination as he and Jackie spent long stretches huddled in animated conversation. This didn't immediately change anything of a political nature between the countries, but it opened a more personal door between the president and his international foe, leading to deeper correspondence over the following years.

Despite the world's fascination with the first lady, she was unable to find peace with her husband. She knew of Jack's womanizing from the beginning, but thought her love could change him. She believed he would see the pain it caused her and the dangerous position it put him in. It used to be barely enough that he was discreet, but even that had changed over the years as his philandering continued. After they moved into the White House, it was her pattern to leave often and stay away for extended periods. She needed more varied and private surroundings, and could not bear to be around Jack when she knew he was cheating on her. She knew he was his father's son, as she had had plenty of opportunity to observe the old man's ways. When she was last in Greece, she had felt like simply staying there. *They will think me a fool in the future,* she thought, *because everyone will know. The Secret Service keeps logs of everyone who comes and goes. Does Jack really think the logs won't be available to someone at some time?* Besides, the Secret Service knew. She could see it in the eyes and the protective bearing of the agents on her own detail. They knew she was being cheated on, and their knowing increased her humiliation.

Although she was devastated by the loss of her child, she had been confused and eventually encouraged by Jack's reaction. She had never seen him respond so emotionally. It had been frightening at the time, but she hoped he was finally grappling with the wall that had separated them. While in Greece, she had contemplated a separation from Jack, but it produced a vision of such a bereft and lonely future, she dismissed it. Perhaps he was beginning to see how his actions affected their marriage. She was sure something deep had shifted, and she wanted to do whatever she could to support him in that. She knew she would always take that chance, the chance based on the hope that he could be a different husband to her.

* * *

And that was how she found herself today, gliding down crowded Dallas streets through throngs of well-wishers calling out their names, hoping for a glance, for a moment of recognition from the president of the United States—or his wife.

Entering the first few blocks of the downtown area with its sun-drenched new buildings, the entire entourage was aware that this was a special groundswell of support from the Dallas community. The twelve blocks from Harwood to Houston streets were packed with people whose vocal welcome echoed off the vertical canyons of concrete and glass. It was exhilarating. For most people, this would be the first and last time they would see the president of the United States in the flesh.

Dave Powers, asked earlier by the president about the crowds and how many had come out for him, said, "For you? About as many as turned out the last time you were here, but a hundred thousand more have come to look at Jackie." Even though they would joke about it at gatherings, Dave was right and everyone knew it. In her own publicity-shy reserve, she was a driving force behind his popularity—their popularity.

But the euphoric was mixed with the ominous. In the business district between Akard and Field streets, three middle-aged office workers stood behind a large plate glass window on the second floor: a woman flanked by two men. The men, wearing white shirts with cuffed short sleeves, thin black ties, and close-cropped hair, waited till the president looked their way, and raised their hands to give him the finger as he passed. There were a few catcalls. A sign reading "Help Kennedy stamp out Democracy" was unfurled on a side street as the motorcade rolled slowly by. A silent, angry face could be seen here and there in the crowd.

Looking over at Jackie, JFK was proud to be here, and his usually reticent wife seemed to be feeling the same. He had worried that she might be uncomfortable with the entire campaigning experience, but now she was hooked. He could tell. The adrenaline rush of the crowds and the waves of joy and enthusiasm washing over the pair were genuinely affecting.

The motorcade was finishing the ride through the tower-lined main streets of Dallas to thunderous applause. It was none too soon for Jack, as the procaine that he had had injected before departing the plane, enabling him to endure the long motorcade, was wearing off. He could feel the edges of heavy pain returning to his lower back. He would need attention before the luncheon.

Toward the end of the business district, the crowds thinned as the motorcade approached Houston Street. There would be a short jog around Dealey Plaza, then a race to the Trade Mart a few miles away. The limo emerged from the last block of cheering crowds, giving the motorcade's occupants a respite from the deafening attention. From the middle jump seat, an elated Mrs. Connally turned to speak to Kennedy, "You sure can't say Dallas doesn't love you, Mr. President!"

A smiling JFK responded, "No, you can't."

But as the car inched left around the last tight turn onto Elm Street, Jack wondered just how much love would be expressed by the members of the Dallas community attending the upcoming luncheon after he took them to task for the city's extremism. He figured there just might be a bit less of it to go around.

Chapter 4

Goldwater 1964
—*Republican campaign sticker*

Goldwater 1864
—*Democratic campaign sticker*

September/October 1964
Air Force One

To claim that Patrick and JFK developed a friendship during the 1964 campaign would be an overstatement. In fact, Patrick had no idea what their relationship was, but one thing was certain: it was enough of a connection, obscure as it might seem, to get him a regular seat on Air Force One.

After his first hitchhike on the president's plane, Patrick again found himself cleared to fly on Air Force One in Zeke Tackman's place. Salinger had off-handedly informed him of his upgrade as journalists milled about the State Department auditorium after JFK's bi-monthly press conference. Patrick was standing apart from a small group of reporters surrounding the press secretary, asking questions about the next month's schedule of campaign stops. Usually an aide fielded such questions, but somehow Salinger had gotten himself cornered. Patrick stood between him and the door, and as Pierre pulled away to leave, he dropped the invitation in his normal brusque style. "Hey, Hennessey. You're cleared on AF One while Tackman's gone. Be on time." All Patrick had time to respond in his surprise was a pair of raised eyebrows.

Patrick flew three more times on the president's plane from late August through the first week of September, but to his disappointment, he never even saw Kennedy while on the flights. The press boarded early, whereas JFK was whisked aboard at the last minute, signaling the flight's departure. For those in the aft section, a glimpse of the president while in-flight didn't occur unless one was summoned to the front of the plane. Patrick's initial excitement slowly dissipated as his hopes of meeting with Kennedy again diminished with each successive flight.

Zeke's return two weeks later required Patrick to relinquish the seat. He assumed that was the undistinguished end to his moment near the nucleus of government. He was again banished to flying the Following Zoo when fortune shone upon him, and flying commercial when it didn't. His prestige at the *Post* rose and fell somewhat in sync with his seating assignments. But even though he was bumped from Air Force One, his editors gave him greater latitude to follow the president's itinerary during the '64 election in hopes that lightning would strike again. And it did.

Shortly after his reluctant re-entry into the ranks of scrambling journalists, another seat opened on Air Force One. A stringer from the *Tampa Star-Sentinel* got crocked on a long cross-country flight. Had he remained quietly inebriated, he would have survived his embarrassing condition, since it was matched by many of his fellow passengers. But he raucously descended into an ugly political diatribe about the declining state of the country and ended with a dismissal of the Kennedy brothers' support for "them damn uppity southern niggers." When Kennedy was informed, the journalist's press pass was revoked and Patrick was given a permanent seat in the journalists' corral in the aft section. He received the notification in the usual curt manner, with a note through Salinger's aide: *Hennessey, you're in seat 26D for the duration, P. Salinger. P.S. Stay sober!*

Patrick was elated, as was his editor. An Air Force One passport gave him more prestige in the journalism corps and the opportunity to legitimately interview the president on behalf of the *Post*. He was moving up in the ranks, but due more to a pleasant acceptance by JFK than to Patrick's hard-boiled reporting. He hoped he was developing a friendship with the president, one-sided and imaginary though it might be. But even with his new seat assignment, he still found himself just a passenger when it came to presidential interaction.

* * *

The 1964 Republican National Convention was held from July 13-16 at the Cow Palace in San Francisco, eight months after the assassination attempt in Dallas. Conservative Barry Goldwater, the senator from Arizona, bested eastern liberal Nelson Rockefeller for the nomination. Just before the California primary, Rockefeller divorced his wife of many years and remarried, oblivious to the fatal impact it would have. He watched helplessly as his well-financed march to the Republican coronation evaporated.

Richard Nixon, the former Eisenhower vice president who had been bloodied after losing the 1960 election to Kennedy and then the 1962 election for governor of California, sat out this contest, offering up Goldwater to the forthcoming debacle.

Politically, Goldwater was a shadowy partner of the Massachusetts candy manufacturer, Robert Welsh, founder of the ultra-conservative John Birch Society. Welch had mythologized John Birch—the American Baptist missionary-turned-spy who was murdered by communist forces in China in 1945—into a modern Paul Revere of sorts, a man who had tried to warn the country of an upcoming communist takeover "covered up" by complicit members in the U.S. government. These supposedly included President Eisenhower, Supreme Court Justice Earl Warren, Secretary of State George Marshall (responsible for the Marshall Plan reconstruction of Europe after World War II) and a host of others in the State Department and government. Mr. Welch labeled all as treasonous agents of Red China and the Soviet Union.

Much of Goldwater's initial Senate campaign money came from Welch and Dallas billionaire oil tycoon H.L. Hunt, another financier of hard right movements. Even when Goldwater became a national public figure and distanced himself from their more extreme positions, he benefited from and supported their causes and candidates. The *Chicago Daily News* stated that Goldwater had "the invaluable ability to give latent, fear-borne prejudice a patina of respectability and plausibility."

Much of Goldwater's support was also fueled by resistance to the civil rights movement. And with every national protest that turned violent, and every claim that the civil rights movement was infiltrated by communists, Republicans hoped more people would shift to the conservative stance espoused by Goldwater's supporters. Their calls for moderation were a pretext, aiming to limit the spread of integration under the guise of restoring peace and harmony. Kennedy was held responsible for the racial strife because he defined the issue in moral terms and publicly supported Martin Luther King, Jr. There was hope in the Goldwater camp that Kennedy's comfortable electoral lead would evaporate if racial unrest persisted. And into this breach, on his horse Sunny, his supporters fervently hoped, would ride the tanned Arizona senator.

But when Nelson Rockefeller rose to deliver his prime-time speech asking for moderation, he was thunderously booed off the stage by Goldwater supporters. A near riot ensued on the floor of the Cow Palace as Goldwater accepted the nomination, stating, "Extremism in the defense of liberty is no vice." Richard Nixon, no paragon of moral considerations himself, did not even stand to support the nomination after the speech. The entire fiasco was telecast by the three major networks in prime time and doomed Goldwater's campaign before he even walked out of the hall, setting him up for failure on a grand scale come November.

The 1964 Democratic National Convention was held in New York City at Madison Square Garden from August 10-13. In comparison, it was a subdued affair—a sign of the confusing times. The national Trials had begun, jolting the public with emerging evidence of treason within their government. The recently passed Civil Rights Act had not ushered in a utopian response. Instead, there were riots when long pent-up frustrations erupted in New Jersey, New York City, Philadelphia, Cleveland, and Chicago. The "long, hot summer of 1964" brought an edgy atmosphere to the convention. But even so, it lasted the usual four days, culminating in a nominating speech for John Kennedy by Hubert Humphrey that was as friendly, emotional, and even comical as it was endless.

* * *

Kennedy and Goldwater, good friends from their years in the Senate, had mentioned a number of times, even before the Dallas shooting, that they wanted to change the format of electioneering. They wanted to set a different tone, go much further into the issues, and alter the whole nature of running for office. So they suggested there be a long series of debates to allow a full airing of the issues. The debates between Nixon and Kennedy had been a good start toward this national conversation, but they wanted to take it further and establish a refreshingly civilized method of competing. After their respective conventions, Goldwater and JFK publicly agreed to a schedule of ten debates, to be held over the course of the two months leading into the elections on the first Tuesday in November. These were staged across the country with roughly two sessions, a few days apart, every ten days. In between, the candidates often flew together on the president's plane from one location to the next.

Patrick had been given his temporary seat on Air Force One just after the first pair of debates in Houston and Denver. He was given his permanent seat on Air Force One in the middle of the second set of debates between Philadelphia and Kansas City. Goldwater had flown with Kennedy between these two cities as he had for the previous pair of debates. Patrick and all the other correspondents on the plane knew the candidates were up front, and drooled in unison at the thought of listening in on their conversation. It made the flights oddly frustrating, so near and yet so far—twelve rows and a galley section to be exact—from the center of their known universe of politics. Occasionally an aide would reluctantly drop back into the press section, whisper into a reporter's ear, and both would bolt toward the front, the aide to avoid interaction and the reporter to gain it. Patrick kept one eye on the column he was writing and the other toward the front aisle in case a fore-section messenger should come his way. This continued during the flights between Phoenix and San Francisco for the third round of debates, with still no summons for Patrick.

On the flight between Orlando and Boston, he was writing an article about the communication styles of the two men and how they were shaping national opinions, not only of the candidates themselves, but of the beliefs they represented. The *John & Barry Show*, as it was coming to be called on the street, was a fascinating interplay to watch.

The Kennedy-Goldwater debates were curious in their congeniality. Goldwater, considered by many to be intemperate and cranky, was an honorable man whom Kennedy enjoyed and respected. A vast gulf divided the two on issues, but amiability connected them personally, a disarmingly unusual aura for a presidential campaign.

With the attempted killing of a United States president and the ongoing Trials that were digging through the intrigue, it would have been easy to demonize any candidate who challenged the president so soon after his near demise. It was a testament to the character of both men that they handled the situation with candor and class, and both gained stature from the exposure. Goldwater could have been a laughingstock, a figure of derision for challenging a sitting president who probably could not be defeated. It was for this reason that Nixon made no moves to garner the Republican nomination that year. As a hard-headed Machiavellian realist, he knew his chances of election were in the low single digits. Why be embarrassed by John Kennedy, again? But these 1964 debates were having the odd effect of raising Goldwater's standing among the public at large while lessening the influence of his ideas. It seemed to shift him from a threatening proponent of radical intentions to a well-meaning but misguided mouthpiece for zealotry.

In debate, Goldwater's message was tempered and deflated by the president's ability to see the many facets of national and international situations, and to bring them into focus for average Americans. Compared to Kennedy, with his sophisticated intellect and grasp of the complexity of the issues, Goldwater was perceived as a generally good-natured but too often hot-headed reactionary casting an intolerant shadow. Separately they each commanded a certain degree of admiration, but when seen together, Goldwater's dimmed by comparison.

Patrick was focusing his column this week on the passage of the Civil Rights Act. Kennedy had proposed the Act before the Dallas shooting, and Vice President Johnson had expertly shepherded it through a reluctant Congress while the president was recuperating at his Florida home. Goldwater had taken a "principled" stand in voting against it because of a small section of the bill that he felt overreached, and had quickly been labeled a racist, a label Kennedy publicly rejected. He knew of Goldwater's prescient efforts to integrate organizations under his control years earlier. But Kennedy suggested that unyielding "principled" stands were not always the best route to take and were often guises for less than stellar intentions. In their exchange just hours earlier in Orlando, Goldwater could only rigidly hold to his previous opinions and retreat to the need to remain true to his principles. During the debates, the camera lingered on Goldwater's handsome but hard visage as JFK elaborated on his reasoning. Patrick thought it was a telling moment. The public began to associate Goldwater's handsome and forthright demeanor with an underlying hardness of spirit that would dog him the entire campaign. A bit too intemperate for national leadership, was the emerging consensus. With Goldwater, the....

"Mr. Hennessey?"

Patrick looked up from his writing. He had become completely engrossed in his article and had missed the approach of one of the president's aides.

"Yes?" he said, a bit surprised, and aware now that others were watching the exchange.

"You've been invited forward," whispered the aide.

Patrick needed no further encouragement. He folded up his tray, stuffed the unfinished article into the seat pocket in front of him, and nearly jumped out of his aisle seat to follow the aide.

Patrick wound his way forward, past the galley and aide sections into the privileged territory. Even though he had hoped for this encounter, now that it was imminent he was nervous. Would he be in the hot seat again? He had mentally rehearsed a few witty rejoinders to questions the president might ask. But when he arrived up front, the area was filled with almost a dozen aides and campaign advisors, all squeezed into the forward section around the four seats, two of which held the president and Barry Goldwater. As he approached, he could see the president sitting to his left in the fore chair, facing aft. He had a small cigar in hand that he hadn't gotten around to lighting. Sitting to his right with a slightly wary expression was Barry Goldwater , drink in hand, listening to someone talking. Patrick squeezed his way into the group and leaned against one of the bulkheads to get a clearer view. Salinger glanced over as he arrived. Kennedy looked up from his thoughts, his gaze lingering directly on Patrick for a moment. Although he gave no other outward sign, Patrick knew he had been acknowledged.

"You trying to write a damn novel, Smitty, or do you want the facts?" said Barry, shaking his head at a reporter's question. There were already a few journalists up front, including Merriman Smith. "I've said a hundred times I am not in favor of nuclear aggression."

"Well sir, that comment you made about 'lobbing one into the men's room of the Kremlin,'" said the persistent mustachioed reporter. "That *would* get the American public spooked, wouldn't you agree?" Smith had long been the United Press International's White House reporter and had had a recent moment of notoriety. In the press wire-car near the front of the motorcade in Dallas, he had clutched the only radio-phone in the vehicle and dictated to his UPI editors the flash report of the shooting of the president. Days later, he had proudly lifted his shirt to show the bruises from the pummeling he'd received from the two other reporters in the car who had vainly tried to wrest the mike from his hands to get off reports of their own. Reporting, besides promoting divorce and alcoholism from long periods on the road, could also be a contact sport.

"No, I would not agree," responded Barry, showing more than a tinge of irritation toward the questioner. "That was an off-the-cuff remark that you should know not to take at face value." Barry did not suffer fools lightly, but it didn't take much for Goldwater to make a media faux pas. When questioned by a *Chicago Tribune* reporter about his ability to be president, he said, "Doggone it, I'm not even sure that I've got the brains to be president of the United States." Opinions others felt best kept closely guarded, Goldwater eagerly shared with the public.

"Off-the-cuff? Other statements could be construed as worse, and they were on the record," said Smith.

"Hardly, Smitty," responded Barry.

"Sir? On *Issues and Answers* only a few months ago, you suggested using atomic weapons to defoliate the jungles in Vietnam," said Smith incredulously as he flipped through his notepad. It was unclear whether he really felt shocked or was just trying to bait Goldwater, a common tactic on the campaign trail.

"Clean low-yield bombs, so as not to endanger life," responded Barry, speaking as if to a child. He took off his signature large black-rimmed glasses to emphasize his point as he leaned in closer to Smith. On the first flight between debates a month ago, Kennedy and others were engaged in more light-hearted discussions than this one, and at the end of the flight, he and all his aides donned thick black-rimmed glasses in a humorous parting shot at Barry.

"There is no such thing as a clean atomic bomb, and there are people in those jungles!" responded Smith, now clearly alarmed.

"Communists, Smitty! And they use the jungle for cover. No jungle, no cover," said Goldwater, clearly annoyed that the reporter could not understand the simplicity of the issue at hand.

The president had been sitting back, silently watching what was becoming a charged interchange between the two. "Barry," he interrupted, the sharp Boston intonations so dissimilar to Barry's Arizonan earthiness. "If you're ever in this position," he said with a slight gesture of his hand indicating the presidential plane and all that it encompassed, "off-the-cuff remarks are suicide. And you never, *never*," he emphasized, "utter them within fifty feet of guys with press passes." He directed this last to Mr. Smith with whom he had cultivated a friendship over his years in the Oval Office.

But Smith continued along the same track. "Even if that was just an off-camera throwaway, how about your comments that you would never negotiate with communists? You've gone so far as to refuse to even open lines of communication with Khrushchev. Don't you think it would help to at least talk with your counterpart in the Soviet government?"

"I see no reason," repeated Barry, as he had many times before. "Khrushchev knows exactly what he needs to do. Endlessly jawboning with the man won't accomplish a thing."

"Well, I would have to disagree with you there, Barry," interjected JFK matter-of-factly.

"Why is that not a monumental surprise?" smiled Barry.

"Yes, well," replied Kennedy with a slight grin. "You already know I'd had lengthy exchanges with Khrushchev prior to the Cuban missile crisis two years ago. If it weren't for those communications, I don't think there would have been any chance of resolving that issue without a military exchange. It was within a hair's breadth of getting out of control and going over to the generals as it was. I was damned happy to have spent the time chatting him up, no matter how steep the barriers between our positions. The stakes are too high when the downside is nuclear holocaust." Kennedy looked at his unlit cigar and returned it to a snap-pouch he had pulled from his pocket. "You are aware, Barry," he said while still looking down, "that had hostilities begun, Arizona would also have been within range of Cuba's nuclear missiles?"

"There is nothing there worth the effort, not like the Eastern seaboard," quipped Barry in his gravelly voice. Smith and the president exchanged glances, wholly accustomed to Barry's propensity to shoot from the lip, even after the warning just a moment before. If this last comment, even known to be made in jest, were to be broadcast, neither the well-tanned residents of Arizona nor the residents of the East Coast would be thrilled.

"Right, the Eastern seaboard that you suggested be sawed off and allowed to float out to sea," laughed Kennedy. It was a comment Barry had made at a press conference in 1961 expressing his frustration with eastern liberals. "Barry, that's where I live, and incidentally, I should warn you that's where we're headed right now." The plane was on its way to Boston, Kennedy's home turf.

"Well, obviously no one followed my sage advice," said Goldwater, smiling.

"Oh, by the way Barry, I wanted to respond to your accusation that I provoked the Cuban missile crisis to influence the fall midterm elections in '62 to the Democrats' advantage. I'm surprised you didn't claim that in my zeal for re-election I also staged the assassination attempt, but cut it a bit close." Goldwater had made the missile crisis statement at the Seattle Coliseum to an adoring crowd that still could not quite follow him to that length of absurdity. The comment had gotten out and made the rounds. Kennedy refused to respond to it in a public venue to avoid lending it an air of legitimacy.

"Well, that was one I should have pulled back," admitted Barry quietly, raising his hands in a gesture of submission.

Patrick could see the tattooed glyph on Goldwater's left palm, four large dots and a semi-circle, an anglicized symbol of brotherhood with the Indian tribes of the American Southwest. It was rumored that Goldwater could even cuss in Navaho.

As Patrick looked about the group, he recognized Richard Kleindienst, one of Goldwater's campaign advisors. He was wearing a familiar campaign button—*Au H_2O for President*—the atomic symbols for gold and water. Democrats had come back with *Ice H_2O* to go along with the *Coldwater on Barry* segment of their campaign. The official "In Your Heart, You Know He's Right" Goldwater slogan had now been morphed by Democrats to "In Your Heart, You Know He Might," referring to the fear that he might actually bluster America into a nuclear exchange.

"So did your friendly status with Khrushchev help any in preventing the slaughter of those 422 South Vietnamese by the communists?" asked Goldwater, pulling the conversation back to communism. Just last week a grave had been found filled with villagers who had supported the South Vietnamese government. They'd been shot execution style—a setback announced in the middle of the last pair of debates. Goldwater was well aware that the president's view on Vietnam conflicted dramatically with his own. Goldwater saw South Vietnam as a bulwark America was morally required to defend against the encroaching forces of world communism. This domino theory postulated that each successive country that fell to communism brought it that much closer to our shores. Kennedy's quest with the North Vietnamese for a fair and bloodless handoff of authority was nearly treasonous in Goldwater's eyes. He always brought it up in debates and conversations. It was one area where their friendship was sorely tried.

Patrick was well aware of Goldwater's anticommunist leanings and his support for communist purges in America. Although Goldwater did not support the extreme elements that accused Eisenhower of being a communist sympathizer, he had supported Joe McCarthy and his inquisitional investigation and refused to vote for his censure in the Senate.

"I find the Vietminh actions very unfortunate, Barry," replied Kennedy. "Even so, I don't feel that we can step into the middle of that mess militarily and hope to accomplish anything. That struggle has for too long been defined as a war against communism, which I do not believe it is. The

French military could not withstand the Vietnamese desire for unity, and I am afraid that we would either have to destroy their country completely or experience the same fate as the French. I am not willing to exterminate the North Vietnamese for what is essentially their desire for unification, even though it is confusingly intertwined with support from China and the Soviets."

"Well, you're taking a hell of a gamble to prove a pretty imaginary point," barked Barry gruffly. "The Joint Chiefs and almost all of the military say you're wrong."

"They had the same opinion regarding the Cuban missile crisis," responded the president dryly.

"Well, I think you messed up there, too! We should have gone in and flattened Castro. We'd hardly have needed to lift a little finger to do it."

"And at what cost, Barry? A nuclear exchange? Ten, twenty, fifty million dead? A radiation cloud ringing the planet?" said the president, exasperated at the argument that had raged for years.

"They would have backed down! You never even tried," claimed Goldwater. "Hell, for that matter, you should have solved that problem years ago at the Bay of Pigs!" Before the assassination attempt Goldwater had often professed his support of a military "second wave" to overthrow Castro's regime after the bungled Bay of Pigs invasion years earlier. However, since the Trials were showing involvement of anti-Castro paramilitary individuals in the shooting of the president, Goldwater had gone silent on encouraging their re-arming.

The president just shook his head. "Barry, not everything has a military solution. This isn't a John Wayne movie where we can throw American military power at every problem in the world and magically produce utopian results. Real life is more complex and ambiguous. This is true regarding Cuba as well as Vietnam, and in both I am taking a different approach, toward both Castro and Ho Chi Minh."

"You're being taken in by those slippery bastards, Jack," said Barry. "You're making some of the most frivolous bets in American history and the results, in my opinion, will be an unmitigated disaster. Had you done it right, we would have an America-friendly government in Cuba this very minute. *And*," he stated even more forcefully, "we should be bombing the goddamn hell out of North Vietnam, and I mean right now! You mark my words, it will be a far bigger disaster within another five years, with the communists flooding into Cambodia, Laos, and Thailand. Then someone will have to clean up the mess from all these feel-good negotiations and carry out a real war!"

Emotions had gotten hot. Kleindienst motioned to Goldwater during the uncomfortable pause to look over a few papers. As they conferred, Kennedy talked to Pierre Salinger. Patrick could not hear what they were saying, but Kennedy seemed insistent and deliberate. After a few minutes Kleindienst sat back in his seat, but Salinger remained in discussion with the president.

"Senator Goldwater, sir?" spoke up Patrick. Barry looked over. "Patrick Hennessey, *Washington Post*," he introduced himself. As he received an acknowledging glance from Barry, he said, "Sir, just yesterday a number of people were arrested in Philadelphia, Mississippi, for the killing of those three civil rights workers who had gone missing and were then found murdered. I wonder if you would comment on that in relation to your vote regarding the Civil Rights Act of this last year?"

"Well, Mr....?"

"Hennessey, sir," answered Patrick. "The *Post*."

"Yeah, Hennessey, as you should know, I have been a strong supporter of civil rights over the years," started Goldwater.

"But you voted against the Civil Rights Act, sir," interjected Mr. Smith brusquely.

"I am quite aware of my vote, and you are quite aware of why I voted that way, Smitty," said Goldwater. His manner indicated that was the last he wished to hear from him. Returning his attention to Patrick, he continued, "I strongly support the Negroes and their rights as equal members of society. But I do *not* believe the federal government should be in the business of dictating to the states how that balance should be achieved. I voted against the Civil Rights Act because it overreached and intruded into the cultures of individual states and their rights to come to their own changes—voluntarily. You cannot dictate humanitarianism. And regardless of what a bunch of over-idealistic college kids might believe, you cannot force open a person's heart to accept equality of the races. The authorities in states that have difficulties with this issue should be able to work it out without the federal government bearing down on them."

JFK put his hand on Salinger's sleeve to indicate a moment of pause as he became aware of the conversation brewing. He was looking at Patrick now.

"But, sir," said Patrick evenly, "the eighteen people indicted included the chief of police, numerous police deputies, the town's mayor, and its main business leaders, basically the entire civil authority structure of Philadelphia, Mississippi. All are members of the Ku Klux Klan. From these indictments it would seem this town, with county and state support, was promoting the murder of these three college students who were trying to inform Negroes of their right to vote. Many are left wondering how segregationist states can be trusted to address this problem if it is the members of the state and local governments who perpetrate the crime. Who else *but* the federal government would be able to step in and demand an accounting?"

"I trust that incident is an aberration for this area," said the senator sadly, "and even though it is tragic, it can be resolved within Mississippi's legal system. It might take time for this to play out, but I am certain that it will."

"Sir," continued Patrick, "Governor Johnson of Mississippi stated that the NAACP stood for 'niggers, apes, alligators, coons and possums.' If you were a Negro whose entire life, and that of your family, has been lived under the thumb of brutal racist thugs running your state, your county, and your own town, how long do you think you should wait before striking back, since you are receiving no civil protection?"

"Are you suggesting that these Negroes should riot, Mr. Hennessey?"

"Mr. Goldwater, respectfully sir, you speak of the individual rights of man toward freedom and the up-by-the-bootstraps approach to getting ahead—you know, not counting on the government for a handout. Well, doesn't that apply in this situation? I am suggesting, sir, that they already live *within* a riot, one directed by their communities against them. Their resistance would simply be standing up for their rights as human beings." Patrick was well aware of turning Goldwater's words against him, but he wanted to show that those statements held a price.

A steward came back from the pilot's compartment and raised his outstretched hand to indicate five minutes. They only had a short time before getting back to their seats.

Kennedy interjected, "Barry, I believe it's the government's role to provide assistance where the individual cannot. That's why I threw federal weight behind integration. Some states, many of which are supporting your candidacy, I might add, are belligerently against any form of integration. Now how long are these people supposed to wait?"

"Mr. President, with all due respect, don't lecture me about the condition of the Negro. Long before these civil rights issues became national campaign fodder with the likes of Mr. King marching into southern towns and raising a ruckus, I desegregated my National Guard unit in Arizona. It was not the popular thing to do. I desegregated my business in Phoenix, long before it was the popular thing to do. And I supported civil rights, as a member of the NAACP, I might add, long before you realized it was even an issue. So don't lecture me about Negro rights. Why, Mr. President, you came late to the party. I've been there for years."

The aide again came back toward the tight group with a bit more urgency this time. "Sir, we are landing shortly and everyone needs to get back to their seats."

"Barry," responded the president before everyone scattered, "I respect your past actions and I know at heart you're on the right side of this. But go further and make civil rights a federal issue. You're seen as a pawn of the segregationists and southern racists whose support you enjoy now, but you'll regret it later. And I may have come to the civil rights party late, as you say, but why are you leaving early?"

* * *

During the final weeks of the campaign, JFK's television ads showed footage from the Republican National Convention in which the furious crowd booed Rockefeller's calls for moderation and greeted Goldwater's endorsement of extremism. They lingered for an endless thirty seconds on the convention floor melee, with a simple "John Kennedy for President" tag at the end.

Kennedy won the 1964 election with one of the most lopsided votes in American history, second only to Franklin Roosevelt's win in 1936 during the reconstruction years after the Great Depression.

$$Chapter\ 5$$

No single individual or coalition of racketeers
dominates organized crime across the country.
—*J. Edgar Hoover*

If we do not, on a national scale, attack organized criminals with
weapons and techniques as effective as their own, they will destroy us.
—*Robert Francis Kennedy, The Enemy Within*

Friday, November 22, 1963
Hickory Hill, Virginia

Yesterday, Robert Kennedy's entire day had been taken up with crime
bosses—Carlos Marcello, Sam Giancana, Santos Trafficante, and Jimmy
Hoffa, to name but a few. Kennedy had made the dismantling of organized crime rings such as La Cosa Nostra, the Mafia, the Syndicate, the
Outfit, and the Mob one of his primary goals as Attorney General of the
United States. With his brother holding the presidency, he was given free
reign to pursue this objective. The crime bosses and a catalog of thugs with
Sicilian and Americanized family names were the targets. Yesterday he
had hosted a meeting at the Justice Department of about forty federal attorneys from almost every state across the country, at which they detailed
the status of federal cases against the Mob. They plotted ways to increase
pressure on crime syndicates and limit their infiltration into labor unions
and established businesses. They charted strategies for current trials and
future investigations. They formulated more effective ways to use infor-
mants who had penetrated the closed ranks of organized crime. *Omerta*,
the Mafia's code of silence, had kept them well below the national radar for
decades. Bobby Kennedy had spent years identifying, exposing, and then
prosecuting their activities—and the task had just begun.

This morning, Friday, Robert had reconvened the group. But due to
yesterday's progress, the unseasonably warm DC weather, and the approaching weekend, he ended the meeting before noon. It allowed the visiting department heads time for a leisurely lunch and a chance to fly home
on an earlier shuttle. Robert and his attorneys clocked fifteen-hour days

as a rule, so a break in the schedule was welcome. Robert Morgenthau, the U.S. Attorney for New York, and Silvio Mollo, the chief of Morgenthau's criminal division, were invited to Bobby's home, Hickory Hill, for an informal resumption of talks around the pool. Morgenthau and Mollo shared a car driving over to the estate.

* * *

Hickory Hill was a pre-Civil War estate in McLean, Virginia, with a long and storied history of occupants. It was anchored by a large white mansion situated among lovely rolling hills on six and a half acres. It had been the Civil War battle headquarters of General George B. McClellan, the secretive and dilatory leader of the Union forces who was a genius at assembling and organizing large armies, but reluctant to actually advance them in battle. General McClellan, with a tendency toward Napoleonic grandeur, would inexplicably pontificate to the press about his lack of any desire to be an American dictator. But more noticeable was his lack of the esteemed French general's natural abilities in battle. He was eventually relieved by President Lincoln in favor of an officer who actually pressed the fight.

A more recent owner was Robert H. Jackson, Solicitor General, Attorney General, and later a Supreme Court Justice appointed by Franklin Delano Roosevelt just before the outbreak of World War II. After the war he participated in the creation of the International Military Tribunal. As one of the American representatives in the Nuremberg trials, he was the chief prosecutor of Nazi criminals Hermann Goering and Rudolf Hess.

In 1953, Hickory Hill became the home of John and Jacqueline Kennedy. Four years later, the premises became a constant reminder of their loss after the miscarriage of John and Jackie's second child, and Robert purchased it from them. Bobby, Ethel and their five children moved in as Jackie and John moved to a smaller house in Georgetown.

Hickory Hill was a perfect fit for the large, rambunctious household of John's younger brother. A growing family was a natural extension of his Irish Catholic upbringing. They could now burst out into the semi-wilds of Virginia with a manifest destiny befitting their position as part of the emerging Kennedy clan. The family expanded with three more children, the estate with added wings, barns, guest and servant quarters, and a second small beginners' swimming pool, and their collection of critters with ducks, turtles, lizards, chickens, dogs, cats, horses, ponies, rabbits, goats, and pigs.

* * *

Robert returned home first and took a quick swim in the backyard pool. Ethel, Robert's exuberant wife, greeted Morgenthau and Mollo's arrival a few minutes later with her usual infectious enthusiasm. They were told to make themselves at home as lunch would be served shortly.

"I hope you're okay with tuna fish sandwiches," she said without a hint of sheepishness, "It's Friday, and being a good gaggle of Catholics who don't want to go to hell, we can't eat meat today. Bobby will be down in a minute. He's changing."

"Love fish, don't we, Boss?" Mollo assured her with a nod to Morgenthau. Everyone called Morganthau "the Boss." Head of the New York office, he was a tall, tousled, hard-boiled introvert. Although he rarely tried cases himself, he was a brilliant attorney who excelled in organization and strategy. Respected and lionized by his staff, he directed the prosecution of white collar and organized crime with gusto and would constantly instruct his staff to "follow the flow of the money." Never known for elegance in his fashion choices, the story goes he was found one day in Abercrombie & Fitch trying on one of their most expensive suits. The sales clerk praised its appearance and asked if he would like to purchase it. "It is a beautiful suit," said Morgenthau, "but what I'd really like is a list of everyone who's bought one."

They wandered out to the pool around back, staring into its crisp blue waters on what had become a sensuous and summery fall day. It disconcerted the senses to have so much warmth in the air while having so much of autumn's oranges and reds in the surrounding trees that had yet to drop their leaves in deference to the approaching winter. Morgenthau had been to Hickory Hill a few times, but it was Mollo's first invitation. He had been down from New York only once, and that trip hadn't included a lunch break at the attorney general's home. As promised, there was a gaggle of kids. He could not distinguish the attorney general's brood from the visiting neighbors, but from the quantity he assumed there were both. Renovation work was in progress about fifty yards away across the pasture, with scaffolding set up against the barn. A pair of painters was applying a fresh coat of off-white to the shutters and old wood.

While walking through the house and out to the pool, Morganthau pondered his concept of home in comparison to RFK's. He personally liked returning to a haven of quiet, away from the day's work, allowing an interlude of peace and serenity. It rejuvenated him for the long run of hand-to-hand combat to come. It felt that way sometimes, as he spent his days struggling against the criminal element in a war of depositions, subpoenas, trials and judgments with fixed deadlines and withering opposition from the other side, and even sometimes from his own. But RFK left the intense battery of pressures at the Justice Department to return to the boisterous hyperactivity of family life. Robert delighted in coming to a home bustling with activity—children running around the house, dogs and cats in tow, jumping on him and wrestling with him upon his arrival, neighborhood children playing with his own, Ethel directing the whole unruly mob with her obvious pleasure at being in the center of the storm. Home released him from his buttoned up, prosecutorial, power-wielding position in the Capital. He seemed to thrive on the rough-and-tumble interaction with its lack of boundaries and restrictions, whereas Morgenthau would find it exhausting.

"If you didn't work day to day with the guy, you'd think he was a veterinarian, not an AG," commented Mollo while they watched six kids run across the expansive horse pasture, three of the smaller ones lagging behind and three large dogs darting in and out around them. A pair of ducks trailed behind. Two horses and a pony stood by the far fence, keeping their distance from the fray. "When I was on my way down to DC the first time, during that meeting in '62, I wasn't prepared to be impressed with him at all. You know, just a Kennedy kid cashing in on his brother's fame and his father's bankroll. That's how I was thinking." Recognizing talent, Morganthau had made Mollo head of the Criminal Division. He was a tough, by-the-book prosecutor. He tried cases and trained new prosecutors, molding them in the science and artistry of lawyering. He was both smart and street smart, which made him a real asset in the crime division.

"Yeah, I could tell," responded Morgenthau as they watched the children's haphazard passage toward the far fence.

"And then when I had that run-in with him that first day...I told you 'bout that. I just couldn't figure when he was kidding or serious. I thought, Jesus, this guy is an arrogant prick. Well, all that's changed. Seeing him work over Hoffa in those hearings, I must say, he's got balls. Hoffa's no school girl."

"Sometimes when I see him in his different worlds," responded Morgenthau, "like here at the house compared to at Justice, I'd swear there were a few different people living inside that body. He's got some seriously rough edges. I get the feeling with Robert, he's still putting the pieces together."

"What's he, forty or so?" asked Mollo.

"Thirty-eight," said Morgenthau. "In fact, his birthday was two days ago. Had a little party for him at Justice. They gave him a punching bag with the name "Hoffa" and a face stenciled on it. Said he could work him over in the office before working him over in court. He thought it was a riot. Pretty damn young to be doing what he's doing."

Bobby came up behind them from the patio door, toweling his hair from showering after his dip in the pool. He had changed into dry clothes.

"So where's Sandy?" asked Morgenthau, still looking at the pool, sensing his arrival.

"Sandy?" asked Mollo.

Morgenthau turned around to look at Bobby. "Yeah, Sandy. Sandy the Sea Lion."

"Hmm, Sandy. Well, ah...Sandy has moved out. He was donated to the National Aquarium," said Bobby while glancing over at Mollo with a wan smile, his Boston accent ever present.

"The aquarium?" said Morgenthau.

"A sea lion? You had a sea lion in your pool?" asked Mollo incredulously.

Ethel brought out a heaping tray of tuna sandwiches, planting them on the patio table before retreating into the kitchen. Bobby, Morgenthau, and Mollo seated themselves casually around the perimeter.

"Well, it seems that Sandy got a little too excited by the female swimmers and, well...he nearly drowned Mrs. Lasketer over the summer with a rather, how should I say it, 'male show of affection.'" Bobby was smiling as he tossed the towel on a nearby chaise, sat down, and piled a few sections of tuna fish and white bread on his plate. Ethel came back with a bucket of clam chowder and a large pitcher of iced tea. A helper brought bowls, glasses, and silverware. "So we figured it might be best if he was allowed to work out some of those issues with other sea lions. Besides, he was getting pretty big. Too much for the pool anymore."

"Oh, sorry to hear it," grimaced Morgenthau in mock seriousness. "I kind of liked his barking and clapping. The splashing was a bit much. Wouldn't catch me in the pool when he was around. Sure he just went for the ladies? Not a switch hitter? "

"No, no, he was straight as an arrow. Don't you think so, Ethel?" Bobby inquired of his wife, who stood over him pouring iced tea into their glasses.

"Really, Bobby, as if I would know," she said, obviously enjoying being a part of the exchange.

"I think deep down Mrs. Lasketer was disappointed to see him go," Robert continued. "They truly seemed to be hitting it off. I think there was a real attraction blooming there. Didn't you notice the way she looked at him, Ethel?" Ethel just rolled her eyes at her guests and walked back inside.

They munched on sandwiches and got right to business. Robert seldom took time off or came to a complete rest. He was far more than just the criminal enforcer for the Justice Department. Previous to his presidential appointment, amid charges of nepotism, he had been his brother's 1960 campaign organizer. He was a master of organization, a quick study in getting to the heart of any matter and above all, loyal directly to the president. "Get Bobby" was a familiar order to the Oval Office switchboard operator, as he was the first person called during any serious emergency. The presidency was sometimes referred to as the "Brothers Kennedy." RFK was an instrumental voice of reason and prudence in the Berlin crisis, in the Cuban missile crisis, and in obtaining the release of the prisoners held by Castro from the failed invasion at the Bay of Pigs. His time-consuming hands-on involvement with Martin Luther King, Jr. and the explosive Civil Rights movement caused a tectonic shift in his personal views on race and poverty. Many of these events happened concurrently, a full plate that would have kept a whole committee of individuals well fed. But this was the standard daily fare of the current attorney general. The early sixties were trying times.

"So, Hoffa?" questioned Robert as he ran his hands through his still wet hair.

"Hoffa's just about over the edge here," chuckled Mollo. "I heard he thinks the FBI sprinkles metallic dust on his clothes so they can track his every move from miles away. He's getting strangely paranoid. And pretty vocal about it."

"Good. Metal dust, fairy dust, whatever ties him in knots is fine with me," said Robert.

"You know Robert, I think you should take Partin's testimony to heart," said Morgenthau. Edward Partin was a recent mobster turned informant. He turned states' evidence regarding a $20,000 payment for

Partin to tamper with the jury at Hoffa's 1962 trial. "He was pretty clear about Hoffa's threats to bomb your car or have you picked off while you drive around on your own. I think—"

"No bodyguards. I won't give in to that. Pretty soon they'll think they can make a few threats and I'll run for cover. I won't give them the satisfaction, you know that," said Robert.

"But they threatened to stake out the house here. Hoffa talked about taking you out with a high-powered rifle while you swam in the pool. They obviously have done their homework on this. I mean they know you have a pool. It's more than just you—your family could be hurt. I really think you should take some precautions," urged Morganthau. All three were aware of the phone calls to Bobby's house. Voices on the other end of the line describing what hydrochloric acid thrown in a face could do. Voices mentioning the exact route taken by Robert's children to school.

"And Partin passed his lie detector test. This is solid stuff," added Mollo.

"You know how Hoover would react. He's already all over my expenses for use of the FBI for anything personal. If I were to get a few bodyguards from the ranks, he would find a way to parade it in the press showing I was cowering up here. I won't give him that."

"To hell with Hoover! This is a real threat. Use the Secret Service. They can be discreet, but do something." Morganthau was emphatic. "You know when I sit in on some of these depositions with Tony 'Pro' and Vito Gallisone, it gives me the creeps. I get a sense that, beyond their braggadocio and the heavily cologned swagger, they really have no sense of humanity. It was extinguished long ago, if it was ever there. They'd take you out in a minute if they could, and wouldn't care a whit if one of your kids got in the way. I worry about you out here, and driving around alone. You've got balls, Bobby, but don't take it too far. They just see that as a challenge."

* * *

Robert Kennedy had arrived at the position of attorney general with a deeply rooted determination to target and expose organized crime, which he considered an unrecognized danger to the American social and business fabric—a danger that was purposely ignored by J. Edgar Hoover's FBI. Robert simultaneously pursued the heads of the secret Mafioso families and their intrusion into organized labor via union leaders. For this he received the undying hatred of the Mafia and their henchman. During his three years as attorney general, RFK had increased indictments and convictions of organized crime figures almost tenfold over the previous AG.

Hoover, the aging head of the FBI, had avoided not only the investigation and prosecution of the Mob, but for many years, even the acknowledgment of its existence. Hoover's passion was communism. He played the red-scare fears of post-war America to the hilt, seeing commies under every stone, in every university, at every civil rights march, and within every progressive movement. By the time Robert Kennedy assumed the attorney general's office, Hoover had thoroughly infiltrated the American Communist Party. In fact, if it weren't for the largess of the dues-paying FBI undercover agents, it would have collapsed from lack of funds and interest. But Hoover had built his reputation as America's number one crime fighter upon his fixation with the undoing of godless communism and wasn't about to let go of such a sweet deal. And with his preoccupation with pinkos and their ilk, he had little time to notice the rise of the Mob. Or did he?

It was believed by many that Hoover, the master blackmailer, was actually in the pocket of the underworld. He had lived with and doted on his mother till he was forty-three, and was a strict moralist who spent a great deal of his time exposing, or threatening to expose, the sexual or homosexual liaisons of those in business or politics. Yet he was a closet homosexual himself. His lifelong companion, Clyde Tolson, the Associate Director of the FBI, was well-known to be his partner. It was an unusual twist of psychology that, closeted as he was regarding his own homosexuality, he was driven to expose the same propensity in others. When it was mentioned in passing at the Justice Department that Tolson was in the hospital having an operation, Robert Kennedy asked, "What was it, a hysterectomy?" It was rumored that the Mob had the goods on Hoover in the form of explicit photographs taken during one of his many vacations to Las Vegas "comped" by the casino heads.

Hoover was a sinister riddle—frightened of flies and germs, but not of presidential or congressional inquiries. He was a mendacious, racist, anti-Semitic, bureaucratic marvel who held such power in DC that he was unassailable in the fiefdom he had carved out with the help of a massive police force, of which he was the sole and sacrosanct head. He cultivated, through a sycophantic press, the image of respectability and purity as America's number-one crime fighter, chief sheriff, bank-robbing-bandit nabber, and law enforcer. And, of course, he loved and supported the Boy Scouts of America.

In November 1957, during Robert Kennedy's term as chief counsel of the Senate Rackets Committee, suspicious of a large gathering of limousines at a private estate in the small town of Apalachin in upstate New York, the local police set up a roadblock. When the meeting members realized they were under scrutiny, they scattered. Some were caught in the underbrush and nearby woods; sixty were stopped at a small roadblock and required to give identification. Another forty holed up in the house, but were identified by the license plates on their parked limos. They were fingered as the heads of the American Mafia, attending the annual confab they had attended without discovery for nearly twenty-five years. This major and very public exposure reached national news and eventually drafted Hoover as a reluctant warrior in the fight against organized crime.

Though Hoover was a constant adversary within the administration, there was no shortage of external targets for Robert Kennedy's assault on organized crime.

Jimmy Riddle Hoffa was the head of the Teamsters Union. He had risen to power in the early days of union organizing, when dedication to the plight of the workingman was required to counter big business's demand for long hours at low pay with lousy working conditions and nonexistent job security. Hoffa, street smart and a quick study, became a leading figure in the empowerment of the workers during the 1940s and '50s. He rose in the Teamsters Union as a pugnacious voice and violent fighter, and assumed the leadership after former president Dave Beck was imprisoned for larceny and tax evasion—the result of an earlier rackets investigation by Robert Kennedy.

With Beck behind bars, Hoffa became the Teamsters' leader in 1957, and the next target of Robert Kennedy. Hoffa was a short, heavily built street fighter who answered violent union-busting tactics with similarly harsh tactics of his own. And as he gained prominence for the Union, he developed a symbiotic relation with the Mob. Hoffa needed the syndicates to help with "security measures" such as brutal beatings, destruction of property and intimidating opponents, while the Mob wanted access to the vast river of money generated by dues-paying union members. For all he did as organizer and fighter for the workingman, Hoffa's inclusion of the Mob in union activities undermined the original motives for unionizing and destroyed his positive accomplishments with organized labor.

Robert Kennedy and Jimmy Hoffa were oddly akin. Under different conditions, with a common enemy, they probably would have complemented each other or at least been competitors toward the same goal. Both were blunt, aggressive, and demanding of themselves and their associates. They had similar ironic streaks of humor, didn't smoke or drink, were risk-takers, and prided themselves on their physical prowess. Entering court during one of the trial proceedings, they were overheard boasting about who could do the most push-ups. They met inadvertently in DC restaurants a couple of times and almost came to blows over Hoffa's taunting and Kennedy's responses. But with Robert's passionate and sometimes puritanical zeal for justice, and Hoffa's open and unrepentant association with the underworld as a strong-armed adjunct to doing business, there was no common ground to be shared. Like reflections seen through a morally clouded mirror, these determined twins, having taken divergent roads from birth and having applied the same abilities toward different purposes, found themselves on an unavoidable collision as their chosen paths intersected.

Just before enlisting to aid his brother in the 1960 presidential campaign, Kennedy wrote a book, *The Enemy Within*, detailing the dangers of the rise of organized crime. He sent a copy to Hoffa with the inscription "To Jimmy. I'm sending you this book so you won't have to use union funds to buy one. Bobby."

Over the next three years as attorney general, Robert brought Hoffa before Rackets Committee hearings and then to trial for prosecution. But the wily Hoffa always seemed to slip through the government's grasp, whether due to expert legal defense, procedural setbacks, missing witnesses, or suspiciously hung juries. Most recently, a deadlocked jury had again sprung Hoffa after the Test Fleet Corporation trial for taking illegal payments through a truck leasing firm set up under the maiden names of Hoffa's wife and an associate. Shortly thereafter, Hoffa was indicted for jury tampering by intimidation and bribery. The war between Hoffa and Robert Kennedy continued, but this time it looked like the charges would stick.

Bobby also struck at the heart of organized crime by attacking its leaders.

Carlos "The Little Man" Marcello was born in Tunisia to Sicilian parents who became naturalized citizens after they moved to the United States. Carlos never applied for citizenship. He instead claimed to be of Guatemalan descent, and carried a Guatemalan passport. Although Hoover's FBI referred to Marcello as just an inoffensive seller of tomatoes, he was in reality much more. The Louisiana Director of the New Orleans Metro Crime Commission, Aaron Kohn, had long ago enlightened Robert as to the extent of the bribery, illegal slots, drug trafficking, and murders in which Marcello had been involved. He was convicted on a number of counts and was ordered to be deported in 1953. But he lingered. With appeals, bribed judges, legal obfuscation achieved through intimidation, and a very large bankroll, he managed to extend his stay in the United States, ad infinitum it would seem. Bobby was aware of his temerity and mocking defiance of the judges and the legal system.

In early 1961, a few months after his appointment as AG and eleven years after Marcello's court-ordered deportation, Bobby had Marcello picked up at his quarterly check-in at the Immigration and Naturalization Office in New Orleans, and flown directly to Guatemala and deposited there. No phone calls, no lawyers. It was one of Bobby's opening salvos in his years-long battle with the Mob. Marcello, finding himself in a foreign country for which his passport and papers were forged, was not only apoplectic with anger, but was summarily bounced to El Salvador by indifferent authorities, then from El Salvador to Honduras where, after a lengthy stay and much difficulty, he managed to make his way back to New Orleans. On arrival, he was picked up for illegal entry and passport forgery. Back on home soil, he was able to use his legal wits to do long battle with the Justice Department, during which time, through the creative use of money and intimidation, he avoided convictions. After his unplanned Central American travels, his hatred for Robert Kennedy knew no bounds. A trial had recently concluded in New Orleans, and Bobby waited on the verdict with seasoned apprehension.

* * *

"What about New Orleans? Marcello's verdict comes down today, right? Any word?" asked Bobby.

"The case was handed to the jury a couple of hours ago, but nothing yet," said Morgenthau grimly. "Getting a conviction down there would be a miracle. He owns that town, and probably every member of that jury."

"If that *bahstahd* walks, we start again. We have enough on him for half a dozen charges—no let-up. Besides, if he's full-time keeping us at bay, the less time he's got to go out and kill somebody."

"He may walk, but it won't be far. We've got the feebies sitting on him twenty-four hours a day," said Mollo, using the nickname for the FBI.

"Yeah, I know, but I want that prick in a prison cell. A Central American vacation isn't good enough this time," said Robert without humor.

There was a stir at the door to the patio. Ethel had been on her way out to be with the men for a while, but was diverted by the maid with a phone call. Bobby could see her talking with obvious exasperation in her face. She looked up to notice Bobby eyeing her and said, covering the mouthpiece to the phone with her free hand, "It's the Director."

Bobby excused himself and walked over to take the call. Morgenthau and Mollo remained at the patio table, looking out across the pasture. They were glad they had come to Hickory Hill to enjoy this last gift of summer warmth. Morganthau's gaze was attracted by a commotion at the barn far across the field. He tapped Mollo on the arm and gestured in that direction. It appeared one of the painters had fallen off the scaffold. The other man stood looking down at him with his hand over his mouth. The scaffold was about six feet high. Morgenthau lazily watched and wondered what they were up to. What kind of painter falls off his scaffolding while the other just watches? The fallen painter got up, at first limping and then, with obvious discomfort, running toward the house. He was holding a box in his hand and yelling something impossible to make out.

Bobby had his hand on the phone while Ethel, with hers still over the mouthpiece, said, "It's Hoover. I told him you were having lunch. All he said was 'It's urgent.' That man!" Ethel was quite familiar with the FBI Director and there was little love lost between them.

Morgenthau sensed something was wrong. The painter was in obvious distress but was still running as fast as he could across the field separating the barn from the main house. A short man with minimal apparent athleticism, he pushed himself with little personal regard, yelling something about "hot" while holding out what looked like a radio.

Morgenthau looked quizzically at Mollo. "Can you hear what he's saying?"

"No," said Mollo, "Wait, he says he's been shot? Oh God! The president! He says the president's been shot! The president's been shot!" They both jumped up and looked at Robert. He stood by the door, looking at the ground with his hand to his forehead, the other holding the phone to his ear. He was ashen.

"I have news for you," Hoover said in short rapid-fire speech.

"What?" said Robert Kennedy.

"The president has been shot." He said it coldly and impersonally, as if reading names from a phone book. Bobby's first response was a mixture of confusion and up-welling anger toward Hoover's cruelty.

"What?! I.... Is it serious? I..." stammered Bobby.

"I think it's serious. I am endeavoring to get details. I'll call you back when I get more." And he simply hung up.

What? What had Hoover said? That couldn't be! Bobby felt a staggering bolt of fear run through him as the blood drained from his face. He couldn't think of any response. He must be wrong. Hoover must be wrong!

The painter had arrived at the patio panting from exertion. "The president...was...shot! He was in Dallas and...got shot in his car!" he said through gasping breaths.

Bobby cried out, "Jack has been shot?!"

"If it's on the radio, it must be on the TV," said Mollo. They all dashed into the library in a state of disbelief. Ethel turned on the set. It took an eternity for the tubes to warm up and the black and white picture to appear. When it filled the screen, there was an ongoing report from a very sober Walter Cronkite. He reported the evening news. Seeing him onscreen in the middle of the day was not a good sign.

"...from CBS News. This just in from Dallas, Texas. President Kennedy appears to have been shot while his motorcade was passing though the downtown business district. Initial reports claim the president has been seriously wounded." There was a short pause while Cronkite was handed a paper. "Further information has just come in. President Kennedy has been shot. An assassination attempt may have left the president mortally wounded. After three shots rang out, the limousine carrying the president reportedly raced toward the nearest hospital. I repeat, today in Dallas, Texas, an assassination attempt on the life of President Kennedy has left him seriously wounded. He is being raced to a local hospital. Stay tuned to CBS News for further details."

Cronkite meant to end the broadcast, but for a moment the cameras remained live. Viewers could see Mr. Cronkite remove his glasses and rub his eyes. There was pandemonium in the background, with the voices of reporters and news staff heard over the open microphone while they rushed across the set. A short musical jingle began, then the image of a steaming cup of coffee and "It takes more than an instant to make a real cup of coffee, that's why Nescafe takes...." It was a surreal interlude cut short as Cronkite returned.

"We have further details of the shocking events in Dallas, Texas. The president has been shot while driving through downtown Dallas in an open-topped limousine. Three shots rang out during passage through a small plaza at the end of the motorcade route. The president was hit at least once. Governor Connolly, also in the car with Mr. Kennedy, was hit at least once. The limo raced to nearby Parkland Medical Hospital where the president was rushed into an emergency room. Doctors are working on him as I speak, but we have no word on his condition. Stay tuned to CBS News for further details."

There were numerous people around the TV by this point as the house staff had all rushed into the library—hands to mouths and over eyes, some sobbing and some frozen in disbelief. A palpable anguish enveloped the room.

Bobby went quickly to the phone. He called the White House switchboard, but it was busy. He tried again, and then again. He got through on the fourth try.

"This is Robert Kennedy. I am calling from Hickory Hill. Keep this line open and do not allow it to be broken at any time. Do you understand?"

"Yes, Mr. Kennedy," responded the operator. She was familiar with Bobby's voice, as she had routed many a call to him over the years. It sounded as if she had been crying.

"I want you to get me Robert McNamara immediately. I will hold," he said.

"Yes, sir. I will try. The lines are completely jammed in DC. It's like everyone in town picked up their phone at the same moment."

"Just keep trying. I will keep this line open. I will also call on our second line and will want to keep that open as well. Do you understand?"

"Yes, sir."

Bobby stood transfixed, staring out the porch door with the receiver in his hand. He was furious and devastated at the same time. Emotion welled up, but he kept it down with a supreme force of will. This couldn't be true. It just wasn't possible. He had just talked to Jack earlier today. He was in Fort Worth getting ready to head to Dallas. He mentioned the crowds were much better than he had expected, and that Connally and Yardborough were going to patch up their differences in a tolerable manner, at least till the next elections. All had been so normal and jocular. Jack was having a good time down there.

"Mr. Kennedy! Mr. Kennedy, are you there?"

"Yes! Yes," said Robert, coming back to the present.

"I have Secretary of Defense McNamara on the phone." There was a short static crackle.

"Bobby! Bobby, I just heard. Do you have any word? All I've got is what's on TV."

"Hoover called, said that he would call back, but I know only the same. Listen, Mac. I want to get down there. I need to be in Dallas. Can you scramble a military jet from Andrews? I can be there in under an hour."

"Yeah, let me make a call and get right back to you."

"And wait, Mac, is there any activity on the board? With the Soviets I mean? Is this something bigger?" Bobby somehow had the presence of mind to see the larger picture, that this could be an opening salvo in a more ambitious plan.

"No. We checked the minute we heard and we're scrambling for info. But it appears completely quiet. No troop movements in days and nothing at all today. We have some fresh U-2 photos and they show nothing. If the Russians are behind this, they're being awfully quiet about it. I just don't see a thing, but we're on it with a microscope."

"Okay."

"I have an urgent meeting convening in minutes with the Joint Chiefs. Maxwell's here. We'll be going to high alert status, but there's nothing showing up right now," added McNamara. "I'll call you right back about the flight." He hung up.

"Is there anything I can do?" asked Morgenthau. He walked over to Bobby. Bobby just stood there for a moment, looking out at the pasture through the porch door. His enjoyment of such a beautiful reminder of summer had vanished completely and was replaced with a staggering weight of fear and grief. "I always thought it would have been me," said Bobby gravely. "I just always thought they'd come after me, not Jack."

The phone rang. Bobby picked it up, thinking it was McNamara calling back. It was Hoover.

"The president has been severely injured. It looks like he's dying. He lost a lot of blood," stated Hoover in clipped indifferent inflections. "Shot a couple of times in the back, we think. He's being wheeled in for surgery. I don't have anything further for now."

"Is he at Parkland Hospital?" Bobby had seen mention of this on TV.

"Yes."

"Is there any word on—"

"Mrs. Kennedy was also hit. She's in surgery too. I don't have anything further for now."

"What! Is she—" But the line was dead. Hoover had hung up.

Chapter 6

History will be kind to me for I intend to write it.
—*Sir Winston Churchill*

The great French Marshall Lyautey once asked his gardener to plant a tree. The gardener objected that the tree was slow growing and would not reach maturity for 100 years. The Marshall replied, "In that case, there is no time to lose; plant it this afternoon."
—*John F. Kennedy*

Thursday, September 12, 1968
Washington, D.C.

Early in the morning, Patrick drove his middle aged Ford Fairlane into DC and parked at the *Post*. He had a number of articles that needed attention, requiring some time at his typewriter and phone following up sources. This was a standard part of his workday. He enjoyed newspaper work most of the time, as it afforded him a mix of working conditions. Some days were spent calling sources to authenticate, either on or off the record, points he was making. When his ear was raw from holding the phone to it, he could always make an excuse to get out and meet in person. He liked both parts of the job, but not the stressful deadlines. All of Washington was in a constant news frenzy. It was not so much getting a lead on a story, but getting the facts and the verification to back it up, that was the tedious and sometimes exasperating portion of his day.

Today he was trying to get confirmation of a quote by Spiro Agnew, who had allegedly stated that the recent U.S. negotiations with the North Vietnamese regarding merging the governments of the South and the North were "a weak-kneed Chamberlainesque appeasement, typical of the nugatory un-American nature of this dissolute administration." Agnew had said it to a group of lobbyists and reporters while slipping on his golf glove, preparing for a round at the prestigious Alexandria Club in Virginia. Patrick's profession was words and writing, but he sheepishly admitted to looking up "nugatory" in the office dictionary. He so enjoyed following Spiro, who could always be counted on to enliven a political season by stepping up to the edge of a verbal cliff, then blithely dropping off.

Keeping close tabs on the vice presidential portion of this campaign was also an educational experience that invariably expanded his vocabulary.

But Patrick's attention today was not fully engaged by campaign proceedings, as his 11:00 a.m. meeting with Kennedy loomed large in his mind.

* * *

The *Post's* offices were situated a half dozen blocks north of the White House, and with the still warm but approaching fall weather, he decided to walk the distance to the East Wing entrance, gaining a little extra time to think. He stopped off at a deli along the way and picked up a bagel, pocketing it in his coat for later as he neared the White House.

The added walking time gave him little relief from his nervousness. He kept slipping into a feeling of unreality. Had he really been called to the White House for a meeting with the president of the United States? Maybe Evelyn Lincoln was calling a different Patrick Hennessey, and Patrick would be ushered into the East Wing and sequestered from the other visitors while White House Security was called. Maybe the appointment had been abandoned like a bit of chaff in the wind and no one had bothered to notify him. He had told no one of the meeting, partly because of Mrs. Lincoln's request, and partly because he was so uncertain as to its nature. He hadn't even told Devona, his editor.

He arrived at the East Wing guard station even earlier than requested. As he came around the turn to the entrance, he was greeted by a throbbing mass of grammar school students and their harried teachers. Two hundred children, the overactive spores of humanity, were lined up along the wrought iron fence that stretched fifty yards from the guard gate. More were getting off a pair of Greyhound buses parked along the staging area to the south. They radiated a chaotic, barely suppressed energy that accentuated Patrick's unease. He got in the line at the entry kiosk.

"Name and identification, please," said the sharply dressed Marine guard as Patrick's turn came to approach the window.

"Patrick Hennessey." He handed over his driver's license.

The guard shuffled though a clipboard thick with papers. "Yes, the Lake Tapawingo Elementary School group. Why, you're just outside of Independence, Missouri," stated the Marine pleasantly.

"Well, not at the moment," responded Patrick. "Ah, Truman's stomping grounds, though, when we're at home," he added recovering quickly. He had better play the part.

"Your students are assembled in group two, just along the fence to the left," said the guard, pointing toward the seething mass of fledgling political scientists behind Patrick. He handed over an admission ticket. "Have a good tour." Did the guard know he was packed in with a group of children he had never met? Was he in on the ruse of a secret White House visitor? Or was Patrick just imagining that a knowing smile flitted across the Marine's face as he handed Patrick the small ticket?

Patrick turned and walked along the fence till he came to the space between groups two and three, demarcated by a small hand-traced sign on blue cardboard, the number three held up with a competent air by a girl in the following group. He queued up behind a young straggler of his assigned class who also seemed to be feeling a bit out of place, judging by his quiet demeanor and downcast eyes. He peeked up from the high collar of his unneeded winter coat as Patrick lined up behind him. The boy seemed to withdraw a bit further into himself at the presence of another adult, and a stranger at that. Patrick stood, warming in the early sun, wondering at the incongruity of his presence here.

"What's your name?" asked Patrick, breaking the awkward silence after a few minutes.

The boy looked up. "William," he mumbled quietly.

"Don't worry, William. It gets better," said Patrick, smiling conspiratorially. He had been painfully shy himself when he was younger.

He took the paper bag out of his pocket, broke the bagel in half, and handed a piece to the boy. After a moment of looking up at his face, William graced him with a slight smile as he took the offering.

The tour finally began, snaking through the Visitor's Entrance, the Library and Gallery Hall, and then into the large East Room. All the while Patrick brought up the rear, following young William as the tour guide talked of some of the history surrounding a building that had been at the center of American development for the last 170 years.

The White House was modeled after Leinster House in Dublin, Ireland. James Hoban, an Irish-American tradesman, was chosen through a design competition early in George Washington's term to begin construction in 1792. Washington lived only to see the exterior shell completed. John Adams, the second president, not all that interested in the pomp of palatial living, made numerous design changes, had some of the stone-carved nude figures removed from over the mantelpieces, and moved in for three months before being voted out of office. It wasn't until almost ten years after ground was broken that Thomas Jefferson, the third president, actually moved in for the duration of his term. Jefferson was an architect in his own right, and made renovations to the main house and to the overall design and layout of Washington to impart a more Roman effect with an added French flair rather than the original English style. Years later, in the War of 1812, after marching through the capital of their revolutionary colony, the British unceremoniously burned "The President's House," as it was called at the time, to its exterior stone shell, but not before the invading troops partook of the remainder of a fine meal abandoned by the fleeing members of President James Madison's household. By 1818, the war with Britain long since won, the President's House was rebuilt and reoccupied. Over the ensuing years it was expanded, remodeled, renovated, thoroughly deconstructed and reconstructed by Truman, then further expanded and re-renovated. Indoor plumbing was added, oil lamps were replaced with gas and then electric light, central heating and air conditioning were installed, a basement bomb shelter was constructed, and eventually telephones, televisions, and teletypes made their appearance.

Recently, following Truman's workmanlike reconstruction and Eisenhower's long neglect during his eight-year stay, Jackie Kennedy spearheaded a much needed major renovation during the first years of JFK's term. It was lauded by many as a rebirth of the importance and the appearance of such a symbol of the American seat of government. More than a building, it was the materialization of an idea, a physical "bricks and mortar" representation of democracy. With all its renovations, additions, and makeovers, it architecturally mimicked the changing nature of the republic itself.

By the time the tour proceeded through the East Room, with Patrick trailing the Lake Tapawingo Elementary School class, he was wondering if his fears of abandonment might be realized. He met no contacts. Was this to be a dry run after all? But as he rounded the door to the Cross Hall entrance, a balding, brown pinstripe- suited man stepped out from the doorway to greet intercept him. Patrick had not noticed him standing quietly near a Marine guard.

"Mr. Hennessey, I presume," he said with twinkling good humor, fully aware of Patrick's humorous position as an interloping adult in the group. "Are you enjoying your class tour?" Patrick recognized him immediately as they shook hands. Dave Powers was the president's close friend and confidant. It was one of his main jobs to greet visitors to the president and

calm their jittery nerves while ushering them into the Oval Office. Patrick
had seen him in the background at presidential events but never up close,
except on an Air Force One flight a few years ago.

"Yes, it's been an education," replied Patrick, nodding to his young
friend, William. The boy had turned to watch the interchange while he
was ushered onward by his teachers.

"Made a friend from what—Missouri, is it?" asked Dave.

"We shared a bagel," said Patrick, "and a bashful childhood."

Dave moved Patrick through the marbled expanse of the elegant Cross
Hall and toward the stairs off the main White House entrance that led up
to the private quarters of the first family. "So I hear Ben Bradlee is about to
take over at the *Post*," said Powers. The man was charm itself. Patrick could
see why he was such a valued friend of the president. He said the last with
a conspiratorial squint, knowing full well that this was inside information
which even Patrick, who worked at the *Post*, had probably heard only as
vague rumors.

"Dave, you're ahead of me on that one. Nobody tells me anything. In
fact," offered Patrick, leaning in with what he hoped was a matching clandestine twinkle whispered, "I don't even know why I'm here."

Powers laughed infectiously; his face was marked with lines that
showed its familiarity with good humor. "Well," he said, looking about
in mock secrecy, as they were already part way up the stairs and no one
was nearby to hear, "I think you're going to enjoy this." He chuckled again
at Patrick's unknowing. Patrick laughed, too. He could see why Kennedy
employed the man as a greeter. He was feeling conspiratorially at ease already.

As they walked up the red-carpeted stairs off the White House's grand
entry, Patrick marveled at the gilt-framed portraits of Hoover, Wilson,
Truman, and Roosevelt that graced the landings. Mrs. Kennedy had restored a regal charm that even Patrick, no expert on anything fashionable
or architectural, could feel and see. He took in his surroundings while
Powers, aware of the effect from having escorted many other guests, let
the stroll impart a feeling of grandeur and suspense. They walked up to
the Central Hall foyer on the second floor, and Powers ushered Patrick
into the Treaty Room.

"Mr. Hennessey, have a seat and the president will be with you in a few
minutes." And with that, Powers retreated down the hall toward the West
Wing, leaving the door open.

Left alone, Patrick didn't quite know what to do. He'd never been inside the private quarters of the White House. He looked about the room and studied the many paintings on the walls. He looked out the window over the balcony Truman had added toward the south lawn. He could just see the edge of the crowds awaiting entrance into the East Wing tour he had just left. In the center of the deep forest green-carpeted room was an elongated table with seven chairs pulled in around it. An eighth had been sitting at the head toward the door, but was now snugged into a corner near the fireplace. This room was one of the results of Jackie Kennedy's renovations, with General Grant's imposing table resurrected from storage to grace the focal central spot. It was an elegant setting, with a huge chandelier hanging overhead. JFK had signed the Nuclear Test Ban Treaty here in '63 and then the surprise Nuclear Non-Proliferation Treaty in '66. Eisenhower had used it for a card-playing room with his pals—bridge they told everyone, although it was always assumed to be poker.

Patrick sat down in one of the chairs toward the end of the table near the door. He was fiddling with one of the table's drawers when he heard footfalls coming down the carpeted hall. But before he had time to lose the calm imparted by his greeter, in walked Dave Powers again, this time pushing the president before him in a wheelchair. Patrick had already risen out of his seat before the president's remonstrations could be acknowledged.

"Mr. President."

"Mr. Hennessey," said JFK. "Please, please be seated. No ceremony *heah*. It is so good of you to come. I trust you enjoyed the tour," he responded humorously as he reached out his hand to shake Patrick's.

The Boston accent, so familiar to the nation from the many public addresses over the years, was even more pronounced up close, as was the president's age. Looking at JFK across the table, Patrick was taken aback by his lined face—indications of age and stress not so obvious at a distance in press and TV images. It had been three years since Patrick had been close enough to reach out and touch the man. Kennedy was graying at the temples, with a lightening of his brown hair to whitish blond at the borders. He had lines and noticeable bags under his eyes. There was a sense of mental vitality but physical wear from enduring the pain that had become more publicly known, especially the deterioration of his lower back. Occasionally wheelchair bound when out of sight of the press, he'd had to adjust to some limitations. He was worn from all the damage that had accumulated in his body from a lifetime of difficult medical conditions and the injuries from the shooting. It was rumored he had some very bad days.

He still appeared in public as a robust and healthy president. And at times, when his back pain eased, either on its own unpredictable schedule or with the help of painkillers, he could feel his old self. The press corps was aware of and complicit in the image of a healed man who was fully recovered. For press conferences, if in pain, he would be already standing at the podium talking to an aide when the reporters filed in. And for other situations he would stoically endure the pain of standing for as long as he could, always with an aide nearby to assist if it ever became necessary. It hadn't so far, and although the nation still saw him as a healthy president with war wounds that occasionally flared up, there were cracks in the facade. The public was becoming gradually more aware of the depth of the president's infirmities and injuries. His spirits, at least from what Patrick could glean, had not flagged along with his physical condition, and his wit, mental acuity, and commanding presence had not diminished at all. In fact, Patrick felt a more sagacious, worldly demeanor emanating from the man, an estimation shared by many observers, in both public and private settings.

"Well, I'm sure you're curious as to why I asked to meet you here, Mr. Hennessey, so I'll get right to the point," began the president, leaning in. "What have you got going over the next, say, year and a half?"

"Sorry...?" asked Patrick, unsure as to the context of the question.

"I want to hire you to write my memoirs," asserted the president, sitting back.

Patrick opened his mouth to say something, but nothing came out.

The president seemed to enjoy Patrick's surprise. "I've been following you, Mr. Hennessey, reading your articles and books. Incidentally, I enjoyed your treatment of Goldwater in your new book—what is it, *Returning to a New Home*? You gave him a fair shake, something I didn't expect from the way you confronted him on my plane that day during the debates. A good man. I'm sure he'll be re-elected to the Senate." Knowing full well that Patrick was in the throes of confusion, he threw in matter-of-factly, "So you're in?"

"But—what about Sorensen, or Schlesinger, or Mailer?" blurted Patrick, suggesting other writers who he assumed had an inside track to the president. "Manchester?" he added feebly. He was completely flummoxed by the offer. There were rumors going about the newsroom that the president was interviewing for an author to write his official biography. But these meetings were made through Kenny O'Donnell, his appointments secretary. That was a sure way *not* to keep the meeting secret, as it was an ongoing game in Washington to decipher who was meeting with the president and why. And the normal appointments secretary route was very visible. Patrick was startled also that the president knew of his upcoming book and had even read it. It was not yet published. How had he gotten a copy of the draft?

"All good choices, all probably going to write their own books," said Kennedy dismissively. Most of the talent in his administration was assumed to be planning tomes of their own. Certainly Sorensen, Schlesinger, McNamara, and a host of others would do so. Kennedy had asked all of them to refrain from publishing before the term was complete, but he understood not only the need for each of their positions to provide an explanation for historical purposes, but also the monetary and social appeal. As long as they did not capitalize during his tenure, he felt that their due.

Kennedy, with raised eyebrows, looked over at Dave Powers, who had quietly retired to a chair by the side of the room near the fireplace. "Dave," he inquired with a smile creeping up on his face, "you writing a book?"

"The thought has lingered suggestively on me mind, Mr. President," responded Dave straight-faced with a hint of Irish brogue. Obviously a private joke between them.

"I thought you might be writing your own book, sir?" said Patrick questioningly, beginning to get a handle on the situation. He was here to be offered a position, not reproached for issues around his latest publication.

"Well, there are reasons to forego that at this time," said the president. Patrick had noticed the still strong grip when he shook the president's hand. But for just a second his gaze flickered down to the president's right hand where it rested on the arm of his wheelchair.

"Yes," said Mr. Kennedy, acknowledging Patrick's involuntary glance. "It would seem I have a little more damage than first thought." He raised his hand and rubbed his fingers together. "To sit and write for any length of time is a real pain in the ass." He said this with frustration as he looked over at Dave. "I had been playing around with taping the whole thing on a Dictaphone, but...." Kennedy waved the thought away as if it was an annoyance he had already dealt with too many times in the past.

Patrick had heard rumors the president was losing some motor control of his right hand. The shots in his upper chest near his shoulder had left nerve damage that had not fully healed. Kennedy also suffered from Addison's disease, leaving him with poor powers of self-repair. Like Roosevelt, though, he was incredibly stoic when it came to any public show of weakness or infirmity and would go to practiced lengths to appear full of "*vigah*." But in reality he was damaged.

The president leaned back in his chair and looked at Patrick. "So, are you in, Mr. Hennessey?

"Of course you *ah*," replied the president, answering his own question.

I think I am, thought Patrick.

The president went on talking, ignoring Patrick's lack of response. "It will be a bestseller, I assure you. We can deal with the particulars later, but I'm sure they'll be satisfactory." The president leaned in again. "My suggestion would be to meet on a regular basis over the next few months. First we'll have a test run. A few meets at the White House for starters—"

"But, sir," interrupted Patrick, "I'm not a ghostwriter." He surprised himself with the comment. He was just getting his head around the idea of writing the memoirs of the president of the United States. Was he crushing any chance he had of being in this plum position by refusing to submerge his own authorship? "I'm not sure I understand the offer, Mr. President," he said nervously. "Am I to be doing this without acknowledgment?"

The president, stopped mid-sentence, leaned back and tapped his fingers thoughtfully on the wheelchair arm. Kennedy could see that Patrick could not allow himself to be pushed. There was pride at work here. *All the better*, he thought. "This will be *my* book, Mr. Hennessey, but that being the case, you will receive full acknowledgment as a co-author. I will have the final say on its content and the time of its publication. My intention is to discuss with you the major topics of this administration, uncut so to speak. I will not censor what I may say to you, mainly for fluidity of our exchange. But I will, almost surely, censor myself afterwards in the final release for publication. And I hold that right without negotiation."

"I understand," responded Patrick thoughtfully. He realized that all the preparations he'd been making over the last six months for a third book, an examination of the interplay between the president, his brother Robert, and Fidel Castro during their exquisite dance toward Cuban rapprochement might have to be shelved for now.

"I've picked you because of your writing style, Mr. Hennessey, and the way you treat your subjects, as I noted earlier with your handling of Goldwater. Also because of your approach and political leanings. You write with—how should I put this—humanity, and a dose of hard-headed political pragmatism.

"Now I want to give you some time to think about it, but I will need your answer shortly. So how about we meet again next week for your decision?" The president was not surprised to see that his guest was still in a state of confusion.

Patrick was still in shock and was glad that he didn't have to say yes so quickly. It seemed unseemly, unprofessional in some way or other, even though he knew his answer already. "That would be just fine, and thank you, sir," was all he could say, but it appeared from his relaxed demeanor that the president was satisfied with his response.

"Mrs. Lincoln will give you another call. She knows my schedule. I'll look forward to seeing you in a week, but I want you to keep this very private for now." And with that, he reached out to shake Patrick's hand. The job interview, if that's what it had been, was over. Dave Powers, familiar with the president's perfunctory cues, had already risen and begun to guide the wheelchair around. Patrick stood quickly as they moved toward the door. "Oh, and by the way," said the president, pausing before he exited, "I already talked it over with your boss, Ben Bradlee. He's all for it. Says you'll be just the man for the job."

Dave Powers wheeled the president from the room. "Just let yourself back out through the tour line," said Dave over his shoulder with a nod.

Patrick had risen and was left standing in the empty Treaty Room. He walked back down the White House entrance stairs, hardly noticing anything this time in contrast to his arrival. He walked past a few Marines stationed off the Entry Hall and then tagged along with a tour group until he could peel away and exit again at the east tour gate. Wandering out into the warm fall air, finding himself standing on a corner off Pennsylvania Avenue, he was lost in thought and uncertain of his destination. He needed to think, needed some time to let himself absorb the event that had just transpired. He didn't want to go back to the hubbub of his office at the *Post*. Wandering aimlessly down city sidewalks wouldn't do either. He started walking east down Pennsylvania, and then hailed a cab to take him toward the Capitol Building.

Sitting in the back of the taxi, Patrick was aware of the magnitude of the offer just presented to him. In the summer of 1961, only six months into Kennedy's presidential term, Elie Abel of *The New York Times* proposed writing a book about the decision-making methods of the new administration. This was after the Bay of Pigs fiasco, the disastrous summit in Vienna with Khrushchev, and the subsequent masonry-walled separation of East and West Berlin that had heightened tensions with the Soviets to the point of real fears regarding an outbreak of nuclear war. In fact, the administration had proposed a citizen's initiative to construct personal bomb shelters to weather the possible upcoming holocaust. To that proposal, JFK had responded acidly, "Why would anyone write a book about an administration that has nothing to show for itself but a string of disasters?" During that time, JFK was plagued by severe back troubles and heavy concerns that his presidency was taking a disastrously incompetent turn.

What a difference between then and now. JFK was confident and relaxed. And, although of course some would always disagree, his administration was showing every sign of being a great success both here and abroad. Historians were placing him in the company of Lincoln and Jefferson. And Patrick was being interviewed, if that was the term for his summons to the White House, for the position of author to write a memoir for this presidency. Interviewed was not the right word. It seemed that Kennedy had already decided. The rumored writers and their very public meetings were a ruse. It would seem that JFK was trying his best to keep others in the dark about who his author would be, at the same time protecting Patrick from the harsh glare of public scrutiny if it were known that he had been chosen. He wondered if Kennedy had asked anyone else. Maybe others were quizzed and had rejected the advance. Hardly! It was a prize assignment, once in a lifetime, and he knew it. The president seemed certain, even to the point of asking Ben Bradlee, his boss, to basically hand him over to the president. Patrick would have felt miffed at his transfer, like a piece of chattel, if he weren't so honored.

Patrick thought also about *Profiles in Courage*, the Pulitzer Prize-winning book JFK had written while recovering from an earlier failed back operation in 1955. He had vehemently professed his authorship, yet did acknowledge that Sorenson and other aides had assisted him greatly in the research and framework for the book. JFK's previous publication was a bit similar to Patrick's. It took a number of subjects and related their courageous stances in trying times, similar to the thrust of Patrick's first book

regarding targets of the McCarthy hearings. He hadn't realized the simi-
larities until just now. Maybe the similarity with his own style had been
the reason for the president's choosing him. Patrick wanted to think that
his own style was a bit more accessible. JFK was a classical writer steeped
in a traditionalist's approach to prose. Elegant and informative, it lacked
the warmth that would invite broader consumption by the public. JFK
had also written a short publication, *Reconsidering America*, during his period of convalescence in Florida after the Dallas shooting. It dealt mainly
with a rethinking of the issues pertaining to communism, the Cold War,
and Southeast Asia. But for his memoirs the president might want a larger
range of subject matter, and true to his nature and that of the fifties, he
might possibly be reluctant to seem too self-absorbed if he were writing
only about himself. He was expert at commenting on issues of a political
and social nature, but might be constrained when writing along personal
lines. And maybe that also folded into the president's choice, as Patrick's
was a more personal style.

Patrick also wondered about the timing. It was rather late in Kennedy's
second term to begin such a project. Why had he waited until now to
begin? Patrick picked up a sense of urgency from the president. Maybe
he had another writer who had been working with him already but had
terminated the project. Patrick didn't think so, but couldn't be sure. He'd
had no direct contact with the president over the years. Actually, he really
had no definitive idea why he was chosen. He was not so self-absorbed as
to miss the fact that there were dozens of writers who could competently
fill the bill. JFK had his own reasons, and that was fine with Patrick.

In fact, it was splendid, he thought with a chill of excitement.

* * *

Patrick got out on First Street, paid the fare, and walked up the west steps
into the Great Hall entrance of the Library of Congress. It was his home
away from home, the place he navigated to when he needed time to think.
He did research using current administration documents at the National
Archives, which he had just passed on Pennsylvania Avenue. But it was
here, in the Library of Congress, that he liked to work. To the unending
frustration of his former girlfriend, Katherine, he had spent so many hours
here, researching his articles and later his books, that he might just as well
have taken up residence. Who really needed an apartment anyway?

Referred to as "the book palace of the American people" by Ainsworth
Spofford, one of its foremost librarians, Patrick thought the Library of

Congress to be one of the most beautiful buildings in the capitol. Its resplendent architecture and sculptures of famous poets, philosophers, and artists looking down from every arch and face of the edifice conspired to create an aura of intelligent probing with an historical component. Commentary claimed it to be the greatest repository of human knowledge ever assembled, with tens of millions of books in hundreds of languages along hundreds of miles of shelf space. For Patrick, the environment just lent itself to investigation and contemplation. The realization that truly great minds had used this same facility for research further inspired his thoughtful state of mind. As he usually did when he walked down the hall, Patrick looked up at the inscriptions on the vaulted ceilings and frescoed walls and picked out one to read.

They are never alone that are accompanied with noble thoughts.

The main Reading Room at the heart of the Library seemed to Patrick to be a sanctuary in every sense of the word. Under the domed copper roof, rising 160 feet from the floor, the interior was ringed by statues of famous men, looking down, it seemed, on those below, contemplating the thoughts of generations of humanity. The light coming through the arched clerestory windows high above the floor gave the interior a golden glow, reflecting off the ruby-tinted marble columns and the dome's mosaic-tiled interior surface. Patrick felt that just by entering the building his IQ rose twenty points. (He had mentioned this to his friend and fellow reporter at the *Post*, Mackie Flynn. "Well, we can round up and that should make it an even 80," he'd responded.) Patrick would often sit at one of the Reading Room's dark oak desks to clarify and deepen his perceptions. It was a cerebral stew in which he could simmer for hours. Using the library's resources to pursue little-known facts, he could while away a good portion of the day lost in intellectual activity within the ethereal quiet.

Patrick was well aware that the kind of information he would need to investigate, such as the transcripts of the Congressional Sedition Hearings, had not yet been consigned to the Library. They were held at the National Archives Building. He would need to sift through related material there as well, but whenever possible he planned to come to the Library for his writing, if not his research.

The Reading Room had continuous desk space that circled the room. The desks radiated from the central submittal and pick-up station like tree rings from the heartwood, providing room for over a hundred people to sit quietly reading and writing. It was more than half full today. He walked along the aisles of card catalogs on one side, picking through their contents for a publication he sought, and then stepped up to the submittal station.

The submittal desk was located in the middle of the circular rotunda at the main floor of the Library. It was the focal point for requesting and receiving the bundled packages of documentation from the bowels of the Library and its associated buildings. Items were transferred up to the Reading Room by what Patrick imagined as invisible minions toiling away in their underground book-lined vaults. They would receive the approved request form via a pneumatic tube from this central station and respond accordingly. After a thirty-minute wait, the materials would magically plop down on the receiving conveyor to be picked up by the requesting party.

Patrick paused to stare at the attractive woman behind the desk.

"What?" whispered the woman a little too harshly as Patrick looked around her and then questioningly at her.

"Where's Barry?" whispered Patrick loudly.

"He's been promoted. He took a position at the National Archives," said the woman, shushing him at the same time. Barry had been Patrick's compatriot at the Library. When Patrick would ask for certain documents, Barry would go beyond the obligations of his duty, reaching further into the subterranean caverns of the repository and pulling forth gems that Patrick often didn't even know existed. The main attraction of the Library was also its main obstacle. It housed so much information that even knowing where to begin one's search could prove an entry barrier too steep for the unmotivated to overcome. Barry had eased that impediment considerably as an unspoken partner in Patrick's research. It was a partnership he had taken for granted.

"He's gone? Permanently?" asked Patrick, feeling panicky.

"Unless he gets canned from the Archives. It was an assistant directorship. Can't say no to that," she said, indifferent to Patrick's plight. "Besides, he was overqualified to be here." Was she inadvertently implying to Patrick that Barry's replacement, this unpleasant woman standing before him, was under-qualified?

Patrick stood back while another library patron submitted a request for some documents, then laid his request sheet on the counter. The woman picked it up with a quick look at its contents and slipped it into a pneumatic cylinder. "This one should come quickly," she said to no one in particular. *Well, at least she knew enough for that*, he thought resentfully.

He lingered a moment at the desk watching her before her questioning glare caused him to back away.

Damn it, Barry!

Patrick seated himself at one of the open desk spaces within view of the central station, but a few rows away. He took out a writing pad. Since he was going to be meeting regularly with the president, he figured he would keep notes of all their interactions, so he might as well get a start. Time passed quickly and when he looked up, he saw that his return tray had been filled. His request was ready for pick-up at the central station.

He gathered up his package, signing for it at the counter under the woman's distracted supervision, as there were a few others filling out and submitting requests. He had wanted to ask if there was some way to contact Barry, but thought better of it. What good would that do at this point? If he was gone, he was gone. Maybe he could track him down when next he was at the Archives. But Patrick paused again. He wanted to ask her something, but with her previous unfriendly behavior, he could think of no good opening.

Seated again, Patrick looked through the compendium of articles he had just picked up. Published by Marvin Weeks, a friend and reporter at *The New York Times*, they were a serialized account of the cascade of events surrounding the shooting in Dallas nearly five years earlier. Released as an anniversary summary of what had transpired since, they aimed to put the events of that period in perspective. Weeks had an inside line to the investigation through Robert Kennedy's Justice Department. During the Trials, Mr. Weeks released regular updates explaining the inner workings of the commissions. It was rumored that the attorney general even used him to leak pertinent information when the situation required.

* * *

USCPASIC – America on Trial
- by Marvin Weeks

Washington, D.C. On November 22, 1963, the President of the United States, after having been stalked for months, was nearly assassinated in a well-organized ambush in Dealey Plaza.

The United States Congressional Presidential Assassination and Sedition Investigation Commission (USCPASIC) was commissioned by special decree from Congress to ferret out the truth of that day. Jettisoning some of the cumbersome acronym, the work of the Senate and House committees, sub-committees and numerous investigatory groups examining the events of Nov 22, 1963, were initially referred to as the PASI Hearings, or more commonly just "the Trials."

Coming to terms with the events that transpired on that fall day in Dallas, Texas, has been an intense undertaking for the American public. The sheer opacity of the clandestine services created a great deal of difficulty in separating the wheat from the chaff, so to speak, of the corrupted individuals working within otherwise benign organizations. The Byzantine nature of the CIA and the authoritarian structure at the FBI under the late John Edgar Hoover were also a great impediment to a clear understanding of these events.

To define the depths to which the CIA had gone in obscuring its role in this national event begs for terms stronger than duplicitous or treasonous. Even Lewis Carroll's Alice would be impressed by the layers of obfuscation that were purposely placed before every investigatory team. Down the rabbit hole indeed! And to think that this was an organization created to protect America's interests! It was the bastardized child of a well-meaning parent that needed to be euthanized before it could do any greater harm. Yet, is there any greater harm than realizing some of its own were exposed as attempting to assassinate the president of the United States, and then finding the entire top of the organization trying, for bureaucratic survival, to obscure its involvement? President Kennedy stated early in his first term that he wished to "break the CIA into a thousand pieces and scatter it in the wind." He finally got his chance.

J. Edgar Hoover, the director of the FBI, has had his leadership of that august organization exposed as bordering upon the clinically insane. Hoover, with questions lingering even now around his death, was the true power broker in Washington, D.C. Secretly accumulating data on nearly every important personage in American society, he misused the police force at his disposal to cement his place of power and twist the dynamics of governing to insure that his will be done. It has been sobering for the American public to realize what had already been suspected in the halls of government and industry—that the Federal Bureau of Investigation was so corrupt that nearly half of its activities were secretly and illegally directed toward maintaining surveillance on its our own people.

After his return from Dallas, Attorney General Robert Kennedy quickly laid out the initial framework of this national investigation. His background, with many years investigating organized crime, gave him insight into the most effective construction of the committees. The overlap with Mafia figures previously under investigation was an added benefit, allowing a continuing examination of previously indicted individuals already well known to the Justice Department and their involvement in the shooting of the president.

So let's begin to unravel a portion of this maze....

The report went on to detail the makeup of the many committees, some of their overlapping responsibilities and the blizzard of subpoenas for individuals both in and out of government. It detailed convictions and incarcerations of those sentenced, indicating that some of the indicted had gone missing; a few of these having perished either by their own hand or that of another. The recruitment by a small band of CIA operatives of select Mafia members and a handful of anti-Castro Cubans was explicitly detailed as far as the information led. There were still many unanswered questions, as the CIA, skilled in secrecy and obfuscation, lived up to its core directive even while being dismembered.

Patrick never ceased to be amazed by the scope of the Trials. Most times the true depth of government malfeasance is deliberately obscured after a cursory investigation gets uncomfortably close to the truth. But for some reason, call it a national emotional catharsis, the near death of John Kennedy had prompted a real investigation. And in their legislative zeal, directed by a truly outraged public and a fiercely motivated attorney general, Congress had delved deeply. It was a fascinating time to be a reporter. Watching the system self-correct was something Patrick would never have thought possible, but yet it had happened. The public demanded an accounting and actually got one.

* * *

After almost two hours of reading, and this only the first of Weeks' reports, Patrick was ready to call it a day. He returned his articles to the front desk, dropping them in the return bin. He still had work to do at the Post this afternoon before he could go home to Falls Church, but for some reason he could not just walk away. He lingered at the submittal station in front of the librarian, maybe unconsciously wanting to make an impression.

"I'm doing research," he stated, unasked, to which he thought he noticed a slight indifferent twitch of her lips. "Presidential issues, Kennedy, etc., etc.," he trailed off. The words escaped from his mouth like small children bolting clumsily from a mistakenly unlatched door.

"Just like everyone else here?" she responded acerbically as she glanced almost imperceptibly toward the hall, filled to near capacity by now with studious members. He heard a confusing mix of distaste and amusement in her voice.

She had him sign the request slip and gave him his receipt. While he lingered over his signature, she finished up another member's request sheet, slipped it into an empty capsule, and placed it in the pneumatic tube on the side of the wall near her station. Her hands economically and gracefully closed the lid of the device as if she had done it a thousand times before. But the image that would come unbidden to Patrick's mind numerous times over the ensuing days was the stretch of her soft cashmere sweater across the lift of her breast as she turned, and the tightening of her calf as she shifted to slip the cartridge into its opening on the side wall.

When she turned back to Patrick, he handed her the signed slip and then reached his hand out and said, "Thank you. It was nice to meet you."

"But…you didn't," she said recoiling slightly, unsure whether to touch the offered appendage.

Patrick's extended hand was withering from exposure, like a limb bared to the frigid air found only at the higher elevation of some alpine slope. He was about to protectively pull it in, hoping to salvage it from the ravages of frostbite, when she mechanically grasped it, shook it once as if to rid it of accumulated dust, and then let it go.

"Oh, well," he mumbled. *God damn it, Barry!*

* * *

The temperatures had warmed and it was a wonderful early fall afternoon in the Capital. Patrick walked all the way from the Library of Congress to his car parked at the *Post*, drinking in the day, still thinking of his meeting with the president and his non-meeting with the attractive librarian. *He hadn't even asked her name*, he thought sheepishly.

After a bit of work at the *Post*, he drove back to his apartment in Falls Church, picking up some Chinese food at The Golden Tong on the way. More Peking duck with rice for him tonight. He dumped his briefcase and some papers on the kitchen table, got a beer from the nearly empty fridge, and took his boxes of food to sit and eat in front of the TV. He thought about calling his editor. She had known he was in contact with Evelyn Lincoln almost a week ago and had pestered him twice already, pretending to call about his upcoming book publication. But he knew she secretly craved information about what the contact with the president's secretary had meant. He knew she would call him again and just as he was thinking the thought, the phone rang. He picked it up.

"Hello," he said, thinking about how he was going to play her.

"Mr. Hennessey?" inquired the voice quickly.

"Yes," said Patrick in shocked recognition. He quickly sat up in his chair, spilling a bit of Peking duck juice on his trousers.

"Jack Kennedy *heah*. I wanted to—"

"I agree. Sir, I'm in," said Patrick, without even pausing to listen to what the president was going to say.

There was quiet on the other end of the line, then a chuckle. "You'd already decided today when we met at the White House, hadn't you?"

"Well, yes, sir. Actually I had," admitted Patrick.

"You sneaky little *bahstahd*!" blurted the president laughing. "Well, I'd thought so. Reluctant to appear eager? Holding out for better terms maybe?"

"No, sir. I was just...well, a bit shocked. Your offer wasn't at all what I was expecting. I regretted not having agreed before you'd even left the room."

The president chuckled again. "Okay," he said emphatically, as if the agreement was now formalized. "Mrs. Lincoln will be our go-between, and she'll call you to set up times. At least in DC we'll need to meet in the same manner, so I hope no one notices how fond you're going to become of the White House tours. Please keep this quiet."

"Yes, sir. Sir, I have one request. I have worked on all my books with my editor, Devona Williams at Brown and Martin. I would very much like to work with her on this project as well," Patrick said carefully. "She is entirely circumspect," he added.

The president paused on the other end. "If you trust she can keep this completely to herself, and I mean completely, then that will be all right. But you swear her to secrecy, do you hear? That's for both our benefits," said the president.

"Yes, sir."

"I'll also be sending you some items at the Library of Congress. They'll be slipped into your bundles, but they will need to stay there, as some of it is not for release yet. I figured with our mutual fondness for the place, it would be a safe spot to examine some of the documents you'll need for the book. I'm looking forward to working together," the president said in conclusion.

"Thank you, sir."

The line clicked quiet, but Patrick could still hear the humor in the president's voice at his last comment. How did JFK know he was fond of the Library of Congress?

He couldn't wait to call and tell Devona of his coup. He'd torment her with the details, letting them out, drip by insufficient drip.

Chapter 7

I submit to you that if a man hasn't discovered something he will die for, he isn't fit to live.
—*Martin Luther King*

There was an immeasurable distance between the quick and the dead: they did not seem to belong to the same species; and it was strange to think that but a little while before, they had spoken and moved and eaten and laughed.
—*W. Somerset Maugham, Of Human Bondage*

Friday Evening, November 22, 1963
Dallas, Texas

At Hickory Hill, most were overcome by shock—and a powerful impulse that denied the reality of such an occurrence. But on the television screen just moments before, David Brinkley of NBC had been in such a rattled state of barely controlled hysteria that it became more and more probable to read the worst into the situation. The president might be dead, killed by an assassin. On a lovely day in Dallas, Texas, all that they had worked so hard to achieve over the last three years might have been snuffed out in a few seconds.

Robert's estate became an early clearinghouse for information. Rather than driving to headquarters at Langley, CIA Director John McCone immediately raced from his nearby home in Arlington to huddle with the attorney general. The president had recently brought him onboard to run the CIA after the previous director, Allen Dulles, was fired over the Bay of Pigs fiasco. He was a man whom Bobby trusted. But he was not a member of the CIA's "old boys" network. McCone had only recently taken the mantle of leadership, whereas longtime agency stalwarts such as Richard Helms and William Colby, immune to the revolving door of politically appointed figureheads, were the real power brokers.

"What was the CIA's involvement?" was the hard first question to McCone. Robert was very familiar with CIA activities, as he had been intimately involved in the planning of numerous covert operations. He was quite aware of its dark underside as well the agency's hatred for his brother as a result of his having cut the CIA off from its normally unrestricted avenues to power. McCone assured Robert that the agency had nothing to do with the attempt on the president's life. But Bobby, from his own experience trying to corral the Agency's feral activities, knew that his friend probably had no idea what might really be afoot.

About fifteen minutes after the second call from Hoover, Robert was handed the receiver again. Ethel Kennedy had been working the phone on one of their multiple house lines to get through to Parkland Medical. After finally penetrating the disarray of the DC and Parkland switchboards, she was connected to the triage desk at Parkland, just doors from the operating room, where the phone was handed to Colton Mays, the Secret Service agent in charge of protecting the president. Mays, his suit and shirt bloodied, was standing outside the hospital door where the president, fully sedated and hardly breathing, was in surgery. Immediately upon the first shots being fired, Mays had bravely sprinted ahead and jumped into the motorcade limo to protect the president and first lady.

Only half an hour earlier, a fellow agent had been carefully ejected from the operating room. In a moment of panic he had barged in, waving his gun while stalking around the room, seeking to prevent further danger to the president. He was still envisioning assassins that he had failed to perceive in Dealey Plaza. He was calmly shooed out by the head nurse, who slowly and deliberately pointed to each doctor in the room, stating matter-of-factly, "He's okay. He's okay. He's okay. Now put that gun away so we can get to work."

Now relegated to uselessly guarding the operating room door, Mays was utterly bewildered to hear the voice of the president speaking to him over the phone in his clipped Boston accent. It took a few seconds of dislocated confusion to realize he was talking not to John Kennedy, but his brother, the attorney general.

"Colton, I said how bad is it? This is Robert Kennedy."

Colton quickly recovered. "Sir? Sir, he's in surgery right now. There are four surgeons in with him. Admiral Burkley is there also. We have two agents scrubbed and present as well."

"But how *is* he?" demanded Robert.

"Sir, we...we just don't know. He was hit at least once. He lost a lot of blood. He wasn't conscious when they brought him in. They quickly prepped him in the emergency room then wheeled him into surgery. We—"

"How the fuck did this happen!" screamed Bobby into the receiver.

"Where the hell was the fucking Service?"

Colton could hardly come up with a response. He was devastated by the events of the last forty minutes. A few damn gunshots had turned his world into an utter nightmare, and he was doing everything in his power to stanch the flow of chaos that reigned within him and around him. "Sir," he said after a long pause, "...we failed." It was all he could come up with.

It wasn't poor communication that prevented Robert from learning his brother's condition. The doctors had feverishly converged on the emergency room after "stat" bulletins notified the entire complex that all surgeons were needed in the triage area at once. They were treating Mr. Kennedy, Mrs. Kennedy, and the governor. They simply didn't know how the president was doing. He was badly injured, and the orderlies were grim-faced in their travels in and out of the operating room. The Secret Service was recovering from their initial confusion. The hospital was being cordoned off and a widening perimeter of control was being extended from the operating room, which was the nexus of their attention, out to the admitting areas, up into the adjacent floors, out to the hospital grounds and beyond.

"Mrs. Kennedy? How bad is she?" demanded the voice on the phone after a short pause.

"She appears to be okay. A minor gunshot wound to her neck. She lost a lot of blood. They're giving her a transfusion. She is about to go into the OR also, just for safety, but the wound appears minor." Colton was glad to be able to salvage at least a slightly reassuring report.

There was a muffled commotion on Robert's end of the line. He came back on. "I'm coming down *theah*. I'll be leaving from Andrews as soon as I can get to the base. Colton, we do not know who or how many are involved with this shooting. You must protect the president! You have to lock down that damn hospital! Do you understand how imperative this is, Mr. Mays?"

"Yes, sir. We're locked down tight here," answered Colton. Robert hung up abruptly. He had not asked about Governor Connally.

Robert had made the decision to travel unhesitatingly. Even though he was much needed as a rock of emotional support by his family, he was manifestly drawn to the center of the action and felt an unquestioned need to be in Dallas. While Bobby was talking to Mays, McNamara had called back to say a flight was being readied at Andrews Air Force Base that could leave in less than an hour with a hastily assembled group of agents and investigators to provide support and protection for the president. A chopper had already been sent to pick up the attorney general at Hickory Hill and should arrive in moments. The flight from Andrews would wait for Robert if he decided to make it.

Robert was met at Andrews by Justice Department lawyers and U.S. Marshals. The FBI was flying a group of more than twenty hastily assembled agents to assist—or more likely wrest—control of the investigation from the Dallas Police. All safety regulations were abandoned. There had been no time to load up the cargo bays properly, and there were stacks of forensic gear, weapons, overnight bags, and other equipment littering the aisles, stuffed in corners, clogging the seats and overhead compartments. Four surgeons from Bethesda Naval Hospital had been rushed over to fly to Dallas to provide what was considered the best medical treatment available, although their expertise would languish in frustration at 35,000 feet while the real work was being done by the less eminent surgeons already on the scene at Parkland.

Strategic Air Command was on heightened alert. There was a dramatic realignment underway directing military personnel to their war stance positions. Friday afternoon found almost half of the Air Force brass scattered across the country, as many had already departed for the weekend. Pulling them back to the capitol was a logistical nightmare that was compounded by the breakdown of the Washington, D.C., phone system at the time it was most needed. Military personnel had to report to the nearest base just to acquire a secure open line in order to call DC to receive deployment orders.

Bedlam reigned on the national scene as unconfirmable rumors flared like wildfire across the country: The president was dead. The first lady was dead. Lyndon Johnson, the vice president, was either injured through gunfire or downed by a heart attack. Governor Connally was dead. The Secret Service had had a firefight with assassins in Dealey Plaza that spread across parts of downtown Dallas, littered with dead and wounded. The Soviets, preparing for a nuclear strike, had taken out the president, the vice president, and the next two heads of state in the line of succession—Speaker of the House John McCormack and President Pro Tempore of the Senate, Carl T. Hayden. The Washington, D.C., phone system had been sabotaged to prevent communication. The diplomatic flight from Honolulu to Japan, carrying most of the top members of the U.S. Cabinet to a high level meeting, had been intercepted by Soviet fighters and shot down. The

U.S. government was being decapitated in order to prevent an organized military response.

The truth became unrecognizable. But the White House Situation Room stepped in as the clearinghouse for communication, radiating a sense of order and transmitting clarifying bulletins to the national media every few minutes.

The American military was poised at its highest alert level, but there appeared to be no organized foreign threat, as there was no discernible movement of Soviet forces either on the ground or in the air.

LBJ was safe, and he was flying back to DC on Air Force Two. He had been spirited to Love Field in Dallas under heavy Secret Service protection, and then flown back to the capital accompanied by a special Air Guard attachment. Johnson was considered too exposed on the ground in Dallas and, with the stricken president at the same location, created too great a concentration of executive power. And, in fact, he passed Robert Kennedy's DC-to-Dallas flight somewhere over western Tennessee. Air Force Two was landing at Andrews Air Force Base at almost the same time Robert Kennedy touched down at Love Field in Dallas.

Congressman McCormack and Senator Hayden were easily located after a quick search. Seventy-two-year-old McCormack was at the U.S. House restaurant lunching with a few aides and congressmen. "My God, what are we coming to?" he said when two reporters rushed to his table to inform him of the shooting in Dallas. The restaurant was further electrified when it was announced moments later that the vice president had also been shot and that Secret Service agents were rushing to protect McCormack, the new president of the United States. It hit him like a freight train. He was probably one of the few in DC who sincerely hoped not to ascend to the highest office. Shocked, now *President* McCormack stood to go back to his office, but collapsed back into his seat from a severe attack of vertigo. Just a few moments later, he learned Johnson was safe and returning to DC. McCormack had tasted the presidency for about sixty seconds, but now reverted to second-in-line, even that not a position he had seriously considered until now.

Senator Hayden, fourth in line for the presidency, was quickly found at the Senate Office Building. The eighty-six-year-old "silent senator" was the most senior and longest serving member, with fifty-one years in Congress. The wisdom of having the oldest member in line to assume authority in the case of disaster is always questionable. Hayden, an aging leader who wielded his power quietly, disdained public exposure. When asked later what he might do if he were to find himself president through succession, he stated, "I'd call Congress together, have the House elect a new speaker, and then I'd resign and let him become president."

The diplomats aboard the flight to Japan were safe and had been in constant contact with the White House Situation Room. The flight was directed to return to Honolulu, where its Cabinet-level passengers were split up and rerouted to Dallas and DC.

The unanswered question, though, was the one most important— what was the condition of the president of the United States? And for that there was only maddeningly incomplete information. Some of the worst news was true: John Kennedy had been shot and rushed to Parkland Medical Center, only a few miles from the end of the motorcade route. Two Roman Catholic priests had been admitted to the emergency room before surgery and remained with the president. It was assumed Kennedy was being given Extreme Unction, the last rites of his Catholic faith, which could only mean he was close to death or, more frightening, already dead. He had been in surgery for hours with no word from the attending physicians. Even the White House Situation Room, in direct contact with the Parkland Medical team, had no clear answer as to his condition other than that his wounds were "severe" and his condition was "critical."

During the three long hours it took to fly to Dallas, constant updates kept the passengers on Robert's flight as informed as possible, but there had been no real answer to the most pressing question. As they were touching down on the Love Field runway, a bulletin came over the plane's radio-phone. JFK was out of surgery. He had not regained consciousness. His medical condition was critical.

* * *

It was 6:05 p.m. when the emergency military flight dropped through a dramatic canyon of cotton and gravel thunderheads to land at Love Field in Dallas, Texas. The front and rear fuselage doors were lifting before the jet came fully to a stop. Robert Kennedy, grim-faced, his tie askew, his sleeves rolled above the elbows, stood at the rear exit of the Dash 80. The stewards secured the opening doors, and the ground crews positioned the wheeled ramps against the fuselage. The Dash 80 was a commercial passenger jet reconditioned to transport government personnel and top brass around the United States and overseas. It was now packed with Secret Service agents, FBI special agents, a large U.S. Marshal contingent, four medical specialists from Bethesda Naval Hospital, numerous aides—and the Attorney General of the United States.

A medium-height, thickly-built man with curly dark hair wearing a heat-rumpled suit coat waited uneasily at the base of the portable stair ramp as the passengers began filing out the plane door. He held his sunglasses in a gnarled hand. The attorney general was first off. "Mr. Kennedy, sir, I'm Secret Service Agent Jiggs Dansant. I have a detail of agents here to provide you with protection while you are in Dallas. We—"

"I will not be in need of your services," interrupted Robert, stone-faced, as he continued walking.

"Sir, I must request that you allow us to provide protection." The agent backpedaled, keeping up with Robert's hurried pace as he continued walking. Jiggs had a flat puggish face that could, at kinder moments, be called roguishly masculine. Just now it held a scowling, pained expression. He was unsure of his position in making demands of the attorney general, the brother to the president, especially at such an emotional moment. But he was also accustomed to the expression of authority and was adamant. "Sir, I have been strictly ordered not to let you out of our protective custody. Please, sir. We are as of yet unaware of the extent of the conditions present here in Dallas, and—"

"Mr...?" asked Robert.

"Dansant, sir."

"Mr. Dansant, the Service fucked up today!" blistered Robert as he halted in the middle of the tarmac, boring into the agent in front of him. He had spent bitter hours contemplating the nature of the shooting and was well aware of the Secret Service's failure to provide protection. But he was also aware of how difficult his brother had made their assignment. Jack had thwarted them at every turn and resented their intrusion into his free-wheeling lifestyle. A constant war of wills determined how much freedom the president could wrest from their ubiquitous presence. Robert had not been afforded protection in the past even though encouraged to request it, and he was loath at the moment to shift his position. But in watching the agent in front of him, nearly pleading, he was tipped to adjust his stance. The man was just asking to be allowed to assist in protecting the president's brother, at least for the moment. There was surely an avalanche of guilt in the tight-knit brotherhood of his professional companions, and there was so much unknown as to the extent of the assassination plot and the potential that this was just the opening salvo of a much broader conspiracy. Also, the agent's transport was immediately available.

"You can drive me directly to Parkland Medical Center," Robert said looking directly at Jiggs, "but you will stay the hell out of my way!"

"Yes, sir," responded Jiggs, shaken but relieved, taking Robert's statement as assent. "We have a car ready for you." He directed Robert to the open back door of an idling black Buick. Bags were quickly thrown into the open trunk as Robert instead opened the front passenger door and got in. Jiggs stuttered for a moment. Not about to test his luck, he quickly jumped into the driver's seat as two agents and an aide piled into the back. A car with agents and another aide pulled out just behind them.

It was only a ten–minute, two–mile ride to Parkland Medical Center. Police at every intersection directed traffic and secured roads to provide direct access between Love Field and Parkland. Caught unaware by the initial shooting, the Secret Service was not about to falter at this point. They engaged the Dallas Police and the Texas State Patrol to cordon off large sections of the thoroughfares around the medical center and redirect nonessential traffic, which was increasing at an alarming rate, to alternate side roads. It was obvious that traffic was a mess, but Cedar Springs Road, Inwood Road, and Harry Hines Boulevard, all restricted to vehicles coming and going from Parkland Medical to Love Field, were nearly devoid of traffic. It made for a short ride.

"What do you know about his condition?" asked Robert immediately after Jiggs had pulled out of the terminal and onto Cedar Springs Road.

"Sir, we just heard on the radio that he's out of surgery, but they are skimpy on detail. We don't know his condition," said Jiggs. "The doctors have been working on him for hours. They wheeled him right into the emergency room, and then, in five minutes, over to Operating Room One. He was still there when I left to come here to meet you. He was shot at least once, maybe twice. Middle-upper-back shot. He lost a lot of blood. The whole back of that limo was drenched. With Colton Mays jumping on the president as the limo sped up, and all the blood from Governor Connally and probably Mrs. Kennedy, it was a real mess."

"I listen to the radio too, Mr. Dansant. What else?" said Robert Kennedy harshly.

"They've been circumspect. At first they seemed to think—at least this is what I heard—that the president's wounds were not too severe and they could patch him up. But after they were in for a while, one of the nurses came out for some extra blood and whispered that he wasn't responding well. It should have been easier, but something was going wrong. That's all I heard. They've been quiet since. Had the president's doctor in there the whole time and then a bunch of specialists. I was told that some specialists were being flown in from DC."

"They're following us. They were on the plane," added Robert.

Robert could guess what was wrong. Jack, unknown to but a few, was taking a wide array of drugs, some probably that even Robert didn't know about. And even with Dr. Burkley's intimate knowledge of JKF's pharmacology, it would no doubt confound the doctors treating him. Robert thought he was quite familiar with JFK's medical condition, but had been shocked recently to discover the multitude of drugs his brother was ingesting and injecting into his ravaged system. His ailments were manifold, and his self-medication was a matching cornucopia of treatments. For most of his life he had been sickly, with a wide array of symptoms that from early youth had defied analysis. He had been in and out of hospitals and world-renowned clinics dozens of times for treatments. But even with his family's wealth and the best doctors available, his illnesses were never fully diagnosed. To treat constant stomach and intestinal pains, which had arrested his growth and left him rail-thin as a youth, he had been taking oral and under-the-skin steroid implants with testosterone injections to aid in weight gain. His cortisone treatment had ravaged his immune system, which required regular doses of antibiotics to stave off infections and illness. His adrenals had failed, and he was diagnosed with Addison's disease. His lower back had degenerated to the point that he was nearly crippled, and that was after a failed major surgery that implanted and then removed a steel plate that fused his lower spine. Three times he had been given last rites by the Catholic Church when his ailments seemed to wash him over the edge. But each time he rallied. Behind the veneer of *"vigah"* so ardently espoused by the president, there was a man who for most of his life had coped as best he could with debilitating pain, stoically creating an image of high health and vitality. Some days his back pain prevented him from bending over to put on his own shoes. Few people outside of close friends and immediate family were even aware of his ailments, let alone their severity. He never complained. To cope, he went outside of the medical establishment, using injections of barely legal drugs supplied surreptitiously by willing conspirators. His most recent unsanctioned source of treatment was Dr. Max Jacobson. Robert had stumbled upon his brother's stash a few months earlier and, surprised to learn of the secret avenue of treatment he was taking, confronted him with his dangerous pattern. Jack had responded, "I don't care if it's horse piss, Robert, it works." Robert had palmed a vial of the substance and had it covertly analyzed at an FBI lab. It was a mix of amphetamines and vitamins with a number of other unidentifiable substances.

During the flight, Robert again contacted Colton Mays at Parkland and instructed him to find Dr. Jacobson, get a detailed recipe for the concoctions he had been injecting into the president, and get that information to Admiral Burkley. He was sure that Jacobson was in one of the following cars or at least somewhere close to JFK. "And Colton, beat it out of the *bahstahd* if you have to."

"And Mrs. Kennedy?" asked Robert as they turned onto Inwood Road.

"Ends up the first lady was hit during the ride in the limo, just no one realized it. There was so much blood in the car, all over the place really with the president and Governor Connally, that no one thought to ask about her. She was tough. Holding Lancer—I mean the president—she was right there the whole time. She even helped get him out of the car and onto the gurney. Wouldn't let go of him for a second and wouldn't let anyone get in between them. She was leaning over the gurney talking to him, even though he was totally out of it. It wasn't till they were half-way down the hall to the emergency room that she just stumbled and fell over. Everyone thought she had just tripped, but she had fainted from loss of blood. Ends up she had a gunshot wound to the neck, just above her shoulder line under her dress collar, and it nicked a vein. A lot of the blood on her clothes was hers, not just the president's. When she fell, she hit her head pretty hard on the concrete wall going down. Fortunately, she was kind of wedged in with everyone else crowded around the gurney, so she didn't fall to the floor. They think she may have a slight concussion. But she's out of surgery. It was just a light wound with stitches, but they had to do a blood transfusion. She's sedated. I don't think they'll be able to keep her down long, though."

While he was speaking, Jiggs was still remembering what he had seen moments after the president's arrival at Parkland. He had been directed to help clean out the limo. Frightening amounts of blood, from the president, the first lady, and Governor Connally, covered the front and back seats. On the carpeted floor, between the two seats, was a perfect bright red rose. It was probably from the bouquet that Jackie had been given at

Love Field where the motorcade had begun. It was centered in a large puddle of dark red-brown blood. Starkly beautiful, it seemed untouched and just floating.

"Why didn't anyone take her aside?" Robert's voice was rising in angry frustration.

"No one realized she was injured or in shock. She seemed so lucid and in charge. Besides, she's the first lady. No one had the balls to tell her to back off and take a seat. I mean, who was going to pry her away from the president and tell her to sit down? It would have made a real scene, and she seemed fine. I mean, not fine, but...." His words had begun coming in a rush, but they just petered out.

"Yeah, okay...," said Robert, hearing the anguish in the agent's voice.

"Probably by the time she got in with the doctors they would have had to separate them, so maybe it was good it happened by itself—I mean not good really, just—well...." Jiggs seemed like a tough agent, but he had been shaken by the day's events and was not used to briefing the AG. He was doing the best he could, but was over-talking and falling into defensiveness. He felt guilty about what had occurred. It was his job as an agent to protect the president, and he had failed. They had all failed miserably.

"Where were you during all this?" asked Robert.

"I was closing up the early part of the motorcade protection from Love Field, since the president had long since passed through. We were on our way out of Dallas to Austin, getting ready for the motorcade down there this afternoon. We got a Code 3 over the car radio while we were sitting on the runway at Love grabbing lunch, waiting for our flight to load. We hightailed it back to Parkland and got here just a little after the president was wheeled in."

They turned onto Harry Hines Boulevard, where thirteen stories of the brown-gray Parkland Medical Center loomed ahead. Even though it was a newer structure, it had a despairingly dusty, sun-baked appearance. There were police cars lining every available gap on the side of the road as well as a number parked askew on the grassy verge near the entry. A number of them still had their doors open, showing the haste with which they were abandoned. There were hundreds of people lining the sidewalk and grassy embankments behind the newly erected barricades off the Lo-fland Street turn. These weren't police or government personnel, but men, women, and a few children all clustered together, watching the cars racing in and out and staring toward the hospital buildings. Robert Kennedy watched them as the car slowed to turn in to the medical facility grounds. They were a silent, somber group, some holding flowers and many with tear-streaked faces. Robert looked over at Jiggs.

"They've been coming since the networks started to carry the story," the agent volunteered quietly. "We expect more."

The pair of cars carrying the attorney general and his escorts pulled into the emergency room entry, stopping short and to the side of the ambulance bays. The backseat occupants piled out quickly and shut the doors. Jiggs shut off the engine, but Robert paused a moment, sitting in the front seat of the car as the ticking engine cooled. Both he and Jiggs were silent as they stared out the windshield at the imposing view of the hospital. Jiggs thought the president's brother was reluctant to go in and face what he was about to see, but Robert surprised him.

"Look, Mr. Dansant..."

"Sir?"

"I appreciate everything you're doing," said Robert turning to look at him. "And you might not realize it, but the president does also; he's said that to me a number of times. I just wanted you to be aware of that." He was thinking again about how difficult Jack always made it on his Secret Service detail. He didn't like to have them around, but he needed them just the same. It was always a touchy situation. And in light of what had occurred today, maybe it was time to listen to what Morgenthau had said and rethink his own vulnerability.

"Thank you," said Jiggs somberly to the attorney general who was quickly exiting the car.

* * *

It was unseasonably hot in Dallas. The heat descended in the early evening with an eerie quiet, as though it had expended its energy during the midday sun and was now languishing, exhausted, waiting for night to arrive. No air movement, just heavy, humid, de-oxygenated molecules that inadequately filled the lungs during a breath. The dampening effect of the leaden air made the hubbub of activity around the hospital more pronounced and a little surreal. The sounds of police talking, the crackle of car radios, and the passing and unloading of cars that were arriving and departing took on an odd quality. It was like listening through air that was too lazy to adequately carry vibration, so it clipped off segments of each audio stream in a dreary, haphazard manner.

The agonizing chaos of the first two hours of the assault on Parkland, because that's how an impersonal observer could most easily describe it, had quieted. Parkland was a fully operational hospital that treated and repaired the citizens of Dallas to the tune of over 250 admissions per day. The emergency room was not just waiting empty and expectant when the president was rushed in for care. There were patients in both emergency bays as well as in half of the curtained booths in the Minor Medical section. They were startled when, delayed by a communications snafu, a 601 Code 3 arrival—very important person, highest emergency—was imminent. They had only a few moments to digest the rare call and were unprepared when the phalanx of cars raced into the partially occupied emergency bays, sirens blaring, to disgorge a host of demanding and arrogant business-suited men who literally took over the entire floor. Normal arrivals to the bays were pretty quiet, since the ambulance drivers usually silenced their sirens when they turned in off Harry Hines Boulevard. But this group blared their way right up to the emergency room entrance, startling everyone. Patients were unceremoniously spirited out of the area. A middle-aged man being treated for laceration injuries was nearly dragged toward the doors leading to the adjacent wing. An FBI agent, already at Parkland and approaching the emergency bay a little too intently, was smacked in the face with a gun butt by a Secret Service agent, breaking the man's jaw as he was forced out of the way. All non-governmental and non-staff occupants were flushed from the emergency area within a minute.

Vice President Lyndon Johnson, exiting a following car after having been sat upon by a protective agent all the way from Dealey Plaza to the hospital, was manhandled into an isolated room and surrounded by Secret Service agents.

Governor Connally was lying injured and bleeding profusely across the middle jump seats of the Lincoln Continental. To the horror of Nellie Connally, cradling him in her lap, he was nearly trampled by hospital staff and agents trying to extricate JFK from the rear seat, until it became obvious that the governor would need to be moved first in order to get to the president. Within a minute, there were dozens of police, Secret Service agents, motorcade politicians, Kennedy staff, and local and national newsmen swarming the area, not to mention the crowds that began to gather just to watch the unfolding scene. Agents and orderlies lifted the president out, newsmen raced toward the phones, police cordoned off the entry as the invasion clogged the hallways and overran what moments before had been a bland but orderly health care facility.

By the time the attorney general arrived, five hours after the event, order had been imposed. The Dallas police set barricades restricting access to the perimeter of the building. A growing armada of Secret Service agents, State Patrol, and Dallas police covered all entries and exits. The warren of hallways, patient elevators, freight elevators, roof, emergency exits, and underground walkways connecting the Emergency area with the rest of the hospital complex were either closed or restricted. Medical personnel were being screened against lists provided by the hospital administration to determine who did and didn't have essential business in the wing in which the president and first lady were being treated. Parkland was being segregated, isolating activities involving the U.S. president from everything else.

As the Secret Service were made aware of Mrs. Kennedy's wound, and hopeful there would be a presidential recovery, the second, third, and fourth floors were hastily evacuated. JFK was to be moved to Intensive Care on the third floor, but the floors above and below in that entire wing of Parkland were cleared, providing a cocoon of protection. One elevator was reserved exclusively for his use, to be stationed, doors open, either on the first floor by the operating theater or on the third floor near his room, depending upon his location.

Transferring so many patients created an immediate upheaval in the Dallas medical community. The most critical patients were relocated to upper floors in the complex to remain near specialized care. Higher priority but non-critical cases were directed to nearby Methodist Dallas Medical Center. Lower priority patients went to the adjacent care centers in the Parkland Medical complex as well as to other facilities in Dallas.

* * *

Robert Kennedy got out of the car and headed toward the stairs leading up to the emergency entrance. Informed by the Secret Service of Robert's expected arrival, Kenny O'Donnell was waiting for him. Both Robert and JFK's close friend as well as JFK's appointments secretary, Kenny was always with the president either in DC or during his travels. A stern no-nonsense organizer of the president's daily activities, he thrived on the intensity of his position as gatekeeper to the Oval Office when at the Capital, or to the president's personal space when on the road. His title as Appointments Secretary belied his close association with JFK as both confidant and political advisor who closely guarded the president's daily timetable, determining who would get precious face time with the president. Along with Dave Powers and Larry O'Brien, he was a member of what the press had dubbed "the Irish Mafia" and presented a daunting obstacle to many a senator or congressman who thought his rank should allow him immediate access to the president. O'Donnell was also a close friend of Robert's, as they had roomed together at Harvard and played for years on its football team. It was through Robert that he became involved with the Kennedy political machine. Bobby and Kenny shared an almost extra-sensory awareness of one another's feelings and thoughts. Having known each other for so many years, first in the thick of college athletics and then later in the political arena, little needed to be spoken. A nod, gesture, truncated phrase, or animated look evoked the necessary communication. Like icebergs whose major mass is hidden from view, the two men's agreement after a seemingly wordless exchange would leave others wondering what they had missed.

"Heard he's out of surgery," said Robert somberly without greeting as he moved quickly with Kenny through the waiting area. To Robert, Kenny seemed drawn and haggard, noticeably aged since he had seen him just a few days earlier.

"Just moved up to the third floor. Intensive Care." said Kenny. He led Robert around the side of the emergency area, skirting most of it as they bounded up two flights of stairs to the third floor. Jiggs followed close behind.

"Dallas cops got the shooter," said Kenny over his shoulder. " A pouty little prick. Caught him hiding in a theater downtown."

"Yeah, heard on the flight. Still just one?" asked Bobby.

"So far."

The hallway outside JFK's room was unusually quiet. All of the patients previously housed there were gone.

Robert felt a visceral reaction on entering the wards of the hospital that he had missed when quickly passing through the emergency room downstairs. How many times had he visited his brother in facilities just like this? The institutional blandness, the fluorescent lights, the concrete walls, the hushed conversations. The banal environment effectively shrouded any vestige of human spirit. But it was the smell that assaulted the senses so. There was something profoundly invasive about the odor of sickness and death. The olfactory emanations of the healing arts—antiseptic, pungent, and uric—carry the underlying emanations of humans in their most helpless and mortal condition. JFK, unknown to any but his closest family and doctors, had spent much of his life in just such places, and Bobby had come to loathe both the nature of their hold on his brother and the fear that sprang like an electric current through his gut when he entered their confines.

There were Secret Service agents at all the exits and at each side of the door to the president's room. Intense but quiet activity filled the hall as nurses and orderlies set up supplies and equipment in the adjacent rooms. There were subdued glances from all around as they became aware that the president's brother had arrived. They pulled back perceptibly to make way for him. Kenny stepped up to the entry, acknowledged the agents standing there, and stepped aside. Robert hesitated a moment and entered.

Robert was a strong man. He would have to be to contain the many facets of his energetic nature that clamored for expression. Many thought of him as a harsh and demanding public figure, arrogant and prickly when confronted, even more so when protecting his brother. But this public face was only half the story. Those who knew him intimately were well aware of his shy and softhearted side, the fiercely loyal friend, the devoted family man, the lover of nature and animals, and the contradictions of these numerous selves that vied for prominence and eventual balance. But the image that greeted him, although he thought he had prepared himself, took his breath away. Just last night his vibrant brother had been laughing and joking on the phone about the unexpectedly positive greeting in Texas; now he lay immobile on a single wide hospital bed, wrapped in bandages from his neck down to his waist. His upper torso was tented in a translucent sheet of plastic. His face, what could be seen of it through the condensation-clouded surface, was pale. His eyes were closed, his head turned slightly to one side. Robert couldn't see any sign of life.

Dave Powers, Jack's closest friend and companion, sat in a chair at the side of the bed. His elbows resting on his knees and his face partially resting in his clasped hands, he seemed to be looking off into his anguished thoughts as much as toward the president prone before him. His suit was still bloodied from helping lift the president from the back seat of the limousine.

Equipment flanked the president's bed, with tubes dangling from a number of IVs dripping fluids into his body. Wires ran from under the plastic hood to equipment on stainless steel trolleys along a sidewall. An oscilloscope displayed a jumping fluorescent green blip that faded after each bounce. Dials and gauges were attached at the edges of the clear tent with tubes running to a pair of steel tanks tucked near the back of the bed at the wall. This was one of the larger rooms on the floor, which normally had a second bed with a separating curtain. That other bed had been removed to allow for more space, making the room appear under-occupied and somewhat cavernous. An air conditioning unit hummed at the window. His brother's left hand, lying waxen and motionless by his side on the white bed sheet, extended just a few inches beyond the plastic draping. The same hand that pointed and chopped through the air during his public speeches and personal meetings now seemed like an escapee that hadn't the energy to flee further; it lay inanimate. It was not so different in color from the sheet supporting it.

Two doctors with clipboards huddled together. On the opposite side of the bed, a stout middle-aged nurse, dressed in white with a small white cap pinned to her hair, was tucking in the sheets and establishing order over the IVs and other equipment. She looked up as Robert entered and then inquiringly toward the two doctors, who immediately became aware of Robert's arrival. Robert at first didn't recognize Dr. Burkley, his brother's personal physician, in his blood-flecked white smock and operating room attire. The pale blue paper surgical mask still hung from his neck. Robert had always seen him in his starched naval uniform, either at the White House or with his brother on a number of personal occasions.

"Mr. Attorney General, we are so sorry," Dr. Buckley half-whispered as he quietly approached Robert.

Dave rose and greeted Robert with a pained glance, and came over to stand beside him. Special Assistant to the president, Dave was, more importantly, a close friend. Dave was Old Irish—an impish, lovable sort of man whose humorous comments could disarm most situations. But today, standing solemnly next to Robert, he was speechless. Robert couldn't take his eyes off his brother lying prone before him. He folded one arm in front of his chest while his other hand rose involuntarily to his mouth. He could hardly see any sign of breathing. Why wasn't his chest moving, damn it?

"Tell me," said Robert, his mouth dry, shifting his gaze between Dave and Dr. Burkley as he walked to the side of the bed to lay his hand on his brother's.

"The president has had a very significant gunshot wound," started Dr. Burkley, glancing first at Bobby and then down at the president. "We believe he was hit once in the back, below his right shoulder. The bullet went entirely through his body. His chest wound is very serious. The operation was difficult. Dr. Marshall did a very good job. He's the resident surgeon. I assisted. But the shot was very damaging." Dr. Burkley was not sure how far to go with the description of the president's condition. "Dr. Marshall is downstairs washing up and should be in his office. The X-rays are there. He can tell you more. I can take you down there," he said. Bobby nodded. Burkley told the other doctor he would be in Dr. Marshall's office and to page him immediately if any changes occurred. Dave stayed in the room. Robert took a lingering look at his fallen brother, then quickly followed Dr. Burkley out the door and down the hall.

* * *

Dr. August Marshall III had planned all week to go to the Trade Mart luncheon, just a few blocks away, to hear the president's speech and mingle a bit with the top crust of Dallas. But at the last minute he had to fill in for the chief of surgery, Dr. Shires, who was attending a surgical convention in Galveston. He was disappointed not to attend the luncheon, but not because he was a Kennedy fan. Though he was a Democrat, he hadn't even voted for the guy—too "Boston liberal" for his political taste. Rather, Dr. Marshall just wanted to take a break from his heavy workload and socialize the afternoon away. He had an intense schedule, and it was a rare opportunity when he could scavenge personal time. His wife, Dora, had gone anyway while he had to cover for Shires here at The Park.

While eating in the hospital cafeteria a few hours earlier, he was shocked to hear Dr. Shires paged over the intercom. The chief of surgery was never paged; instead, a personal messenger was always sent. Dr. Marshall immediately answered on the cafeteria phone and was informed of the wounding of a member of the presidential motorcade. The victim was being rushed to Parkland. The doctor abandoned his chicken salad sandwich and ran out of the cafeteria. At that point he really hadn't started to worry; there just hadn't been time.

The president had already been wheeled on a gurney into the crowded emergency room when Dr. Marshall came running in, stethoscope in hand. He was shocked to see *this* man lying bloodied and motionless on the stainless steel table in front of him.

What appeared to be half the hospital's surgical staff had also converged in the frenzied confines of the emergency room. Dr. Marshall remembered Drs. Jones, Carrico, Perry, Crenshaw, Baxter, and McClelland all arriving at about the same moment. Amongst all there was a moment of pause as they realized the identity of the man lying in front of them.

He was still almost fully dressed. His suit coat had been removed, and although unconscious, he was fully recognizable as the man they had seen numerous times on television or in the press—John F. Kennedy. Their respect for the man and his office momentarily collided with their normal, well-practiced efficiency in such circumstances, and they hesitated an instant before cutting through and ripping off his shirt and trousers.

But after that moment's stutter, their medical training kicked in. Incisions were made to the ankle and arm to start intravenous drips of Ringer's Lactate for hemorrhagic shock. Dr. Marshall ordered the crowded room be cleared of agents and aides, as the congestion was restricting their normal workflow. One of the nurses had to practically drag a gun-wielding Secret Service agent out. Admiral Burkley presented himself as the president's personal physician, and as the clothing and back brace were fully removed and surface palpations begun, he quickly informed Dr. Marshall of the patient's medical history and essential blood chemistry. Kennedy was immediately administered Solu-Cortef hydrocortisone intravenously, and the chief endocrinologist and his team were paged. The president was wheeled into X-ray and then directly into the operating room.

Marshall had always loved the operating room. Love might seem an inappropriate word for his affinity for cutting open and repairing human flesh. But if total concentration, deep expectation, and a constant preoccupation with all the wonderful intricacies of the body's physical construction weren't love, then he was uncertain how to describe it. And during the surgery, thank god, his obsession with perfection simply took over. This was the part of his life where all his skills and attention were totally focused, as death was literally a missed heartbeat away. Middling concerns were pushed aside while he worked the room: the patient, the anesthesiologist, the nurses, the assistants, and the banks of equipment on the surrounding walls. There was a feeling of adrenaline, concentration, and urgency that he could find nowhere else. The Parkland doctors were a well-trained trauma team familiar with a wide range of physical mayhem. Had the president arrived at any other facility in Dallas, he would have hardly had a chance.

But now Dr. Marshall was worried. By God, he had just operated on patient #24740, the president of the United States! The man had been literally torn apart inside, and it was his skill that had reassembled him downstairs in Op One. Not a bad job, and better, he felt, than most anyone else was capable of. But now it was over and the mental dikes holding back his personal thoughts and worries had been breached. This was going to make or break him. If, God forbid, he had screwed up anything—*anything*—they would tear him to pieces in the medical community, not to mention the national press.

* * *

With his thoughts elsewhere, Dr. Marshall was startled when, after a brief knock on his door, Attorney General Robert Kennedy was ushered into his office. The president's personal physician, who had assisted in the operation, accompanied him. Mr. Kennedy was shorter than his brother, slightly stooped, it seemed, and smaller than the doctor had expected. But his size belied his energy, something like a coiled spring whose discharge had yet to be released. The large room seemed full even with only the three of them.

"Dr. Marshall, this is Robert Kennedy," said Dr. Burkley. "He's just flown in from Washington. He's been up to the room with the president, but I wanted you to talk to him about the operation and the president's condition."

Robert immediately reached out and shook the doctor's hand in greeting. "Doctor," said Robert in acknowledgment. He glanced at the wall of X-rays that the doctor had been facing when he walked in. "My brother's?"

"Yes, I was just looking them over," he said, pausing. "Do you want to go through this right now?" He looked from one to the other, wondering if Kennedy was prepared to hear what he was going to say.

"Yes, now would be fine," Robert responded directly.

"Well," started Dr. Marshall, "the president—your brother—is badly wounded. It appears he was shot with a high-powered rifle. He lost a great deal of blood. We used fourteen pints during the operation. The projectile entered through his back and tore through the right shoulder muscle and part of the bone structure of the shoulder blade, then through the lower right lung, through the thoracic cavity, and then split a rib on the way out. Plowing through all the muscle and organs caused significant internal damage. We picked out numerous bullet fragments, a whole host of them really, while we were cleaning up the wound and before sewing him back up. The exit area at the front upper rib cage showed a number of skin punctures from bullet fragment exits and possibly from a small piece of bone. There was significant muscle and epidermal trauma as well from the force of the concussive exit velocity."

As Dr. Marshall spoke, he also observed Mr. Kennedy for signs of how bluntly to proceed. He would always tailor this type of discussion to the individual. Some people were squeamish about a medical evaluation, and even though sincerely wanting to know the condition of a loved one, would noticeably recoil from the information—averting their eyes, shifting their feet, and visibly suffering, unconsciously begging for it to be over. Mr. Kennedy was totally present and alert, and although the set of his mouth and the rhythm of his breathing indicated he was anguished, he was absorbing every word the doctor uttered.

"His right lung was severely damaged, ruptured and partially shredded really, with a significant portion needing to be removed. It wasn't a full lobectomy, but more than half of his right lung, remnants mostly, was taken out. We had to manually breathe him with an Ambu bag when he was brought in to provide initial ventilation, as well as assisting his breathing during the operation." Dr. Marshall reached over and picked up a ballpoint pen from his desk. "You see here, this inconsistent mass in the X-ray that was taken before the operation," he stepped over to the X-rays mounted on the wall, moving his pen in circular motions along the celluloid. "This is the location of the right lung cavity. This area should be rather clear with even gradations in the X-ray, similar to the lung cavity on the left side. Instead, it shows density variations that indicate a region filled with debris from the damaged bone, flesh, and muscle pulverized along the bullet's trajectory.

"The damage throughout his right thoracic cavity was substantial. We entered his chest from under the right arm as well as through the already damaged rib cage, cleaned out the wound, removed bullet and bone fragments, and closed off his right lung. I closed off all the severed arteries in his lung so as to prevent internal bleeding, and then sewed him up in layers as we exited the wounded area."

"Are you experienced specifically with gunshot wounds, Doctor?" asked Robert.

"We get sometimes a dozen a week here. We're the major trauma center for the Dallas area, and get a parade of knife and gunshot wounds as well as every other sort of medical trauma. Here, if you look closer at the X-ray, you can see further indication of the bullet's path." Dr. Marshall selected one of the films clipped to the light wall and, rearranging a few of the sheets, brought the selected one into the central position. "This shows an oblique front view of the president's torso. Along this line is the assumed path of the projectile, as there is a trail of significant internal damage." Dr. Marshall traced along the bright and dark sections of the film with his pen. "Do you see this?" He pointed at a grouping of bright specks all around the damaged area. It resembled a shower of sparks on the X-ray film. "These are minute lead fragments. I've seen this before on a few gunshot wounds. Some doctors refer to it as a lead snowstorm. It's an indicator of the type of bullet used, a fragmentation bullet that's designed to disintegrate as it passes through the soft fleshy portions of a target. It explodes, really, leaving pieces of itself imbedded in the flesh as the bullet fragments and deteriorates. It creates this sunburst trail on an X-ray, and in the body it creates a trail of destruction."

"Is this unusual?" asked Robert.

"Not necessarily. I think it just indicates the type of bullet used. I'm not a ballistics expert, now, so I might be wrong about all this. It's just that I've seen it numerous times. I tried to remove all accessible fragments without causing undue trauma to the patient, but I don't assume I got them all. The remaining pieces are very small, though, as you can see in this X-ray taken just after the operation was completed. We'll run another X-ray set later to assess how much is remaining, but I think it should be minimal considering the accumulated mass of the pieces I removed. From talking with Dr. Shaw, I had the impression Governor Connally's wounds fortunately did not include lead debris to the extent of the president's. Maybe the bullet just held together better, or was a different type of bullet altogether."

Dr. Marshall paused, thoughtfully staring at the X-rays on the wall.

"What else?" said Robert, knowing there was more.

The doctor seemed to want to choose his words carefully, but candor won out. "There is something strange about this wound. I hunted as a kid with my dad and I know a little about firearms. After treating missile penetrations, you get a feel after a while for the genre. We treat so many gunshots here. I mean...this is Dallas, everyone has a gun. The entry wound on Mr. Kennedy was a rectangular 1/2 inch by 1/4 inch tear through the upper back at the lower edge of his shoulder blade. In a normal projectile wound, the bullet enters the skin as a tight circular incision with a clear-cut diameter and then proceeds to do its internal damage. But this was different. Something may have caused it to wobble, or tumble end over end, rather than corkscrewing like a football pass. I would have thought it was deflected before it hit the president, but in talking to Dr. Shaw, I learned

Governor Connally's wound was similar, if not worse. His entry wound was the same width, but a longer 1-1/2 inch rectangular impact, indicating that it hit flatter during the tumbling cycle. A strange entry wound for both men. Fortunately the impact missed the president's shoulder joint proper, but unfortunately plowed through bone into the lung and chest cavity before exiting through the middle of the upper rib. A bullet like that wreaks havoc in the process. Entering flatter, it carries a greater impact, creating a messy wound rather than a clean penetrating incision."

The Doctor wondered if he might have overstepped his bounds in talking about aspects other than those directly medical. But he had the complete attention of the younger Kennedy and sensed that he was very interested in hearing whatever was said. "The operation was long. We had him opened up for almost four hours. It went as well as it could, considering the damage, but," the doctor paused, "there are other issues."

"What?" asked Robert, fully aware of what was coming.

"Your brother has a complex physiology. Fortunately, Dr. Burkley was present and alerted us to the president's blood chemistry. According to my calculations, he has severe adrenal deficiency, negligible from a practical point of view. That drawback alone would make survival of any sort of major medical trauma a fifty-fifty proposition. If Dr. Burkley weren't here, your brother would be dead now, as we had no idea of the severity of his condition. Dr. Burkley administered cortisone before the operation and monitored his blood chemistry levels during the surgery to try to stabilize him. We had an endocrinology team in there the whole time monitoring his chemical balance.

"But, your brother has other rather substantial ailments. His back is a mess and he takes painkillers, Procaine and probably others, on a regular basis. He's taking steroids and testosterone, antihistamines, antispasmodics, and a variety of other medications. He is also taking God-knows-what in that concoction from that—what's his name, that Jacobson doctor, that has an amphetamine base. The man is a walking chemistry lab. If this was not a life and death situation and I had seen his blood chemistry earlier, I would have kept him stabilized and sent him over to detox for a few weeks before starting any type of normal operation. Even though we had an endocrinologist present, he should have had a full metabolic work-up before such a major operation. But we had no choice. If we had not operated immediately, he would have expired within half an hour.

"Now that the operation is over, there is the potentially more dangerous period of postoperative infection. He is tremendously susceptible due to the suppression of his immune system from his adrenal deficiency and his steroid tabs and injections. He, well.... Well you probably know all this already."

"Yes," nodded Bobby. He used to tease his brother when his family was around: *Pity the poor mosquito that would bite Jack.* "Yes, I'm well aware." Robert was looking at the X-rays on the wall. "Thank you," said Robert. "Dr. Burkley said you did an excellent job and was very impressed." He turned to face the surgeon. "I'm glad it was you on rotation.

"The press will be hounding you for comments regarding what has happened here today. I would appreciate that you say nothing. There are national and international considerations that must be taken into account. The wrong word or phrasing could have significant repercussions. When we do release information, we need to do it in a controlled manner, as I am sure you are aware in your position. We'll need to make a public statement and I'll talk to you about that before it occurs. But for now, keep this information entirely to yourself regarding the president's operation, condition, and previous ailments."

Robert turned and took a long look at the series of X-rays on the wall. Without turning back to face Dr. Marshall, he asked, "What's your feeling about my brother's chances, Doctor?"

"Mr. Kennedy," he said quietly after a thoughtful pause, "I did all I could for the president, and I know that your specialists are here to take over his care. I'll be briefing them right after I talk to you. But I fear that your brother's wounds may not be survivable."

Chapter 8

Of course the people don't want war. But after all, it's the leaders of the country who determine the policy, and it's always a simple matter to drag the people along whether it's a democracy, a fascist dictatorship, a parliament, or a communist dictatorship. Voice or no voice, the people can always be brought to the bidding of the leaders. That is easy. All you have to do is tell them they are being attacked, and denounce the pacifists for lack of patriotism and exposing the country to greater danger.
—*Hermann Goering, 2nd in command of the Third Reich, Nuremberg Trials*

Every gun that is made, every warship launched, every rocket fired signifies in the final sense, a theft from those who hunger and are not fed, those who are cold and are not clothed. This world in arms is not spending money alone. It is spending the sweat of its laborers, the genius of its scientists, the hopes of its children. This is not a way of life at all in any true sense. Under the clouds of war, it is humanity hanging on a cross of iron.
—*Dwight D. Eisenhower, U.S. President, Republican Party*

Tuesday September 17, 1968
White House

"It's not that hard to get a country to go to war. In fact, it's damned easy."

Kennedy sat back on Grant's sofa in the Treaty Room at the White House. He was in a serious and reflective mood. He seemed a bit angry, not with Patrick or anyone in particular, but at the issues he was discussing.

"You can look through history and see the ease with which the martial passions of an unsuspecting population are inflamed. What's hard is *preventing* a country from going to war when the military and their supporters are able to prey on fearful and emotional triggers to arouse patriotic bloodlust in a population. I know because I had to stop the United States from going to war over Cuba twice during my first term—the Bay of Pigs and the Cuban missile crisis. I also removed our troops from Vietnam and have worked most of my second term to come to a peaceful resolution of that conflict, against, I might add, the railings of the military brass."

This was the second meeting between Patrick and the president. They had conversed for a short time on the previous Thursday, going over contractual agreements, particulars of their scheduling, and the president's vision of what he hoped to accomplish with his memoirs. Both then and today, Kennedy had sauntered in unaided for his meeting. Although he seemed unaffected by the pain in his back, as he did not need the assistance of a wheelchair, Patrick observed that he sat down gingerly on the couch after their greeting.

At the previous meeting, Dave Powers sat with them for a few minutes, but today Patrick sat alone with JFK in the rich quiet of the deep green-carpeted room. The president seemed pensive. He launched right into his comments after sitting down. Patrick wondered if this would be the normal pattern of their sessions.

"The military is created to fight," continued the president in his crisp Boston accent as he lit up one of his thin cigars. "And so it should be. That's its reason for being. But if you ask it to find a solution to a problem, it will be a military solution. You go to your military when you need to go to war, but not to solve problems that have other, more complex dimensions. If you react militarily before all other—and I mean *all* other—possibilities are thoroughly exhausted, then chances are you create a whole new set of problems, often more daunting than the original ones. You may find yourself wishing for the return of your initial dilemma, because the unholy mess you've created through military force may be far more tragic and intractable.

"Now, don't get me wrong about the military. We need a strong military in these crucial times, and I fought hard to keep our armed forces strong, even to the point of being considered a hawk in the early years of my presidency. World tensions could have boiled over into a globe-encompassing war more easily than at any time in our history. The entire equation of warfare changed with the introduction of nuclear weapons at the end of World War II. Any false move—a technological slip-up, an errant commander intent on attack, a swarm of birds misidentified by radar as an incoming bomber squadron—all these things and more could trip the hair-trigger upon which our defense rests, and in so doing provide for the annihilation of not only our enemies, but also of ourselves—with hardly a moment to reflect. We need a strong military so that words can be backed up by strength, if needed; but the best military, in my opinion, is the one never used."

Patrick took notes, but the president had also provided a Dictaphone for recording their conversations. It sat on a small table between the two men. Its use had been agreed upon last week. The reels were to be transcribed by Mrs. Lincoln or one of her secretaries and a typed packet would be given to Patrick during their next meeting. This would allow Patrick to weave the president's comments directly into the narrative of the book.

"We need to step back a bit to understand the forces at work here. For the most part, a president is not fully free to act in just any way he chooses. There are constraints," said Kennedy, pausing to look directly at Patrick. "Now, what I'm about to tell you has been alluded to but not released, so it's for your information alone at this point. I am not yet sure of its inclusion in the final book." He paused again, pondering what he was about to say, "During the Cuban missile crisis, I made what was, at the time, a secret deal with the Soviets to remove our Jupiter missiles from Turkey." He paused again to gauge Patrick's reaction, which was surprise—as much surprise at the information, which Kennedy and his administration had vehemently denied many times when it had been suggested by the press, as surprise that JFK would be admitting as much to him now.

"That action needs to be put into perspective," said the president, sliding an ashtray on the end table at his side closer to him . He flicked the ash of his cigar into it. "With the flight of Sputnik at the end of 1957, the Soviets shocked the world. They were the first to launch a satellite into orbit. It was a tiny little basketball-sized thing, but that little payload created a torrid response. Most observers assumed this meant the Soviets were far ahead of us in rocket technology and would soon be able to rain a swarm of nuclear missiles down upon American soil. Then, in a month, the Soviets sent up another satellite payload; this time it was a dog. The American people were afraid we would soon be at the mercy of the Russian bear. Our European allies were frightened; they had no protection from the rising Soviet menace. The world assumed that the communists dominated space.

"One of Eisenhower's responses was to position nuclear-tipped missiles: the Thors in England, and the Jupiters in Italy and Turkey. It was a muddled plan. In some cases it allowed for these nukes to be launched without American oversight. They were also placed above ground, which wasn't so bad in England, as they were on military bases. But in Italy and Turkey there were over fifty of them scattered around the countryside, and anyone with a rifle and a grudge could take potshots at them if they so desired. And remember, Turkey is a country with a communist element that comprises a quarter of the population. There were even reports of lightning strikes causing accidental partial armings.

"At the beginning of my term, we discussed removing those missiles completely, but knew it was a tactic that would anger the Turks. They were members of NATO who looked at the placement of those missiles on their soil as a sort of national treasure. There were other constraints to their removal as well, but in the end we regretted our inaction. Those missiles were right on the Soviet border, on a hair-trigger, so to speak, pointed directly at the their heartland.

"So is it any wonder the Soviets responded to our Turkish missile presence by placing missiles of their own in Cuba? Move for move, they were trying to match our offensive posturing. To the Soviets, there was no difference in magnitude between the threat the Cuban missiles posed to the United States mainland and the threat the Jupiter missiles in Turkey posed to the Soviets' homeland. What no one wanted to admit was that the Soviets were playing catch-up to western military movements, and were not necessarily being confrontational from sheer belligerence. You see, except for the more senior members of the military, few realized the United States had *overwhelming* dominance in nuclear delivery ability. The so called 'missile gap' bandied about in the political campaigns assumed that the United States was lagging behind in nuclear missile delivery potential and therefore at the mercy of the Russians in the case of a nuclear exchange. It was a farce. In fact the 'missile gap' was the reverse.

"We had such a substantial military lead at the time we could have decimated the Soviet Union and all her strategic counter-attack forces with hardly the fear of even an errant nuke of theirs reaching U.S. soil. Their missiles were above ground and land-based. We knew exactly, from our U-2 flights, where each and every one of them was located. Their attack bombers were so slow that, in the six to twelve hours it would take them to arrive after flying over Alaska, we would have hours of fighter sorties and intercept time to blow them from the sky a dozen times over. Theirs was also a suicide mission, as they had no midair refueling capabilities and no land-based refueling stops. It would be a one-way flight for all their crews. Their submarines were noisy, diesel-powered, short-range boats far inferior to ours with no refueling stations either. The Joint Chiefs were certain that almost all of the Soviet Union's nuclear forces could be eliminated with nary a blow landed on American or, for that matter, European cities. We had a fifteen- or twenty-to-one advantage in almost every way. But how many times do you need to atomize an enemy city?

"And with this comes the quandary. That much power begs for usage. The temptation to exercise it is great, while the benefits are illusory. We had overwhelming superiority in every theater of operation—so much so that the militaristic inclination of the American generals was almost impossible to restrain.

"Returning to Sputnik for a moment.... The launch of Sputnik had made a great publicity splash, but it did not translate into Soviet military missile superiority. In fact, it was just the opposite. It was a calculated bluff for the weak hand they were holding. The military brass here knew it, and that knowledge drove them to distraction.

"They wanted a reason for a nuclear war because they felt that if we had one then, while the Soviets were at a severe disadvantage, we could be done with them once and for all. It was an insane idea," said the president with obvious disgust, "but first-strike scenarios were bandied about with locker-room jocularity by the Joint Chiefs.

"When I avoided direct U.S. support of a military invasion of Cuba during the Bay of Pigs fiasco, I was lambasted by the military and the community of Cuban expatriates living in this country for cowardice, for weakness," said the president, still angered at the thought. "When I avoided a military confrontation during the Cuban missile crisis, I was *excoriated* by the Joint Chiefs, to the point that I was afraid there could be a mutiny. But fortunately, when I sidestepped an escalation of the conflict in Vietnam, the military brass had already been weakened, or I would surely have been impeached. Such is the tightrope a president walks while avoiding war.

"Earlier in my first term, I promoted the filming of the movie *Seven Days in May*, allowing it to be filmed on White House grounds, to try to bring to the attention of the American people the danger the military chiefs represented at that time. Burt Lancaster did a bang-up job of crystallizing the attitude of the Joint Chiefs present on my staff with his super-patriot rhetoric. There is a politicization of the military leadership at that level that twists its priorities, concentrating its energies on a bureaucratic desire for self-expansion and power, with the most polarizing figures rising to the top. Now realize that I single out the upper levels of the military and not our men in uniform. I was in the military myself and I respect the service these men give to their country. But with the chiefs, it's a whole different ball game.

"Now, the United States was so overwhelmingly ahead of the Soviets they feared a first strike coming from us would obliterate their homeland. A fear, I might add, that was not unfounded considering the mentality of the military chiefs in our country. Do you remember the movie that was released in 1964, *Dr. Strangelove?*" asked the president.

"Sure," said Patrick, "*How I Learned to Stop Worrying and Love the Bomb.*" He smiled at the humorous title. He had seen the movie a couple of times, finding it disturbingly enthralling.

"You remember the deranged general?" asked Kennedy.

"Yeah, the main character, the maniacal officer intent on total destruction of the USSR—worried about the Soviets sapping the precious bodily fluids of American citizens," responded Patrick.

"Right. He was depicted initiating a nuclear shooting war with the Soviets by circumventing presidential authority and running Air Force bombers past their fail-safe points. Well, that character was modeled after General Curtis LeMay, the Air Force Chief of Staff. *My* Chief of Staff! In *my* administration!" said the president nearly incredulous at the thought. "And, as strange a caricature as that movie presented, it was not off the mark," continued Kennedy. "I canned him at the start of my second administration, but he's back, running with George Wallace for vice president. Ousting him during the early years of my presidency would not have been possible. It would have caused an insurrection in the military. In a recent campaign stop—in Memphis, I think—he mentioned he still wanted to 'drop a few nuclear bombs on someone deserving.'

"But back to the missile issue." The president snuffed out the remnants of his cigar in the nearby ashtray and continued. "So on our side we had the military brass yearning to strike. The Soviets were well aware of their weakness in regard to nuclear parity. They had no similarly lethal weapons in place to threaten the United States mainland as our Polaris submarines, our silo-based ICBMs, and finally, the British, Italian, and Turkish missiles did to threaten the Soviet homeland. So they were simply creating a balance in opposing forces. We, of course, did not see it that way at all.

"In order to quell the furor, without bringing it to a nuclear exchange that would have been apocalyptic in scale, we, Bobby and I, made a back-channel agreement with the Soviets through Georgi Bolshakov, a contact we'd used in previous discussions with the Soviets. Khrushchev would stand down and remove the missiles from Cuba, and in exchange, the United States would remove the missiles from Turkey. The Jupiter missile part of the deal would come to fruition in six months only if the Cuban stand-down was satisfactory, and if this quid pro quo was not revealed. Otherwise all deals were off and it would be vehemently denied.

"Now, what would have been the reason to 'stand on principle,' so to speak, and refuse to remove those outdated missiles? The Soviets were correct in their assessment of the danger poised on their borders. And I could not deny the danger they presented, as I had already said as much previously in a number of meetings regarding their positioning. To stubbornly refuse to act reasonably could have instigated a nuclear exchange. Had we moved on the Cubans, the Soviets would have moved on West Berlin. The international chessboard contained more players than just those using gunboat diplomacy off the Florida coast. The hard-right military forces in Khrushchev's Kremlin, similar to those in the United States, were hell-bent on preserving their national pride and were not about to back down from a conflict. And it would have been a conflict without any meaning whatsoever, other than misguided pride.

"So we made the deal." Kennedy, with his legs crossed and one arm over the back of the sofa, was staring out the window at the South Lawn while recounting much of what he had just been saying. He was surprisingly calm in his remembrance of the conflicts surrounding the Office of the President.

"And it worked. I appeared more formidable than I really was. I truly felt that the removal of the Turkish Jupiters was a reasonable demand. But I could not express that publicly at the time due to the inflamed nature of the standoff. In the United States, there is a strong, harsh, and unreasonable right-wing element at work.

"That has been revealed quite vividly from the investigations into who the plotters were and why they attempted to eliminate me from power in Dallas years ago. Few people realized at the time how powerful and elemental that force was in our society. If I had acknowledged the Jupiter missile deal at the time, I feared there might have been a coup or I would have been impeached, such is the ferocity of the hatred toward any sort of reasonable give and take between the superpowers. Any accommodation is seen as treasonous capitulation.

"We quietly dismantled the missiles, photographing their dismemberment and removal to prove our compliance to the Soviets. The SS-4s and 5s were similarly removed from Cuban soil and shipped back to Russia.

"We've lost nothing really in the removal of our Jupiter missiles. From a balance of power perspective, we have far greater accuracy and stealth from our Polaris submarine-based strike platform. And in reality, I sleep easier knowing that severe weather in Turkey will not translate into a volley of nuclear missiles headed toward Moscow." The president paused. Patrick thought he might be wrapping it up for their first session when he slowly leaned forward on the couch as if he might be ready to stand and leave.

"And now here comes the kicker," he stated quietly, looking at Patrick. He had been waiting for this moment, Patrick realized, and was ready to surprise him. "Our intelligence had accurately assessed the presence of the forty-five or more Soviet nuclear intermediate range SS-4 and SS-5 missiles that were either operational, or nearly so, on Cuban soil. We knew there were anti-aircraft SAM missiles at shore and inland batteries as well. What we *didn't* know at the time," emphasized the president intently, "was there were over one hundred operational tactical nuclear weapons that were positioned in anticipation of an American invasion of that island. Had we responded militarily and launched an invasion, our forces would have been decimated, along with the incineration of Cuba and the southeastern United States."

"What!" Patrick was staggered. He had lived through the Cuban missile crisis, watching it unfold on television screens and through the many tense press conferences given by the president and other administration officials during that two-week period. Honestly, at the time even Patrick thought it would be a reasonable idea to invade the small island country, for all the difficulties it had been causing. He felt foolish and even guilty now, knowing that his desire, had it become the national policy, might possibly have led to his death and the near complete destruction of a significant portion of the country. And to think that his own acceptance regarding the invasion of their southern neighbor was magnified a thousand times by the military's pressure upon Kennedy to go to war.

"How could that be?" asked Patrick. "There was never any mention of that in the press or...." Patrick trailed off, trying to grasp the enormity of the events that had transpired less than six years ago.

"None of us knew," said the president sitting back, apparently satisfied with Patrick's reaction. "The Soviets never mentioned a thing. I don't even think the Cubans were going to mention it, but Castro's bravado got the better of him." The president smiled ruefully at the thought of Castro being tripped into revealing information.

"Castro was being berated by a member of our delegation for accepting the newer trade agreements, as being the whipping boy of the Americas or something to that effect. It was an offhand, thoughtless remark. Well, Castro whipped out the outrageous claim that he would have decimated the American forces had they stepped one foot on the 'glorious soil of the Cuban motherland' or some such nonsense. Anyway, he divulged the fact they had been waiting and ready for an American attack. In fact, it was the first thing for which they had prepared. Before setting up the longer range SS-4s and 5s, they already had shoreline batteries all along the north portion of the island to both repel an invading force and to strike deep into the American south. These included twenty-five-mile-range Luna nuclear missiles as well as scaled-down pilotless MiG fighters outfitted with nuclear bombs used as cruise missiles, to fly by radio control with well over a hundred-mile range. They also had longer-range bombers stationed on the island with nuclear weapons capability. We've since had the information confirmed privately to our satisfaction through our Soviet contacts, as well as pictures of the construction and then dismantling of the sites along the coastline where the missiles were originally positioned.

"The information deeply shocked all of us. Had we succumbed to the urge to strike Cuba militarily, we would have lost most of the Southern and Gulf State cities in a nuclear holocaust, because at the time, Castro was intent on wreaking as much havoc as possible if we invaded his country. It would have been a worldwide calamity. It would have decimated our invading force, which would have comprised over a hundred thousand troops, a significant portion of our military. The destruction would have reached deep into the heart of the American southeast, killing millions and rendering that part of America uninhabitable for decades or even centuries to come. It would most probably have eliminated America as a superpower—that is, if our ensuing nuclear retaliation against the Soviets and their response did not kill us all in the process. Cuba, including our Guantanamo military base, would probably have been completely destroyed. We were *far, far* closer to the destruction of civilization as we know it than any of us had realized. It would have been just devastating." The president had said the last with a great deliberation. He watched Patrick's response.

"My God," said Patrick sitting back in his chair. He rubbed his face with his hands. The information was staggering, and he, a seasoned Washington reporter, had had no idea. He needed to think about what the president had just revealed to him.

To his credit, Kennedy did not seem to be taking personal credit for his decision—a decision that, unknown to him or to anyone else in the free world, had averted the destruction of the planet. He was oddly philosophical about it, knowing he had followed what he thought to be the only reasonable course, one that in retrospect had inadvertently avoided a holocaust. Instead he appeared to marvel along with Patrick at what had been avoided. He seemed as confounded by our human luck as anyone, even though it was largely he who was responsible for the avoidance of such a global calamity.

With a soft knock on the door, Dave Powers poked his head through, "Cabinet meeting in five minutes, sir."

Kennedy looked at his watch. "I think we're done here for today," he said as he slowly rose to his feet. He seemed to be aware of the hollow feeling the thought of a barely avoided war had produced in Patrick, and paused to talk a bit more.

"There is the nature of military power and then the nature of moral power," he added as he faced Patrick before leaving. "Understanding when and where to use each is important. The use of military power is only effective under certain extreme conditions where other options have been abandoned. But moral power is far more persuasive and far more effective. It does not injure people, but enlivens them and confronts their prejudices. It may be frustratingly slow-acting, but in the long run it exchanges beliefs, not bullets. Moral persuasion is more long-lasting, and if, out of necessity, used with military force, it can be extremely powerful. But if military force is used alone, with a mocking nod to a moralistic cause that is not grounded in reason and truth, it will have detrimental effects indeed." He paused for a moment looking at Patrick.

"Next week, Mr. Hennessey," said the president shaking Patrick's hand. He still used the formality, but because of the way he emphasized it, Patrick thought he was doing it for light-hearted effect rather than stuffy protocol.

"Yes, sir," responded Patrick soberly.

* * *

Patrick left his morning meeting with the president and took his time strolling toward the Library of Congress. The president's information regarding the hairsbreadth avoidance of a nuclear Armageddon only six short years ago had shaken him to his core. He and other members of his reporting profession had only a partial realization of how close the nation had come to utter destruction. Like a ship slowly passing through a heavily mined strait, its passengers argued on deck, unaware of the deathly dangers that lurked just below the surface. It was hard to imagine they had come so close to annihilation.

Patrick had not been to the Library of Congress since his first encounter with the new brusque librarian. He had been to the Archives a number of times doing document research and had even tracked down his old friend Barry, who was now working there. Patrick had to admit that Barry was overqualified to be at the Reading Room desk, just as his prickly replacement had said, and after talking for a bit Patrick found that he was just as helpful to Patrick's research at the Archives as he had been at the Library.

But the Library was Patrick's inspirational home. Today, although he was ready to spend some time writing, he felt a nagging reluctance mixed with excitement at the idea of returning to the scene of his earlier snubbing. He had thought of her often over the last week, this attractive librarian, and was scheming for a way to meet. But as he entered the domed Reading Room and the hushed quiet of its embrace, he felt his nerve slip. He circled the central reader's station from the cover of the card catalog aisle a number of times, sneaking glances her way as he tried to gather his wits to make some manner of impression. Patrick knew his limitations in this regard. He hated to admit it, relinquishing some of his male pride in the process, but he was a hormone-addled member of the human race, deeply flustered when approaching a woman he was attracted to. And by his second circumnavigation of the card catalog aisle, it was difficult to come to a more manly conclusion, which further undercut his resolve. But after of bit of pathetic meandering, he pulled up and went directly into the fray. He approached her position from the right flank with the trepidation General Lee probably felt approaching Grant at Appomattox, though with little of the general's bravado.

He had tried to calculate his arrival to be direct and private, but his timing was off and he was undercut by two other patrons who slipped in front of him while he dithered. They both had complicated requests and were obviously not experienced users of the library's system. Imagine, asking for a copy of *The Linguist's Guide to Slavic Pronunciations* without having first looked it up in the card catalog! What was this woman thinking?

After a few long moments, the Slavic wordsmith's request satisfied, the librarian moved on to the next patron's request—"Publications showing the effects of Greek and Roman architecture on public buildings in Washington?" Maybe this guy should just go outside and take a walk down to the Mall and back, looking around at the many examples of classical architecture, and stop wasting their time. Patrick was getting impatient and it probably showed. She glanced up at him for a moment, taking his measure. Oh-oh.

Standing slightly to the side, waiting anxiously as she handled the request of the architectural non-scholar, he had a long moment to observe her close-up without interruption. He was charmed by her presence. She was concentrating intently on the assistance she was giving. He was concentrating intently on her. A strand of her long dark hair fell toward her face, escaping confinement behind her splendidly shaped ear, as she leaned in to look at the patron's request. She brushed it back unconsciously, pulling one of her hands off its task of rifling expertly through the 3x5 card catalog drawer in front of her. He watched her attentively as the errant string of hair was slipped efficiently back behind her ear. But then as she leaned forward again it would insolently escape, only a few moments later, in a sort of follicular rebellion, creeping stealthily forward across the side of her glasses—glasses that were far too blocky and incongruous next to the soft curve of her neck and the light fuzz exposed by the reflected light at the base of her ear. The lock of hair would come to rest, triumphantly touching the curve of her cheek in a moment of successful escape. The lock slid along what, at second glance, appeared to be deliberately unattractive glass frames that rested bulkily on her delicate nose, like an old dump truck parked in the middle of a perfectly manicured Japanese garden.

As lost in concentration as he was, he pulled his gaze away to take stock of her personal items on the desk around her. What he assumed to be her pocketbook was tucked into the shelf visible just to the side of her desk. A bulky bulging thing, it looked more like an overstuffed suitcase than a stylish contribution to her tidy appearance. He noticed the title of some personal reading material on the desk to her side, *A Short Etymological Dictionary of Modern English*. It was a densely arcane bit of esoteric literature. If that was the short version, at about ten pounds, Patrick would hate to see the full edition. He shifted his gaze to look about some more. When his eyes returned to her, she was quietly watching him.

"Boy, that looks like pretty exciting reading," he blurted out, intuitively sensing that he would regret it before the last syllable even passed his drying lips. The patron before him had finished, and she was looking at him while he had been hungrily distracted, gawking about her habitat.

She stood directly before him, looking him squarely in the eyes. With a slight forward tilt of her head, she pushed the reading glasses down on her nose to get a better view of him. The dump truck had shifted position.

There was an interminable pause. It was during this juncture that Patrick was hooked, as if he wasn't already, this short moment when the boundary of cool indifference shifts to the personal. And even before he could acknowledge the thought, the feeling had already affected his nervous system. It was the no man's land where Patrick stepped into a space reserved for the vulnerable as opposed to the guarded, although you wouldn't know it from her response. Her eyes bored into his. "Do you know that sarcasm is the lowest form of humor?"

"Uh, I think actually I heard that somewhere." Oh, this was *not* starting well, Patrick feared.

"Then why did you say that?"

He wasn't prepared for being quizzed so directly, and honesty just popped out of his mouth. "Well, I was embarrassed, I was trying to think of some way to introduce myself. I'm rather pathetic when it comes to attractive women."

"Oh, and what is that? Is that more sarcasm?"

"No, that was self-deprecating humor, with a hint of...well...a compliment. I always thought women found men who could laugh at themselves interesting."

"I believe self-deprecation is the second lowest form of humor. That is, if it's humor at all. Though equally unsuccessful, I'd think you might want to stick with sarcasm."

"I'll take that under advisement," replied Patrick. Was she enjoying this? Patrick couldn't tell.

"Are you a lawyer?"

"No," said Patrick, exasperated, wondering if there was any hope of success in an exchange with this woman. This was not going the way he had hoped. Women were always out of season for him.

"Then why did you say 'under advisement'? That's a lawyerly term."

"Well, I was trying a little more humor. Obviously not my strong suit." *Did she get the pun?*

"It would seem." She wasn't exactly smiling, but he sensed at least some enjoyment reflected in her voice.

Without taking his eyes off her, Patrick handed her the slip from the card catalog he had been holding in his hand during the entire exchange. It included the identifying prefixes that JFK had given him for documents he was to peruse in the privacy of the Library, as well as some choices of his own. She looked it over and turned to drop it in the pneumatic sleeve while keeping him carefully in view. He half turned to depart, but couldn't help himself and turned. "Well, I think I'll just wait for my order. I'll be sitting in the corner, bleeding from my wounds. You don't mind, do you?"

"Will I need to send over the janitor for cleanup?" Certainly there was a hint of levity in her response, wasn't there?

"No, I'm very neat," he added with more sarcasm. She obviously wouldn't approve.

Patrick retreated to a desk a few aisles away from the central station to regain some composure and to settle into his task at hand. As he sat, he glanced back at the librarian, but she quickly looked away.

He wanted to get down on paper his communication with Kennedy: his comments about his first-term hostilities with the military and the balancing act of the competing agendas within a large and vital nation such as the United States. Such leadership was a Herculean task that no one man could adequately encompass. Patrick was glad it was not he who was required to make the Solomonic decisions necessary in such a high-visibility position. But he especially wanted to write about what he had felt regarding the final information about the unknown Cuban missiles. He just couldn't understand how such a dramatic development as this had not been previously discovered or reported upon by the press. It was historic.

He also wondered about the dynamics of his exchange with JFK this morning. "Exchange" was a generous description of the nearly word-perfect exposition the president had delivered during their first meeting. Like a dam of pent-up knowledge, the floodgates had opened, releasing a reservoir of information. Patrick wondered if it was to be like this during their entire time—JFK expounding, and Patrick listening in rapt attention. It didn't give him a lot to do. But it was early, only their first exchange. He would see how it played out. Certainly, he could find more to contribute. But Patrick wondered if contribution was part of his job description.

He had worked on his piece for about half an hour before coming up for breath when he noticed his package was in the receiving bin at the central desk. He ambled over for the pickup. She was alone. He silently gave her his request slip and she matched it to his bundle. He figured maybe silence would be a better alternative in his developing strategy. She gathered his materials, but as she was handing them to Patrick she paused, her hand still holding the packet.

"Hmmm. This isn't the usual call code for CASIC or at least not one

I'm familiar with. E842.9 is the usual prefix. This has an EK822.7 prefix," she whispered in her library voice. There was a little tug of war, as they were both holding opposite ends of the documents.

"Ah, well, it's some of the minutes from an auxiliary oversight committee. It's not so commonly known is all. Just some of the side issues regarding how the main committee had been formed, membership decisions, parameters, rules of order for the investigation. Background mostly," whispered Patrick. He had already planned how to respond if anything were to be questioned. He was aware from the way the top file was wrapped that this was probably one of the special packages he had been told to expect from the bowels of the Library. It was not something he wanted to have a discussion about.

"I wasn't aware there was an oversight committee. What's it called?" She looked closely at the thick manila envelope with the twine-bound flap, wondering over its marking code.

"The PASI hearings do not have an oversight committee," inserted a barely hushed voice over his shoulder. "It is its own oversight committee. It was formulated by special decree from Congress in order to consolidate all investigative activities under one umbrella of organizational teamwork in a manner that would facilitate a decisive explanation of the conditions around the assassination and the sedition infiltrating our government that was played out on November 22. It—"

Patrick recognized Professor Hamillon from George Washington University. He was a resident researcher who could be found almost all hours of the day either in the Reading Room of the Library of Congress, the Adams Building Reading Room, or the National Archives. A tall, wiry man with thickened glasses from his years buried in books, he was sarcastically referred to as "the ferret" by Barry. The professor's historical renditions of current events were so long-winded that he was rarely read or quoted. His Faulknerian style, even when whispering, was even more pronounced than that of the author himself. In his articles, he rarely wrote a sentence that started and ended on the same page, and in conversation, he rarely completed a commentary before the patience of his audience was exhausted. Patrick avoided him whenever possible.

"Shhh," shushed the librarian. She glanced at Patrick and noticed the subtle shake of his head. They had a moment of eye contact. He thought he detected a sinister grin.

"On second thought," she confided softly to the professor with a genial smile as she tried to look around Patrick, "tell me more, Mr. Hamillon." Everyone seemed to know the ferret. It was the first moment in their interactions when Patrick was sure she was enjoying herself.

"Well," started the professor, as he tried unsuccessfully to edge around Patrick and get a little closer to the desk in order not to have to raise his voice, "during its initial stages, the creation of the committee was a contentious task, made all the more difficult by the reluctance of the Federal Bureau of Investigation and the Central Intelligence Agency to share their raw data or even participate in the more public nature of the investigation because, as we all now know, they had some serious skeletons they desired remain well hidden. But in regard to this erroneous idea of a side committee whose creation would provide oversight, there is really no designation—"

"I am sure we are all interested in sharing your vast knowledge regarding this matter, professor," interrupted Patrick as he inserted himself more directly between the librarian and the professor, "but I have some time constraints for my research today." As he said this, he looked more pleadingly at the woman in front of him. It was not a joking glance. "I *really* must get to work right now," he said more urgently in a low voice. They were both still holding on to the package.

"Well, the committees were formed with the express requirement that all information be centrally configured in order to—" continued the professor.

"Well, hmm, maybe I do recognize this," she reconsidered after a moment's pause. "It is a sort of sidebar to the investigations, if I remember. Something about research into the participants to be sure there was a thorough balance on the committee." She gazed quizzically at Patrick.

"Oh, I must disagree with your conclusion, Miss," whispered the professor in quick response to her comment, his voice rising. "There was little if any discussion of a public or private nature that could possibly allow one to come to that conclusion, and I should know, as I am intimately aware of all the committee's creations as well as sub-committees that were created and disbanded over the years, delving into side issues regarding, as a few examples, the shooting itself, the gathered forensic evidence that evaded the FBI's initial submittals, the witnesses whose testimony was impounded, and a—"

"Shhh!" shushed the librarian more emphatically. After a long moment of furrowed study aimed at Patrick, she released her hold on the packet to his grateful nod. Patrick slipped it under his arm as he retreated from the desk under the professor's inquisitive gaze. He had no desire to extend this conversation, and he passed with a noncommittal nod.

* * *

That did not go well, thought Patrick as he returned to his seat. He was uncertain what he should do regarding the librarian's obvious curiosity. He would need to think about this some more, and possibly talk to the president about finding a method for a more private exchange. But he was eager to look at the documents the packet contained. He opened the top flap by unwinding the twine from the nibs that held it shut and pulled out a few bundles of stapled reports and some loose documents. There was a handwritten note on the top;

> Hennessey,
> As we discussed, these documents are for your perusal and not for direct quotation. When writing your drafts, please note the areas where these documents have been used for attribution as they may get pulled from the final. Fun reading, though, I am sure you will agree. Be sure that these packets I will be sending are repackaged as you received them and are observed by yourself to be fully inserted in the conveyance system at the Central Reading Desk before your departure. I had to pry them away from the agencies for your viewing. They are for no other eyes.

There was no signature.

There were three reports in the packet: *Cuban Tactical Nuclear Missile Deterrence: The Latin American Theater*; *Soviet Nuclear Readiness and Alert Levels: The Cuban Crisis*; and *Permissive Action Links: Minuteman ICBMs*. He read them all.

The first two were detailed reports supporting the discussion between JFK and Patrick. Included were position papers generated by the CIA, and internal Soviet audits that showed the nature of the missiles arrayed against the United States at the time of the Cuban missile crisis, their capabilities, damage potentials, and eventual dismantling and removal.

The two Cuban reports showed that the Castro regime had been delivered an array of nuclear response choices the United States had been completely unaware of at the time. This included the SS-4s and 5s, the Il-28 bomber, the Luna missiles, and the pilotless FKR MiG. This was presented by Castro, reviewed by the CIA, and then confirmed with documented proof from a mix of CIA intelligence and KGB documentation supplied by the Cubans.

Patrick wondered how the Soviet documents had come to light. Were they from Castro? Did he want the United States to know how close they had come to blows? What did it say about Cuba's relationship with the Soviets, that Castro was releasing to the United States top-secret Soviet position papers and documents?

The third report regarded the nuclear codes and creation of the Permissive Action Links system for preventing the unapproved launch of nuclear ICBMs. This was not fully relevant to what they were discussing, but possibly pertained in an ancillary manner since they had been discussing Cuban acceptance of Soviet nuclear missiles on their island nation. Although the report had no codes or direct information, it detailed the layers of fail-safe protections that were built into the American nuclear arsenal, making it nearly impossible to launch one of the silo-based Minuteman missiles without full Presidential and Joint Chiefs approval.

No matter how one looked at all the information contained in these reports, it was obvious the world had lingered on the precipice of destruction, its leaders playing with toys of their own creation that they really didn't know how to control and that could easily have led to complete destruction. It was sobering reading.

Patrick made a lot of notes and would be careful to keep this information highlighted in any of his further writings. After a few hours of reading, he carefully repackaged the documents in their original packet, rebound it with twine, and, gathering up his gear, approached the central reading station.

He noticed a little plaque now on the desk in front of her. It had not been there before. Maybe they had finally had one made up, or it had just gotten delivered to her desk. Her name was Jenna. He lingered a moment looking at the plaque and then at her face. She looked back as if daring him to use it in a sentence. *Why, your name is Jenna*, or *Well thank you, Jenna*, or *You might want to get some better glasses, Jenna*. He was careful to watch that the conveyor swallowed the packet. The minions in the basement would appreciate its return.

She noticed his lingering gaze as it shifted from the packet's slow advance into the conveyor enclosure to the nametag displayed so prominently on her desk. She must be wondering at his odd behavior, which she must by now think to be his normal mode of interaction. He opened his mouth and imagined she was rising to the occasion with a particularly cutting response.

But all he said was, "Thank you, for earlier." He felt still a little shaken by the information he had received. But just as he was about to leave he turned, "Oh, I didn't make a mess, no need for the janitor...Jenna."

Chapter 9

We have only to believe. And the more threatening and irreducible
reality appears, the more firmly and desperately we must believe.
Then, little by little, we shall see the universal horror unbend,
and then smile upon us, and then take us in its more than human arms.
—*Pierre Teilhard De Chardin*

A sin takes on new and real terrors
when there seems a chance that it is going to be found out.
—*Mark Twain*

Saturday morning , November 23, 1963
Dallas, Texas

On Friday evening, after his arrival and initial conference with Dr. Marshall, Bobby went to see Jackie. For protection, and in consultation with the Secret Service, the medical staff had placed her in a room on the third floor, just down the hall from the president. She was asleep, having been sedated for the procedure to close the bullet wound to her neck and given a transfusion to replace the blood she had lost. Two Secret Service agents at the door nodded to Bobby as he entered. He knew from talking with Kenny earlier that she was all right, just sleeping, so he wasn't as wary upon entering. Inside were a doctor and nurse talking quietly over a chart. Mary Gallagher, Jackie's assistant, was sitting beside the bed. Jackie was also in a standard-issue hospital bed in a room cleared of its second station to provide more privacy. But instead of seeming more spacious, it just felt barren.

She had a white bandage over a dark swelling on her upper left forehead near the hairline, which showed the impact from having struck the concrete wall when she fell while helping wheel in the gurney holding Jack. Her hair was a tangled dark mass.

"Mr. Kennedy, I'm Dr. Janets," whispered the doctor, reaching out to shake hands.

"How is she doing?" asked Robert quietly as he looked down at her. Pale and looking so small, she slept quietly.

The doctor had a boyish appearance, with bristling blond crew-cut hair and a neat white smock, but upon closer examination was more middle-aged than he first appeared. A neat row of colored pens lined his breast pocket. "She had a shallow penetrating gunshot wound to the neck just at the crease where it connects near the shoulder muscle," he said, pointing to the spot on his own neck near his starched white collar. "It broke the skin in a one-and-a-quarter-inch trough, grazing the trapezoid muscle and a vein in the process. We don't know if she didn't realize she'd been shot in the shock of the event, or if she just didn't pay it any mind. But she'd been slowly losing blood since the time the limousine was in the plaza. It didn't catch up with her till she had gotten out of the car and was walking down the hall." The doctor appeared to be a little in awe of his patient, possibly more for who she was than what she had just done, although it could have been both. He also seemed a little impressed with his own abilities as doctor and entertained the faintly self-important air of one who is old enough to recognize his developing talents, but not yet wise enough to realize their inherent limits in the face of life's vagaries. "By that time she had lost quite a bit of blood and simply fainted when the exertion of pushing the gurney was too much for her. There wasn't enough blood getting to the brain for it to function properly. Quite impressive really. I sutured the grazing wound. The bullet removed a section of epidermal layer, slightly damaging the dermal layer below, but I tried to be very neat. There unfortunately will be a scar, but I think it'll be minimal."

"And the wound on her forehead?" asked Robert, still speaking softly.

"It appears minor. We don't think she suffered a concussion, at least not in severity that would cause a hematoma—a blood clot on the brain," interjected Dr. Janets to be sure Robert was following the medical terminology, "—or even any memory loss," he continued. "Her initial unconsciousness was caused by blood loss. That's the reason she fainted. We took two sets of X-rays, one before and one after the suturing and blood transfusion in the operating room, to be sure there was no blood clot. We especially wanted to be sure that with her blood pressure back up to normal, there was no blood vessel leakage that might have gone undetected. We saw no sign at all of any blood pooling in either set. When she wakes, a better test will be to see if she fully remembers what happened up till the time she fell. If she does, there was no brain trauma." The doctor paused, looking at the patient. "Although, I guess in other ways it might be a better thing if she does not fully remember what occurred."

Bobby was watching Jackie sleeping as the doctor spoke. There was a bank of equipment on the wall beside her bed, and to one side was an oscilloscope, the phosphorescent green blip bouncing silently to her rhythmic heartbeat.

"Mrs. Kennedy will most certainly have a severe headache at first, and she will probably be weak over the next few days from the blood loss and shock, but she should be fine with rest," finished the doctor.

Bobby was sure that as soon as she awoke, rest would be the last thing she would be taking. So he let her sleep. She might be upset that she had not been roused earlier, but there was nothing she could do at the moment, and there would be time later for her to sit with him and share the trauma of Jack's dying. She looked so peaceful lying there, as if nothing of the last many hours had happened. He wondered for a moment where she could be in her dreams, to appear so restfully content, somehow oblivious to the events that would re-engulf her as soon as she woke. He asked the doctor to let her sleep and to inform him as soon as she stirred.

* * *

The presidency is more than just the man who occupies the office, and the White House is more than just an address on Pennsylvania Avenue. The White House communications system follows the president wherever he goes. There should be a secure phone within fifty feet of the president at all times, but usually it was closer. At any location where he will remain for even one day, the Army Signal Corps sets up a complete communications switchboard manned by a small platoon of experienced communications operatives who open and maintain direct links to every important national location and personage. During Kennedy's travels through Dallas, one switchboard was set up at the Texas Hotel in Fort Worth on the lower floor and manned by no fewer than sixteen active technicians and operators. At the time of the shooting one was being set up at the Austin Hotel, as that was to be his next stop after a flight out of Dallas following the luncheon and speech at the Trade Mart.

All that changed when Kennedy was injured. The entire communications apparatus was re-established in five rooms on the far corridor of the second floor of the hospital, off the service elevator, one floor below Kennedy's. It supplied direct links with the White House and every major administration operative across the United States. The "traveling White House" had all the capabilities of the best technology available at the time. It was in heavy use.

Bobby used it to make his many evening calls, both on the private and the more secure scrambled lines. He called Ethel numerous times, informing her of Jack's condition and his own feelings about what had happened to his brother. He talked to his children to calm their fears. He called Nicholas Katzenbach, the assistant attorney general, and ceded to him many responsibilities for day-to-day operations as acting attorney general for the foreseeable future. He knew that he would be absorbed with caring for his brother and did not want this to jeopardize the multitude of complex decisions regarding issues not directly related to the assassination attempt. He could not focus on both while Jack was incapacitated.

Earlier he had called his brother, Senator Ted Kennedy, to talk with him about Jack's condition and to ask him to keep in communication with Bobby's family at Hickory Hill while he was away. His intention was to stay in Dallas as long as needed, and he had no idea at the moment how long that would be.

Then he called his mother, Rose. He had already talked to her once before leaving for Dallas, and then again after he was briefed on Jack's condition at Parkland. But he knew she needed more.

Joseph Kennedy, Sr. had not been told. The family had instituted an elaborate hoax to prevent their invalid father, hobbled and muted by a stroke only two years earlier, from learning of the shooting. They were afraid that in his delicate condition, the shock might trigger another stroke or heart attack that would kill him. They eliminated all sources of information from his daily environment. Unable to deactivate the power switch and prevent him from viewing one of the favorite news programs he watched every day, they had torn the wires out of the back panel of the television when it was inadvertently turned on and warming up. The house was culled of newspapers. Instructions were given to his nurse and attendant to avoid making any mention of Dallas until they could find a way to break the news in a manner that would be least distressing. Edward Kennedy was coming up from DC to help. By the time Bobby had called back late in the evening, Joseph Sr. was still uninformed but mighty suspicious. Since he was wheelchair bound and nearly mute, he could communicate only by frustrated stroke-restricted gestures and piercing glances. But with his mind still sharp, he knew something was very wrong.

Rose was unsure if she should come to Dallas. She desperately wanted to, but she was torn between caring for her invalid husband and being with her injured son. She would need to stay in Cape Cod until her husband was informed, and then decide. A doctor was at the compound in case it all went bad.

And finally, in the dark early hours of Saturday morning, Bobby called Chief U.S. Marshal Jim McShane. He asked the chief to provide unobtrusive U.S. Marshal protection for his family. McShane, a man whom Bobby trusted implicitly, approved of it as an excellent idea. The chief was grateful that RFK had called, since he would otherwise have had a hard time explaining the phalanx of marshals already surrounding the Hickory Hill estate. They had arrived less than an hour after the Dallas shooting. In fact, the local Fairfax County Police Department, unsummoned, had surrounded the property with every available officer within moments of the shooting of the president. They had held the property until the federal marshals arrived a short time later to provide more permanent protection.

* * *

John Kennedy was well attended. Had he not been president, his personal wealth would have seen to that. But because he was the center of national and international attention at this moment in history, his caregivers would have moved mountains if that's what was required for his recovery. He was cared for by the Parkland Medical team during the first frenzied hours of trauma, and then additionally by a team of surgeons and doctors flown in to scrupulously pursue any further treatments that might improve his chances of survival. But, unfortunately, there are limits to medical intervention, and at a certain point, care and maintenance peak and can be increased no more. Nothing was denied him during his period of unconsciousness, but what was most recommended after the initial operations and treatments was rest and observation.

At Parkland Medical Center, especially on the third floor, the frenetic pace that normally accompanied the presidential entourage had abruptly subsided. The momentum and exuberance of the campaign swing through Texas had been stilled by the sense of grief permeating the hot, heavy Texas air. A hundred and fifty grains of lead and copper, fashioned into a tiny projectile, had changed the course of history, and no one knew down which road it was heading.

Bobby had talked to the doctors almost too many times by now. There was nothing they could add to the knowledge he had accumulated regarding the condition and care of his brother. They were exhausted and he was exhausted, but even so, he was unable to rest. So it was well after Friday midnight and deep into Saturday morning, after six or seven hours of intensive appeals to and demands of the medical staff, innumerable calls to family and associates, and numerous staccato hallway conferences with Kenny and Pierre, that Bobby ran out of actions to take, things he could actually *do*.

Jackie was still asleep in her room a few doors down the hall. Dave Powers sat in a chair near the president's bed, nodding off at times but refusing to lie down in one of the nearby rooms with beds set up for members of the president's entourage. Kenny O'Donnell was in and out as well, but he had a great deal to do communicating with DC regarding the conditions developing at Parkland and the confused immobility of a leaderless government. Nurses and doctors came and went regularly to check vital signs, read the charts, and have quiet conversations among themselves. Bobby, Kenny, and Dave were aware from the doctors' tone that there was nothing new to report.

Bobby spent more and more of his time beside Jack as the night progressed and available avenues of activity diminished. Jack was barely hanging on. His respiration was labored and he had not moved.

Sinking into a chair by the east window in Jack's room, Bobby had time to ponder the tragic events swirling around him. He could hardly believe how much had changed since he was sitting by his pool at Hickory Hill with Morganthau and Mollo earlier the previous day, talking of departmental business in the warm fall sun of a Washington afternoon. The entire fabric of the world was rent, not just for him personally, but for an entire country. It was nearly impossible to mentally encompass the worldwide repercussions of the possible death of his brother, an American president.

Robert had been threatened early and often due to his zeal in exposing and eliminating the power and reach of the Mafia. He had assumed he himself would be the target for killing, if anyone was. So it was with deeply self-critical feelings that he watched his brother lying in the bed across the room, unconscious and slipping away. He should be there, not Jack.

There was intense speculation in the media about who was responsible. The information filtering through official channels about the shooting indicated a consensus emerging that a man named Oswald had planned it alone. He acted alone, fired alone and was caught alone. There seemed to be no one else involved. Dallas Police Chief Curry stated in unequivocal terms that Oswald was the only shooter and had no accomplices. It seemed an incongruous comment to Bobby. How could they possibly know so soon? FBI director J. Edgar Hoover was being paraphrased over radio and television saying that Oswald was the only shooter, although he had not come out and directly said so himself.

But Bobby was not so sure. He had been talking to the doctors and others in the motorcade. And even though he had not said as much to any of them, he was wondering if further accomplices would be found. He had not intended at this point to even try to decipher the motives or means of the would-be assassin or assassins. Yet, in his frequent discussions with both Dr. Marshall and the experts from Bethesda, he was beginning to doubt what was emerging as the accepted public version—a version that had been released without even consulting the president's physicians. How could Hoover know that it was a lone gunman if he did not have firsthand knowledge of the actual wounds? And since there had been no FBI inter- rogation of either Dr. Marshall or the physicians who had flown in from DC with Bobby, how could the director of the FBI have come to this conclusion? Maybe it was being said to allay fears that there was a foreign component to it. Maybe there was more going on than Bobby was aware of. He had been fully occupied caring for his brother and would hear most information in passing from conversations with Kenny or Pierre. All else was just swirling about outside his periphery.

Earlier in the evening, he had found himself alone with Dave Powers watching over the president. They sat quietly for a while, both slowly sink- ing into the realization that their world had been shattered.

"You know he was warned away from Dallas," said Dave eventually. "I was there when Fulbright told him not to go. He would have come any- way, I think, even if he hadda believed the senator."

"Yeah," said Bobby, "probably so." Bobby could faintly hear his broth- er's breathing through the hooded plastic tent over his bed. "Did you know he'd gotten more than seven hundred death threats just this year?"

"Yeah," said Dave, "we talked about that once. I didn't know the num- ber, but while we were swimming in the pool at the White House, he men- tioned it. Said the Secret Service had a few mailbags full of 'em, all saying the same thing in one way or another—that he was as good as dead. I think for a moment I saw him worried about it. But then he just shrugged it off and never mentioned it again." They sat for a while. "I watched it all," continued Dave, seeming to replay it in his thoughts. "It was like the world slowed to a stop between when those shots came down and when anyone moved. I saw it from the car right behind his, but was as stuck in my seat as any of 'em. Just couldn't make sense of it."

"You think it was the guy up in the book warehouse?" asked Bobby. "I mean, just him?"

"No. No. I heard it from the front. Think I saw some smoke up near the trees," said Dave.

"They're saying the guy in the warehouse was the only one," said Bobby neutrally.

"I'd watch *them* real close on this, Bobby. I'd watch them *real* close."

Kenny's response earlier that evening had been even more direct. While he was standing in the corridor outside the communications room, word had come over the line that Police Chief Curry had declared over the radio Oswald was a lone gunman. Kenny had been talking to Bobby about conditions back in DC when Salinger came out and quoted Curry to them.

"Horseshit!" said Kenny emphatically. "How the fuck would Curry know that? That little Oswald prick in two places at once? He ain't Jesus Christ."

Bobby looked at him, wanting more.

"Look, there were shots from the front," continued Kenny. "You can bet your ass on that, Bobby. I saw 'em. So did a dozen others. Christ, even the cops went up the bank to that fence line ahead of the limo to flush 'em out."

Bobby sat for a long time thinking about all that had occurred, trying to bring some order to his shock-numbed mind and the jumble of thoughts, feelings, and fears. So much had happened so quickly. It was his responsibility to remain strong and focused. But as the evening progressed into morning—those hours in the morning when it is so easy to wake from a fitful sleep and feel the mind sliding helplessly into cascading thoughts of worry and self-deprecation, those hours when it seems the darkness outside has taken hold of whatever feelings are bright and positive and tilted them toward incessant and repetitive worry, those dark hours when the human personality seems so pathetically small in the face of the frightening cruelty of an impersonal world—Bobby descended slowly into realms that he had not allowed himself time for in the busyness of caring for his brother, his almost lost brother, dying only a few feet from where he was sitting.

He feared there was something terrible awaiting him. Something that he needed to accept. He knew what it was. He might lose his brother, that was a real possibility. A brother whom he trusted and believed in with all his heart and soul. A brother to whom he had given his life, subsuming his own desires and wishes, to serve him and what he represented to the best of his ability. He loved his brother and was not reluctant to state to anyone that he thought Jack was the greatest person he knew. The crucible in which he had grown his life was defined by service to his family and, most paramount, to his brother.

And yet, there is a flip side to such unconditional surrender to the service of another. And that harsh reality presented itself now. Bobby had lived a life deferred. And it was this that lay waiting at the base of his distress. He had given so much of himself in service to his brother's dreams that, if his brother were to die, he would lose not only Jack, but also, in large measure, himself. In giving himself over to the service of an ideal, an ideal realized through another, he had given himself away. No one would think of Robert Kennedy as a man out of touch with or removed from himself, but in a way, that was what he was discovering as he sat by the window of a third floor room of an impersonal American hospital with its bland wall coverings, antiseptic overlay of musty odors, old furniture, and traffic-worn interior. He prayed fervently for Jack's recovery, not simply for the tender love he held in his heart for the man, but also because he simply did not know how to deal with what little would remain if Jack were to die.

* * *

The sky was a brilliant furnace of light. The sun shone so harshly that she could hardly open her eyes to view the ecstatic crowds that had gathered along the motorway. She wanted to hold her hands in front of her face and peek through her fingers to see their faces, but knew she shouldn't. The light coruscating off the mirrored walls of the multi-storied buildings lining the street augmented the already blinding illumination of the day. It seemed to envelop her in a drenching, penetrating, nearly painful brilliance no matter which way she turned. She felt exhilarated and yet somewhat frightened at the same time. How was she to look at all the people screaming out Jack's and her names, to share in their happiness, if she couldn't see them? They were so joyous, and yet she could not fully partake in their emotions. She needed to look at them. They were nearly invisible in the white hot radiance, yet she could feel their pressing, their needing. A needing for Jack? Or a needing for her? She didn't know. She had a pair of sunglasses in her lap, but Jack had twice already asked her to take them off. "They want to see your eyes," he had said. "You can't be separating yourself from them." So she had complied each time. But now it was just too much. She was unable to distinguish even those near the car as its large bulk sliced delicately through throngs of well-wishers. She was unsure if Jack was looking her way, but she just had to see what was going on around her, even though a foreboding mingled with her eagerness. She raised the sunglasses to her eyes for a quick peek.

As she flipped the glasses up to her face, the dazzling brilliance was replaced by a darkness so extreme that she was again blinded, but this time due to a dearth of illumination rather than excess. The crowds were stilled, making not a sound. The car's movement had slowed. There was an ominous cast to what light was beginning to flicker through her adjusting eyes. Just ahead of the limo in which they were riding was a line of tightly marching Marines, their numbers extending entirely across the broad avenue, morbidly splendid in their dress attire, stretching out as far as she could see down the thoroughfare, marching as if to a funeral cadence. She could see the white mist condensing from their breath as they stepped in unison to an unnatural military gait. A single drumbeat echoed. Where were all the people she was hoping to see? There they were. There were so, so many of them. They were packed along the sidewalks and completely filled the side streets. Their numbers extended as far as she could see, wrapped in their heavy black coats with their dark, somber stares. She grew frightened. She could feel their emotion, their sadness, the well of loss whose depth she feared to fathom. Her attention shifted to her right as she noticed the hulking mane of a beautiful black stallion, saddled and anointed, its mane flowing with a stately grace. But it had no rider. The polished leather saddle was empty. The majestic steed was walking, almost prancing alongside the car right beside Jack, who quickly flung his hands to his throat in an awkward manner. "Was his tie too tight?" she was thinking as his head erupted in a burst of blood and matter splattered her face and glasses, preventing her again from seeing anything, concussing against the side of her body and drenching her hair and clothing in a slimy red mist. She screamed and cried at the horror of the sight and the assault on her body, and reaching out she could feel nothing but the cloth of Jack's suit as he fell toward her—bloodied, destroyed, dead. She knew he was gone and she could not stop the sobs that welled up in her throat as she clutched at the blood-saturated cloth of Jack's suit coat. No! No! No!....

Jackie woke, crushing in her hands the clean white sheets at the corner of the bed. They were wet with tears, her tears, as she clutched and cried with a manic need to hold on to them. She had had a dream. There was a horse, a bloodied horse? What was it that had terrified her so? The fear and the pain that had enveloped her body and mind with a terrifying power were slowly receding, but a deep, overwhelming sadness persisted, as if the world had shifted and all that remained was sorrow. She was confused about where she was. She had traveled so much over the years and was used to waking in unfamiliar surroundings: a hotel room in an American or foreign city, the White House, Hyannisport, their house in Georgetown or at Glen Orr. But this seemed different somehow. She began to feel relieved that her night terrors were just that, a nightmare receding into the reaches of unconsciousness where she would gladly not follow. But no sooner were the departing shudders of a perilous dream appreciated than the reality of her location bloomed in her mind. There had been a shooting. She was in a hospital. Jack!?

* * *

Early Saturday morning, a nurse partially opened the door of the president's room and leaned in. "Sir, Mrs. Kennedy is waking up," she whispered softly to Bobby, who was sitting silently in a chair near the window.

"Thank you," said Bobby, aroused from his thoughts. The nurse wondered if he had been awake all night. Bobby had talked to Dr. Janets a few times during the course of the evening about Jackie's condition and received always the same reassuring reply, "She's sleeping normally and seems to be fine."

Bobby left the room and walked down the hall. When he entered Jackie's room, she was already sitting up in bed, her gown loosely wrapped around her, impatiently allowing herself to be examined by Dr. Janets. Mary Gallagher had been with her all night and had gone to fetch the doctor when she noticed Jackie's turbulent waking. The first lady was looking more disheveled than he had ever seen her. The large white bandage on her neck was more visible from this angle. It had a slightly yellowed stain at the center. Dr. Janets was asking her to track a small penlight with her eyes, but when Bobby walked in she turned her head and looked at him instead. She saw a young man stooped and saddened, with tousled hair and a dirty, wrinkled white shirt, sleeves rolled above the elbows. Tired, red-rimmed eyes indicated he was both physically exhausted and mentally spent. Robert and Jackie had always been close. She felt he was her protector as well as his brother's, and their trust and feelings for each other were very dear.

"Jack?" she asked tentatively.

Bobby could see the fear and intensity in her eyes. He exchanged a glance with the doctor.

"She appears okay, but not too much exertion please. She does need to rest," Janets said, knowing it was a fruitless and probably foolish thing to say. The young doctor had become uncomfortably aware that he was dealing with the first lady in the flesh and that his position of importance had ended. She had been unconscious when he had treated her injuries in the emergency room, and it wasn't until just this morning that his nervous demeanor reflected his newly understood position.

Bobby came over and sat on the bed next to her as the doctor and Mary Gallagher left them for a while, closing the door behind them.

"Jack is alive. He's in bad shape though," said Bobby. Jackie closed her eyes and seemed to breathe with deliberate effort. "He was in surgery for about four hours after he was brought in. He has a bullet wound to the chest and had a portion of his right lung removed. He's not conscious and hasn't been since they brought him in." Bobby wanted to give it to her straight. He was well aware Jackie was not the "delicate debutante" presented by the press. He, as well as anyone who had dealt with the first lady over the years, knew her refined girlish personality misdirected attention from her strong and perceptive nature.

"What are the doctors saying?" she asked, eyes still closed. For some reason she had thought Jack was dead, that all hope was gone. She had woken only moments before with an overwhelming sense of loss and despair.

"They just don't know. Under normal conditions this thing would be survivable, but very tough. With Jack's history, there are too many unknowns. The operation went well. It's a question of whether he can turn the corner. And for now they don't know how he'll respond." As Bobby spoke the words to her, a close and loved friend, he felt his defenses slip. He had shown no weakness over the last twenty hours, but in reciting just this small amount of information to Jackie, his voice caught a number of times, and he looked away as he finished. "The specialists who came down from DC are trying to be upbeat, but I know the surgeon thinks his chances are damn slim."

Intensely shy yet powerfully driven, Bobby had a personality that some people thought cavalier, but those who were close saw a different person altogether. Even though he had been fully in charge of numerous campaigns for Jack, for senator and then president, when he met with groups he had difficulty making eye contact. He was somewhat hyperactive in his serenity. With his toe tapping, or a pencil flicking in his hand, he would maintain a composed countenance during meetings or interviews, and then erupt with blunt and direct instructions and observations. Two parts of him seemed to be at war. He was deeply gentle at the core, yet cloaked in a sheath of muscular will. It was as if his own power was somewhat foreign to him, and he was not yet balanced and integrated in its expression. It took quite a while for people to get close, but when they were accepted and trusted within the boundaries of his self-protection, he would support and encourage them with all the might of his relentless drive.

Jackie was well within his protective perimeter and had been since early on in their relationship. She was an outsider in the Kennedy clan, not prone to athletic exuberance nor the thrill of political competition. She wasn't martial in her expression and rarely shared in the sporting free-for-alls that were a mainstay of the Kennedy gatherings. Competition was not her deity, as she valued a more refined manner of expression that set her a bit apart from the family and their roughhousing. Her plight resonated with Bobby, as he was outwardly the enforcer yet inwardly a sensitive soul who could see from both sides of his competitive upbringing.

She put her hand on his. "I need to see him," she stated, and started to gather her robe about her slowly.

Bobby breathed deeply and squeezed her hand. "Okay. He's just a few doors down the hall. The hospital's been partially emptied and we have the whole floor. How do you feel?" he asked.

"I'm a bit woozy, and my head aches, but I'll be okay. I just need to be in there."

"Let me get the nurse back in to get you some clothes, then we can walk over there together."

When Jackie went in to see Jack, she said little, but instead walked to his bed, sat on its side so as not to disturb him, picked up his hand and held it as he lay unresponsive. She stayed there for a long time, stroking his uninjured arm, rearranging slight ruffles in sheets whose landscape had been rearranged countless times before by the head nurse and others. She talked to him quietly, patiently, encouragingly, as a wife to a husband, as lovers do, willing her healing intentions toward him, her caring, her love.

* * *

Bobby retreated quietly out of the room while Jackie ministered to her husband. As he closed the door, he was greeted by Kenny O'Donnell, who had come striding down the hall.

"There's a call for you from Johnson," said Kenny. "He asked that you take it on a secure line."

"Right," said Bobby. "I'll be downstairs for a while making some other calls, too. Jackie's in with Jack. You might give them some time."

"Okay," nodded Kenny.

Bobby walked down the hall toward the exit stairway, which was the conduit being used for travel between the third floor, where Jackie and the president were quartered, and the second floor, filled with communications and security offices. Jiggs, Bobby's new Secret Service agent, had unobtrusively stationed himself at the juncture near the stairwell door to be able to keep an eye on Bobby without intruding. Bobby had been aware of Jiggs' watchful presence and was grateful for his skill at remaining in the background while still monitoring Bobby's movements. Up until now, since their introduction on the ride from Love Field, the sum total of their communications had consisted of nodding acknowledgments with hardly a word of conversation between the two.

Jiggs opened the door and followed Bobby down the stairwell to the second floor, and stayed outside while Bobby entered one of the rooms used for private calls. It was the secure room, with a scrambled phone directly to the White House switchboard. Jiggs had made this same trip numerous times the previous evening due to all the calls Bobby had made, but few of those were in the secure room. Closing the door, Bobby walked into what had been a patient's room, now nearly stripped of furniture. He sat down and took the receiver off one of the three phones sitting on the room's lone desk.

"The attorney general for the vice president," he announced.

"Yes, sir, Mr. Kennedy, he's waiting for your call," the operator responded immediately.

There were a few clicks on the line as he waited. He looked around the small room. There was a desk with a few wooden chairs in the nearly empty space. Heavily painted, dun-colored concrete block walls gave the place a drab, despairing quality. A faded print of a floral scene hung on the wall opposite the window facing the courtyard. The blinds were partially closed, keeping out some of the effects of the Texas morning sun.

Bobby's rapport with Lyndon Johnson had never been good. They tolerated each other. They had started off on a poor footing right from the beginning. In 1960, the day after Jack's nomination at the Democratic National Convention, the horse-trading melee of choosing a vice president to run with Kennedy was just getting underway. Jack had offered the position to Johnson. Everyone in the president's inner circle thought it was a face-saving gesture for the senate leader and would be turned down. But to everyone's surprise, except possibly Jack's, Johnson accepted. The liberal and labor wings were aghast that JFK would even think of endorsing the conservative Johnson. But it was a clever and pragmatic solution to a number of vexing problems with the election. For one, it brought Johnson, a Southern conservative, into the fold with all his votes and supporters, helping to ensure a large Southern voting block shifting to Kennedy. It also removed Johnson from his powerful Senate leadership position, allowing Senator Mike Mansfield, a close ally, to move up and take his place. JFK was going to need a supportive Senate leader after election to get his progressive ideas through Congress, and he had concluded early on that Johnson was not right for the post. When asked about the unusual move and the possibility that Johnson could transition up into the presidency under adverse conditions, Kennedy responded, "I'm a young man. I don't plan to die in office."

But there was an indelicate moment of both indecision and poor communication when it was thought Jack was backing away from accepting Johnson as his second in command. Bobby had gone to meet Johnson in his hotel room and told him it was not appropriate for him to be on the ticket with his brother Jack, that it would be best if Johnson declined the offer. Insulted and shocked at being courted and then rejected, Lyndon had immediately called Jack, and in an emotional exchange, expressed his unequivocal desire to be vice president with Kennedy. After apologies for all the confused miscommunication, JFK accepted Johnson. But Johnson nursed an undercurrent of bitterness toward "that little prick Bobby" that was never really dislodged.

By his nature, Johnson always felt a world apart from the Kennedys' patrician ways, due to his rural Texas upbringing. There probably never would have been an easy relationship between the two. The passionately progressive activities pursued by Robert Kennedy grated against Johnson's conservative "good old boy" worldview. In the current administration, the pragmatic mediation of the president kept the two at bay. But Johnson felt it was Bobby, not Jack, who had tried to dislodge him from the vice presidency, and that cemented a lasting enmity between the two, covered by a tense geniality when in each other's presence.

The phone line clicked again and the vice president's voice was in Bobby's ear.

"Bobby? How you doin' down there?" inquired Lyndon Johnson soothingly in his heavy Texan drawl. It was a speech inflection that Bobby was becoming accustomed to in dealing with the staff at the Dallas hospital during the last twenty-four hours.

"Lyndon, I'm fine," replied Bobby slowly. "I'm sure they're keeping you up to speed on Jack's condition. Nothing's really changed, we're all just waiting."

"I wanted to first of all say how sorry I am for all that happened down there yesterday," Lyndon said sincerely. "I'm totally shocked and saddened for your brother. Lady Bird and I want to tell you that we're sayin' prayers for John and that we're devastated by the events of the past twenty-four hours. If there is anything we can do, you just name it, as we want to help in any way we can. How are you holdin' up, partner?"

"Thank you, Lyndon. Well, I've found there's little to do here at this point. The doctors did a good job, but Jack's pretty well shot up." Bobby had no intention of sharing his feelings with the vice president.

"How is Jackie? God, that was awful, that that lovely lady should get caught up in all this!"

"She seems to be okay. Just a flesh wound to her neck, but she was sedated all night. She's up and around. She's in with the president right now." Bobby changed tack. "What's it like back there in DC?"

"As you know, we're in a jimmy back here. You know how it is, there's a thousand people asking questions and we have no one making any decisions. Now, I don't want to move into any territory that would be imprudent for me to transgress, but there's a logjam here without anyone taking charge, and...well, it could get dicey." Johnson had shifted into a more serious and less affected tone.

"I realize the problem. I've been talking with Nick Katzenbach about it," said Bobby, referring to the assistant attorney general, "and it seems to be a pretty gray area." There were serious issues regarding the dynamics of who should be making decisions. Johnson was the vice president, but without the death of the president, he had no real authority to act and needed to be very circumspect and not appear to be interfering or grabbing for power—a situation that Johnson, an astute student of politics and history, knew could come back to haunt him if the president were to recover. "There is no clear transfer of power while Jack is unconscious," Bobby did not want to say *until my brother dies.*

"Yes...yes...that's my position entirely. I—"

"Lyndon, I'll be here with my brother until he recovers. I'll retain my position as the attorney general, but I've given Nick authority over existing department issues, so my distraction won't affect operations. But regarding policy decisions, it's a questionable area we're in right now."

"I hear you, Bobby. I do. But there are some issues that have been brought to my attention by Mr. Hoover that I think require us to come together and make a decision. And by us I mean as few as absolutely necessary. Have you talked with J. Edgar today?" Pleasantries over, the soothing tone had departed from Lyndon's voice.

"No, I spoke with him before coming to Dallas, but not since." Bobby remembered the curt pair of calls from Hoover callously informing him of the shooting as he stood by the pool at Hickory Hill, only twenty-four hours ago.

"Well, he has done some damn fine detective work over at the Bureau and has come to a few serious discoveries. Now, you know they got that fella Oswald, right?"

"Yes, Lyndon. I'm up to speed on all that. I have a couple of Justice Department lawyers at the Dallas Police station keeping tabs on that mess."

"You do? Ah well, that's...that's good, that's good. Now you must know they found the gun that was used up on the sixth floor of that book storage building."

"Yes, I've heard that."

"Hoover has told me some other facts as well. It seems Oswald had bought a gun through Chicago by mail order for about twenty dollars and had it sent to himself under an alias. Hoover has all the information about this as well as fingerprints on the rifle and copies of the receipts for the gun. He thinks the case against this Oswald is convincing but not very... very strong legally. Now here is the—"

"Lyndon, I've watched a little of the events at the Dallas Police Station on the television here," interrupted Bobby. "I also have some men there observing, and must say, the handling of the whole affair by these local police is terrible. Oswald is being dragged through the halls of a station packed with reporters and who knows what, like a trophy. It's entirely unprofessional. There's no legal protocol being followed. He was shown at one point asking for a lawyer, but I don't believe he has had one appointed, even though he's being questioned. Now, if this is the guy that shot my brother, I frankly don't give a goddamn about how he's treated. But from a legal point of view, he has grounds to have all the interrogation information deleted from evidence. It's amateur hour over there, and the whole world is watching."

"I hear you on that, Bobby. Oswald claimed police brutality right off. The problem is the Dallas Police have a reputation of being...well, a little overzealous, if you know what I mean. Some prisoners have ended up in the hospital after being questioned, and they didn't want that to come down on 'em, so they went overboard the other way and are trying to look fair and open. You know, parading him around to show he's still breathin' and all."

"Lyndon, that'll come back to haunt them, to haunt us all. They need to get Oswald out of there so this is all handled legally."

"Well, I think that is the plan, as they were going to do that real soon, kinda keepin' the timing secret. I was told by Hoover they plan to get him over to the county jail. But Bobby, here's the thing we need to talk about, the reason I called...." He could hear Johnson taking a steadying breath. "It would appear there is a very bad twist to this whole affair that has come to light from some diggin' Hoover did in FBI field files when they learned the name Oswald. It seems this Oswald fella took a trip to Mexico City about two months ago, in September and, I think, October..."

"This year?" asked Bobby.

"Yes, absolutely, this year."

"How do they know that?"

"Well, I'll tell ya, while he was there, the CIA, you know they're keepin' tabs on the embassies down there. Anyway, they got a tape from a couple of phone conversations and some pictures of this Oswald guy, damn him, comin' out of the Cuban Embassy. But they also got tapes from the phone calls he made. It seems the CIA has a super-secret program in Mexico stakin' out all the foreign embassies, tappin' their phones, buggin' their rooms, and who knows what else. I'd never heard about it, I tell you, but they can tell who's takin' a piss and how much of it's hittin' the bowl. Anyway, this fella Oswald was at the Cuban Embassy talkin' over the phone to a man at the Soviet Embassy. They were chit-chattin' about visas and passports and all 'cause Oswald, he wanted to go to Russia but stop off in

Cuba on the way. But see, here's the kicker. This guy Oswald was talkin' to was a Russkie named Kostikov. And Hoover says they know for a fact that even though this Kostikov fella is just listed as an attaché, he's really head of their security forces for the entire western hemisphere. Now, these security forces use assassination as one of their main tools of operation and—"

"Wait, you're sure this was Oswald?" said Bobby, with a jolt of panic in his voice. He rubbed his forehead with his free hand as he began to understand the implications of all this.

"Yep, yep, they got voice tapes and a picture of him comin' and goin'."

"The CIA and FBI knew about this two months ago? Why didn't they pick up on this?"

"Well now, Bobby, that's a good question, and I don't know the answer, but what I'm gettin' at is this. Why would Oswald be talkin' to the head of the assassination squad for the Russkies? And if Kostikov is the head of the assassination team, as Hoover firmly believes, why would he agree to talk to a guy about a visa? It means this might not be just some stupid crackpot sittin' in a window down there in Dallas with a rifle. There could be a whole other dimension to this, way bigger than what we had thought at first. You know how emotional everyone is. The American people, well, they really love your brother. The public is in kind of a state of shock right now. I mean, aren't we all? But if they come out of it to the news that the Soviets and the Cubans planned your brother's shooting, then all bets are off. Now I think we've got to be takin' this out of the arena where they're testifying that Khrushchev and Castro did this and did that, ignitin' public bedlam and kickin' us into a war that can kill forty million Americans in an hour."

"Do you have anything else to go on? Are you sure of this information from Hoover?" Bobby distrusted Hoover, and even though he was technically Bobby's subordinate, it did not really play out that way in the actual workings of DC politics. Asking Lyndon for an assessment of Hoover was a nonstarter. Lyndon and J. Edgar had been bosom buddies for many years, and some of their back channel dealings were of a questionable nature.

"Well, I trust the man to do an excellent job in this area. You know as well as I do, he's a bulldog getting the goods on those Commies," said Lyndon in support of his friend. "You know if this gets out, it'll cause an uproar. It'd be the last thing John would want, you know, a war started because he was shot. A war that he's spent his whole damn time in office avoiding. I'm sure, Bobby, that you know what this could mean."

"Damn it, Lyndon, are you sure about this?" Bobby didn't know what to believe. If true, and if this information became public, there could be a disastrous national emotional response. Bobby was beginning to understand the consequences of releasing this information.

"I am, Bobby. I am. And that's why I'm callin'. We have got to come up with somethin' to head this off at the pass. There're already some of the DC papers callin' for a congressional investigation—you know, the *Post*, and others. If this goes to Congress it'll get out of hand. You know as well as I do that we got some real hotheads over there. Now, I asked Mr. Hoover when I spoke to him to try to use his influence at the *Post* to quiet this down for now. But it's gettin' so we have to do something to control this or it'll explode all around us."

"What do you have in mind?" asked Bobby, still not sure of the track this was taking.

"Well, we need to contain this thing. There's no tellin' what—"

"Did the Soviets know they had a compromised phone system? They must suspect that sort of thing these days." Bobby was still trying to get his head around this new information.

"That I don't know, but Hoover said it was one of the CIA's closest held secrets."

"If they did know, why the hell would they be letting this Kostikov guy and Oswald even talk over their phones?" pondered Bobby, thinking out loud.

"Well, I don't know about all that double thinkin', double agents and all, but I do know this needs to be knocked down. I was suggestin' to J. Edgar that we set up a commission to investigate this shooting. Now I think you know this is a state affair and not a federal crime, the shooting of a president. I know it's a weird omission in the federal legalities, but that's the way it is. Because of that, it should be handled in Texas by Texas authorities. I could get the attorney general down there, Waggoner Carr, to convene a special state commission, but use the FBI resources to handle the investigatin' side of the inquiry. That way it would carry some weight."

"Yes, I know there's no law making it a federal crime to shoot a president. I've been talking to Nick about it. I have one question. If Oswald was in Mexico City talking with someone who was known to be the head of the assassination team for the Soviets, and the CIA and FBI were aware of this two months before he shot the president, why was he not investigated and followed?" Bobby was still trying to figure the angles.

"Well, Bobby, I just don't have an answer for that." Lyndon seemed to be getting a little exasperated at the line of questioning Bobby was following.

"Lyndon, what you're asking is that I help herd this investigation into a state court and tie it up with an FBI investigation to try and quell any indication that there was a wider involvement beyond the role of this Oswald guy." Bobby's voice was rising. "You're suggesting that I agree to pin this on Oswald to avoid it going any further, all based on this information from Hoover. You realize, I am sure, that this is my brother we're talking about!" said Bobby angrily. "But more important, this is the president of the goddamn United States! You want to try to fix this investigation? Is that what you're saying?" Bobby was both appalled at the presentation of such an idea and simultaneously aware that, if this information was true, the exposure of a communist plot to kill the U.S. president would almost surely precipitate a military response. And without Jack there to moderate the hard-nosed military, there was no way they could be reigned in during a situation like this.

"I hear ya, Bobby, and I know this is a bitch. But what can we do?" Lyndon was also getting hot. "If the press gets hold of this, or it goes to a wide-open congressional investigation—because Bobby, that's the alternative—then this will explode! You know how high emotions are running right now. We can't contain it if we let it get away from us at the start. We have to decide now, or I tell ya this could blow up in our faces. I mean, we are talkin' a possible escalation to war, and if it went nuclear, there could be millions dead. I talked to McNamara. The Russkies and Cubans are on high alert. They are sittin' on the trigger, and if we don't calm this down we could all be dead in a week!" Johnson was scared. Bobby could hear it in his breathing and the way he clipped his words.

The line was quiet for a moment as both Bobby and Lyndon digested what had just been said. "I need to talk with Hoover about this," said Bobby. "I need more information. I can't make a decision with just this. I'll call back after we talk."

"Okay, but we gotta move on this, Bobby." There was an extended moment of silence and then a click as the connection was severed. Bobby slowly placed the black receiver in its cradle as he stared at the wall, trying to take in what was being asked of him—to agree to cover up the attempt-

162 *The Memoirs of John F. Kennedy*

ed assassination of the president of the United States, his own brother.

Bobby picked up the phone to put a call through to Hoover, but instead replaced the handset, got up from the desk and started to pace about the room, then went out and walked up and down the hall. He passed Jiggs, who just looked over at him as he left but remained stationary at the door. Bobby needed to think. How would it benefit Castro to kill an American president? Castro was belligerent, but not suicidal. He knew that if this information got out, and it would, the United States would invade Cuba and use all its resources to violently depose him. The military chiefs would not be stopped on this one. President Kennedy had spent thirteen long days in October of last year trying to defuse a military escalation with nuclear-fortified Cuba, and just barely beat back the machinations of the Joint Chiefs of Staff, who were arguing for launching a full-scale invasion. What would prompt the Cuban leader to move ahead with such a self-destructive scheme?

Even though it was a hushed-up secret, the FBI and the CIA knew Jack had been using a backchannel intermediary to respond to Castro's preliminary overtures of peace with the United States. As far as Bobby knew, these avenues were still active. And what about Hoover's sources? Bobby had never trusted the prickly head of the Bureau, and in the murky dealings of the clandestine services, Bobby was never really sure what distorted version of the truth he was getting. And why hadn't the FBI followed up on Oswald if his contacts with a Soviet assassin had been registered months ago? Why was Oswald just walking around loose this whole time?

Bobby went back in and called Hoover at the Justice Department, ironically at an office that was just a few doors down the hall from his own when he was in Washington.

"Director's office." It was Helen Gandy, Hoover's longtime personal secretary.

"Put me through to the Director, Helen," said Bobby. This was a call he often made. When in his normal location at his office in the Justice Department, he would call Hoover on a direct line, bypassing Hoover's prissy, protective secretary, a line that he had demanded be installed. But calling from Dallas, he needed to rout through her.

"I'll see if he's in, Mr. Kennedy," responded Helen impersonally, as if she wouldn't know, what with him being in the next room. There was a short pause while Bobby was on hold.

"Hoover," came the staccato bark into the phone. There were no pleas-antries exchanged between these two men. They had worked together, or more accurately, against each other, for years now, and there was little need to disguise their mutual contempt.

"The vice president informed me that you have information regarding Mr. Oswald from months ago in Mexico City. He mentioned you were going to talk to the *Washington Post* and try to clamp this down for now," stated Bobby.

"Well, he did mention that to me."

"And did you take any action?"

"I don't have any influence with the *Post* because, frankly, I don't read it. I view it like the *Daily Worker,*" he said pugnaciously. Hoover had a rapid-fire monotone manner of speaking that reduced most sentences to inflectionless representations of data.

"Right. A communist rag, the *Washington Post*?" The *Daily Worker* was the Communist Party newspaper in the United States. Bobby always found Hoover's bigoted, single-minded obsession with communism in-credible.

"That's absolutely correct, Mr. Attorney General."

"Let me ask you, Mr. Hoover. I've heard that this man Oswald was a Marine and then a defector to the Soviet Union, and that he then re-turned to the United States only a year or so later."

"How did you hear about that?" responded Hoover suspiciously.

"I have two of my assistants at the Dallas Police Department, and they've kept me informed of what's going on there."

"I see. Well—"

"Is it not the FBI's practice to keep all defectors on a watch list that's flagged whenever there's an activity somewhere that brings their names or actions to the Bureau's attention? I believe that is standard procedure. Was the FBI aware of this recent taped conversation, or group of conversa-tions? There was more than one, wasn't there?"

"Yes, there were actually several of them on different dates during September and October. They occurred in Mexico City, and the tapes re-mained at the CIA station there. The CIA cabled the FBI notification of these contacts," stated Hoover.

"Then with all this advance notice, and the flag on Mr. Oswald's file, why did this man escape the attention of the FBI?"

"Well, Mr. Kennedy, yes, there is, in most cases, a FLASH on these accounts that transfers this information to a Security Index, but for some reason this FLASH was removed. There seems to have been a mistake made, and I can assure you we're taking action against the dereliction of procedure by a number of agents involved with missing the Oswald connection. I can assure you they will be punished for—"

"That is not what I am asking. What I would like to know is how this man did not raise the attention of the FBI. There was a flag on his file, correct?" Bobby was pressing.

"Yes, there was, for a number of years."

"You say it as if his status changed. Is he not still flagged?"

"That's a matter we are looking at rather closely."

"Meaning what, exactly?" Extracting information from his supposed subordinate was always a chore and most times only partially successful. Hoover had been piqued, right from the beginning of Bobby's tenure, at having to relay information through the attorney general rather than going directly to the president, as was his wont in previous administrations. He was curt and intransigent as a rule, and that was on good days. But regarding this issue, Bobby would press as far as needed.

"Mr. Oswald's file flag was removed," said Hoover with a note of defiance in his voice.

"By whom?" demanded Bobby, losing patience.

"The special agent in charge of foreign espionage, Gavin Needham. Believe me, his punishment has already been addressed, and—"

"Why did he remove it?" interrupted Bobby.

"We're not yet sure about that," said Hoover. He was getting peeved at being treated like an underling, especially by the younger Bobby Kennedy. "He's being interviewed and I'm waiting for a report on exactly what happened."

"When was it removed?"

"Uh, well...that's the difficulty—"

"Mr. Hoover!" demanded the attorney general into the phone. "When was the flag on Oswald's file removed?"

"The flag was removed on October 9, shortly before cable notification by the CIA of the first call recorded at the embassy in Mexico City. It was not reinstated since that time. Therefore none of the calls activated any alarms within the Bureau. The information was placed on file, but Mr. Oswald was not placed on the Security Index for follow-up."

"How *shortly* before being cabled was this FLASH removed?" demanded Bobby.

There was a silence on the other end. "Mr. Hoover! How recently was—?"

"A few hours," inserted Hoover sharply.

"A few *hours* before!" exploded Bobby loudly into the mouthpiece. "He'd been on the fucking watch list for what, three or four years, and was removed just hours before he surfaced at the Soviet Embassy in Mexico City, talking to a Soviet assassin!"

"That is correct."

Bobby could hardly find the words to express his outrage. "And even if the alarms were not activated, wouldn't it be in the best interest of the American government to ascertain why an American, *any* American, would be talking with and leaving messages for a goddamn Russian agent who is the head of fucking assassinations? What was the Bureau doing on this? I want more answers on this, Mr. Hoover, and I expect when I call again, you *will* have them!"

There was a short pause and the line clicked dead. Bobby was sure if he were able to listen to the Director's utterance at this moment, it would have been a big "Fuck you, Bobby Kennedy!"

Bobby then called Robert McNamara, Jack's hard-headed secretary of defense. He and Bobby had a good rapport and talked often and candidly. Bobby needed more input and was going to go wherever he could to get it. McNamara needed to be tracked down at the Pentagon, and took the line after a few minutes. Bobby used the time to calm down after the exchange with Hoover.

"McNamara here," came the crisp response over the phone.

"Mac, this is Bobby."

"Bobby," said McNamara kindly. "How is Jack?"

"Mac, it's not good. He's in bad shape, and the doctors can't predict this one," said Bobby quietly. He was aware of the affection and sincere connection between the secretary and his brother.

"Damn it, Bobby, I'm sorry!" said McNamara. Bobby filled him in on some of the details about the president's injuries and on Jackie's condition as well.

"Mac," said Bobby after a moment, "I need some answers here. There are a lot of rumors flying around about this being more than just Oswald, maybe a plot, maybe international influence. I need to know what you know over there at the Pentagon. I know I asked you already, but what do you make of the Russians, and for that matter the Cubans? I know they're on military alert, but is there anything more you can tell me?"

"Well, Bobby, we've been watching them real close and should be getting some Soviet film pretty soon. We sent up a bevy of U-2 flights timed to catch them as the sun came up. The film has to be flown all the way back here to be studied, but that's being done as we speak. As I mentioned earlier, the Soviets have ratcheted up their defensive positions and would appear, from other sources of information, to be on high alert. It seems to be all of a defensive posture, though."

"Do you think it was anticipated? I mean, does their activity appear to be a response to the shooting or are there indications of pre-activity? I guess what I'm asking is, can you tell if they knew ahead of time that this was coming?"

"The previous photos we had, which were only a day before the shooting, showed nothing out of the ordinary. We've looked them over closely, and if the Soviets knew ahead of time, that knowledge didn't precipitate any significant troop movements or missile launch preparation activities. They've upped their alert status, but there does not seem to be an overwhelming call to arms.

"Now, the rub here is the same problem we had during the Cuban missile crisis, namely who's in charge over there. Khrushchev may have most of the reins, but that doesn't mean he has them all. Leadership in Russia, as you know from experience, is enigmatic. There may be a group of KGB or military hard-liners who've set this up, and may be just standing back and watching it unfold, hoping as they did during the Cuban embargo stand-off, for an escalation to a military confrontation. If that's the case, our seeing no military buildup would not mean that they weren't behind this thing in Dallas. It might just mean the politicos and the general military command were not informed. A more likely scenario I would think, *if* they planned this thing.

"The Cubans, on the other hand, seem to be hyperactive in getting into defensive positions. We had U-2s over them early this morning and have already been looking at those shots. My guys get the impression they were caught completely off guard by all this and are scrambling to get into position. Now this could be a similar situation, with a small group of plotters hoping to draw the country into a confrontation. But with the Cubans, that would be an unlikely scenario. The leadership channels there are pretty well established.

"Now, I would assume that if either of them had a part in this, it would've been kept hushed. It would probably be held in a tight circle of people in each country, but especially Russia. They know we watch them and they respond accordingly, but I'm thinking they wouldn't have shown their hand so blatantly as to do a pre-buildup. It would make it too obvious. They're not stupid."

"But could they hide any preliminary preparations for a response to an event like this?" asked Bobby.

"I'm sure they couldn't hide the most egregious indicators, troop movements and the like, but there are certainly more subtle things that they could, at least for a while. The thing is that the more subtle indicators—soft information from people on the ground—are only gained from agents and observers, and that information is slower to come in." McNamara paused. "Now, I know this isn't as helpful as it could be, but we are working on the military side of things and, from a military perspective, there is no indication that the Soviets are following this up with any other actions. I personally get the feeling they're taking only half measures in order not to inflame the situation. As I said, they're not stupid."

"And how about the Cubans?" asked Bobby.

"Well, they're in a somewhat hopeless situation. They'd be idiots, in my opinion, to foment something like this and then think they could do anything at all to stop a U.S. invasion were the information to get out that they had a part, any part at all, in shooting the president of the United States."

"How about if they figured they could hush it up? I can't see how they would, as we found their secret missile installations just a year ago. Could they have not learned that lesson?" asked Bobby.

"Well, Bobby, the way information leaks across borders, I think by now they'd know that'd be a deadly game of craps," replied McNamara somberly.

"Yeah, that's my feeling too."

"We're looking at all of this, Bobby."

"I know you are. And thanks, Mac. Call me if you get anything more, will you?" said Bobby.

"I sure will. And Bobby? " added McNamara sincerely, "We are all pulling for Jack."

"Hoover."

Bobby had called the Director again and, after passing through the Mrs. Gandy gauntlet, was connected to the FBI Director.

"Mr. Hoover, what answers do you have regarding the Oswald file?" demanded Robert.

"The situation was caused by a reorganizational mistake," Hoover began bluntly, with hardly a moment between the asking of the question and the answer. He had obviously been working on the issue in the hour or more since the last call. "The Office of Espionage and Foreign Services was in the process of reviewing individuals who had defected to the Soviet Union and then returned. The list was prioritized with those at the top being individuals who had shown a propensity to be involved with communist-related activities. There was a cutoff point, determined by available manpower, regarding those who would be referred to the Security Index and those whose threshold of activity did not warrant further observation. Oswald did not make that cut. There had been no activity in regard to this individual for almost the entire time since he'd returned to the United States, approximately one and a half years ago. It was for this reason there was no Bureau reaction to his name surfacing in regard to the Mexico City activities. This is an unacceptable situation, and the agents in charge will be demoted with pay cuts. The flagging system has been re-evaluated in the light of the shooting of the president and the cutoff threshold has been removed."

Hoover had spoken, it seemed, without taking a single breath.

"How could this have happened just at this time? It would seem to be *most* coincidental," said Robert sarcastically.

"It is entirely coincidental. It was an agency foul-up. There is, I'm afraid, no excuse for this."

Did Hoover just acknowledge a mistake? Was that a moderate attempt at an apology? It caught Bobby off guard. "What about the fact that no one pursued the issue even though there wasn't a flag on Oswald?" asked Bobby. "I mean, if it had been Joe Smith talking to the head of the Soviet assassinations squad in Mexico City, would we not have followed up on Mr. Smith, flagged file or not?"

"That is true," said Hoover a bit more quietly. Was Bobby detecting a note of contrition, albeit ever so slight, in Hoover's tone? "There has been a bureaucratic foul-up here that's had the worst possible repercussions, and believe me, there will be punishments meted out. The information forwarded to the Bureau was sent to the espionage section. It was assumed by that section to have been dealt with by a special team from the previous flag on Oswald's file. There was still paperwork showing this to be the case. But since the cutoff point, as I previously mentioned, had been adjusted just hours before, the information was not transferred through to the proper agents. It stayed in holding, with each of the two groups thinking the other had taken the issue in hand. It was a very serious—the *most* serious possible—botch of protocol for which, as I mentioned, there will be significant career repercussion for all the agents involved. I realize this does not correct the issue of the president's shooting," said Hoover. "We have already corrected this deficiency, though," he added.

Bobby did not know what to say. Hoover's tone bordered on conciliatory. Was he admitting a mistake? He had worked with the man for three years now and had never had an occasion in which the Director had acknowledged a deficiency in the Bureau's actions, and most especially not in his own. This was surprising new territory and left Bobby wondering at the seriousness of the implications regarding Soviet and/or Cuban involvement. If it was enough to bring Hoover to a state of—not self-, but at least Bureau—reproach, then the implications were severe. Bobby needed a moment to readjust.

"Mr. Hoover, how certain are you of this contact between Oswald and the Soviet in the Mexico Embassy? And for that matter, the Bureau's certainty of the true nature and activities of this man Kostikov?" Bobby's tone had eased.

"I'm absolutely certain of both the repeated contact between Oswald and Kostikov, and Kostikov's true activities. We have been watching Mr. Kostikov for a number of years and are sure of his involvement with Department Thirteen. That's the name of the assassination group of which he's the leading member. His fingerprints are on a number of killings in South and Central America. We also have the tapes of Oswald initiating calls and speaking with him four times while Mr. Oswald was in Mexico City between September 27 and October 1. There is no doubt of this connection."

"What was the content of those tapes?" asked Bobby.

"They contain a number of stilted conversations about visas, travel dates, and permissions to enter Cuba via Mexico. They were with subordinates at the embassy as well as Mr. Kostikov himself. The exchange was odd and seemingly forced, as if it might have been in code. They spoke only of mundane matters," recited Hoover. "What we are still unaware of is the extent of co-conspirators, if there were any, and the extent of the involvement of other extra-nationals. We are concerned, as the vice president has probably stated to you, about information getting out that this was an international plot with members of the Soviet and Cuban governments taking a leading role, possibly for payback. This information could necessitate a military response, in my opinion, that would almost certainly lead to a nuclear confrontation, judging from the mood of the country right now."

"Payback?" asked Bobby.

"Excuse me?"

"You said 'payback,' Mr. Hoover."

"Well, I would assume that the Cubans were well aware of efforts to eliminate Castro from power," said Hoover.

So Hoover knew about Mongoose, thought Bobby.

"I would think the Cubans might have been trying to act first to avoid self-destruction," said Hoover.

Bobby was startled that Hoover had alluded to the clandestine program Bobby initiated years ago through the CIA to eliminate Castro. Operation Mongoose was an abject failure, muddled by foolish plans for disruption of the Cuban economy and the Cuban military, subversion of Castro's hold on power, and a general program to topple the Cuban ruler. After the Bay of Pigs, it had escalated over the years to become an obsession with Jack and Bobby, to change the head of state in the small southern island. After the Cuban missile crisis, it had been abandoned, at least as far as Bobby knew. But with the murky dealings of the CIA, it was hard to know what was and wasn't in operation. Bobby didn't want to go down that path with Hoover. It was a surprise that he knew about it, but then Hoover seemed to know more than God.

"And what would the FBI do to mitigate this information?" asked Bobby, returning to the issue at hand. Mitigate? So lawyerly. How about *shove the whole goddamn thing under the rug and conspire to lie about what happened to his brother*, he thought. He could hardly believe the words coming out of his mouth. How could he condone restricting the investigation in order to isolate Oswald as the attempted assassin? How could he not?

"We will lead this investigation to the conclusion Oswald operated independently," stated Hoover matter-of-factly. "That is not problematic.

Our greater concern at this point is expediency. This direction needs to be taken immediately, or there's no telling where a public investigation will lead."

Bobby could sense, throughout this entire conversation, a distinct shift in Hoover's attitude. He was apologetic, an almost unnatural condition for the director, and behind this Bobby thought he sensed fear. The thought of a looming nuclear exchange appeared to have sobered even the hardest of Washington's power brokers.

"And what about the real assassins? If the Soviets had a hand in the shooting of the president, what will we do to find them?" He had wanted to say to punish them, to kill them.

"We will have to take up that matter at a future time," said Hoover with a bit of hesitancy. He seemed surprised at Bobby's tack on this, or maybe had just not thought that far ahead. "We can certainly do so, but it needs to be done quietly and without public acknowledgement."

"Thank you, Mr. Director. I'll consult with the vice president immediately." There was a pause, and the line went dead.

Bobby stepped wearily out into the corridor. He felt an overwhelming desire to retreat, to lay down this load—to leave such a choice to someone else. But he knew he could not. He leaned back against the door he had just closed behind him and stood motionless, one arm folded across his chest and one hand cradling his forehead. Jiggs, who was standing on the opposite wall a few yards away, looked at him with concern. Even though he'd used a closed room with a secure phone, it was probable that Jiggs had heard some of the conversation. Maybe that was why he had moved a little down the hall, away from the door. This was a hospital after all, not built with the soundproofed construction that would usually be required for such communications.

Bobby knew he needed to make a decision, but he just couldn't bring himself to do so. He was being asked to approve, at least tacitly, a plan to prevent an investigation into his brother's shooting, to conceal the assumption that it was planned and executed by America's arch communist enemies, the Soviet Union in conjunction with Cuba. Revealing such a link would surely bring about a military confrontation, and Bobby was pragmatic enough to realize that this would play directly into the hands of the military hawks, who would escalate until there was no turning back. Jack had been so effective at reining them in during the Cuban missile crisis, relentlessly probing and deciphering the Soviet responses, keeping the military on a tight leash while he cautiously negotiated a way off the path to a mutually assured destruction. But without Jack to take the leadership role—in fact with no one clearly in the executive position—there was no way to stop the military's influence. Johnson certainly couldn't. This shooting would lead to war, a war that the nation and world had been so frightened of unleashing, a war that would create unimaginable suffering and death. Bobby thought of all those grammar school children who had been drilled to hide under their desks as a placebo for protection. They would be incinerated along with their class members, their neighbors, and their friends for blocks and blocks of city streets, with similar scenes of destruction playing out in major cities all along the eastern and western seaboards. Was the exposure of conspirators worth the elimination of New York and all its inhabitants—or Moscow, for that matter—in a flesh-searing fireball? All of these people, hundreds of thousands or even millions, were relative innocents, far removed from the machinations and intrigues of political and military leaders.

If he couldn't prevent such a horrible scenario, should he call Ethel and have her move the family out of DC? How could he do that and not inform the rest of the population? He remembered the guilty embarrassment he had felt when members of the elite Washington corps had been issued passes for the bunkered retreat in the Virginia hills during the Cuban missile crisis, passes he and his family had received, but others on his staff had not. He and Ethel had refused them, Jackie as well. And that was during a period of drawn-out negotiations. This would be sudden and apocalyptic. It would be mayhem. No wonder Hoover and LBJ were frightened. They had had a bit more time to contemplate the consequences of this information becoming public, and had come to similar conclusions regarding the ghastly effects of a nuclear exchange in reaction to the shooting of one man, albeit the president of the United States.

Hadn't World War I started along eerily similar lines, the shooting death of Archduke Ferdinand during a Sarajevo motorcade? The repercussions of his killing escalated along ever-increasing levels of engagement, until nation after nation was drawn in, and years of fighting engulfed the entire world. Who could say it wouldn't happen again, and this time with nuclear weapons, not "just" mustard gas and endless trench warfare? Escalation would be swift and irrevocable. It would take a nuclear-tipped missile only about half an hour from launch in the United States to reach into the heart of Russia, obliterating an entire city. In a similar time span, one from Russia would reach the United States with the same deadly effect. No one could un-push the button if it began. It would take an inconceivably short time to destroy one another's nations, and only a madman could think that recovery would be swift, or even possible. Yet there were such madmen, and they held positions of authority in this country. Bobby had met them many times in the halls of the White House during previous crises, men like Curtis LeMay, the bombastically aggressive Air Force Chief of Staff, whose mission in life was to use the arsenal of weaponry he had so passionately helped assemble in the form of the Strategic Air Command. Who would stop men like this if Jack was not there to do so? Bobby didn't have the power or position as attorney general—and Jack was lying unconscious, his presidential powers unavailable, in a bed upstairs.

Oh God, Jack! thought Bobby, *Please wake up! Please don't die!*

There was a commotion a few doors down the hall as an aide came out of the main communications room and almost turned to go up the stairwell until he saw Robert Kennedy standing in the doorway. "There's a call for you, sir. Vice President Johnson is on the line."

Bobby looked up slowly and nodded. "I'll take it in here." He gestured toward the room he had just left. Bobby's gaze traveled to Jiggs, who was standing between him and the aide. They looked somberly at each other for a long moment. Was that fear etched on Jiggs' tired face? Bobby turned and went in.

"Bobby, this is Lyndon," came the voice over the line as soon as Bobby sat down wearily at the desk and again picked up the phone.

"Yes, Lyndon, I'm here," responded Bobby.

"I *am* sorry to have to press you 'bout this. I know you need more time, we all do. But I've been talkin' with Hoover and there's scuttlebutt that the *Post* for sure and maybe even *The New York Times* are going to come out with an editorial tomorrow morning callin' for a congressional investigation to look into the confusion around the shooting of the president. Now if this happens, there ain't no way to stop a subpoena-empowered committee from gettin' the information about Oswald and this Mexico City angle. And if that happens, my friend, we are on a shit ride to hell, make no mistake." Bobby could hear Lyndon breathing hard, and there was a tremor in his voice. "Now, I have talked to Hoover, and he said you had concerns about the accuracy of this information the FBI has, and he said to you, and he said it again to me, and I believe 'im, that this is rock-solid. Just rock-solid. The Soviets and the Cubans are up to their asses in this. When this becomes public knowledge—and it will, you know how reporters are—it'll turn into an ugly circus here." Lyndon had been talking with a great deal of emotion, but paused as he quieted down and spoke with sincere pleading. "Now, Bobby, I know you love your brother, and I understand that, truly I do. But I am askin' you, with full knowledge, mind you, of what it is I'm really requestin' here, Bobby, that for the benefit of this country, to let us go ahead and quiet the waters here. Hoover is ready to come out with a statement sayin' his investigation has led to conclusive proof that Oswald was the only shooter. We need to know you're with us on this." The connection was quiet as Johnson waited on the other end for an answer.

After a few moments he repeated his request. "Bobby, *please* talk to me 'bout this! Do I have your consent?" pleaded the vice president.

There was a long pause on the line, to the point that Bobby could hear the intake of air. Lyndon was about to ask if he was still there when Bobby quietly spoke his one-word answer into the phone.

"Yes."

Chapter 10

John Kennedy is a realist brilliantly disguised as a romantic;
Robert Kennedy a romantic stubbornly disguised as a realist.
—Arthur M. Schlesinger, Jr.

The greatest threat to our world and its peace comes from those who want war,
who prepare for it, and who, by holding out vague promises of future peace or by
instilling fear of foreign aggression, try to make us accomplices to their plans.
—Hermann Hesse

Saturday, September 28, 1968
Glen Ora, Virginia

"Mr. Hennessey?" The U.S. Marshal leaned down to the window of Patrick's light blue Ford Fairlane. "We've been expecting you," he said. "Got some ID there, Patrick?"

Patrick handed over his driver's license and *Washington Post* press pass. It was still a curiosity to see a U.S. Marshal, rather than a Secret Service agent, guarding the president of the United States. But after the events in Dallas, the Secret Service's presidential protection mandate was rescinded. Organized under the U.S. Treasury Department, their role as the guardians of the executive branch was always a curious anomaly. Revelations from the Trials determined that their protection of the president had been exceedingly lax. As Attorney General, Robert Kennedy had been toying with the idea of absorbing the protection of his brother into the Justice Department anyway. After Dallas, he created a division at Justice solely for protection of the president. The U.S. Marshals Service was already a far more muscular department under the young AG, and it seemed prudent, with the times, to absorb the existing Secret Service into its fold. Some of the agents who were devoted to the First Family were retained on a case-by-case basis. Along with an overhauled Federal Bureau of Investigation, the fit seemed natural, as more transparent information sharing solved some of the previous issues of intransigent non-communication between the FBI and the Secret Service.

"Okay, you're good. Why don't you pull up and park by that white horse trailer, this side of the second barn," said the marshal as he handed back the two cards and directed Patrick toward one of the buildings up the gravel drive toward his right. "The main house entrance is over to the left, but the presidential party is grouping over there at the far end of the fence line." The marshal pointed across a long pasture to a small group gathered near a few golf carts. "By the way, interesting vehicle color, Mr. Hennessey. Special order?"

"Uhm...well, no," said Patrick, cringing a bit, "I bought it used."

Patrick's Friday mid-morning White House meeting with the president had been changed. He had received a call at his apartment late Thursday evening from Evelyn Lincoln. It was going to be a beautiful fall weekend by all accounts, and the Chief Executive was getting out of DC. Patrick was instructed to meet him Saturday morning at Glen Ora, in horsey country, just an hour and a half drive from of the capital in Middleburg, Virginia. The presidential secretary gave directions to the 400-acre estate that the president and first lady occupied during their retreats from Washington. The president had arrived the evening before on Marine One, the presidential helicopter service. From the gatehouse entrance, Patrick could see the gleaming metal bird sitting quietly in an upper pasture a little beyond the main house. Patrick had driven the distance. It was turning into a beautiful day. With the changing leaves, the rolling hills of Virginia in the early morning light, and minimal traffic, the drive had been stunning.

"The president suggests you bring an overnight bag—and your golf clubs," Mrs. Lincoln had said in their closing exchange Thursday night.

Patrick pulled his car over to the barn and parked, then got out and stretched a little. There was a commotion across the way, and in the quiet morning mist he could make out some talking and laughter. It seemed his arrival had been noticed, as a golf cart was coming his way along the gravel drive that stretched across the long entry to the front of the house and around the wood-railed horse pastures that extended down to the tree line hundreds of yards away. The cart came to a screeching stop behind Patrick's car, spewing gravel.

"Mr. Hennessey," announced the president jovially, accenting the formal introduction in his most humorous Bostonian accent, "you *did* bring your clubs, right?" The president was dressed in khakis and a thick crew sweater.

"Yes, sir. In the trunk," he said, as he hurriedly popped the back with his key.

"Load them on the back and let's get to work. We have a lot to accomplish this morning." The president was in high spirits. His energetic banter brought a smile to Patrick's face as he quickly pulled his clanking bag of clubs from the trunk. While the president rambled on, Patrick strapped them snugly to the back of the cart, next to the black leather bag with the White House insignia. "How was the drive? I wouldn't know about that anymore, as I have my own helicopter limousine service now. You might want to try it when you get the royalties from our book. It's a great way to see the world." Patrick pulled out his shoes, closed the trunk, and jumped into the seat beside the president.

"How's your game?" asked Kennedy.

"Working my way down the eighties, sir," boasted Patrick with a bit of pride.

"Well," scowled the president, "I guess that will have to do." He tore off in his golf cart as if he were working his way toward a land speed record. The governor on the motor would only allow about eighteen miles per hour, but the president was going to get every bit of speed he could wring from the puny engine.

"The first order of business is to soundly defeat you and your partners, Senator Fulbright and our British Ambassador, at a round of golf," said the president matter-of-factly. "It's going to be a merciless endeavor, with none of the leniency I've shown in my recent pardons. The only charitable aspect will be the amount of money that you, the kind senator, and Britain's ambassador will owe me by the end of the round." The president was referring to some of the pardons that had been recently granted to a few of the conspirators caught up in the long series of national trials.

They drove toward the main house, passing below its front porch before going farther on to the small assembled group. But when they got close to the house, the screen door opened and a woman came walking out onto the veranda. She was holding the hand of her youngest boy, who was waddling his way out the opening, a mug of coffee in her other hand as she elbowed open the door. She had on riding boots, with a bulky sweater and her hair was windblown. The president screeched to a stop at the base of the steps, again spewing an arc of gravel.

"Jackie," called out the president, "I'd like you to meet Mr. Patrick Hennessey. I told you about him. He's writing my bestseller." Patrick was stunned to be introduced to the first lady, as he hadn't been expecting her to be present. He should have, as this was her favorite retreat and the reason that the president spent weekends here. Her hands were full as she gave him an acknowledging smile, but the president was off again before Patrick was able to respond with more than a startled "hello" that trailed off behind him. They quickly rounded the drive and pulled up to the waiting party.

The assembled crew was preparing for their outing as only golfers can—adjusting their tight one-handed leather gloves, picking debris from their spiked shoes, clearing the imagined grit from the grooves of their irons. These were men at the height of their influence, using the pretext of sport as a companion to power. The president skidded to a halt next to the three carts and got out. He seemed energetic today, and from the way he was moving, Patrick would not have thought there were any physical ailments plaguing the president. He looked quite nimble and pain-free. Patrick thought of the comments on the seriousness of the man's back injuries and the stories that he often took painkillers for temporary relief. It seemed this might be one of those times.

"Gentlemen, I'd like to introduce the last member of our fivesome, Patrick Hennessey. He and I are having a few interviews together, may want to turn it into a book, although that is still hush-hush for now. You probably know him as a reporter with the *Post*," said the president conspiratorially, as an aside, "so you may want to watch what you say. Any moment he might revert to form, with your unintended comments ending up on the front page of tomorrow's edition."

"I'm off the clock, I promise you," said Patrick, raising his hands in surrender. He was well aware how stilted conversation could become if it was perceived that there was a chance it would find its way into print.

"This is Senator Bill Fulbright, Ambassador David Ormsby-Gore, and, of course, Red Fay, Under-Secretary to the Navy," said the president as Patrick shook hands during the introductions. "Now besides soundly trumping the three of you on the president's private course, I'll be badgering the senator and ambassador for political purposes during the game, attempting to translate my course advantage to a political one. It's never worked in the past, but hope springs eternal, does it not?"

"In your mind sir, that's a good thing. The hope part, I mean, as the reality part might be a bit of a disappointment," said Ormsby-Gore. The Ambassador was a genial man, upstandingly British from bearing to speech. Tall and thin with thinning swept-back hair, he had a warm quality that invited friendship. His acquaintance with John and Jackie Kennedy spanned many years. He nearly lived at the White House for the amount

of time they spent together, which afforded the two nations an unusual
degree of cooperation. They were obviously comfortable in each other's
company and could banter roughly between themselves like brothers.

"I look forward to your usual harassment, sir," said Senator Fulbright,
smiling, "although, as in the past, the effects might be difficult to discern."
The sixty-two-year-old senator from Arkansas was a longtime ally of Mr.
Kennedy's and was instrumental in cementing Congressional approval for
the peace process and negotiations in Paris with the North Vietnamese.
He was one of Kennedy's conduits to the Senate and had political leanings
similar to the president's regarding international affairs, although he was
still reluctant to fully embrace Civil Rights integration. Patrick especially
remembered his stand against Joe McCarthy years earlier, and the senator's part in calling for his eventual censure. No one in this group, except
probably Patrick, was cowed by proximity to the president of the United
States. The repartee of long-term friends seemed the mode of conversation.

"Now, even though golf was rumored to have been invented in the
British Isles, that heritage has not rubbed off in any appreciable manner on
the play of our ambassador," said the president, pulling on his golf glove.
"And for that reason, Hennessey, he will be plinking away with your squad
for wagering purposes. On the other hand, Senator Fulbright here is an
accomplished golfer, having spent many hours on the links, which in no
way, sir, implies the slightest dereliction of duty from your Congressional
responsibilities. He will be a formidable foe. In addition, Mr. Hennessey,
I might add, is a ringer. Why, he told me on the short drive over here that
he easily and regularly breaks eighty and looks forward to embarrassing
us all."

"Has the president already been messing around in your head, son?"
said the senator, seeing Patrick's look of surprise at the total distortion of
his earlier comment. "Be careful, he will connive and bluster in any way
possible to gain an advantage. You can't trust him or let your guard down
even for a moment. And I say this as a lifetime member of the same political party; as someone who even foolishly voted for him in the last election."

"And would again if I were running for a third term," said the president. "Why, that damned Constitution has been a nagging hindrance my
entire time in office."

"But even in deference to your aggregate greater abilities in the game," continued the president, "Redhead and I still see fit to take on the three of you. It will be a struggle to compete, but I think we can bear up under the strain," cajoled the president as he looked over at his agreeable partner, who solemnly nodded his head in affirmation. "Speaking of which, I think we should clarify the terms."

The senator rolled his eyes and an audible moan erupted from the ambassador. They were obviously familiar with the president's upcoming wagering terms.

"Now, since I'm a bit rusty, not having played recently due to a crushing workload—unlike, I might add, our senator here—I think you might find it in your hearts to spot Red and me a stroke per hole." There were sounds of protest from the senator and ambassador. "So," continued the president, undeterred, "how about a dollar a hole, with side bets of fifty cents for longest drive, first on the green, closest to the pin, least number of putts, and first in the hole. Ties carry over to the next hole. Birdies are worth two dollars. Now, a few additional course-specific rules. Hitting a cow, if it is over a hundred yards away, is two strokes off, but within that range adds two strokes. Hitting a horse, on the other hand, adds five strokes to your score no matter how near or far and includes a two dollar penalty paid to each other player at the time of said occurrence. There is also an official presidential gag order on any discussion of an equestrian direct hit, as Jackie would string me up if she were to hear of it. All clear? Okay." The president had rattled off the rules as if he had done so many times in the past. Except for the horse and cow addition, Patrick was familiar in one way or another with all of them. Keeping track though, added a whole other dimension to the game and might require a separate accounting sheet. "Shall we begin?" continued the president brightly.

"Not with one stroke per hole advantage," inserted Fulbright. "I may have made the mistake of voting for you last term, but with you holding the course record, I believe we should get the added stroke per hole." The senator held firm.

"I'd have to second that motion unless, of course, I am going to be playing on the president's squad, in which case I would agree with whatever he says," added Ormsby-Gore.

"All right, all right! If you insist, we'll play it even up," said the president, seeing that taking the middle road would be the best advantage he could gain. He had played with Fulbright and Ormsby-Gore numerous times in the past. They knew his wheedling. "Now, shall we begin?"

"So what is par for this course?" asked Patrick.

"We'd have to say it's an imaginary number plucked from the sky by presidential directive," offered Ormsby-Gore in his clipped British accent. "No one really knows."

"Although it may be with a desire to frighten my competition here, I will have to admit holding the course record of forty-four," boasted the president with obvious pride, "over five holes."

"Five holes?" said Patrick. "That's a par nine per hole."

"If you're lucky," responded the president. "If you're not lucky, well, it can be a long and costly day. I might add that, except for the fifth hole, a birdie is an eight."

An eight! thought Patrick.

He was a bit perplexed as he looked around. He didn't actually see a golf course. He had thought they were going to drive off to some local links. There was a small trail that went off toward the woods, but no visible tees, fairways, or the normal accouterments of golfing.

He'd heard about a private course Mrs. Kennedy had had created at the estate for the president's pleasure. Jack had never really been a part of the horsey set; his weak back made it a painful challenge to ride. Early in 1961, she had asked a local farmer to close-crop the meadows in a particularly meandering area of the 400-acre estate to create a three-hole course. It was supposed to be rough, very rough, with moments of relief from hazards only at the tee areas and the small greens. In many ways it was a reminder of the origins of golf, meandering through wind-swept Scottish sheep pastures. The grassy fairways, at their kindest, were rumored to be about four inches deep. It had been expanded to four holes soon after, and then to five after the Kennedys returned to Glen Ora during their second term.

The owners from whom the First Family leased the property had been reluctant to renew, because of concerns that the property was being overrun by presidential activities, so the Kennedys' return after the birth of their fourth child was unexpected. They had already begun construction on a home nearby, which they were going to name Wexford, after the county of his ancestors in Ireland. But after the assassination attempt and a realization that greater security was required, for which Wexford was found wanting, the Glen Ora owners had consented to lease the property for a second term. Jack enjoyed his stays now, as he could bring along his golf buddies and carouse in the wooded hills of the estate without the prying eyes of photographers or press.

Most people had no idea there was a course hidden away in these woods, and Patrick had to admit there were no indications that gave it away other than the presence of their carts.

They all piled into the vehicles and wound their way up the trail Patrick had noticed. Besides the carts with the golfers, there was a cart with a group of local boys who had been recruited to carry the president's and his guests' clubs. Kennedy's back prevented any weight-bearing activities, and the local youths were more than eager to be drummed into presidential service. Following, ahead, and all around, it seemed to Patrick, were members of the U.S. Marshals Executive Detail, so it was a small platoon that drove the short hundred yards to the first tee. Most of the course could be walked, but there were a few longer runs between holes that excused the luxury of motorized travel.

Patrick had golfed for years, mostly at public courses in DC and Virginia, and occasionally, when invited, at private links. He had picked up the disease from his Uncle Duncan who, upon his return from Ireland, brought with him, like a viral infection jumping national boundaries, an addiction to the game. They played often in Patrick's youth, with long conversations on the course about his uncle's time on the Emerald Isle and the attempts of the FBI and the McCarthy commission to pressure him to their will. Their course times were good memories for Patrick. The time spent on the links developed into a semi-passion for Patrick as he took to local courses on weekends. He was becoming familiar with the mid-eighties, even shooting a legitimate seventy-nine one glorious day at the municipal course in DC—no gimmes, no mulligans.

* * *

But this course was different right from the start. Where was the green? The first tee was a small mowed grassy space only a half dozen yards square. Two small orbs with the presidential seal were spaced across the opening to indicate the tee-off position. From the first tee, the terrain sloped uphill to the right through an open expanse of rocky pasture that extended for about one hundred fifty yards before ending abruptly at a dense copse of trees. It appeared there might be an opening beyond, but it was by no means obvious.

"See that gap between the trees?" pointed Kennedy, to Patrick's obvious confusion, as he had been looking in the wrong direction.

"Not really."

"Well, when you're up closer it's a bit more obvious," said Kennedy with little hint of levity.

"It's across a rock-filled meadow. How do I avoid the rocks?" asked Patrick, still not able to find the opening in the tree line.

"Well, Hennessey, you just aim around them."

They threw a tee between the five of them to determine the order for the first hole. Patrick was last. The ambassador and senator got off two relatively clean soft iron shots, straight and playable. They both laid up in front of the wall of trees without being unduly diverted by the rocky ground.

JFK stepped up to the tee box and took an easy swing, landing his ball near the shots of the senator and ambassador. He had graceful form with a natural, fluid arc. Patrick realized the rumors about his golf game were true. Before him, President Eisenhower had spent many a day sneaking off from the White House to get in an afternoon round, and paid for it dearly. He was mocked as the Duffer in Chief, the presidency said to be his barely tolerated second job—as long as the weather did not allow for a full eighteen holes. Kennedy and the Democrats ran against his "old fogey" image during their 1960 campaign, suggesting that they would never resort to such a foolishly patrician waste of time. But the success of their negative portrayal of Ike left Kennedy having to hide his love of the game and even restrict any mention of golf during his first term. Photos of him on a golf course or swinging a club were not allowed. It was rumored that he was a scratch player, and from the graceful drive off the first tee, Patrick could see it might be true.

Red Fay also got off a clean shot, although his hit a rock and ricocheted directly into the woods on the left side of the fairway, only to ricochet again back onto the course. He was congratulated by the president for having such keen local knowledge.

When Patrick's turn arrived, he was nervous. He had clocked a significant body of time on golf courses and felt comfortable with his game, but shooting with the likes of the president and his friends was an entirely different animal. It had an unnerving effect. Most professional competitors would hold that it was the first shot from the tee, under the glare of the TV cameras and following crowds, that was the hardest. Most just wanted to tee off and connect with a shot that got them as far away as possible from the glare. Patrick was no different. He was ruffled from the moment his turn approached. He botched it, topping it off the tee. It jumped vertically and landed about twenty yards down the fairway, bouncing off a few rocks and coming to rest in a patch of weeds—although in fact everything appeared to be a patch of weeds. There was silence as everyone selected their next club and, with caddies trailing, began the trek to their balls.

"You're lucky there are no ladies' tees, Hennessey," said the president as he passed Patrick.

Red Fay, so called because of his typically Irish hair, was still standing at the golf cart while Patrick exchanged his club. Red had been the president's friend since their days running PT boats around the Pacific during the Second World War and, with his position as Under-Secretary of the Navy, he'd had a lot of access to the president over the years. He noticed Patrick's confusion at the president's comment.

"See, when we play, if you don't get your shot off the tee past the ladies' box, you have to play the rest of the hole with your pecker hanging out," he stated matter-of-factly. "On a public course it can be rather embarrassing. Really affects your relationship with the president, you know. Always having an image of you in that state of, well, undress. Probably doesn't help your game any either, or so I'm told. You remember Percival Montgomery, that junior congressman from Georgia?"

"No, not really," said Patrick.

"Exactly," nodded Red, and walked away.

He took the next shot, as he was furthest from the pin, wherever that might be. Patrick was beginning to suspect its location was a closely guarded secret. He made it up to the tree line and took only two more shots to get through. He did find the narrow gap, but his ball bounced off a branch in the process. The senator and the president went through on their second shots, and Red followed on his fourth with Patrick. The pasture behind the tree-lined barrier revealed a tiny expanse of green carpet about two hundred and fifty yards beyond. The peaceful little green, with a flag flying out of the hole, beckoned alluringly. Getting to it was the rub, as there was a marshy expanse around two-thirds of it.

Kennedy's last shot had hit a meadow fence post and bounced back. It was now a little behind Patrick's ball in relation to the green. He and Patrick stood together waiting for Ormsby-Gore, who was on the other side of the "fairway," attempting to extricate himself from a nasty pile of rocks in which he was embedded.

"Did you read the two articles on the Cuban missile batteries?" Kennedy asked, not taking his eyes off the ambassador and his dilemma.

"Yes," said Patrick, a little surprised at the non-sequitur, "and I still find it shocking. How is it that no one knows about that yet?"

"It's surprising it hadn't leaked earlier, but it will. We'll see to that," he asserted. "How about the article on the nuclear fail-safe codes?"

"Yes, I read that too," responded Patrick. "Sometimes I wonder how the human race has managed to survive this long without someone pulling the trigger, even if just because of a short circuit in a piece of equipment in a basement at NORAD."

"That's why I like you, Hennessey," said the president glancing over at Patrick, "always looking on the bright side."

Patrick chuckled. With the ambassador out of his rocky cage, the president lofted a clean shot toward the pin, landing just short of the water, only thirty yards from the green. Patrick followed with a clean shot of his own landing not twenty feet from the president's ball. They looked at each other.

"I'm hoping to make a little lunch money," said Patrick, "just in case the book doesn't sell."

It was the president's turn to laugh.

On his next shot, Patrick dumped his ball into the drink, twice. The president overshot and went off the tiny green and into trees behind. Both the ambassador and the senator spent time getting intimately acquainted with the hole's water hazard. Red lost two balls, one in the woods and the other mysteriously disappearing right from the middle of the fairway. By the time they were actually on the green, no one lay under ten strokes. Fortunately, there were no out of bounds penalties, because in reality everything in between the tee and the green appeared to be in some manner of rough whose boundaries could not be adequately defined.

While watching the others play, Patrick noticed Kennedy occasionally shaking out his right hand, as if trying to loosen up a cramp. It was an idiosyncrasy he repeated numerous times. He never mentioned it and did it only when he was not the center of attention. Patrick thought it might have something to do with the damage to his arm from the shooting years ago.

Though Patrick was one of the last to the green, the flag was still in place, but it wasn't until he was up near it that he realized its markings. He pulled out its tail end to get a clearer look. *Castro* was written in block letters.

"These used to be small Confederate flags," said Ormsby-Gore, coming up behind Patrick. "Jackie had them made up. But when the civil rights issues started showing up in the southern states, she figured it might be best to get rid of them. Hence the renaming."

"Why Castro?" asked Patrick.

"Well, it's a pitifully tiny little piece of green real estate surrounded by a water hazard. It's the entry to the course closest to the house, with a run-up that can ruin your whole day," said the president, who had finally put his last shot on the green. "You know, Castro challenged me to a game of golf," said the president, "in a round-about way."

"Here we go," protested Ormsby-Gore.

"No, this is real, don't laugh," said the president. "He and Che Guevara had heard Eisenhower and I were golfers. So, never to be outdone, Mr. Cuban Machismo himself and Che, both of them in army boots and fatigues, shot a round of golf at a course across the bay from Havana. They declared themselves experts when the round was over, claiming they could easily defeat the capitalist American presidents. It wasn't till an AP reporter got hold of one of the caddies that they found out the score. Over one-fifty for Castro and a masterly one-twenty-seven for Che. Too bad we couldn't have a match to decide the next election down there. It would be delicious—golf as a kingmaker in international affairs. Much saner way to decide world politics, don't you think?"

They all one- and two-putted for scores of eleven through fourteen. They summed up the wagering and Patrick found himself in the middle of the pack.

* * *

The young caddies lugged their bags from the carts toward the next tee, across a short grassy incline. They seemed very attentive to the president, never allowing him to lift anything heavier than a club. Like the first, this hole gave no hint of a green at its end. There was a narrow fairway—a generous term for the less obstructed area between the tree lines—that turned gradually toward the left as it sloped downhill. Whatever was around the far bend was not visible.

"So, are we the only victims you subject to this course, Mr. President?" said Senator Fulbright. "I would think it a better political move to share this with Republican members of Congress, since it's such a discouraging experience."

"I have tried to be bipartisan," said Kennedy, "but I believe hardship is best savored with close friends."

"Does the vice president play?" asked Patrick.

"Lyndon can hold a club," replied the president, pausing from his warm-up swings. "He can also make swinging motions, but calling it golfing would be a serious mistake. We attempted a game in Palm Springs after I was elected," recalled the president. "We played a round. He made three to four hundred swings, taking mulligan after mulligan until he settled on a shot he liked. He cajoled the ball in a way only Lyndon could, sweet-talking and swearing it into submission. Watching him play was painful to my very core. I was never sure whether he was swinging at the ball, tilling the soil for planting, or killing a swarm of rattlesnakes."

"You know, I play a lot of golf, as you so thoughtfully reminded me earlier, Mr. President," said Senator Fulbright, "but I've never heard of the vice president playing."

"My VP has no passion but politics. A shame, really, as it leaves him little else to lean on. He lives and breathes for the bartering, and the seduction and domination of rivals. A few other interests would do him no harm."

"I've been worried about that man's health," said the senator. There was a little over a month until the presidential election. "It wasn't all that good to start. He drinks coffee and Fresca all day, works endless hours, drives himself and everyone around him to exhaustion. Do you really think he has enough left in him to go the distance? I mean, four years in that position can age a man, as you well know—although it hasn't had any visible effect on you, Mr. President," he added quickly, with patronizing insincerity and a wink at Patrick.

"Your pandering is noted, senator, but will not affect the sums of money you will owe me at the end of this round," said Kennedy. "Lyndon has an unquenchable thirst for the presidency. He can draw energy from dirt if need be. But I wonder the same thing—can he carry a full term? I don't know," said the president thoughtfully. "Hennessey, it's appropriate that you should ask about Lyndon, as we're on the vice president's hole right now."

"Oh, really?" exclaimed Patrick looking around for a hint of why.

"You notice there is a gentle curve to the left as we go downhill?"

"Sure."

"Well, beyond those trees is a sharp dogleg right. That's my VP," quipped the president.

"What I find hard to understand is his teaming up with Bobby," said Ormsby-Gore. "They despise each other, and that might be expressing it gently. It pained me to watch them at the convention, forced smiles and clasped raised hands, accepting the nomination. It was probably the greatest distance two people can stand apart and still have a small patch of skin touching. I'm often half thinking they might break into a fistfight at any moment. You must have had a hand in that union."

"Hardly the tiniest of suggestions," noted Kennedy innocently. "I would never, ever interfere in the selection of a candidate for public office."

"I believe thou dost protest too much," said the senator, laughing at the sheer cheek of the statement.

"The way Lyndon shepherded the civil rights and social bills through a deadlocked Congress was mighty impressive," added Kennedy. "He deserves his chance."

They played down to the green, and, sure enough, following the gentle left bend in the fairway, a sharp dogleg right descended into a marshy quagmire.

"I probably should mention, this is Hoover's hole," announced the president as they approached the next tee box.

The third hole, if at all possible, was the worst so far. Along the lower right side of the rocky fairway, a dense tree-lined thicket looked as if it could absorb all natural light as well as any golf ball that tended its way. And tend they did, as the sloped rocky fairway eventually bounced all their balls toward its black expanse. Along the left uphill side was a split rail fence dividing the shorter cropped fairway and the three-foot-high grass pasture that extended a hundred yards or more beyond.

The U.S. Marshals, as unobtrusive as fullbacks in a kindergarten class, were deployed around the president, even on his own property. With assault rifles slung over their backs, they scanned the perimeter of the fairways ahead and behind the golfing party. Patrick had seen a couple of burly, conservatively dressed men, wires hanging from their ears, lurking quietly in the trees on the first two holes when he was scouring for lost balls. He suspected they gave the president assistance locating errant shots. They would stand near them, looking off toward the horizon as if providing protection from foreign dangers until the president approached, at which time they would silently move on. They never seemed to be around when Patrick was searching for his own hooks and slices. But on this hole, even the marshal's detail seemed to disappear into the opaque darkness of the trees along the fairway.

Having won the last hole, Red Fay teed off first, hooking one directly into the thick of the grass beyond the left fence. "That ball is lost as sure as the next election will be by our dear friend Mr. Nixon," he announced.

The president was up next. He powered a long shot that flew straight down the fairway, only to bounce off the rocky surface directly into the trees on the right. There was a short pause, then everyone watched as the ball mysteriously bounced back in bounds toward the direction of the green. Patrick looked around, but no one said anything. "Nice shot, Mr. President," muttered Patrick suspiciously.

"Local knowledge," he deadpanned, studiously flicking some of the grass divot off his wood.

The British Ambassador's shot was timid but lucky. It hit a rock and bounced well forward, gaining far more distance than would have been thought likely. The senator's and Patrick's balls both penetrated the dark expanse of uncut lumber on the right, never again to see the light of day.

"Well, it makes good sense," said Kennedy in explanation, continuing with the discussion of LBJ and Bobby as they walked along the fairway together. "LBJ still has some standing in the South and can at least pull a bit of our remaining support there. His work on Medicare and poverty programs also has a lot of purchase. But it's in the way he championed civil rights issues—the Civil Rights and Voters Rights acts—that you could really see his stature grow. Couple that with Bobby and the prestige he's gained from his part in the Trials, his roving ambassadorial work with the North Vietnamese in Paris, and then the public debates with Castro, and the pairing works. There's been a complete realignment of the South, as you well know, senator."

"True," said Fulbright.

"I mentioned that we'd probably lost the Southern vote for a generation when Lyndon and I jointly signed the final Civil Rights Bill," the president continued. "But Wallace pulling in the segregationist vote has yanked the rug right out from under Nixon. I'm inclined to think it'll come around for the Democrats in the future."

"Unfortunately, I don't share your opinion on that, sir" said the senator from Arkansas. "The Civil Rights legislation has moved too quickly. We've had three long summers of inner-city violence, and I fear that one day things could really erupt. And I mean serious riots, not just these little brush fires and skirmishes we've been having. Do you realize what would have happened back in April if the Reverend King had been killed in that shooting in Memphis? This country would have ignited like a stack of dry kindling."

"Were Hoover still in charge at the FBI, that attempt might have succeeded," said Kennedy. "He had a real hard-on for King, even tried blackmailing him out of the Civil Rights movement. Did you know that? But King wouldn't budge. Hoover would've sat on his hands had he known someone was stalking King. You know, the Reverend's quietly had federal protection for the last two years," said the president as an aside to the senator. "He might chafe under it, but it's probably saved his life."

Patrick knew Courtney Evans had succeeded Hoover after his death, rearranging and slowly introducing a different culture to the calcified agency. Evans had been a trusted liaison between the prickly former director and Robert Kennedy during his term as attorney general. He was elevated to the directorship after Hoover's sudden demise in early '65.

"The frustrations playing out in the Negro communities are, I believe, an unfortunate but natural extension of the deep changes that are occurring," said the president. "This is not going to be an easy transition, no matter what we do. And putting it off till later won't work either. Legitimate civil rights issues go straight to the heart of our culture, and if we don't get it right once and for all, then it will only lead to more serious upheaval later on."

"I've always wondered about Hoover's death. There's something no one is saying, isn't there?" said Ormsby-Gore into the pause in the conversation. "Did he really have a heart attack? Somehow the timing of his death seemed rather too...well, timely."

The president looked thoughtfully at his friend, but did not respond.

The fairway took a near right-angle turn after the first two hundred yards and opened onto a relatively clear expanse up to a raised green only one hundred fifty yards away. But upon closer inspection, the green sat atop a massive rock. Anything short of a perfect shot, and it would bounce off the protective citadel into the surrounding brush. By the time they all arrived at the top, on the green, their scores were in the double digits, although Kennedy, with his course familiarity, and Patrick, who tried to follow him shot for shot, were at the low end of the scale. They had reached the green earlier by overshooting and coming back to it from behind. But the senator, the ambassador, and Red Fay had all been chipping away, trying to assault the stronghold from the front, raising their scores and lowering their spirits in the process.

"A horrible approach through a treacherous path; a pathetic little green sitting on top of a granite lump of stone," said the president as they all stood around the tiny green, somewhat disgusted with their efforts.

"I thought maybe it would be Khrushchev's hole," said Ormsby-Gore.

"No, I renamed it *Hoover* a while back, after Khrushchev, that cantankerous old fart, signed on to the Non-Proliferation Treaty far earlier than we had hoped. And I really think that we can get a Comprehensive Test Ban Treaty in the next few years as well. Then we can avoid all nuclear testing, ground and atmospheric." His comments about the brusque Russian leader revealed a surprising amount of warmth. "So, I felt he deserved better. Khrushchev, that is, not that *bahstahd* Hoover."

* * *

The fourth hole started off as a relief from the first three. It had a wide, forgiving fairway, if you discounted the scattering of local dairy cows. They all got off the tee with generous shots and only one bovine strike. It was a minor thing, really. Senator Fulbright's ball bounced along the ground, clipping the front foreleg of a cow as she munched the fairway grass. The cow looked up for a moment as the ball came to rest a few feet away, wondering if she should be concerned or just eat it. But, deciding the small white orb posed no threat, she went back to her feeding. Since the strike occurred more than a hundred yards out, the senator happily benefited from a two-stroke relief.

They were all near the green in record time, at least compared to the previous three holes, and one could not blame them for thinking about birdies and eagles. But their enthusiasm was quelled when they started to putt. That's when the trouble began. The green had a pleasant appearance from afar, but it had a hard compacted surface with a distinct slope that prevented most putts from doing more than sliding off its surface. For all their ease attaining the green, their balls rested together in a clump at the downhill side.

"A clear and open run up to a deceitful little green whose slippery surface is near impossible to lay a ball on," said Kennedy as he watched the struggles of his playing partners. "And that's why it's been dedicated to Mr. Nixon."

The three- and four-putt green more than made up for the easy access.

* * *

The last hole was a par three, a real par three with no unexpected hazards or hidden obstacles. It looked bad from the tee, barely visible beyond a rise, but opened onto a clean soft green with ample room for putting.

"Khrushchev's hole," announced the president as they stood on the tee looking off to the green only a hundred and thirty yards away. "Recently renamed. It's even more forgiving than it looks, gentlemen."

To a man they made clean shots that landed on or near the green. It was a well-deserved relief from the horrors of the previous four holes. After their shots, as they all walked toward the green, Patrick noted the president's more serious tone. He had started the day in a rush of energy, but was slowing and looking a little less effusive. By the time they had reached the green, Patrick was aware there was something on his mind. They were standing off to the side while the senator and Red Fay lined up their putts.

"Other than to get you depressed, I had another reason for sending over that report on the PAL codes," stated Kennedy while they stood together warming in the autumn sun. "See that fellow over there," he said as he nodded toward a man sitting in one of the golf carts. He wore a military uniform with a bulky briefcase by his side.

Patrick turned and looked. He had noticed the man earlier and wondered about him. His attire did not match that of the U.S. Marshals.

"That man has the football. He, or one of his tag-team members, is my shadow all day, every day. They're no fun, and I've yet to find one who can swing a club. In that heavy satchel on the seat are the codes to launch a nuclear attack on the Soviets. I have about 15-20 minutes, after we get a warning, to decide what sort of response to make. It's a macabre reminder that follows me day and night wherever I go. Ike hardly used it, as the technology wasn't really developed, and the idea that an unauthorized launch could occur was not yet a serious concern. But after the Cuban missile crisis in '62, when we came within a hairsbreadth of letting them all fly, I was worried some over-inspired general would slip from my control and push a few buttons that could not be unpushed. So McNamara and I instituted a thorough review of the chain of command and created a procedure by which a node off the linking chain must be activated in order to permit a launch. That man carries the node. We have hundreds of silo-based ICBMs scattered around the middle of the country, ready for release if I give the word. I carry the codes to unlock it with me at all times," he said as he patted his back pocket, "and hopefully no one will circumvent the whole procedure."

"That is truly frightening," remarked Patrick.

"What? That we are in this predicament, or that I am the one with the codes?" asked the president, trying to get a rise. But Patrick just smiled and refused to respond.

"From those documents, I wanted you to get a good understanding of the efforts we've made to create a virtually foolproof lock on the use of nuclear weapons and the extent that we went to in order to keep it under my control. You probably saw that movie *Fail-Safe*. I was glad that came out, as it showed the precarious posture of men trying to control the weaponry we've created. What was your response to your reading?"

"It was a bit beyond me, sir, but it would seem that circumventing the coded procedures would be like doing brain surgery through the anus. Nearly impossible."

"Hennessey, save it for our book," laughed the president shaking his head. "You do have a way with words. Well, we went to great lengths to create a procedure that could not be circumvented and would give us all at least a degree of confidence that those missiles would remain safely in their holes in the ground, never to see sunlight. Did you feel safer knowing those measures were instituted?"

"Well, I guess."

"Well, you'd be wrong," responded the president softly. "The entire fail safe procedure was a sham. To our tremendous shock, the elaborate measures so painstakingly worked out by the military and nuclear watchdog groups were never fully implemented. The final authorization sequences, the ones that'd be activated by the two men in control of the silos, were never entered into the system. This final link in the chain was deliberately left open so it could be overridden at any time. So in essence, I really had no ability to prevent the launching of nuclear weapons. That power had always been held in reserve by the generals. Always."

"How was that discovered?" asked Patrick, shocked once again by a revelation of the president's burden.

"During the Trials. Much attention was focused on Military Intelligence, and, as one thing led to another, one of the investigators came across SAC correspondence containing questions from silo operators regarding the open code condition. It was hushed up, but there was a paper trail that led back to the top brass. This was quietly forwarded to McNamara."

Patrick was lost in thought for a moment. "Wait a minute! So that's why the generals are disappearing," he exclaimed. One of Patrick's *Washington Post* reporter friends had recently brought to his attention the fact that an inordinate number of military brass had retired. Cashiered was more like it. There seemed to be a methodical reorganization of the structural control of the military going on, without any fanfare from the administration.

The president looked at him closely, and with a frustrated shake of his head added, "Damn. I knew it would get out eventually Who knows? "

"A couple of weeks ago Schillberg talked to me. You know him, he covers the military beat at the *Post*." Kennedy nodded as if he knew the name. "He'd been looking at pay scales and military retirement benefits and found a curious trend of generals recently being put out to pasture. He asked if I'd been aware of it."

"Your shot, Mr. President," said Ormsby-Gore, walking up to where the president and Patrick had been standing with their backs to the green.

Kennedy thought for a moment, probably about how much to convey to Patrick. "I'll talk to you more about this later," he finally concluded. "And Mr. Schillberg will be getting a call. I'm not ready for this to come out yet."

They finished out the round. The president won overall, both in score and monies owed, with a forty-seven. Patrick was second at forty-nine, owing only three dollars to Kennedy (which the president said was a pitifully small amount considering the efforts involved) and a dollar each to Red and Senator Fulbright. He had held his own. Ormsby-Gore was last with a frustrating fifty-eight, which he asserted was a personal sacrifice to maintain friendly relations between the two countries, as it would be impolitic to win on the president's home course.

"I believe there's lunch waiting at the house," said the president, "after which the Ambassador and Mr. Hennessey will be accompanying me to Camp David. By the way senator, I know you have to head back to DC, but you're in my debt for $5.50. Make sure you pay up before you leave. Don't make me sic the Treasury Department on you. You know how indelicate the IRS can be."

"Would you be willing to trade it for a vote on the South American Debt Relief Bill coming up next week in the Senate, sir?" asked Fulbright with a sideways glance at Patrick.

"Sir, it's your debt relief we're talking about at the moment. Pay up!" The president already knew he had the senator's support.

"Patrick, it was a pleasure to meet you. You showed great wisdom today," acknowledged the senator in parting. To Patrick's questioning glance, he explained, "If you don't want to retard your career, never be so foolish as to thrash the leader of the free world in golf, and especially not on his home course."

Chapter 11

For certain is death for the born, and certain is birth for the dead;
Therefore over the inevitable, thou shouldst not grieve.
—*Bhagavad Gita, 300 BC*

One-fifth of the people are against everything all the time.
—*Robert F. Kennedy*

Sunday morning, November 24, 1963
Dallas, Texas

Dressed in a black cassock with a gold-trimmed purple stole covering his surplice, Monsignor Oran Allarty, a Catholic priest from nearby Holy Trinity Parish, was administering benediction. It was Sunday, and he arrived early to administer the sacrament to Robert and others in the Kennedy group who had been huddled for almost two days at Parkland Medical Center, unable to tear themselves away from the unfolding events. Since they were reluctant to travel to receive the sacrament at the nearby church, the Mass came to them. Services completed, the Monsignor softly sprinkled holy water on the plastic oxygen tent and linen covers on John Kennedy's bed, blessing the unconscious president before departing. The clinking of the brass wand against the small metal holy water font and the quietly recited Latin invocation with its rhythmic cadence and confident delivery hinted at a secret wisdom which usually instilled a sense of comfort to those present. Here was a man with a direct link to God, asking for intervention and healing. And if he didn't have pull with the divine to improve the condition of what appeared to everyone there to be a dying president, then who did?

But Robert Kennedy was definitely not feeling comforted. While watching the Monsignor bless his brother, Bobby had disquieting thoughts about the power of plastic and whether it restricted the healing energies of holy water. Did the water need to actually touch the skin to deliver its miraculous effects? Or did the unfathomable powers of the clergy render material separations immaterial to the healing abilities those flecks of water contained?

When Lord Longford, an English Catholic, had suggested writing a book about John Kennedy's faith, Eunice Shriver, Kennedy's sister, responded, "It will be an awfully slim volume." John was a practicing Catholic who took his faith seriously from a familial and cultural view, but with a significant dose of existential detachment. Bobby, on the other hand, had been a devoutly passionate Catholic all of his life. He went to Mass every Sunday and, when travel permitted, would attend and often even help serve early morning Mass if the priest of the parish was short-handed. He believed deeply in the power of God. And through all the adversities of his intense career, he relied on God's best intentions being expressed through his life—his and his brother's. But that faith was being assaulted right now by recent events. Jack had been lying in this bed for almost two days, nearly unmoving. He had not regained consciousness. Death might be only a few shallow, labored breaths away. And Robert, with his abundant will and energy rendered useless, could do nothing but sit and wait.

As the Monsignor departed with a benedictory glance toward Bobby, he walked past one of the many fragrant floral arrangements that decorated the antiseptic room in which the stricken president lay.

Dallas flower shops had started receiving orders within an hour of the president's arrival at Parkland, and they continued until the hospital's entire entry, emergency room bays, waiting rooms, and halls were filled with every conceivable configuration of flower and foliage imaginable.

Complex wreaths on stands were delivered later, arranged through Dallas and Austin florists but originating overseas. "Pour mon ami, mon affection la plus profonde. Mes souhaits les plus sinceres pour votre retablissement...Charles DeGaulle" (For my friend, my deepest affection. My sincerest hopes for recovery.) That arrangement was brought up to Jack's room.

There was concern that the sheer quantity of foliage being delivered to the hospital would overwhelm the staff and prevent normal navigation from room to room. The overflow arrangements were bundled and stacked in corners and closets to keep them out of the way. Many were moved outdoors and quickly succumbed to the unseasonable Texas heat.

Jackie, aware of the situation, and by now feeling somewhat restored, asked her staff to take charge of cataloguing the arrivals and then delivering excess to the rooms of every patient in the hospital. And when the volume still proved too much, they were delivered to surrounding health care centers, especially those that housed patients unceremoniously re-moved from Parkland only a day earlier. For the next week, a nurse or doctor could walk into any room in the hospital and be greeted by the aroma of fresh cut flowers. It had a distinctly reviving effect on the whole atmosphere of Parkland Medical as well as other hospitals in the area.

But the terrible tragedy unfolding in Room 326 of an average Ameri-can hospital—the demise of a young president whose national and world potential were only just beginning to be felt—was juxtaposed with an in-creased sense of beauty, even if only temporary. It did not go unnoticed by the local Dallas residents and the Parkland staff that the love for their fallen leader might be as equally felt by a small town in Gabon, Africa, home of a Peace Corps center, as by the Prime Minister of Sweden, whose country had been assured protection by the United States from the threat-ened domination of the Soviet Union.

As he listened to mass in Jack's room, Bobby's sense of impotence was made all the more unbearable by the events of the previous day. He had made an agonizing decision. He tried to convince himself he had acted for the highest good—the safety of the country, even the safety of the world for that matter, since the effects of a nuclear exchange would not be lim-ited to the United States. And yet the decision gave him no sense of right-ness or justice. His brother had been shot. The man who had probably done the shooting was tied in with the Soviets and the Cubans in an assas-sination plan. But the U.S. government, Bobby's government, was going to cover up all indications of a wider conspiracy for fear of provoking an atomic war. They would pin the shooting on a lone assailant. And Bobby had signed off on the plan. No matter how he tried to look at it, no matter the rigorous logic behind his conclusion, he could not help but feel he had betrayed his brother. It was a Faustian bargain, made even less palatable by the participants with whom he conspired: Hoover and Johnson. Bobby also could not afford to share or even hint at the situation for fear of leak-age to the press, which would destroy whatever good the cover-up might accomplish. It was a burden he would have to bear alone.

* * *

Like a plague of locusts, the world media had descended upon Dallas. Flight after flight of national and international correspondents arrived at Love Field during the days after Kennedy's shooting. Becoming aware there might be a prolonged vigil, the media, to the consternation of the lo-cals, took up residence in Dallas to await the outcome. Pierre Salinger had flown in directly from Honolulu, where the plane carrying the Cabinet members had been returned from their aborted flight to Japan. He arrived late in the evening on November 22.

Crowded into a vacant Parkland lecture room, the press had listened with rapt attention to Assistant Press Secretary Malcolm Kilduff, and later to Pierre Salinger, as they described JFK's injuries, condition, and care. The three major networks, ABC, CBS, and NBC, devoted all their airtime to stories involving the assassination attempt and Kennedy's medical condition.

When it became apparent that the wait for an answer might be longer than anticipated, the networks, needing filler segments after the initial story was covered and re-covered from every angle, found plenty to report. The presumed shooter, a man named Lee Oswald, had been caught within hours and was led about the Dallas Police Station on Friday like a prize calf. Film from the location showed a mob scene of police, newsmen, politicians, and local hangers-on jammed into the station while Oswald was paraded from his cell to an interrogation room and back again through crowded hallways. A detective waded through the throng to his office with the Mannlicher-Carcano rifle, allegedly used by Oswald, raised high over his head.

Bobby and Kenny, watching the television yesterday in the communications room, had seen that mayhem and were appalled. It appeared to be chaos, pure and simple. Irate at such obvious confusion and ineptitude on the part of the local police, Bobby called Nick Katzenbach, the Acting Attorney General, to look into taking control of the investigation in order to re-establish order. Katzenbach was ahead of him on this, but had run into a surprising legal roadblock. Both he and Hoover, in trying to intervene, had discovered that an attempted (or for that matter, successful) presidential assassination was not a federal crime. In fact neither was the killing of a senator, congressman, or vice president, even though the killing of an FBI agent was. It therefore fell under the jurisdiction of the local authorities to investigate and prosecute such offences.

Killing a Secret Service agent was a federal offence. Advocating the overthrow of the government was federal. *Threatening* a president was a federal offense. But the shooting of a president was a federal offense only if it was part of a plot or conspiracy. And only Bobby, Hoover, and Johnson knew that, since the idea of a conspiracy was being quashed, that reason for claiming federal jurisdiction could not be used in the Oswald case.

In fact, from the way it was playing out on television, it appeared that Oswald had more than sufficient grounds to avoid prosecution altogether, just from the inept manner in which he was being treated as a prisoner. He had publicly asked for legal representation numerous times, even on national television, but none was provided. And yet, he was interrogated for hours by the Dallas Police with both Secret Service and FBI agents present. It would be a national travesty if his case were later tossed out by a judge who could do nothing but dismiss it due to police and prosecutorial incompetence. Barefoot Sanders, the U.S. federal attorney in Dallas, was trying to figure a way around this conundrum. He drafted a number of subpoenas, hoping that one might be acceptable to a federal judge who would allow the case and the suspects in custody to be removed from Dallas. With prompting from Washington, he wanted federal agents to be allowed to march into the Dallas Police Station and take their trophy away from them. But his efforts so far were ineffective, as the law was simply not on his side.

Numerous television networks, both American and international, began reporting on the violent subtext of the Dallas community and the role it played in fostering an atmosphere that could incubate an assassin within a democratic country. The BBC created a multi-segment report detailing the rise to prominence of the John Birch Society and the Ku Klux Klan in the Southern states, particularly in Texas. There were a number of revealing interviews, one of which culminated with a sobering comment by a Klan leader proclaiming "a nigger-lovin' president deserves whatever he gits, and that's a fact."

Such negative reporting over the days that followed the shooting could not help but have a devastating effect on the City of Dallas and, more generally, on the State of Texas. Many residents were already appalled at the climate of discord and the "City of Hate" moniker that had been ascribed to their home. Lyndon Johnson, the leading Texas politician, was asked to shore up the local image with some official comments. But his homilies regarding "the great State of Texas" and its ability to "rise to the defense of freedom," recorded by reporters in Washington, fell flat in the face of the more rigorous flailing it was receiving from the general press.

Contrasting with the strident ultraconservatives were the quiet, supportive throngs whose numbers steadily increased on the grounds of Parkland Hospital. In the first night alone, three to four thousand people waited silently outside the medical center—praying, hoping, waiting for word.

And even as people came and went, the number steadily grew until it appeared there were eight to ten thousand keeping vigil by Sunday morning. It was not a boisterous crowd. The silent mass of observers, waiting for the revival of a single man lying in a hospital room above, was a moving sight. It was a larger version of the assemblage Bobby Kennedy had passed the Friday evening of his arrival from Love Field. It brought home to him the effect his brother had had on the American people. By some he was hated, that was true, but by far more, he was loved.

* * *

"Bobby, what do you think about bringing down the children?" asked Jackie.

It was Sunday morning. She was sitting with Bobby and Dave Powers in Room 326. It had been almost two days since Jack had been shot. As much as possible, she had stayed at his bedside since her arrival, and although a great deal was happening in the world outside the walls of Parkland Medical Center, for Jackie and those sitting in the room, nothing had changed. Before them lay the president of the United States, possibly the most powerful man on the planet. No pomp or ceremony, just an unconscious and severely damaged body lying on a standard hospital bed in an ordinary intensive care room. All so mundane. All in stark contrast to the importance of the event in its national and international significance and to the psyche of the American people.

Medical experts pored over the details of the wounds inflicted and the minutiae of the president's operation. The doctors mentioned many times they had done all they could do and at this point it was up to Mr. Kennedy's innate healing process. So after the first two days, most knew they were waiting, not on any medical breakthrough or new treatment, but on the essential mystery that allows for the human spirit to regenerate the flesh and find the strength to go on.

"I have been thinking about this quite a bit," continued Jackie. "I know this is not the best environment for Caroline and John—it's frightening to me, let alone to two little children. It would also be difficult to keep this private, with all the press coverage." She was talking slowly and deliberately, asking for his opinion, but Bobby could tell she had already decided. "You know how much Jack loves the kids. He's a different person when they're around. They connect with him differently. He's more himself."

"Yeah, I know," agreed Bobby. The recent loss of their son Patrick, stillborn just a few months earlier, had staggered both Jack and Jackie. He had always been devoted to his children, but Bobby had noticed recently that Jack seemed more deeply appreciative of Caroline and John-John.

"Well, I want to bring them down. For him. I talked to the doctor this morning. He said that if Jack shows improvement they would remove the oxygen tent, allowing him to breathe more normally. Without the tent it wouldn't be so alarming. To John he would appear to be sleeping. It's Caroline I'm more concerned about. She loves her daddy, but she's getting to the age where she can understand more mature ideas. I'm hoping she'll respond well enough to be able to be near her father without feeling frightened by his condition."

"Where would they stay?" asked Bobby.

"I had Mary Gallagher call Lyndon's office back in Washington. He knows a lot of people here. He said there's a nice house available for us to use only three miles away. The children could stay there with Maude while we spend our time here. They could come and visit regularly, depending on how they react when they first get down here. I guess it all depends on how Jack does over the next few days. I just wanted you to know."

"Okay." Bobby was listening and responding, but his attention seemed elsewhere.

"Bobby, are you alright?" asked Jackie. All of them were going through the grief and shock of what was happening in their own way, but Bobby looked so tired. She had sensed a change in him since yesterday afternoon. Instead of being fully engaged with the events that were occurring, he seemed preoccupied and distant. Maybe he was just beginning to realize the depth of his feelings after the whirlwind of activities the first day. But something else seemed wrong.

"You haven't slept since you've been here, have you?" added Dave. He had seen Bobby the evening before, awake and brooding in the chair by the window in Jack's room. "Bobby, you need to take a break, maybe use one of the extra rooms down the hall and crash for a few hours."

Bobby took a long breath, "I'm okay," he responded, with a wan smile directed at Jackie. "There's just been a lot to deal with."

"You going to give a press conference?" asked Dave. There were rumors flying that Jack was dead or that the family was covering up his real condition. In the current state of affairs, rumors such as these needed to be punctured, as they tended to spread beyond their origins far too quickly. The White House medical specialists, Dr. Burkley and Dr. Kliendorf, gave regular press briefings in the large auditorium off the medical wing of Parkland. It had been specially outfitted as a temporary press hall, serving as a focus for updates and information the administration wanted to release. It mostly involved reports on the medical conditions of the president and first lady, but also strayed into information regarding the police investigation into the shooting. Many in the press were also focusing on the Dallas mindset and exposing the hotbed of ultra-conservatism that had allowed such violence to occur. Pierre had raised the idea of Bobby speaking to them in a nationally televised press conference as Jack had done so many times. It was hoped that Bobby's presence in a similar milieu would help allay fears as well as bring some focus to the widespread uncertainty.

"Yeah. In a half hour or so. In fact, I better go. I need to talk it over with Pierre." As Bobby started to rise, Jackie leaned over and kissed him on the cheek. It was a surprisingly personal show of affection from her.

"You know Jack trusts you," said Jackie looking intently at him. "I'm sure whatever you need to do, he'd have complete faith in your decision." She added, with her hand on his, "And so do I."

Bobby was deeply affected by her support. Did she know what was going on? That he had surrendered his role as defender of his brother and agreed to cover up the investigation to root out his assailants in exchange for a lessening of international tensions? And if she knew all this, would she still have faith in his decision? *How could she?* thought Bobby as he departed.

* * *

Bobby walked down to the second floor, followed by Jiggs, to meet up with Salinger for the short walk between buildings to the hospital amphitheater-cum-press auditorium. The conference location had been switched the day before to remove it somewhat from the care portion of the hospital complex, yet still keep it close enough for the doctors and presidential staff to provide updates when necessary. Pierre was just finishing up and met Bobby in the hall to take the elevator down to the lobby. He had a sheaf of papers in his hands that he had quickly grabbed after ending a hurried call.

"How is he?" asked Pierre.

"Same," said Bobby, not looking at Pierre as they walked.

"Hoover announced Oswald was the only guy. Lone gunman. The press is going to ask you about it down there."

"Yeah, I know."

"What are you going to say?"

"It's their game for now. I'm not in the loop," said Bobby, catching Jiggs' eye for a moment as they turned to go into the elevator. They were uncharacteristically silent for the short one-floor ride. Pierre could see Bobby was exhausted. He seemed to have aged unnaturally over the last year, with all the crises he was handling for the president—juggling the civil rights eruptions, the Cuban missile crisis, the Mafia investigations, the re-election of his brother for a second term, and now his brother's shooting. Much more than one man should be asked to handle, and yet Bobby did all that and more. But it was taking a toll. Pierre knew about Bobby's meeting with Janet Travell, the White House physician, a few weeks before, and that she had told him to take food supplements to attempt to curb his weight loss. He was physically shrinking from the load of all the pressures he was carrying. And yet today, if it was possible, he seemed worse. He had gone beyond reasonable limits before, and always seemed to find a reserve to draw from. But watching him in the quiet privacy of the elevator, Pierre wondered if he had finally overdrawn the account.

The lobby was mostly empty. It was secured by the Secret Service, but there was still some activity, since this was an operating hospital and the patients on the many upper floors still needed attention from the staff. An agent met Bobby and Pierre as they got off.

"Sir, the Mayor and City Manager of Dallas are waiting. They said they knew you were about to give a news conference and wanted to have a word with you if they could."

Bobby glanced over at Pierre as they started to move through the lobby, but Pierre shrugged, indicating he was unaware of their intentions.

"Yeah, where are they?" asked Bobby.

"Right over here," replied the agent, pointing toward the wall of windows near the main door.

Two men were looking toward Bobby and came over when the Secret Service agent gestured to them. *Does everyone in Texas have a damn cowboy hat?* thought Bobby as the approaching men removed theirs.

"Earle Cabell, Mayor of Dallas," said the medium-height man with heavy black-rimmed glasses as he reached out his hand. He looked like a stouter Robert McNamara, with his slicked-back black hair. "And this is...."

"Elgin Crull, City Manager," said the shorter man, completing the introduction. There was a perfunctory shaking of hands. It was obvious that Bobby had time constraints.

"Mr. Kennedy, we are profoundly sorry for your brother, the president, and we truly wish for his speedy recovery," said the mayor. "And we are so sorry for Mrs. Kennedy. We hear she's up and around. Please give that little lady our best wishes." He knew he had only a short interval to have his say, so he started right in. "The city is taking quite a beating from the press, Mr. Kennedy. They're all over us down here. They seem to think the people of Dallas are responsible for this fella Oswald." He grimaced in disgust, glancing at Crull for support. "In fact, you might be interested to know that we're havin' him moved this mornin' over to the county facilities. Chief Curry wanted to sneak him over late last night, but Elgin and I," he said, gesturing to his partner, "we thought it would be much better to do it with the full observation of the press. You know, we don't want to hide nothin' here. Now I think you know that this could've happened anywhere, but we're seeing Dallas singled out as a hateful place. We've had calls comin' in all day cancelin' conventions and pullin' away business from the community, and we were hopin' that you could maybe say a few good words about us in your press conference. Tell the world that the people of Dallas are good people, God-fearin' folks, and maybe help us out a bit." The city manager looked on, nodding his head as the mayor made his points. "This here is a letter signed by a group of upstandin' Dallas business leaders, with some information about Dallas and a request for a good word for us," he said as he handed an envelope to Bobby, who didn't look down as he took it. They had come, literally with hats in hand, to ask Bobby to promote the Dallas business community.

Pierre could see the mayor was about to continue, but Bobby interrupted. He extended his hand slightly and tapped the envelope he had just been handed against the mayor's chest. "Would you mind stepping over here for a moment?" he asked, gesturing to both men as he moved toward a small phone alcove off the main entry.

Pierre had spent a lot of time with Bobby, and the quiet intensity of this simple move scared him. He had seen the attorney general erupt a few times in the past and knew Bobby Kennedy was not beyond having a physical altercation. Pierre shared a worried look with Jiggs.

A few yards away, Bobby turned to the mayor and moved in close, jabbing his finger in the man's chest. "If it weren't for the press and the witnesses standing around, I would punch you in your face so damn hard I would knock you to the floor." Bobby was up close in the mayor's face. "You stand there with your well-to-do arrogance and comfortable racism

and ask me to support you in that, and give Dallas a glowing recommenda-
tion to the nation, while my brother is lying upstairs dying from a product
of your hate." Bobby's raised voice could easily be heard by those nearby.
Pierre could see the man was shocked by Bobby's feral intensity, realizing
he was on the edge of violence.

"Now, I don't—," started the mayor.

"Your town's well-nurtured spite for all that my brother has worked
for has been the cause of all this," continued Bobby, as the mayor tried to
object. "All the hate! All the fucking hate that's coming from your city!"
Bobby's mood was a mix of anger and despair. "And you want me to give
you a good word?" There was a long moment of silent rippling tension
as Bobby stood facing the two men. They stepped back, and he walked
around them toward the door. Pierre and Jiggs followed. With hardly an
added motion, Bobby dropped the envelope in the trash bin on the way
through the exit.

It was a large steamy room in which Robert Kennedy would address
the crowds of reporters and television cameramen from the national and
international press. Bright klieg lights added to the oven-like quality of
the hall, especially on the podium at the front. A dozen large network
cameras lined the walls along the side aisles. Cables and power cords ran
under everyone's feet as perspiring reporters and network anchors vied for
position. The hall was densely packed this morning. Although every scrap
of information regarding John Kennedy's condition was considered important news, having his brother, the attorney general, scheduled to speak
this morning made it a riveting event people around the world would be
watching.

Pierre, Bobby, and Jiggs entered through the guarded back door to
avoid the crush of media at the front. The excited buzz of the crowd increased when word passed that Robert Kennedy was in the building. The
anticipation was short-lived. Without preamble, Bobby made his way
quickly through the aides packed around the back entry and stepped up
to the small lectern where the television lights and microphones were focused. On home sets, the nation viewed the grainy black and white image
of the attorney general as he removed a piece of paper from his suit coat
and unfolded it. Never acclaimed as a public speaker himself, Bobby always admired his brother's ability to charm a crowd. He wished he had
such talents. "Please be seated," he directed. "I have a short statement to

make and will then answer questions."

In front of the quieting crowd, Bobby laid the paper on the lectern and absentmindedly smoothed the wrinkles from the sheet as he seemed to be reaching for the right words to begin. "I only want to speak for a few minutes," he began in his distinctive Boston inflection. "I want to thank the nation for the outpouring of hope and support for President Kennedy. Really, it has been an international outpouring, as we have received communiqués of hope and encouragement from almost every country and national leader around the world." Bobby spoke slowly and strongly, and although he was able to keep his emotions in check, his somber delivery conveyed his feelings. "It is not only my brother who lies in a room of this medical facility, or just the president of our United States of America. No, it is a world leader who lies injured here today. A world leader who has tried to sow hope and justice throughout our country and has tried to bring peace to our strife-torn international family. So, to the people of America and to the people of the world who are watching, I would like to sincerely thank you for your concern and the outpouring of emotion for John Kennedy." He paused and looked into the pool of reporters. "I know you have questions," he said, and nodded to the first hand that went up.

"Mr. Kennedy, could you give us a confirmation of the president's condition? A Catholic priest was seen entering and exiting this morning from the president's wing. Has the president received last rites?" asked a UPI reporter in the front row.

"No, he has not. The priest said the Mass and gave a blessing to the president, but not Extreme Unction, the...uh...last rites of the Catholic faith. Many of the president's closest associates are Catholic, and a local monsignor was asked to come in for all of us since it is Sunday morning. The president's condition is still critical. He has not regained consciousness after the operation. I'm aware that Doctors Kliendorf and Burkley have been keeping the press informed of the president's medical care, so I will not go into that here. But he has been badly wounded, and the doctors are quite concerned about the possibility of infection. But at the moment that problem has not arisen. We are simply, very hopefully, waiting." He pointed to another raised hand.

"If the president were dead, would you tell us?" The question was from the back row, blurted out by what appeared to be a local reporter, given the brimmed hat still on his head.

Bobby paused and looked intently at the man. He was obviously angered by the question. "I would." There was a rustling in the group, as feelings were tense, but this question had overstepped the bounds of taste, even for the press corps.

"There are rumors circulating that the president gave you or others instructions regarding presidential powers and operations when he was lucid and—" began another reporter.

"No, he has not communicated in any way. He has not regained consciousness since his arrival at the hospital and did not speak to anyone during his initial arrival nor during the entire time that I've been here. I realize there is a great deal of concern regarding presidential powers, and the position of Vice President Johnson, and what role he should take in the interim, but there has been no communication at all."

"In the event of the death of Mr. Kennedy, have there been plans made for the transfer of power to Vice President Johnson?"

"I am not thinking along those lines, and we are making no plans for that eventuality. We have well-defined constitutional guidelines that would come into play under those circumstances, but I am not pursuing that line of preparation."

"How has his care been at the hospital? Would it not be better for the president to be treated in a more modern facility?"

"We discussed this very issue early on and dismissed it. The president is too ill to be moved. His condition is precarious, and it was determined that there was too much danger in transporting him, say, to Bethesda Naval Hospital, or any other facility for that matter. We decided instead to bring the expertise and specialized equipment to him. This is not to denigrate in any way the conditions here at Parkland. As you have already been informed, his care has been excellent. His original surgical team, comprising Dr. Marshall and his staff, we've all concurred, did an exceptional job. In fact, I want to personally and publicly thank them for their professionalism."

"Do you feel comfortable having your brother stay here in Dallas for treatment? With all that has happened here, do you feel able to depend on this location for his safety and healing?"

"Yes, I do. I'm glad you brought this up, so let me be clear about this. There are elements here in Dallas that have worked against the aims of this administration since we took office. And even though there will always be differences of opinion about the direction any administration will take, those differences can be aired in a public and civil manner that does not include violence. That is what differentiates our country from those with harshly restrictive governments. The intolerance expressed here in Texas, and especially in Dallas, is born of ignorance. And it is the ignorance of the few, not the many. When my brother rode through Dallas just two short days ago, he was greeted with an overwhelming public expression of support. He called me the night before and spoke of this in very encouraging terms. He was happy with the people of Texas and their abundant welcome. He had not expected to be so appreciated, aware as he was of the numerous recent civil disturbances and the harsh local rhetoric. It is not Dallas that is to blame for my brother's injury, but a very vocal subsection of the Dallas community that seems to equate progressiveness with treason, and reasonable compromise with capitulation. It is to those individuals he came to speak while here, till his voice was silenced. Temporarily silenced," he added.

"We've been told Mrs. Kennedy is awake. Could you describe her condition?"

"Jackie, Mrs. Kennedy, was slightly injured with a bullet wound to the neck. It was minor, but, as you've been informed, it caused a great deal of blood loss. She's doing very well regarding her injuries and has been in with the president continuously since she awoke from sedation early yesterday morning."

"The *Washington Post* and *The New York Times* editorials today called for a Congressional investigation into the shooting of the president. There are many rumors regarding the possibility of foreign ties to Mr. Oswald and the manner in which the investigation is being handled here in Dallas. As attorney general, what is your opinion of this?"

Bobby paused, distressed at the answer he was about to give. "As you are probably aware, this shooting, even though of the president, is a state matter. At this time, it will be handled by the legal system of the State of Texas. That is simply the law. It is too early to try to untangle the reasons for Mr. Oswald's actions, but I firmly believe justice will be served in this investigation. I will do my best to see to that. But at this point I would ask you all to withhold inflammatory statements based upon rumors or partial information. I realize the forces acting upon you all to expose the full story of the events here, but I would ask for patience." Bobby had said the last slowly and deliberately. He looked tired and on the edge of emotion as he spoke, and it was obvious to anyone watching that he was having great difficulty dissociating his feelings from the factual comments he was making. "Thank you. I believe there is nothing more I can add at this time."

He turned and stepped quickly from the platform, leaving behind the paper he had laid on the lectern. An enterprising reporter surreptitiously picked it up in the close-packed jostling of the conference room. To his surprise, it was nearly empty. It appeared to be a note the attorney general had started to his son, encouraging him to be strong in the face of all that was transpiring and to pray for "Uncle Jack."

* * *

Returning through the hospital corridors to Jack's room after the short press conference, Robert first noticed the smell—the odor of aging floral bouquets wafting through the hospital. Their scent overlaid the pungent medicinal aroma of an active medical facility—ammonia and Lysol mixed with roses and chrysanthemums. In the short walk outside into the warm Dallas Sunday morning air, through the passage between buildings to the auditorium, his senses had cleared of the cloying aroma of death. He had not realized how accustomed he had become to the medicinal smells until he re-entered the hospital. Those olfactory agents seemed to permeate every inch of the building, attaching to each molecule as if to be sure all were reminded that this was an arena of profound transformation—either the cessation of life and dreams, or their reprieve by the mercurial grace of God. No matter how long he had had to adjust to being within the walls of this facility, morbidity clung to his spirit like ammonia to his clothing.

Bobby stopped off in the hall to talk with the head nurse, Evey Morgan, the primary caregiver to the president, and then walked into the president's quiet room, saying nothing to Jackie, who looked up as he entered. Dave Powers rested on the sofa. Kenny O'Donnell was sitting by the window. Bobby sat down in a chair next to him. Looking over at Kenny, he was about to ask a question when the door opened again.

"Oswald's been shot!" exclaimed Pierre Salinger excitedly through a surgical mask held up to his face. He was trying to be respectful, but was bursting with alarm. As soon as he leaned in further and saw Bobby and Kenny sitting by the window, he said, "We just saw it on the TV. Some guy just shot Oswald!"

"Oswald?" asked Jackie questioningly, looking from Bobby to Dave Powers. It had been less than two days since Jack's shooting, and even though the rest of the world had been following the news with agonized attention, there had been no such interest from her. She was focused on the health of one man, and had paid little attention to much else.

"The guy they picked up for shooting Ja—for the shooting," said Pierre, unable to even say it out loud.

"I know that, but the police have him," she said, looking from one to the other. "Don't they?"

Bobby and Kenny looked at each other in surprise and simultaneously sprang from their chairs. They exited the room and started to run down the hall. Pierre, already preceding them, ran toward the exit stairs to go down to the press communications room on the second floor. Jiggs was waiting in the hall with the door open, already aware of the commotion.

"The Dallas cops were moving him to the county jail," said Pierre, panting. "They had it all filmed on national television. Some guy just stepped up and plugged him in the gut!" Pierre was not a very athletic man, and with the run up the stairs and through the hall to JFK's room and then the turnaround back to the communications room on the lower floor, he was mostly spent. He quickly lost ground to Kenny and Bobby. They heard his comments as they raced past him. They ran down the stairs two and three at a time. As they burst into the lower hall, they could already see a crowd of people around the door to the communications room. There were four televisions monitoring the three major networks, with the remaining one for the White House cameras in the press auditorium. Bobby and Kenny pushed their way into the crowd.

All three networks were in a state of pandemonium, fruitlessly trying to describe verbally what millions of people had already watched live on NBC. Each network replayed it with its own reporter doing the commentary. "Oh my God! Oh my God! Oswald has been shot! Lee Harvey Oswald has been shot! There is total panic here...absolute pandemonium in the basement at the Dallas Police Headquarters. Police have their guns drawn. But Oswald has been shot!" On the screens, a video replayed the different phases of the shooting. A chaotic scene showed reporters and police struggling with an assailant after the grimacing Oswald recoiled into an accompanying detective. He had been shot in the stomach at close range. Cameras were swung and tilted at weird angles as the scene devolved into confusion. But over it all, an announcer claimed that the accused assassin of President Kennedy was himself being assassinated in the basement of the local police station.

The announcer again came on. "A man lunged from the crowd of detectives around the presumed assailant of President Kennedy. He had a gun in his hand. He quickly jammed it into Mr. Oswald's stomach, fir-

ing one shot. He was wrestled to the ground. An ambulance is arriving...
flashing red lights. Mr. Oswald is lying on the ground...motionless. Now
he is being lifted onto a stretcher...he appears lifeless...his arms limp at
his sides...into the open back hatch. There is blood on the concrete...his
clothing. The ambulance is pulling out...red lights flashing."

They watched some of the pandemonium on the TV as the ambulance picked up Oswald. Kenny grabbed Bobby's arm and tugged him
toward the door. "I bet they're bringing him here," said Kenny, "to Parkland." Again they went running, down another flight of stairs and across
the length of the lower floor toward the emergency bays, the same bays
through which the president had been delivered to Parkland two days earlier. Jiggs was ahead of them. The muffled sound of an ambulance siren
could be heard as it approached. A crowd of agents, police, and hospital
staff had assembled, having been alerted to another important arrival over
the police dispatch.

Jiggs, Kenny, and Bobby arrived at the emergency bay platform just in
time to see the ambulance turning in off Amelia Court. The siren was silenced as the vehicle swung around, screeched to a halt, then backed up to
the entry. Doctors rushed to the back of the ambulance, climbing inside
to work on Oswald right there. After a few moments of feverish attempts
at resuscitation, Oswald was lifted out of the vehicle, set on a gurney, and
quickly wheeled away. He was bloodied and motionless. The detective
seen in the televised shooting was also in the back of the ambulance. He
followed the gurney out of the bay and toward the emergency room. The
empty handcuff that had attached him to Oswald was still dangling from
his wrist.

Jiggs was out on the tarmac between the surrounding cordoned crowds
and the president's brother. Most of the medical staff followed the gurney, while Bobby and Kenny remained on the emergency bay platform,
watching them disappear into the hospital. Ironically, they were following
the same route they had followed only two days earlier with the wounded
president.

The ambulance technician was leaning against the flip-up back door
of the modified station wagon looking grim. Bobby and Kenny dropped
down off the platform to talk to him. "That guy is done," he said, "I heard
the death rattle as we were coming in. There's no mistakin' *that* sound.
They're gonna' go through the motions, but he's dead as a stone."

The technician shut the backdoor of the ambulance, got into the driver's seat, and started to drive off. As he departed, Bobby and Kenny found themselves standing nearly alone on the hot black asphalt of the Parkland Medical Center Emergency bay, partially shaded from the hot sun of a dusty Texas morning by the bay overhang.

"What the *fuck* is going on here?" asked Kenny slowly.

Saying nothing, Bobby just stared intensely into the distance, following the departing driver. But Jiggs, fearfully surveying the crowd beyond the police lines around the ambulance bay, hustled the president's brother back into the protective safety of the hospital confines—out of view of preying eyes and unknown dangers.

Chapter 12

We must face the fact that the United States is neither omnipotent nor omniscient,
that we are only 6 percent of the world's population, that we cannot impose our will
upon the other 94 percent, that we cannot right every wrong nor reverse each adversity,
and that therefore there cannot be an American solution to every world problem.
—*John F. Kennedy, Seattle, 1961*

I used to think that the causes of war were predominantly economic.
I then came to think that they were more psychological. I am now coming to think
that they are decisively personal, arising from the defects and ambitions
of those who have the power to influence the currents of nations.
—*H. Liddell Hart, Military Strategist*

Sunday, September 29, 1968
Camp David, Virginia

More attracted to the cosmopolitan delights of Washington, D.C., and the sailing activities of the Atlantic Coast near his home in Hyannisport, Massachusetts, President Kennedy rarely used the Camp David retreat during the first years of his presidency. Located in the Catoctin Mountains within a two-hour drive of the White House, it had been secretly selected by Franklin Delano Roosevelt during World War II as a retreat from the political and climatic pressures of the city. At an elevation of 1800 feet, it provided a welcome escape from the withering humidity and scheming statecraft of DC in the summer months. It was initially planned as a boys' camp, with six small cabins with bunkbed cots on 143 acres, and included a swimming pool, recreation hall, common showers, and other rough-hewn amenities. Over the years, with successive presidential improvements, it grew into a modestly well-appointed retreat center that provided, if not all the amenities of home, at least a semblance of comfort within a quiet natural setting. Successive presidents were usually charmed by its reflective and soothing environment. Its natural wooded surroundings and long walking trails gave tranquil respite from the harsh public pressures of the Capital.

Perhaps Kennedy's introduction to the retreat, a bleak consultation with former President Eisenhower just after the Bay of Pigs fiasco, left a bad impression. But just before Dallas, he and Jackie had vacated Glen Ora. They had not yet moved into the newer home they were building at nearby Wexford, so they spent many a weekend at Camp David. Jackie even trailered a few of her horses up to the retreat so she could ride the extensive trails around the protected reserve. Since that period, even though they unexpectedly returned to live at Glen Ora, the president had been much more comfortable in the compound. With the help of Jackie's designer eye, he upgraded many of the retreat's structures to give a more refined flavor to the rural camp setting. From that point on, Camp David figured into the presidential agenda for informal meetings with foreign dignitaries. With media pressures removed, their public personas were often softened in the intimate and restful setting. Kennedy invited Khrushchev for a long weekend in late '66, during which the groundwork was laid for the emerging détente between the two Cold War adversaries. It seemed that not a month went by without the press reporting another meeting at Camp David with a foreign dignitary, or a council for some world body with which an agreement was discussed or a treaty signed outside the pressure cooker of the political city below.

It was a half-hour Marine One flight from the White House, and slightly less from Glen Ora. Patrick accompanied the president and British Ambassador David Ormsby-Gore, along with a number of aides, to the mountain retreat after their day of golf. It had been a twilight flight, and even though Patrick was still surprised at his newfound status as a traveler with the president, the novelty of the flight had him staring out the Marine One windows, nearly indifferent to his fellow passengers. Watching the presidential helicopter lift off from the pad at the White House was a common occurrence for reporters on the Capital beat, but being inside the aircraft was something else entirely.

Patrick relished the moment of watching the small set of links on which the presidential party had golfed earlier in the day recede into the surrounding hills as they quickly gained altitude from the pasture at Glen Ora. The orange and red dappled hills were beautiful in their emerging fall colors. He watched intently as the craft was expertly guided to the mountaintop retreat of Camp David, coming to rest on a pad just a short distance from a cluster of structures. He could make out a swimming pool, and the small three-hole golf course that had been constructed at the parklike estate by former President Eisenhower, the Duffer-in-Chief, when he was president.

Kennedy was meeting at Camp David with his staff and representatives of the international team from the Paris Peace Talks regarding the winding down of the Vietnam conflict. Negotiations were being finalized for the United Nations involvement in the upcoming elections there, and Kennedy, Ormsby-Gore, the French Ambassador, and UN representatives were all arriving for the short conference.

Patrick dined with many of the conferees that evening in the dining room at the main lodge and even slipped off to watch a film in the small projection theatre—a relic of the Eisenhower Administration that had been upgraded to satisfy JFK's love of westerns and musicals. Restless, or possibly in pain, the president had quietly exited mid-showing and retired early. Patrick wound his way back to his room in one of the renovated cabins that housed visitors to the compound. A note had been left for him to meet with the president midmorning tomorrow in the study at the main lodge for a book session.

He slept fitfully that night, with dreams of missed golf swings, enraged cows attacking the presidential golf party, and a beautiful but aloof librarian strolling past him, bare arms loaded with books, ignoring his longing stares. It seemed his mind was trying to digest all the events of the past couple of weeks simultaneously but was unable to cram in all the information. Instead, curious details overlapped and magnified, like the small black wristwatch band on Jenna's bare forearm. He found it so enormously appealing, taking on great importance, but making no sense upon waking.

"What do I care if she even has a watch!" he exclaimed at one point in the middle of the night to no one in particular. He was alone in his room.

He woke a number of times before dawn finally arrived, forgetting where he was and how he had gotten there. By the time he came fully awake in the very early Sunday morning light, he was relieved to be able to get up and go outdoors. The camp was silent, vacant except for a few Marine guards who acknowledged his presence with a nod as he walked along the gravel paths around the main buildings. He proceeded deeper into the woods, allowing himself to explore and get lost among the chestnut oaks, red maple, and black birch. It was so very quiet here in the cold, misty morning. The only sound was the crinkling his steps made on the drying leaves that had fallen from the changing trees that were slowly displaying their splendid colors in the rising light. Patrick was reminded how much he loved the outdoors. He had hiked with his father in the forests around Virginia and had loved the solitude found in a quiet natural forest. "A cathedral of nature," his dad used to say, "beats church sermons by a country mile."

Patrick found a bit more order in his thoughts as he walked, the confusing mindstorm of the sleepless night receding. He wondered back on his time spent recently with the president. It had only been a month since he had been approached—no, appointed—as the president's memoirist. They had met several times, mostly at the White House except for yesterday's golf outing at Glen Ora, and he was still trying to get a handle on just who he was dealing with.

Last week he had a curious discussion with Devona, his editor, about how reporters became ensnared in the Kennedy mystique, losing all sense of objectivity. Patrick mentioned he was trying to remain levelheaded and dispassionate in his professional involvement, but was afraid that he was drifting toward the whirlpool of admiration that would ruin his objectivity.

"You're one of the few people I know with 'adoraphobia,' Patrick Hennessey," she had laughingly claimed. "Most reporters would give their first child to be on talking terms with the president of the United States."

"I don't got one," replied Patrick.

"That's because you ignored that poor Katherine girl," she shot back uncharacteristically. "Sometimes I think you have tap water for brains, Patrick Hennessey!" Devona had liked Katherine. They met once when Patrick drove her up to New York for an outing and stopped to drop off some papers at Devona's office. She would often ask how Katherine was, but had stopped mentioning her at all after they split up—until now.

"Um, I have a call on line two," he said in response.

"You don't have a line two," she said, laughing. "And don't worry about getting lost in the presidential puppy-love parade. I don't think you could come unmoored even if you tried. You sometimes seem like an unanchored ship because of the way your interests wander, but I've known for a long time you have a solid steel cable down there. It's just well below the surface."

He hoped she was right, but he was wavering. His time spent with the man was a blur of fascination. JFK's confident charms were so evident, and with the mantle of the presidency upon him, they were magnified tenfold. Patrick often saw advisors and social hangers-on subsumed by his presence, losing a certain vitality of independence. It was something that Patrick resisted, but he was aware of the magnetism pulling toward that end. Oddly, Kennedy seemed to respond to him more energetically when he was being his normal irreverent self than when he was in awe of the man's place and position. It was probably refreshing to have an independent response from someone around him, which made Patrick respect the man for his character, thus dragging him back again into the camp of his doting admirers.

But Patrick could sense there were restricted territories in Kennedy's personality. It was nothing he could put his finger on, but he sensed a wavering between personal and impersonal that reflected more complex motives at work below the surface. Patrick was not so foolish as to think that spending a half-dozen hours a week with a politician of the president's stature would bring him into the inner folds of friendship. JFK had boyhood friends for whom he reserved that circle, and of those Patrick knew little. But he did sense a thawing of the president's reserve, and inklings of openness and friendship that Patrick found compelling.

As he wandered through the crisp autumn leaves, his mind returned to Jenna, the indifferent siren of his tome tomb, the Library of Congress. The woman who haunted the wristwatch compartment in his dreamscape. His thoughts constantly returned to their recent interactions. He was sure there was an interest there, behind her feigned indifference, just as he was sure there was a knowing higher intelligence behind the inexplicable churning of events of the human race. God would certainly not be slipping him the secret decoder ring to the human agenda, but he felt there was at least an odds-on chance Jenna might let him through her front door.

Thinking of his conversation with Devona, he realized one telling difference between his past relationship with Katherine and his imaginary one with Jenna—other than the imaginary part, that is. With Jenna, he had a constant and appealing partner in his thoughts, as she came unbidden in all manner of situations. He would find himself reliving conversations at the Library of Congress, all having a much more positive outcome, of course. This also included imaginary discussions of music, writing, Washington politics, romance, and even library book retrieval criteria—with her in the shared starring role. But with Katherine he had often needed to remind himself to include her in his inner world, as his mind drifted out of her orbit in ways he felt no compelling interest to explore. Even in moments spent with the president, Patrick's mind would slip off to thoughts of sharing the experience with Jenna, and he was sure she would be filled with razor-sharp perceptions.

The sun was beginning to warm the wooded path. The morning mists, both internal and external, were clearing. He was getting hungry, and time had passed quickly. Breakfast and a midmorning meeting with the leader of the free world awaited.

* * *

"We hold the truth that all men are created equal. They are endowed by their Creator with certain unalienable rights, among these are life, liberty, and the pursuit of happiness." The president read from a sheet of paper he was holding. "Recognize that, Hennessey?"

"The Declaration of Independence," replied Patrick. "Sort of."

"Actually spoken by one of our more reviled antagonists, Ho Chi Minh," continued the president as he put the paper back on the side desk. "He uttered those choice phrases, speaking in Vietnamese, on September 2, 1945, in Hanoi's Ba Dinh Square, to a huge crowd of mostly barefoot peasants—hundreds of thousands of them. It was his declaration for a free and united Vietnam, his attempt to notify the United States that he was trying to establish a fair and just society and needed to be released from the oppression of French and Japanese occupation. Vietnam was on the cusp of independence and was groping idealistically for a future path. But because Minh embraced communism as the best bet for the unification of his country and release from foreign intervention, we proceeded to demonize him and every action he took, with little or no understanding of his motives or intentions. America basically sold Vietnam back into bondage, giving back control of the country to the French after the brief flicker of independence they'd carved out of the mayhem of World War II. And that was just one of many moments of politically arrogant blindness from which bloomed much of the trouble we have seen in that poor country.

"It makes one wonder. Here is a foreign leader who knew enough about the American Revolution to invoke its essence in a public display. Now whether that display was for propagandizing, as some would claim, or a sincere expression of their leader's position, it nonetheless demonstrated he had enough understanding of the United States and its history to invoke it at all. We did not know much about Ho Chi Minh, or his country's struggle for independence, or for that matter, anything about Vietnam, yet we were quick to declare them our enemy and engage them in war because they were communists."

President Kennedy and Patrick were sitting in the study at the Main Lodge. It had a rustic interior with open timber walls and an air of cultivated country charm, a feeling usually achieved at great expense. The president sat in his rocking chair, which the U.S. Marshals always delivered to presidential destinations. The gentle movement eased his back pain and allowed him to sit for longer stretches. He seemed more careful today in his physical movements and only motioned for Patrick to have a seat, not rising to greet him when he entered the study. Patrick wondered if Kennedy was paying the physical toll of having had a golf outing the day before, and if he had labored unseen to get to his chair before Patrick's arrival. But the president quickly launched into the subject of the day.

"Southeast Asia has always been a misunderstood region of the world for America," continued Kennedy. "We have unfortunately stamped a Western interpretation on all things oriental, and at times it has served us quite badly. The Korean War was a great lesson in that respect. We battled North Korean and Chinese troops to a tie, re-establishing the original Korean borders after a three-year war at the expense of almost two million lives, over thirty-thousand of which were American, with an equal number injured. That war crystallized our judgment that all things communist were by definition loathsome, and from that basic assumption we developed our foreign policy positions over the next ten years. It was a conclusion that did not serve us well in the Indochina peninsula.

"I don't want to give the impression that I accept communism as a rightful form of government. I find it reprehensible in most ways. But, as I stated in my American University speech in '63, we must learn to live together and use peaceful means to challenge another country's ideology. As western countries, we have nothing to fear from contact with communism. We are militarily strong and, having so many deeply established freedoms, are not converted by their repressive regimes.

"But our belief in a monolithic communism, marching lockstep toward world domination, did not reflect reality. Any observant student of world politics could see that China and the Soviet Union were probably more suspicious of each other than they were of the United States. And the North Vietnamese were in neither camp by their own volition, but more as support for their own nationalism. They wanted their country back, and it was Ho Chi Minh's lifetime endeavor, with the full support of his people, to accomplish that goal. They almost surely would have accepted American assistance toward that end, but we abandoned them to the French."

JFK pulled over a checkerboard from the end of the table between them. "Care to have a game?"

"While we're talking about this?" asked Patrick.

"You don't think the president of the United States is capable of discussing foreign policy and simultaneously beating you at a game of checkers?"

"Well...no, not really."

"We'll see. Besides, this is all on the Dictaphone so you don't need to take notes." The president proceeded to set up the game. It was an intricately inlaid hardwood board of high quality. "A gift from the Brazilian Ambassador," said Kennedy, noticing Patrick examining the pieces, "with each checker lathed from a different species of hardwood. See the tiny inlaid presidential seal on each piece?" Kennedy held up a checker for Patrick to view. "Quite beautiful. A little perk of the presidency. You get a lot of stunning gifts. And of course," he added, "some...well, not so stunning.

"So, that's why the issue of Indochina is so problematic," he continued. "Because we made the wrong choice in 1945, and a litany of boorish decisions afterwards by successive administrations, mine included, we have had to deal with a problem that could have been solved long ago. Ceding Vietnam back to the Vietnamese in '45 would've caused the French serious disappointment, but saved them from years of military struggle, many deaths, and an inglorious defeat at Dien Bien Phu."

Kennedy proceeded to talk as he set up the board. "Choose," he said, holding out two clenched fists with checkers inside. Patrick indicated the president's left hand. "Your move," said Kennedy as he showed the reddish checker. "And remember, once you touch it, you have to move it.

"In order to understand the conditions present in Vietnam, we have to look back at what's occurred there historically. To just call them an aggressive communist nation with a geographic appetite is to miss entirely the point of why they were fighting, why such an undeveloped agrarian-based third world country could beat the French in a century-long struggle, and why Americans are fortunate not to be engaged there in a protracted and consuming land war ten thousand miles from home. I don't want to ignore their expulsion of the Chinese and the Japanese after World War II, but the defeat of the French in '54 was considered the end of the First Indochina War. Vietnam's ten-year-long struggle with the U.S.-dominated South Vietnamese political regime was a kind of simmering Second Indochina War. And, as we all know, after the events in Dallas and the re-election, I refused to introduce combat troops into Vietnam and allow what would probably have developed into a full-blown second Indochina War.

"The French colonized Vietnam in the mid-1800s. Now, I like that word, 'colonization.' It sounds so civilized and forward-thinking. Kipling described colonialism as 'the white man's burden.' But what it really means is the French eliminated the autonomy of the Vietnamese people, sometimes quite brutally. The country's resources were expropriated for French profit, the people's rights were replaced by repression, and their Buddhist culture was supplanted by French Catholicism. Colonialism is a fine-sounding word in the countries that are doing the colonizing, doing the righteous work of civilizing the natives and all that. But to the suppressed people under the thumb of an occupying force that's milking its resources and profiting from its suppression, it's more akin to slavery. And yet America agreed to the reimposition of those conditions after World War II."

They began their game, with Patrick making the opening move.

"There are moments in history when choices can be made and solutions implemented with a minimum of effort. Unexpected circumstances can offer a path around a seemingly insurmountable obstacle, and a significant shift can be encouraged using forces already aligned. They just need a little nudge in an alternate direction. Jujitsu diplomacy, so to speak. In 1945, such a fulcrum point was available and a little wisdom would have prevented a lot of pain.

"But it was not employed. At the end of '63 and into early '64, a similar confluence of events presented the opportunity for a different approach, allowing a shift of momentum toward a diplomatic rather than military engagement. Previously static conditions changed, and then, of course, there was the assassination attempt. Together these events allowed a significant reappraisal of America's affairs in Southeast Asia. We were presented with another fulcrum moment in history that permitted a change of course—and I took it.

"You might want to think a little further ahead, Hennessey," said the president, plucking from the board two pieces he had just captured. The president was quite engaged in what he was saying as he recited his role in the events of Vietnam. Patrick thought he had forgotten about the game entirely, only to have him shift a piece on the board as an afterthought once he paused in his talking.

"I'm on it, Mr. President," replied Patrick. "But when you say '64 presented a fulcrum moment, what do you mean?

"Okay, a little background on the run-up to the events in Dallas, as that date appears to have been the culminating point for all manner of conditions that had been brewing in the first years of my administration regarding our commitment in Southeast Asia. It must be understood there was little knowledge of both *why* we were fighting in Vietnam as well as *what effect* our fighting was having. The entire history of America, and for that matter, Western intervention over there, has been plagued by ignorance and misinformation, and that was no less true in my administration.

"The military's demand for intervention in South Vietnam and for the bombing of North Vietnam was very vocal when I first entered office in '61. The Joint Chiefs predicted a total collapse of our democratic efforts there, with a complete failure of the Diem regime due to the rising North Vietnamese insurgency. The Chiefs wanted to introduce ground combat forces in the South and air strikes on the North. I refused. The meetings were contentious. We finally agreed upon a limited introduction of so called 'advisors,' pilots and troops really, with limitations on the manner in which they could support the South's combat forces. Then, in the so-called Thanksgiving Day Massacre in '61, I stated that I would not approve an increase in combat troops in that conflict and removed my most vocal ideology-bound staff advisors who were constantly recommending the use of unfettered military power. I hoped my reshuffling would encourage the exploration of other avenues of action. Well, that didn't work so well.

"Speaking of which, your game isn't going so well, either. King me," said the president as he moved one of his pieces into the end zone on Patrick's side of the board. Patrick was beginning to get concerned.

"I had to tread carefully regarding restriction of the military. The Joint Chiefs of Staff presented a formidable and reactionary vein of power in the U.S. government. Their advice and proposals were shown over and over again to be completely suspect. During the run-up to the Cuban Bay of Pigs invasion of '61, just months after I'd been in office, I was assured by the CIA and the military that the operation formulated by the previous administration to overthrow Castro was a sure thing—no possibility of failure. Yet, it was revealed only last year that the plan was assumed to be a failure even before it began, and it was supposed that, when things went to hell on the ground, I'd capitulate and call in air strikes, and eventually the marines. Similarly, with the Cuban missile crisis it was difficult to rein in their desire for a second chance at a military invasion of Cuba.

"In the instance of Vietnam, they were a bit more creative in their deception. The Chiefs filtered the information going to McNamara who, as defense secretary, was my man on point. With all their color-coded charts and choreographed briefings, the Chiefs presented a military situation that was always turning in the South's favor, that always showed improving conditions with a sunny outlook just around the corner—progress reports that were about as far from reality as could be imagined. I believe their thinking was that this would give them time to create a military toehold in the region. Similar to the thinking around the Bay of Pigs, they assumed once the boys in uniform were in-country, the president wouldn't allow the mission to fail, and the Chiefs would be able to build on the forces already assembled.

Kennedy and Patrick exchanged moves on the checkerboard, with Patrick's captured pieces piling up to an alarming degree on the president's side of the board. He had two kings now to Patrick's one, and better board advantage with the remaining pieces.

"Under those conditions, with fabricated reports showing steady success and a full victory predicted by '65, it was difficult for me to pull out the sixteen thousand-plus troops that were in-country. But I began to suspect, as time went on, that this rose-colored assessment was unrealistic; there were too many contradictory reports from other sources.

"The field analysts whose data showed a *failing* policy in the country were stymied, too. Contrary to what was being reported to Defense Secretary McNamara, they saw a Vietcong army two to three times larger, a South Vietnamese military that avoided the fight and was rife with deserters, a Diem regime thoroughly out of touch with Vietnamese citizens, and a tidal wave of events sweeping the Vietcong into power. But their data couldn't get past the Chiefs' censors. I proceeded to send additional advisors to decipher what was really happening.

"But due to the nature of the military chain of command and a fear of internal reprisals, the information I received depended almost entirely upon the independence of the individual sent. If he was in uniform, I got back a rosy report, whereas a civilian usually brought back a scenario of gloom and doom. Henry Cabot Lodge, my ambassador at the time, was more committed to CIA intrigues than he was to following my directives. So, I sent Democratic Senate Majority Leader Mike Mansfield to Vietnam in late '62. He came back saying the situation there reminded him of the gaping hole which the French had dug themselves, and he recommended getting our troops out pronto. It got to the point where I asked one pair— General Krulak and State Advisor Joe Mendenhall—who returned in mid-September of '63 with opposite reactions, if they'd even gone to the same goddamn country!"

The president had taken most of Patrick's pieces, and the two remaining were not very effectual. One was a king, harassed on the far side of the board by the president's kings, and the other a standard piece stuck on the edge ready to be pounced upon. It would be over quickly for Patrick unless he could lull the president into a poor move due to lots of repetition.

"Well, where was LBJ during all of this?" asked Patrick. "Didn't he have a good rapport with the Chiefs?"

"Oddly," continued the president, "it later became apparent my vice president, privy to a back-channel source, had more accurate information regarding what was really transpiring in Vietnam than I, but he never deigned to share this with his president. The reason might be that Lyndon, being of a different constitution than myself, thought if I had the real scoop on how badly things were going over there, I might just pack up and leave. So he kept mum."

"Smells of insubordination," offered Patrick.

"True, but it paled in comparison to what occurred on November 22," responded the president with a frown.

"But as I said, it was becoming evident just before my trip to Dallas in '63, that the storybook successes were a fiction. Both McNamara and I, as well as numerous officials who were trying to decipher the events, began to realize we'd been deliberately and methodically deceived. The insurgency was getting stronger, and the Diem regime, a government we had been propping up for many long years, was disintegrating. And then with the suppression of the Buddhist uprising, South Vietnam unraveled. Diem and his brother were removed by a military coup and killed—a coup, I might add, for which we had bumblingly signaled our tacit approval.

"Diem's regime epitomized the contradictions of our involvement in Vietnam. Even an unbiased observer would be hard pressed to determine which regime, the communist North Vietnamese or the American-supported government of the South, was more repressive.

"At the same time I was riding through the streets of Dallas, McNamara and the Joint Chiefs were meeting in Honolulu, hashing out the available options remaining in Vietnam. The recommendations, which I did not receive until after my recovery, were stark—either we pack up and walk away, or we Americanize the war with a massive influx of U.S. combat troops. Neither option was palatable."

The president gave Patrick a withering look as he repeatedly moved his one remaining king back and forth trying to avoid capture. It was fruitless.

"Well, the shooting in Dallas changed everything. The attempted removal of an American president had repercussions around the world, the crux being, who would be in charge—Lyndon Johnson or myself? Would I recover or not, and what aspects of American foreign policy would change if I didn't? Lyndon and I had different personalities and approaches, and from that would radiate a different projection of American influence. The Soviets, Chinese, Vietnamese, and our allies were quite aware of our different temperaments, and after the shock of the shooting settled in, there was little clarity regarding how to proceed. So what mostly transpired was nothing. During the pause everyone waited upon my middling regenerative abilities.

"I had a lot of time to think while I recuperated at my father's house in Palm Beach, Florida. A long introspective reappraisal of a first term is a luxury few presidents ever get. I concluded the Vietnam issue needed to be fully reappraised. It needed to be addressed directly and publicly. Reframing Vietnam as a poor fit for the Domino Theory was essential. That's why the campaign of '64 was so different. I wanted to create a real choice, and let the people, fully apprised of the situation, vote on my proposed course of action, as opposed to Barry Goldwater's. I felt we had a second chance to get it right, but I needed popular support, a decisive election outcome, to move in a new direction.

"And I felt encouraged toward that direction by the tone of the country. In the fall of '63, whenever my speeches veered toward comments regarding peaceful resolution with the Soviets, or nuclear reduction treaties, I'd receive a swell of support and standing ovations. The country was far ahead of the politicians on these issues.

"One of the reasons I wanted you to write my memoirs, Hennessey, was the book you wrote regarding the election cycle of 1964. Your analysis of the forces at play in the Vietnam theatre was perceptive. The articles you wrote at the Post examining some of the issues often ended up on my desk during the campaign, and I appreciated your thoughtful and creative approach toward the entire enterprise. You educated and swayed voters. Too bad you're so lousy at checkers. I hope you can give me a wee bit more challenge in a second game." The president had corralled Patrick's only king and ended the match.

"This is all going according to plan, Mr. President," said Patrick.

"Oh, how's that?"

"My intention from the start was to give you a game, lull you into complacency, then strike," said Patrick, with as much confidence as he could muster. It seemed Kennedy was able to concentrate on the game while discoursing on major policy decision. It was Patrick who was distracted.

Kennedy looked at him with amusement. "Well, I sincerely hope it works out for you, Hennessey. Hopefully your poor performance is not due to lack of ability."

"No sir, not at all," he deadpanned. "And thank you for the compliment. About my articles, I mean."

"You're welcome," said the president. "Choose," he said holding out his clenched hands.

"Defining Vietnam as a war against the spread of communism was a misread of the conditions there. And not properly defining an armed conflict is a recipe for failure. I wasn't willing for America to assume a role analogous to that of the English in the early struggle for American independence: England became enmeshed in a faraway war against one of their colonies that was engulfed in a fight for freedom and self-determination.

"I've come to have a grudging respect for Ho Chi Minh over the last few years. Part of that is from conversations I've had with Bobby, who was the point man for our delegation in Paris. After numerous visits to the North and communications with the Vietnamese, Bobby became convinced Ho was more akin to a Vietnamese George Washington than to a menacing dictator. Bobby mentioned when he first met the man, he couldn't tell him apart from any other peasant he'd met in his travels there—wafer-thin, with the same simple tunic and sandals. We in the West dismissed him as a barefoot, tubercular know-nothing. But in fact, he's highly educated, fluent in seven languages, genuinely self-effacing, and he's devoted his entire life to reunification of his country. The man thoroughly charmed my brother, and a bit of that has rubbed off on me as well.

"Now, it was hard to balance appreciation of the man with his support of communism. But careful analysis by the State Department and more rigorous investigation of the history and comments made by old Uncle Ho led us to believe he was a man who put nationalism—the unification of his country—before support of the Chinese or Soviet brand of communism. And that was the hard thing to swallow. How do we let him off the hook for his long association with a communist regime, a form of government we find the very antithesis of our own, and take into account what appeared to be his desire to also be free of his communist benefactors after he gained freedom for his country? It was similar to Castro being attracted to the Soviets. Castro was deeply mistrusted in Soviet circles for embracing communism as a feint to hide under the umbrella of Soviet military protection, when ideologically he was not really one of theirs. But Ho had been a longtime communist, or at least during his long public career. His devotion was more to his people than to creating a mirror Stalinist government marching in lockstep with Moscow.

"We already had a template for a situation of this sort with Josip Tito of Yugoslavia. He ruled over a communist regime that we kept our hands off of because of his mixed record on freedom and his opposition to Soviet rule even though Yugoslavia was a communist country. We figured a Titoist Vietnam was a viable outcome."

Patrick was making a game of it this time. He had held his own so far and had two kings already, though they were blocked up at the far side of the board.

"So the big question regarding our involvement in Vietnam was how to reverse the momentum of a generation of U.S. hatred of Communism. The complexity of the situation—our well-founded disgust with their policies and human rights abuses as opposed to our ingrained, misinformed clumping of all things communist into one monolithic evil—needed to be expressed. The difficulty then became how to elucidate that distinction. Once that was done, we would be able to disengage from the struggle in Vietnam without raising a fearful ruckus in the American populace that would bring cries of appeasement and cowardice. It's often been mentioned that I had a track record in my first term of being so successfully nasty to Castro that I could choose to accommodate him without inviting overwhelming political reprisals. I'd shown my anticommunist chops, so to speak. I felt the same applied to the conditions present in Vietnam. I'd shown my credentials as a communist antagonist and could therefore carry the trust of the country when choosing to shift from that position.

"This, of course, was displeasing to American military leaders, and I must admit it was a hard decision for me to come to in the first place. But just as I'd enumerated in my '54 speech to the Senate a month before the French fell at Dien Bien Phu, we had no reason to be in Vietnam then, and that still held. We fundamentally had no compelling reason for engaging militarily with Vietnam and fighting what would become a guerrilla war of attrition in the jungles there. We could at best create another South Korea that would need American military support for generations to come, and at worst an embarrassing defeat similar to that of the French."

"You can king me now. *Again*," emphasized the president, moving a piece into the last square on Patrick's side of the board.

"I'll be the devil's advocate here, but why did you conclude that American military prowess would be unable to secure a victory in Vietnam?" asked Patrick.

"There's an old Chinese proverb Senator Fulbright reminded me of a few times," began the president. "*In shallow waters, dragons are the sport of shrimp.* America has a powerful military, but like the French, we'd have been operating out of our depth by plunging into the jungles of Vietnam, a place where real power, of the type projected by the Western forces, would be mired and ineffective. Guerrilla warfare is local and personal. It doesn't translate into victory with the kind of forces America has at its disposal. Like the English during our revolution, we would be out of our element. A common rule of engagement regarding insurgencies requires a strike force ratio of ten to one—ten regular army personnel against one insurgent. And with an estimated one hundred thousand Vietcong in the countryside—not including North Vietnamese regular troops if they were to engage in the South—that would mean one million U.S. troops. There is no sane reason to assume America would engage a million men in Vietnam. And even if we did, how long would they need to stay there to keep the population under control? It would've been a vast military operation with many deaths and little if any positive result to show for it.

"And that's why we reopened the Geneva Talks, though this time we're holding them in Paris. I felt that by re-implementing the agreements from '54 that had guaranteed national South Vietnamese elections in '56, we could stave off a civil war. The Eisenhower Administration, under Allan Dulles, had abandoned those elections when they realized no matter how many hoops the North were required to jump through, and no matter what was required of them to assure fair elections—even including United Nations oversight, to which, I might add, the North agreed—that Ho Chi Minh would still win by an 80% margin. I should be so lucky as to win by such a margin in the States. No one ever has.

"And with an in-country margin like that voting *for* the supposed enemy that you have come to fight, was there any possibility of an American military intervention being successful? Fighting *against* the wishes of the population we were supposedly protecting? Not in our wildest dreams. Liddell Hart, a military strategist I believe you're familiar with, stated that 'Guerrilla war is waged by the few but dependent on the support of many.' And the North Vietnamese had the support of the many in the South.

"I always wondered why the Vietnamese would agree to talks. I mean, the ruse of talks had been pulled on them numerous times in the past," said Patrick, at the same time making a risky move to try to salvage his game.

"Well, I'm certain the Vietnamese saw those talks as a stalling tactic, but were wise enough to understand the need for a bit of calm in order to allow a shift in American politics that would permit a disengagement of American forces. They knew they were gaining momentum at the time. They could have made a serious military push that within a year or more could have overrun the South. But they held back, aware that I was serious about finding a peaceful conclusion. Besides, they understood how a military push would frighten the American hawks and activate our military tripwire, requiring that we come to the aid of the South Vietnamese government we had spent over ten years and billions of dollars supporting. They were not unaware of the nature of American politics.

"And they didn't want a war. They'd been fighting one country or another for so many years they were exhausted from the constant conflict. A poor country always on a war footing has little time or energy for anything else. They didn't want to fight American forces. They didn't want to go through another protracted military confrontation with a Western power. Even though they were boastful of the chances they had for success, they were well aware that a successful outcome, even in their best scenario, would take many years against a powerful war machine that would bring terrible misery to their population. They weren't stupid, but to save face they needed other countries to appear to coax them into negotiation. It was a dance we did, our allies and theirs, during '64, into the presidential contest, and then for a short while afterwards. They'd already gained great prestige in Asia for expelling the French, a major Western power, through direct battle—a feat that astounded much of the Asian continent. They didn't want to lie down for another great power after gaining such respect. But on the other hand they did not want to lose what they'd gained by engaging in a direct war with the United States, whose military was far more powerful than the French.

"Later, in early '65, after Bobby's role in the Trials was coming to a close, he took some time off. Well, that didn't last too long, and on one of his 'vacations' to Europe, he met with some representatives from North Vietnam who invited him to meet with Ho. Negotiations for the meeting went back and forth for diplomatic reasons, but finally we just said 'To hell with it,' and off he went to Hanoi. Got a lot of flack for that, as you can recall."

"Yeah, who can forget that *New York Post* headline, '*Neville—er, Bobby Tours Hanoi.*'"

"Right, that," said Kennedy, nodding.

"But what transpired was historically transformative. Bobby and Ho hit it off remarkably well. They were like brothers from different cultures. I swear I had to remind him he was a Catholic first and not to go native on us and become a Buddhist," said the president jokingly.

From newspaper reports Patrick remembered, Robert Kennedy had been very measured in his public comments regarding Ho Chi Minh and the North Vietnamese.

"But it represented a real breakthrough in the entire connection between our two countries. In my first term, I'd never directly spoken to Mr. Ho Chi Minh or a representative of his government—surprising, when I thought back on it. We were preparing to go to war with them, but we had opened no lines of direct communication. With Khrushchev, as you know from some of the correspondence I shared with you, I had an ongoing letter-fest over a four-year period; but with Ho, nary a word. But—and this might surprise you, Hennessey—Ho and I opened a sort of stuttering correspondence that began shortly after my recovery in '63."

"You did?" questioned Patrick. He had researched the Vietnam issue quite thoroughly, and not a word had come up about back-channel negotiations with Ho Chi Minh.

"Yes. We'd received a letter, while I was still in Dallas recovering, which was a mixture of condolences and a probe toward direct contact. I was unsure of its authenticity, coming from a private post through a French diplomatic pouch, so I returned it, asking for Ho to make a public, somewhat poetic comment in one of his national addresses. He quoted Frost about three weeks later."

"The Christmas address? The one that everyone found so peculiar?" asked Patrick.

"Yes, you remember it?" replied the president.

"It was a piece of *The Mending Wall*, I think," said Patrick. "There was some oblique commentary in the press that the North Vietnamese were getting a bit daft in their penchant for quoting Robert Frost." Patrick remembered it because it had seemed so out of character when Ho had spoken the lines himself, and only that one time. At his age, he rarely gave national addresses, at least none available to Westerners, and he usually sprinkled the ones he did give with Oriental phrasing and proverbs. And on Christmas, instead of a Buddhist holiday.

"*'Before I built a wall, I'd ask to know,'*" began Kennedy, quoting Ho's version of Frost, "*'What I was walling in or walling out, and to whom I was like to give offense. Something there is that doesn't love a wall, that wants it down. And that has made all the difference.'*"

"Yes," said Patrick, "that's it."

"Did you notice the last phrase was from a different poem, *The Road Not Taken*?" asked the president. "Very clever, really. And it proved to me, beyond any doubt, that it was Ho's real note I had received. I cautiously responded with another note. This contact went back and forth a number of times, with eight exchanges in all. It was curious in that we never really shared anything of strategic substance, but the opening of communication initiated an adjustment for both of us. It personalized the decisions we were making, and it shifted my approach on the whole affair. Only myself, Jackie, and Bobby knew of the communications from our side. It included Jackie because it arrived through a correspondence from one of her connections in France."

"No one ever knew about it, at least not that I've heard of," said Patrick, surprised that it hadn't been ferreted out by someone in the press from either the United States or Europe.

"I'm not even sure the Soviets or Chinese knew about it," said Kennedy. "There was never any reference to it in our negotiations, not even an insinuation from their side during the Paris talks."

The president glanced at Patrick with a concerned look on his face as he took the last of Patrick's kings off the board, winning for a second time.

"Three out of five was my original plan, sir," asserted Patrick lamely. He had been so totally absorbed in the revelations regarding Ho's correspondence that he had given little attention to his game. The president obviously used this to his advantage.

"Right," said the president as he reset the board and held out his hands, "It's your time to shine. Choose.

"Well then, when did you actually decide to exit Vietnam?" asked Patrick.

"I must admit I had been conflicted up until November of '63 as to what direction to take," continued Kennedy. "I wanted America out of that part of the world, but the obstacles for an effective disengagement were steep. What it came down to in the end was prestige. Would America's prestige suffer if we were to abandon the South Vietnamese to their fate under a communist regime? Would it adversely affect our standing with our allies if we were to pack up and go home? Would they take it as a lack of commitment on our part to honor our pledge of support, or as lack of resolve, even cowardice on the part of the president?

"Surprisingly, when we started to make rumblings of our intention to negotiate, our allies, France, Britain, and Germany, were distinctly relieved. De Gaulle had already been not-so-secretly maneuvering with the South Vietnamese government to open talks with the North, and was becoming very vocal about it. England came out wholeheartedly in support of talks aimed at disengagement. Our allies were not only supportive in word but in action as well, providing advisors and ambassadors to help smooth the road toward a peaceful solution. They had not wanted to take sides in the first place, saw no validity in the original arguments, and were more than a little relieved at being able to help in the patching up of things.

"And then there were the responses of our two cold war opponents, China and the Soviet Union. We were surprised to find they also were relieved, but for different reasons. The Soviets did not want a proxy war in Vietnam. They didn't want the expense of competing with China to supply military equipment, advisors, and training to the North Vietnamese, especially since they didn't see the North as true communists, but more as nationalists with a communistic governmental structure. They were also not eager to have a shooting war with U.S. forces unfold near their border that might escalate into a clash between the United States and the Soviet Union, as military conflicts are wont to do. But besides all of this, my rapport with Khrushchev had been developing after the Cuban missile crisis. We'd brokered a deal for the Nuclear Test Ban Treaty, we'd come to some grudging acceptance of each other, and we were on the cusp of a détente in all areas of our relations. The Soviets did not want all that jeopardized by the eruption of a war in Vietnam that they'd inexorably be drawn into in unanticipated ways. Khrushchev was supportive of our movement toward talks and pressured the North to come to the table.

"The Chinese response was a bit more muted, but still supportive of talks if the North could prevail in them. Both the United States and China were well aware of each other's military capabilities, as we'd been directly engaged during the Korean War only ten years earlier. They did not want a buildup of American combat troops on their borders. They'd prevailed for the most part against the smaller U.S. army in Korea, but at a tremendous loss of life. They did not want to re-engage American forces.

"They also had a rather delicate relationship with North Vietnam that vacillated between support and antagonism. Vietnam had had to drive them out of the country at the end of World War II. In his travels, Bobby heard a comment Ho had made repeatedly in the past: 'It's better to sniff French shit for a hundred years than to eat China's for a thousand.'"

"North Vietnam did not want to have to rely on either China or the Soviet Union, and the economic and political debt incurred by accepting aid from either or both of those entities would restrict and bind them too closely to governments that in reality they did not want to emulate. They wanted their freedom, not another form of enslavement. So you can see there was a great deal of room to maneuver diplomatically. We had our opening."

"You must've felt relieved to have guided the country away from a war in Vietnam," said Patrick.

"Actually, I was surprised at how easy it was. For years I'd feared the debacle that a failed interventionist policy would cause here in the United States, as well as internationally with our allies. But what actually occurred was quite different. As you well know, this is a vast oversimplification of the complex set of dynamics operating between all our countries, but in essence we realized we needed a more sophisticated and nuanced foreign policy than what we'd been using. The success of the talks in Paris has proven to be a real boon to our foreign relations across the board. We've even been talking of normalizing diplomatic relations and maybe opening an embassy in North Vietnam, eventually—something that would have seemed absurd five years ago. But due to the talks, we're seeing a marginally aligned North Vietnam emerging with a propensity to communicate to a greater world audience. And that includes the United States. Look what happened with France, their long-time foe. They're working together now with a mutual respect for each other, even staging the peace talks in Paris. That couldn't have been dreamed of ten years ago."

"Many have called your decision to negotiate rather than escalate a fig leaf to cover the extraction of U.S. military forces from Vietnam. Is it true that it was used just as an excuse not to engage the North militarily?" asked Patrick, still playing devil's advocate while the president continued to acquire his board pieces.

"From a certain standpoint that is true, but had I admitted it at the time, it would've enraged the dominant military minds of the country. But we had come to the conclusion—based on further investigation after the assassination attempt, reports from advisors sent over to evaluate the conditions developing in-country, and information from our allies—that it was inevitable that the North would merge with the South. It was just a matter of time. It also became obvious that Ho Chi Minh had greater legitimacy than the inept and apathetic government of the South, which we were supporting.

"But the negotiations did let us extract U.S. forces, and saved blood that would surely have been spilled had we introduced land troops. Reprisals toward the Vietnamese who had supported us in the South were the most pressing concern. A great deal of anguish was prevented by the long and drawn-out negotiations that slowed warring interactions and eased tensions. It wasn't perfect by any means, and many died on both sides due to tit-for-tat killings. But I believe on the whole it was a far better resolution than any other we could arrange."

"There were rumors of a strange secret bombing of North Vietnam during the talks. Some thought the entire diplomatic process had been abandoned when those rumors emerged. What was that all about?" asked Patrick. In his research, he had come across numerous unconfirmed comments about a "non-bombing campaign."

Kennedy didn't respond for a moment, and Patrick thought he wasn't going to. Then, surprising Patrick, he reached over and shut off the taping machine. "In mid '65, during the beginning stages of the negotiations," he began slowly, as if unsure about continuing, "there was a reluctance on the side of the North Vietnamese to negotiate. They were in a position of strength. They could watch a steadily disintegrating South and see there was really no need to negotiate at all, just wait and all would come their way. There was a great deal of frustration brewing within my advisory circle that we had taken a terribly wrong course and the negotiations were grinding to a halt. Even Ho Chi Minh, who was open to the Paris talks, could not push his nation further than the generals and population would allow him to move. He couldn't get too far ahead of popular opinion, even in communist North Vietnam. After a great deal of internal discussion, we came up with a plan. We didn't want to be in Vietnam, but the United States could not be dismissed and disengage in such a faceless manner. We wanted neither to enlarge our military confrontation with the North, nor to allow the North to disregard our resolve to emerge from these negotiations with a firm plan in place.

"So we bombed Hanoi, after a breakdown of the talks was precipitated by the North Vietnamese delegation walking out in the middle of the U.S. delegation's presentation of adjusted proposals. It was a secret bombing, never mentioned in the press or alluded to by the U.S. military, but it was very effective. Approximately fifty American fighter-bombers from the Seventh Fleet were dispatched to the North with specific targets in mind, including a representative number of every viable military target: fuel storage facilities, essential bridges, munitions storage, manufacturing facilities, harbor cargo docks, and even the central military headquarters. It was a surprise semi-surgical strike with one major component missing: the detonators. None of the bombs exploded. None caused any damage other than what would be expected from a five hundred-pound sandbag falling from beneath the wing of a military jet. There may have been injuries or even deaths, although the targets had been selected to avoid locations where people would be congregated, and the bombing run occurred at a very early morning hour.

"The strike had been carefully planned to make a statement to the North that the United States had not given up on its position in Vietnam and was not ready to run with its tail between its legs. It was holding in reserve a formidable military power that it was *deciding* not to use. We were at the negotiating table from a position of weakness only because we had *chosen* not to escalate tension in the region to a point that would cross a line that could not be uncrossed.

"One wonders what the Vietnamese thought of the situation—the strangest bombing run in history, probably. At first they might've thought we were inept and our weaponry was faulty. But almost a hundred duds would raise a few questions. We were sure they would investigate the unexploded ordnance, of which there was a great deal lying about, realize the detonators had been deliberately replaced by sand, and that it wasn't a mistake. Just to be sure, we'd also stenciled the phrase 'practice run' on each bomb, some of which I was assured would still be readable.

"We had not announced or acknowledged our actions, and for a number of reasons did not expect the North to do so either. The strike was alluded to in a number of international papers, but the story quickly faded when the United States denied it as too foolish for comment, and the North Vietnamese stated there was no such campaign, as it would have been actively repelled with its batteries of anti-aircraft protection. A month later, at the next scheduled meeting in Paris, both sides arrived and actively resumed negotiations."

Patrick glanced quickly at the Dictaphone, then Kennedy. "In the book? Is this going to be included in the book?"

"I'm afraid not, Hennessey. This information will be excised from our manuscript. It's still far too early to allow it to come out and possibly throw a wrench into our ongoing negotiations. Our official line is that the whole idea is utterly absurd."

Patrick was disappointed, but knew Kennedy was right. "That's amazing! How did the military brass respond?" asked Patrick after a moment.

"To put it mildly, they were none too keen on the idea," said Kennedy, laughing. "McNamara had to put observers on the carriers to be absolutely sure the bombs were disarmed. Needless to say, it was a strange military operation that went completely against the grain of our military personnel. And it was a feint that could only be used once."

"I have a philosophical question," said Patrick, after digesting what had just been revealed. "Not to be morbid, but what do you think would've happened had you not survived Dallas? With Vice President Johnson assuming your position?"

"A legitimate question." He didn't reach over and reactivate the Dictaphone, even though he noticed Patrick glance at it as he began. "I'll never forget the comment Lyndon made after the election of '64 when, by giving us our resounding victory over Goldwater, the nation had basically given us a national referendum to exit Vietnam. He said, 'Why don't you just let the Air Force boys kick those mother-fuckers in the nuts!?' He said this to me while we were riding the White House elevator down to a black-tie dinner in honor of our re-election. I asked how we could do that after the last twelve months of saying otherwise to the public. His response, 'We'll just piss on them a little when nobody's lookin', and when they piss back, we bomb 'em back to the Pliocene era or thereabouts.'

"Johnson, I'm quite certain, would've jumped right into a conflict over there. He would've inherited the same situation I had coming back from the shooting in Dallas, but the conditions for him would've been very different. He would have been a fresh face and would have to prove himself. He hadn't been completely on the sidelines. Remember, he had all the benefits of the very successful domestic and civil rights agenda he directed while I was recuperating. That gained him a great deal of prestige domestically, but he was still an unknown factor internationally. So I think the reputation I had developed of being acceptably harsh on the communists during my tenure would not have transferred to him. He would've had to prove himself from scratch, and because of that he would think he'd need to project a resolute demeanor.

"But there is a more basic reason why I think he would've jumped into Vietnam, and that's due to the basic makeup of the man. He's a Texan, heart and soul. Not that that alone is an indication of his psychological makeup, but I fear that, along with his basic insecurities, would exacerbate his need to appear tough and uncompromising—to prove his mettle. There's a pugnacious pride the man takes in simple and direct actions, and a reluctance to respect the nuances available to him if he chose to look. Unfortunately, he's not one to depersonalize a situation. He'd probably feel a withdrawal of troops from Vietnam would be an unacceptable personal failure and public disgrace. And even though he'd be sure to express it as his executive prerogative, his thinking would be much more in line with that of the Joint Chiefs. I just can't wait to see how the nation reacts when they really see the cowboy they're electing to the office of the presidency. But that's something to talk about another day, after his tenure is over."

"One last question," said Patrick. "You've mentioned how easy it would be to start a war, and you've made a lot of effort to prevent this from occurring. But what about a president, a Commander-in-Chief with all that military power at his disposal, who felt the same way as his military advisors—say, a General Curtis LeMay or Lyman Lemnitzer—who wanted to take hold of that power and unleash it on a designated enemy?" he asked.

"That could be a confluence of dire proportions. Especially without the real need to unleash military power because of a dire threat. Who would stop such a man? Congress could, but they can be corralled by both the upsurgence of the more military-minded members as well as coercion from the Executive Branch. They might eventually come to their senses, but that could easily be too late. Starting the war is easy, finishing it, not so easy. And the cost of getting out of a bad situation can be tragic.

"Now, Eisenhower was a military man, but he understood the dangers implicit in military matters. He led the Allied invasion of Germany during the Second World War. But even he had to keep tabs on the extremists in his administration, warning about them in his departure speech from the White House regarding the fearful power in the Military-Industrial Complex. Actually he was going to call it the Military-Industrial-Congressional Complex, but deleted the last term at the last moment for fear of making a few too many enemies all at once. But he had it right. Those three forces, united toward the wrong purpose, pose a great threat to this nation. The vast resources necessary to create a livable society would be diverted into a never-ending war machine that needs conflict in order to support its being. What would be most frightening is that someone with no military background, who would not have the normal inoculations acquired from having been to war, would use the war machine as his private projection of power. That could present a real danger.

"The American people need to be wary of the drumbeat to war, because it's often misguided. Focusing all our energies on military might as the solution to frightening issues around the globe strangles the resources available for other, more long-term solutions. For what we spend on weapons and troop buildup, we could effect more long-lasting change by eradicating poverty around the world, supporting emerging democracies in foreign countries, building schools, and educating the populations of poverty-stricken nations. That's why we have so robustly expanded the activities of the Peace Corps. The effect it has been having around the globe is substantial. It is the effect of projecting softer power, holding violence in check.

"In a recent *New York Post* article, I was referred to as a 'peace-at-any-price president.' It was said with a hint of distaste for the 'Chamberlainesque' stances I've taken to avoid war. And although they had it right—I will go to great lengths to avoid military involvement—they unfortunately have the wrong perspective. I think I know the difference between selling out the position that America holds in the world as a great power for a transitory peace. I believe America is too strong *not* to seek compromise. And if the negotiation process is difficult and frustrating, then so be it. That's a price worth paying for the avoidance of a conventional or nuclear war. The alternatives are far less palatable, as military conflict is always brutish and often tragic."

Chapter 13

Miracles do not, in fact, break the laws of nature.
—*C. S. Lewis*

The most beautiful experience we can have is the mysterious.
It is the source of all true art and science.
—*Albert Einstein*

Sunday-Thursday, November 24-28, 1963
Dallas, Texas

The weekend's events reverberated through every household in America. Marty Stallart, who lived in Newark, New Jersey, wouldn't have gone to work today, even if it had been Monday. The president had been shot on Friday, and he figured he wouldn't be walking the girders again until he saw how it all panned out. He had purchased a new 23-inch black-and-white TV console with a built-in stereo phonograph only two months ago, over the objections of his wife, Alice. She thought it was an unreasonable extravagance for a family of five on a New Jersey steelworker's paycheck. Her objections had quickly faded, though, as she grew accustomed to spending the early evening hours watching *Gunsmoke* on the large screen while doing her ironing.

Marty, his wife, and three kids had just returned from Mass at the Catholic church. This morning's sermon was short and solemn, reflecting the president's grave condition. Father Mickel had been rather eloquent in his heartfelt address, asking the parishioners to pray for Mr. Kennedy. Even Marty was affected. Afterwards, they stopped off at the bakery to pick up his favorite crumb cake for their Sunday brunch.

The TV had been on almost continuously since he came home early from work late Friday afternoon, and he switched it back on as soon as they walked in the door. Oswald was being moved from the Dallas jail this morning, and Marty was glued to the set while Alice stole glances from the kitchen. He stood with a glass of orange juice in one hand and a plate of crumb cake in the other, watching the diminutive Oswald being led through a cordon of police, all wearing suits and ties with their curious white cowboy hats. It seemed so incomprehensible that some little fella—because he looked so small compared to the hulking lawmen around him—could be such a troublemaker.

Then it happened. A guy in a suit and hat jumped out from the line of reporters and shot Oswald with a pistol, just like that! Marty was so shocked he spilled his OJ, while at the same time blurting, "Holy shit! They shot the little fucker!" Alice would have given her usual plea for better language in front of the children if she were not so stunned herself. Nonetheless, it was pretty much the reaction of the nation as Oswald was publicly murdered, live on national television.

Before the murder of Lee Harvey Oswald by Jack "Ruby" Rubenstein in the basement of the Dallas Police Station on Sunday, November 24, the nation grudgingly accepted that the shooting of the president had been carried out by one man, and that one man was in custody. Even though he professed his innocence numerous times, it appeared to everyone watching the television accounts of the shooting, and that included a large part of the world, that the perpetrator had been caught. Even with some far-fetched rumors about Cuban spies and Soviet conspiracies, most believed the police had their man.

But the murder of Oswald, occurring so quickly after his capture, rescinded that generosity of belief. This generosity had followed Americans home from World War II. A whole generation of citizens had fought a life and death struggle with the dark forces of European Nazism and Pacific imperialism, and had returned home a tested and wiser populace. They had been in it together, struggled together, lost loved ones together, and sacrificed together. The normal tension between a government and its people had eased as they returned home to a land abounding with hopes for peace. The politically somnolent '50s was a product of this relaxed trust.

But with this simple killing—the shooting of an accused presidential assassin on national television in the bowels of a southern police station—the vein of trust abruptly petered out. Most people did not even know it had dissipated, at least not consciously. But in the psychic stew of the underlying oneness of a people, there was a tectonic shift; a long dormant suspicion was aroused. The complacent '50s were at a close; while the nation's guard was down, its trust had been pilfered. What had been a tragic shooting and the capture of his presumed assailant metamorphosed into a more sinister situation that sorely tested the American belief in the government to give an honest account of the events of the last few days. And it was not the *ability* of the government to do so, but the *intention* of the government to do so that was now questioned.

* * *

Bobby had little time to think of the implications of the shooting of his brother's assailant. Along with Kenny and Jiggs, he had been present at the lower ambulance bays when a mortally wounded Oswald was delivered. They were all dumbstruck by the turn of events, but walking back up to Room 326, Bobby was met with a hubbub of activity that consumed his attention. One of the doctors' assistants hurried out of the room and down the stairs while a small crowd of white-smocked doctors and nurses converged in the hallway outside the president's room. Doctor Burkley, who saw Bobby approaching, quickly went down the hall to meet him and pulled him aside.

"Robert, I need to talk to you. The president's exhibiting signs of infection," he said quietly. He explained that Evey Morgan, Jack's primary nurse, had noticed a reddening of the skin during her morning observations. "His breathing seemed a bit labored earlier, but we couldn't tell for sure. Then we discovered swelling and slight pus leakage at the sutured wound on his side." The massive doses of antibiotics he was taking intravenously were not holding back the burgeoning population of bacteria infecting his body.

"The antibiotics? I thought he was taking heavy doses of penicillin and ampicillin," said Bobby.

"He is, but they're just not effective. His previous antibiotic intake has created a kind of immunity. You know how much he relied on them in the past. They slowly lose effectiveness with prolonged usage, which appears to be the case here. We have re-mixed his intravenous flow over the last two days and are giving him very substantial dosages, but we're limited by the potential toxic reactions if the doses are too extreme."

"What're you going to do, doctor? We will not lose my brother!" said Bobby adamantly.

Hearing that Bobby was back, Jackie, looking frightened and pale, had come out to the hall to listen to the conversation.

"We are looking into one possibility," began the doctor cautiously. "It's a new antibiotic, gentamicin. It's been recently isolated and has been very effective, especially against staphylococcus infections and hospital-borne bacteria, as well as, most importantly for us, lung infections. Since he's never used it before, its strength would be undiminished. His infecting bacteria would have no resistance to it."

"So why aren't we using it?"

"It's brand new and untested. It's gone through only the most rudimentary review procedure, and those preliminary studies showed substantial potential for ototoxicity and kidney failure. It's a drug with potent side effects."

"Ototoxicity?" said Bobby.

"Hearing damage. It can damage the inner ear and restrict hearing. The inner ear regulates balance, and its damage can lead to dizziness, disorientation, and possibly other more problematic results. Now—"

"Too dangerous to use?" asked Bobby.

"Well, we tracked down the group that developed it, and the endocrinology team talked to them at length. They were adamant that, if used, dosage needs to start low and built up slowly. They have not yet determined threshold levels of toxicity. It takes twelve to twenty-four hours to see results, so there might be a touchy period in which we need to balance effectiveness with potential toxicity. We don't want to poison the president in our attempts to save him. The dosages are specific to body weight and other conditions. We have to test his blood after administration to see how much of it is being absorbed before we can determine the level of his next dose. We've shared with the developers all the president's medical information so as to get an accurate point to begin, but I need to run this by you first. This drug is not licensed. It hasn't gone through the normal testing procedures. We're using it a couple of years ahead of time, so we're running almost blind on this."

"What other options do we have?"

"We can try to recalibrate his current antibiotic mix."

"But that was already done."

"Numerous times. We were hoping it would be effective, but at this point that strategy shows no long-term potential. He needs something more effective. His body is going through a big chemical change, what with all the drugs previously in his system being flushed out. The newer mix taking their place just isn't cutting it."

"Will they need to re-operate?" asked Jackie.

"Well, the problem is that a second operation would just worsen his weakened condition. Nurse Morgan caught this at an early stage, so we have a little breathing room," said Dr. Burkley.

"But not much," said Bobby, looking at Jackie.

"Not much at all," replied Dr. Burkley.

"What do you think?" Bobby asked her.

"Thinking like Jack, I figure he'd want as much information about it as possible," she paused, "and then he would say 'Go ahead.'"

"Our endo team has been working this angle since early yesterday, just in case, so they're pretty far along, They've already determined the initial dose and the body chemistry tests they need to monitor," said Dr. Burkley. "If you approve, we can start right now."

Bobby looked at Jackie. She nodded her head.

"Yeah, let's start," said Bobby.

* * *

As the afternoon progressed, Chief Nurse Evey Morgan was all quiet business. She monitored the president's fluid levels, checked his heart monitor and respiration, organized his IV tubes, gently prodded and smoothed his sheets while carefully rearranging his bedding. She precisely marked all her findings on the clipboard that was always present for the attending doctors to view. She also monitored the oxygen tent supplying the rich breathing mix to the patient—especially helpful with lung injuries to accelerate regeneration. The quandary was that even though an oxygen-rich environment was at first created by tenting a patient, it quickly deteriorated as the patient exhaled, increasing the percentage of carbon dioxide in the mix, until the beneficial effects of the tented enclosure were nullified by the changing mix of gases. The tent's gauges measuring the balance needed to be watched constantly to determine when it was necessary to clear the covering and start again. It was quickly determined that a better method was needed. One of the doctors had a small, boxed bellows installed at the window with a hose running to the tent, and the exhaust pointed out the window opening. A small flap at the back of the tent was untucked from the bed to allow enough incoming air flow to prevent suction and deflation. This used a great deal more pure oxygen, but after a bit of fiddling, it eliminated the need to clear and restart the cycle every twenty minutes. It also reduced the condensation on the clear plastic, allowing the president to be viewed more closely.

Evey also kept a careful check on blood pressure. With this type of operation, there was always the possibility that a blood vessel grazed by a bullet fragment might not have been detected during the surgery. In the early stages of healing, with blood pressure back up to normal, a vessel wall thinned from projectile impact could swell and burst. This hemorrhage would cause internal bleeding, indicated by a steady drop in blood pressure. The problem could be detected on an X-ray, but they couldn't constantly disturb the fragile condition of the patient by moving him in and out of the X-ray room and on and off the X-ray table. It was part of Evey's job to monitor him closely and note any fluctuation. If there was a drop, X-rays would need to be taken again, possibly requiring reopening the wound to fix the condition—another setback in the president's recovery, and one that she personally willed not to happen.

Evey had been a nurse for almost twenty-one years and had seen a lot during her life in the OR, the ER, and patient care. She didn't cringe at the blood and guts that were a constant companion to caring for the human body. But with this patient it was different. She didn't let on, but she was nervous around Mr. Kennedy. For the moment, it was just his inert body that she dealt with, checking his pulse and breathing, helping the doctors re-dress his wounds. She also worked Jack's body, flexing his joints and rubbing down all his muscles. It was the job of a good nurse to keep the body in motion to maintain blood flow and muscle tone and to prevent bedsores. Lying too long in any one position can quickly allow the skin to develop ulcerations that can become infected and create a life-threatening condition. The normal tossing and turning related to healthy sleeping is not duplicated while in a deep state of unconsciousness. Mr. Kennedy was certainly no different in a bodily sense from the thousands of patients she had ministered to over the years. But she felt deep concern about his awakening. She wasn't sure she would be able to keep her composure at such a juncture. Nonetheless, she was doing everything in her power to encourage his recovery.

Evey found her position most satisfying. There had been a lot of discussion regarding who should care for the president, who would participate in his diagnosis, who would be cleared by the Secret Service even for admittance to the lower three floors of Parkland Medical Center after they had been commandeered, but especially who would have personal access to the president's room and assist directly in his care. The doctors and specialists who had flown down the first day with Robert Kennedy from DC, as well as others who had been quickly assembled from across the country for the president's care, had wanted to exclude anyone not a member of their party.

There was a point early on when Evey thought she'd be pulled off the third floor and sent over to C-Wing to care for all the patients who had been abruptly transferred there on Friday. Transferred? It was more like a fire drill evacuation. She was afraid they'd all have been dumped out on the street and left there, for all the Secret Service agents cared. And if it wasn't for the president's brother that first night, she'd have had a lot more time to spend with her son, Sean, over the weekend and the upcoming holidays. But she just couldn't keep her mouth shut with that doctor flown in specially from the east coast. She thought she'd really made a hash of it, correcting him, and her being just a nurse. She could not keep her mouth shut sometimes, but that brother had surprised her. Just so.

She hadn't noticed him come up the stairs behind her that first night, but instead saw his reflection in the eyes and demeanor of Dr. Ingram, who perked right up.

"Is *theah* a problem *heah*?" Mr. Kennedy had said in that funny Boston way he had of speaking, with the crisp nasal clipping of his disappearing "r"s. He seemed all pinched up in his nose, but didn't seem to notice how odd he sounded.

"No, we're fine here, just straightening out the staff," answered Dr. Ingram, with casual superiority. Straightening out the staff, my behind! She could tell from his eyes, though, that he wasn't feeling too superior in their new company.

If it hadn't been for the look Mr. Kennedy had given her, she might have backed down right there, and now she'd be organizing new room arrangements in C-Wing. But he had turned and looked at her directly, with a questioning expression, as if he actually wanted her opinion. Something she hadn't expected, what with all the gruff men giving orders all day and expecting her to jump aside. It was a man's world in the medical profession. And even though half of them didn't know their stethoscope from a gramophone, it was hardly her place to say so to their faces. It had to be done delicately, indirectly, made to sound like improvements were *their* suggestions, not hers, an art she was practiced at but unable to fully embrace when her dander was up. But the brother wasn't dismissive. And he didn't seem angry at her just because she was here at Parkland, local to Dallas, and part of all the pain that had come down on his brother from the attitudes here. That look gave her permission.

"Sir, I was mentioning that the drugs need to be kept refrigerated. The heat dissipates their effectiveness, and leaving them here in the hall all lined up on the shelves is convenient, but not good practice. This is Texas," she said, referring to the heat and humidity.

Bobby looked at her a moment, then turned to the doctor, saying, "She right?" The attorney general seemed to have been interrupted in the middle of something else, but he was giving this his full attention.

"Well, there might be some reason to suggest that may be necessary," Dr. Ingram said. But she could see he was changing his obstinate stand right in front of her. She had corrected him. In front of the president's brother. She, just a southern nurse, and he, a fancy northern doctor.

"What else?" Mr. Kennedy said, looking back to her. He was genuinely asking.

So she plunged ahead. "I wanted to suggest his bed be moved away from the air conditioning unit at the window. When I was first tucking him in, he had goose bumps on his free arm. His body finds it too cool, so it might need to be turned down as well. Besides, it'll be quieter and it'll avoid condensation buildup on the oxygen tent. He's not looking at the scenery right now, and he'll be needing all his concentration to heal up. He can be moved back later when he wakes up if he wants a view." She paused a moment to see if she was overstepping and should prepare to be relieved of her duties.

"And?" was all he said.

"Well, a lot of equipment was flown in with the new medical team, and I'd recommend that it be thoroughly washed down with antiseptic solution. Everything should be exceptionally clean. The main problem here is going to be infection, and the cleaner we keep everything, the less chance of stray germs entering the room and the better chance we have of preventing complications. I also think anyone not intimately familiar with the president should wear surgical masks when coming and going, and entry should be restricted to only a few people so there is as little chance as possible of stray infection—colds, et cetera—from entering that room." She had stated this all quickly and concisely.

"And what's your name?" asked the brother. He was looking down at the tag she had been given by the Secret Service, allowing her to remain in this part of the hospital.

"Evey Morgan," she replied. "I'm the head nurse here in the emergency wing." Mrs. Morgan was a neat, white-smocked, slightly portly nurse—a plain-talking specimen of the local medical community. She had smooth parchment skin, finely weathered from the Texas sun. Her slightly nervous but direct approach could not disguise her warmth and sincere concern.

Bobby looked at her a moment, thinking, then turned to Dr. Ingram, who had been shifting uncomfortably while she spoke. "Some good points, doctor. You agree?"

"Yes. Um, very helpful." Dr. Ingram, for all his annoyance, knew when to be gracious.

Evey discovered the next morning, when she came in for her shift, that she was assigned full-time solely to the president's detail on the third floor. "The attorney general requested you specifically," the Secret Service agent told her when she checked in with her pass at the anteroom off the nurses' office.

When she had told Sean that Saturday evening, just before he was going to bed, that she was helping take care of the president, he had looked at her with that skeptical nod he had so recently developed—a generous dose of worldly disdain with more than a pinch of all-knowingness. So when had he all of a sudden gotten the world-weary attitude of an old man, him being almost a teenager? Just so. She'd have to pay more attention to him; he was growing up and away from her too fast.

"Are you really taking care of the president?" Sean had asked the next morning, crunching away at a bowl of Cheerios. He still wasn't sure she was being completely straight with him. Sometimes her teasing would confuse him as to which parts of their conversations were real and which were parts that she made up. She'd have to stop doing that. At twelve, he was too old to be treated like a child anymore.

"Yeah. It's me and Mrs. Mergstrom and then a few other nurses they flew in from a Washington, D.C., hospital."

"Is he going to die?" Right to the point, he'd get.

"No!" she replied, rather emphatically, surprising herself. "No, he's not."

* * *

The national press demanded an investigation into what was going on in Dallas after Oswald's nationally televised shooting by a Dallas strip-club owner earlier in the day. What had previously been a veiled concern that Dallas and its law enforcement community were not up to the task of dealing with such a significant event quickly devolved into a demand from all quarters that the investigation be removed from their incompetent hands. The calls for open congressional investigations from newspaper editorials, radio broadcasters, and television commentators were swelling.

Vice President Johnson, now the de facto head of the government, deflected them strongly. More and more decision-making concerns were being shifted toward him simply because there was no one else in charge. The vice president was handling this delicate position deftly. During his frequent press conferences to his "fellow Americans," he was cordial, self-effacing, and excessively reasonable when explaining the actions the government was taking.

Behind the scenes, though, he was classic Johnson—cajoling, demanding, crude, and effective. He sensed a rebirth, a coming-in from the steppes. His isolation from power had been painfully foreign to him over the last three years; he could feel his sails swelling with the new attention. Eyes were turning his way, some reluctantly, some resentfully, but he was feeling the shift—and privately he reveled in it.

But Bobby and Jackie barely acknowledged events unfolding outside Room 326. Bobby had not returned calls from Johnson. The press requested daily briefings from Bobby, but he declined them as well. He made many forays down to the communications area, but mostly to contact his family, to call his wife and his children, and his mother, Rose, informing them of Jack's condition and treatment. The circle Bobby communicated with and confided in was shrinking.

* * *

Sunday afternoon led to Sunday evening. The intravenous administration of gentamicin was begun at a very low dosage, but Jack's condition had only worsened. His wounds showed more puffiness and signs of increasing infection. His breathing was weak and coarse. The doctors were doing what they could to drain the swelling.

Bobby, Jackie, and Dave Powers were constant occupants of the president's hospital room. A priest from a parish in Austin was secretly brought to Parkland medical, sneaked in wearing his street clothes with his clerical collar removed, to give the president Extreme Unction, the Catholic last rites. Bobby was utterly spent. He'd not slept, but for fitful moments, since Thursday night. He'd been up for almost seventy hours, yet he could not give way to lay himself down and release the load he was carrying. His thoughts were morbid, as all indications pointed to the death of his brother. There was hardly any discussion among the trio in the president's room, as they all struggled in their own inner worlds of fear and gloom, trying to maintain a hopeful view in order to hold at bay the terrible reckoning of what would occur if Jack's faint breathing were to quietly cease.

During the early evening, six hours after initially administering it, the doctors incrementally increased the dosage of gentamicin. The president still showed no improvement. The mood in the room had turned extremely somber, reflected in the attitude of the doctors and staff, an aura that was noticed by the more perceptive reporters and observers on the fringes of the hospital personnel. There was no direct comment to the press, but dark forebodings radiated from the third floor.

The crowds on the grounds of Parkland medical facility swelled. The Secret Service estimated more than fifteen thousand people were assembled now, their increase seeming to correspond with the president's declining condition. A flickering of tiny illuminations gave outline to the expanding group. Their candles and lanterns reflected into the cooling Texas twilight as evening descended.

Bobby's nighttime reverie matched his brother's grim condition. Oswald's murder had torn the fabric of Bobby's understanding of the agreement he had made with Johnson and Hoover to restrict the investigation into his brother's shooting. Where on earth did shooting Oswald fit in? Had this been in the works when he agreed to their cover-up of the Soviet and Cuban involvement? Had he unknowingly agreed to killing Jack's assailant? And who was Ruby? Was this a Mob hit? Kenny had been looking into it, and the man sounded connected. If so, was the Mafia somehow involved in the shooting too?

* * *

Rose Kennedy, in sporadic contact with Bobby in Dallas, had so far decided to stay with her husband in Hyannisport. Only a few days before, Joseph, Sr., was finally told by son Edward Kennedy that John had been shot and was possibly mortally wounded. The information had been kept from him until Sunday morning, but he was well aware, even in his debilitated state, that something was very wrong. It was sad to observe a man, once so vibrant and powerful, unable to do anything with the news of his son's shooting than implode upon himself. His pithy and worldly advice had, in many ways, been a source of wisdom for his family, and Jack had often sought "the Ambassador's" opinions on a wide range of subjects. But due to his stroke, his means of expression had been reduced to a mumbled "nooo." Bobby and Jack had become expert over the years at interpreting the gradations of that one-word response to determine whether it was agreement or disagreement. Mr. Kennedy, mostly confined to bed, was still able to move himself about, however jerkily, making signs and gestures to convey his meaning. But after hearing this news, his stoicism could not conceal his devastation. He cried inconsolably upon hearing his son was near death, and then numerous times while watching news reports on the television. His doctors had tried to sedate him, but their efforts failed.

Later that day he resolved to see his son. By hand gestures and staccato words, wheeling his chair to the carport entry, he indicated his desire to be driven to the local airport. Long familiar with his iron-willed nature, his attendant did not attempt to dissuade him. Once there, he directed that he be wheeled toward the structure where their private jet, Caroline, was usually hangared. It was not there, as it was in use elsewhere. He stopped and broke down crying in the middle of the tarmac. One of the wealthiest men in the country, a former ambassador to England, the original chairman of the Securities and Exchange Commission, a man whose personal wealth and savvy had financed and directed his son's bid for Congress, the Senate, and then the Presidency, was powerless to do anything to help his son. His power and influence, acquired through very questionable means and with the accumulation of many enemies and detractors along the way, had propelled one son to the presidency, one to the position of attorney general, and another to the position of senator. But now his disability prevented him from even assisting in his son's recovery or being anything more than a burden on his caregivers. After a few long minutes in the blustery late autumn winds, with the despairing realization of the diminishment of his powers, he turned and was wheeled slowly back to the car for the short, silent ride back to the Hyannisport compound.

* * *

The dusty golden-red glow of a Texas morning sun was just filtering through the curtains in Room 326 when Evey entered it again on Tuesday morning. She had been up all night, checking on him several times every hour. Doctors had been in and out of the room as well, ensuring a constant surveillance of his condition. There had been little to report. Robert hardly noticed Evey as she entered again to smooth the bed sheets, check the fluid levels in his brother's glass IV vials, and closely observe the condition of his wounds. She spent a long time staring at the president's partially wrapped shoulder wound, as the dressing had been opened to allow for cleaning and left that way for better observation. She was bent over by the side of the bed for a long moment, slightly tucking and lifting some of the gauze covering the sutures. She was on the opposite side of the bed from

Bobby, who sat in a chair against the window. Jackie was sitting with her legs curled under her on the couch. Evey came up with a thoughtful look on her face as she glanced across the bed, but it was missed by both Bobby and Jackie, as they were lost in their own thoughts. They had become used to Evey's comings and goings. She left the room quickly without filling out her chart. With this simple deviation from her normal procedure, both Bobby and Jackie suddenly took notice, looking up with questioning expressions. Before there was time for them to wonder out loud, Dr. Burkley and Dr. Kliendorf hurriedly entered the room, followed by Evey. They went quickly to the far side of the bed, and both took a long and probing look at the president's wounds, especially examining the redness and swelling around the sutures. By now, Bobby and Jackie were standing by the bed, looking over Jack to where the doctors were huddled. Bobby saw Evey's face intently observing the doctors as they examined the president. It wasn't fear that was showing—it was tightly reined hope.

"Say something!" was all Jackie could come out with as she watched the two physicians.

Dr. Burkley looked up at her and then at Dr. Kliendorf for concurrence. "The swelling is receding!" he stated excitedly. "Evey—ah...Nurse Morgan has been keeping a close measurement on the inflammation. It is definitely receding. Just a little, mind you, but it is. Wouldn't you agree, Brian?" he asked, looking at Dr. Kliendorf for assurance. "It is receding? The gentamicin looks to be working. It looks promising, but mind you, it's just a little." But Dr. Burkley's face betrayed his careful warning. He looked relieved. He even gave a cautious smile.

Bobby grabbed Jackie and hugged her tightly. "He's going to do it! Jack is going to do it!" he said as much to himself as to Jackie. She had her hand to her mouth. Tears were flowing, tears more from exhausted relief than from joy. Both knew this was just a slight shift, but after so much despair it seemed like a rebirth—at least a rebirth of hope.

Dave Powers whooped, "That's the way *my* president does the job!" he blurted. He hugged both Jackie and Bobby and darted out of the room to find Kenny O'Donnell, who had been in and out all night.

Evey stood at the base of the bed, looking at the still-unconscious president, smiling.

The morning passed quickly. Within the next few hours, after a number of careful observations of the president's wound and a careful count of his blood chemistry, it became more and more obvious he was improving.

His breathing seemed to be less labored and his color looked better. Bobby stayed at the bedside for a couple of hours and then went down to the communications room to call Ethel and Rose to tell them of the positive changes. They were ecstatic. Rose said she would tell "the Ambassador," and said that he might want to come down now. Bobby told her to wait just a while to see how his dad felt before deciding. Besides, he would need to make arrangements for them to stay if they did decide to come. Bobby knew full well that if Rose or Joe wanted to come, they would simply do so, regardless of what he might say. But he was so happy and relieved that he couldn't worry about how that all would play out.

And then Bobby slept, or more accurately, he sat down on the couch in Jack's room and simply slumped over onto its arm. When Kenny noticed, he nodded to Dave Powers, who helped get Bobby up and into the next room, where an unused bed had been waiting for him since he arrived. They pulled off his shoes and, after they laid him down, quietly closed the door as they left. It would be almost fourteen hours, early Wednesday morning, before he woke.

* * *

The shiny veneer of the podium reflected the brilliant stage lights into his eyes as Bobby stood before the masses of people gathered to hear him speak. Tens of thousands stretched as far as he could see into the darkening distance, obscured from his view. He stood waiting for the crowds to settle, but the roaring went on and on. He was not happy to be here. He had not wanted to come and speak. He was frightened to be standing in front of so many people, with the weight of their expectations pressing him. Nothing in his life prepared him to support their desires, their dreams, their needs. Yet they bellowed their approval without pause.

He pulled the paper from his suit pocket and smoothed it on the podium. He could not make out the words he had labored over for so long. They looked like a garbled mass of hieroglyphics. He tried to speak anyway, but the roaring went on and on. It was like a physical pressure on his body that required him to lean into its force in order to remain upright. He wanted to say he was not the person. That he was flawed. That he could not be the repository of their hopes and he would be removing himself from consideration. He spoke into the force of their acclamation, but his words were not heard, even by his own ears; such was the power of the wall of sound directed toward him. He needed to hold onto the podium with all his might to prevent himself from being blown over, but the barrage continued. The tone of it was chang-

ing. The cheering support became a strengthening gale that now changed to a moaning irresistible force as the brunt of the tempest keened around him. His speech had long since blown away. He gripped the podium, as it was the only thing keeping him in place, but the pummeling winds began to tear it from its moorings. In a last moment of shock he felt it give way, and he went spinning off in a backward freefall. Falling, falling, falling....

Bobby woke abruptly, breathing heavily. He felt overwhelmed and frightened. It was pitch dark and an hour past midnight, according to his watch. Realizing where he was, in a Dallas hospital bed, he had a moment of thinking he had been wounded or was sick, such were the disquieting feelings he awoke to. But as his thoughts cleared, he remembered it was Jack who lay wounded in a room nearby. He rose quickly, splashed some water on his face and went out the door.

* * *

"I see you have Service protection," said Kenny. He and Bobby stood in the hall a few doors down from Jack's room. It was Wednesday mid-morning, and the president's condition was improving. Bobby had slept more than half a day after the realization sank in that Jack was rebounding from his infection. He was still unconscious, but the doctors were relieved. It was not only what they were telling him and Jackie about Jack's condition, he could also hear the relief in their voices and see it in their demeanor. They had even removed the oxygen tent earlier that morning, as they felt it was best to let him become used to breathing normally. He was still receiving the new antibiotic, but in small and regulated doses that minimized its potential for harm. There was hope in the air.

"Yeah," said Bobby, "I didn't quite have the heart to ditch him. You know me, a soft touch."

"Oh, absolutely," said Kenny sternly.

"Met me at Love Field when I arrived, been hounding me ever since," he joked. Bobby had actually come to appreciate Jiggs' strong but unobtrusive presence and had intended to talk with him some more, but had not yet had the time.

"Hear what he did?" asked Kenny, nodding in Jiggs's direction. Jiggs was standing toward the end of the hall, another few doors down but out of range of their quiet conversation.

"Uh-uh, what?" asked Bobby.

"He didn't tell you?"

"Tell me what?" Bobby was getting curious.

"Your agent down there kicked some feebie butt," chuckled Kenny, enjoying this. It was good to have something to enjoy. "He was down in the emergency room Friday when Jack was brought in. I think he'd just arrived back from someplace in Dallas. Not on the motorcade detail. I hadn't seen him in the following cars, and he came in a few minutes later. So anyway, he'd planted himself just outside the Operating Room, covering the door facing the hall, when two FBI guys came marching in, advertising their badges way out to here," Kenny held his hand at arm's length, "claiming to be taking over the scene and wanting the Secret Service agents to clear out. Pair of arrogant pricks!" said Kenny intensely, shaking his head. "Well, that poor crew-cut feebie had hardly got three words out before your man clotheslined the first one, layin' him flat on the floor staring at the ceiling. He keeps movin' and pushes the other out the swinging doors they'd just come through and slams him up against the opposite wall with his forearm under the guy's chin. All very fluid and quiet-like. He was good. Intense and over before it hardly began. I was coming back from talking to Lyndon and just happened to walk right up behind it. He moved so fast I hardly saw it. Your man was leaned in real close to the face of the agent he had pinned to the wall and said something like 'Get your fuckin'ass outta here, Martin!' Real close up, seemed he knew the guy."

Kenny was a tough, decorated war veteran, as well as a starring quarterback for Harvard during his college years. He and Bobby had been on the Harvard team together, and were close friends as well as tenacious physical competitors. It wasn't beyond either of them to get into a fight in their earlier days. Both were impressed by people who took action and, having spent so much time on the gridiron, in the war, and in the political trenches, they knew the various ways men expressed their strengths.

"A second Service agent in the emergency area lifts the feebie off the floor and eases him directly out the door behind Jiggs," continued Kenny. "That feebie got up gingerly, but mightily pissed, let me tell you. Said the Bureau would have something to say about this, but backed off." Kenny raised his eyebrows tilting his head down the hall toward Jiggs, "Coulda' used him on the starting squad back at school."

"I had no idea," said Bobby. "He's been real quiet so far, staying out of the way. I wasn't sure what to make of him."

"Did some checking on him," said Kenny, "and it seems your man was an agent."

"FBI?" asked Bobby.

"Yup," nodded Kenny with eyebrows raised. "Seems he had a falling out of some sort. Applied to the Secret Service and, with his background, moved up pretty fast."

"I had no idea," repeated Bobby, looking down the hall at Jiggs.

"You know the Service gave him a code name, now that he's on your detail," Kenny paused. "Brawler," he said with a tight, self-satisfied grin as he folded his arms across his chest.

"What's mine?" asked Bobby a few moments later. He figured he must have gotten listed by now.

"Brethren," said Kenny after a pause, the grin gone as they both stared down the bland corridor.

* * *

Jackie made good on her promise to bring the children to Dallas. It was done quietly, and the press had not so far gotten wind of their arrival. They were slipped in through one of the underground service passages used for equipment storage and power plant service work. Both Caroline and John-John, flanked by Secret Service and their caretaker, Maude Shaw, found it quite exciting to prance through the conduit-lined corridors with the huge boilers and motorized equipment bubbling and whirring all around them. When he arrived at the room, John-John, only three years old, did not understand the situation. He was at first quiet and respectful, mimicking those around him, but his natural exuberance got the better of him, as roughhousing with Bobby and Dave Powers was what he normally expected. He could not understand their reluctance to respond in kind and it required a lot of attention to keep him from becoming unruly.

Caroline, on the other hand, entered very quietly and seemed to be aware that her daddy was not well. She didn't cry when she saw him. He seemed to be asleep, but she sensed it wasn't so. At first she remained a bit distant from her father's bed, sitting close to Jackie on the couch across the room. Jackie let her respond in her own way. She gazed at her father silently. When it was time for them to leave, and although she had said little, she was reluctant to go. Jackie assured her she could come back the next morning, Thanksgiving Day, for another visit.

* * *

"Can I read Daddy a story?" Caroline asked as she entered the next morning. She had obviously spent the evening thinking about her father's condition, and had come to the conclusion he needed her assistance. So she had rummaged through all of the books Mrs. Shaw had brought with them and selected two she felt would be most helpful. Her daddy read to her many nights, and she felt compelled to return the favor. *Dribble Makes a Doodle* and *The Friendly Trees of Victor McGee* were chosen. She carried both of them, one under each arm, serious and determined to be of help.

"That would be just fine," responded Jackie as she picked her up and kissed her. They got another chair from the hallway and stacked a few telephone books and a pillow on it to raise her up high enough to peer over the railings on her father's bed. Jack was breathing normally. John-John played with Colton Mays, his favorite Secret Service agent, in the hallway.

Bobby, Kenny O'Donnell, and Dave Powers were in the room as well, sitting on the couch and the two chairs by the window. They were talking shop. No longer so overwhelmed by Jack's condition, they had reverted to what was most natural—their passion for politics. It was funny how the human psyche worked. It could become used to most anything. A few days ago, sitting in the hospital room beside a fallen president chatting about Washington politics would have seemed unconscionable. But now, with the despair they had shared over the last week lifting, political conversation seemed the best way of returning to normalcy, a bulwark against the possibility of Jack's regressing.

"*This is the story of Victor McGee,*" started Caroline. She was not yet able to read unassisted, but for all appearances seemed to be doing so. This favorite story had been read to her so many times, she had it mostly memorized and only needed to follow along in the book to remind her of the words.

"*Who lives in the forest and sleeps in a tree.*
It wasn't always this way with kind Victor,
He once thought of life as a boa constrictor."

"What happened to Gearhart?" Bobby asked Kenny.

"The Bagman?" asked Dave Powers.

"Yeah. I heard he got turned around last Friday." Ira Gearhart was the military attaché who had the unenviable job of carrying the nuclear launch codes in a thirty-pound satchel never more than a moment away from the president.

"Lyndon has the football," said Kenny.

"So much for its staying with the president at all times," said Bobby.

"*He long ago had a house and a cat,*" continued Caroline. Her soft child's voice was a gentle lilting counterpart to adult discussions in the room. Jackie sat on the couch, alternately watching Caroline and listening to the men's conversation.

"And on his front porch in the sun he had sat.
But he dreamed of a life in the boughs of a tree
Sipping sweet juice from the summer snap-pea."

"Yeah, there was quite a tussle downstairs that first day," said Kenny. "I guess they didn't plan on a situation like this. At first Gearhart wouldn't leave with Lyndon on the plane back to DC. Can't blame him. He has absolute orders not to be out of contact with Jack. But with Jack out cold and the question of whether this whole thing was a Soviet action, he couldn't just sit beside an unconscious man, waiting for incoming. Couple of Lyndon's aides tried to pry him away, but he wouldn't leave the hospital. They had a shoving match down in one of the side emergency rooms. The football was cuffed to his wrist, and I heard one of 'em talking about sawing it off if he wouldn't get on the plane with Johnson. Finally, Johnson came over, and in his compassionate way suggested they have the cuffs surgically removed 'cause he was leaving in twenty minutes and wasn't getting on the plane without the football. 'Course that wouldn't have done him any good, the football without Gearhart and the combination lock codes he has in his head. But that's Lyndon, master of gentle persuasion."

"I heard the guy nearly shit his pants when Johnson told him that," whispered Dave.

"Naw, I heard that too," said Kenny. "But I was there. He still refused, even with Lyndon breathin' down his neck. Tough little bugger. I think that rumor got started by Lyndon himself. Gearhart finally got a call from McNamara telling him it was cleared with the Joint Chiefs that he was to go with Lyndon. "

"So he went?" asked Bobby.

"Yeah. The satchel is with Lyndon," said Kenny. "It's his finger on the trigger now."

"Why am I not comforted by that thought?" said Bobby.

"All his friends had told Victor, 'You must get ahead.'
And this from his pals who looked tired and dead.
But he studied and sweated and for money he worked,
But in the back of his mind those tree-feelings lurked."

"Did you hear the Texas investigation is history?" Kenny asked Bobby.

"Not surprising," replied Bobby, "What with Oswald killed inside the Dallas police station, you'd have to be on holiday from sanity to think Texas could get an investigation right."

"It's probably going to go to the Hill now," said Kenny.

"I wouldn't bet on it," responded Bobby cryptically. He had not shared with anyone, even Kenny or Jackie, the agreement that he had made with Johnson and Hoover for a special investigation that would exclude any reference to the Cuban or Soviet participation in the shooting of his brother.

"You *know* Ruby's made," insisted Kenny. "Made man" was a term used to indicate membership in the Mob. "He just reeks of that scum."

Bobby nodded his head despite himself. He had just gotten a brief from his investigators at Justice showing all the calls Ruby had made in the day and a half before shooting Oswald. It read like a *Who's Who* of underworld connections, a laundry list of names Bobby was familiar with from his Rackets Committee and Mob prosecutions.

"When do you weigh in on it?" asked Kenny, wondering why Bobby had not gotten into the fray. He had figured so far it was a given that Bobby would sit out any involvement while Jack was wavering between life and death. But with Jack improving, thoughts of involvement were returning.

"Sometime later," said Bobby, looking away with a shake of his head.

"But the harder he toiled, and the more he prespired," rhymed Caroline, tripping over the last word while concentrating intently on the page.

"It's *'perspired,'* honey. It means sweating," said Jackie.

"...the more he perspired," continued Caroline.
His arms, legs and shoulders, they got deathly tired.
And each time he moved closer to life's roller coaster,
A limb fell to slumber and was useless as lumber."

"Johnson got blindsided by a reporter yesterday, what's his name, that Hennessey guy from the Post," began Dave, on a different tack. "Asked him off the record why the government wasn't going for a full congressional investigation. Lyndon and J. Edgar were at the White House before a press conference. So get this—Hennessey says, 'So, Mr. Vice President, with the shooting of Oswald in Texas and the dismal track record of the Dallas legal community pursuing this issue, will there be an independent congressional investigation of the shooting of President Kennedy?' And you know what Johnson said, God love his soul? He said, 'Now we can't be checking up on every shooting scrape in the country.' Is that precious or what? 'Every shooting scrape in the country!' God, I wish he'd have been on television saying that. Bye-bye, Lyndon." Dave, like Bobby and Kenny, had little respect for Lyndon.

"Where'd you hear that?" asked Bobby. He shouldn't be by now, but Bobby was still surprised at what could pop out of the vice president's mouth.

"Got it from one of the secretaries who went back to keep tabs on the Oval and liaise with the communications center downstairs. She was walking down the hall when she turned the corner into LBJ's little eruption. You know how he can give you the treatment, one hand on your shoulder and the other with a finger pushing into your chest, all the while hovering over you three inches from your face. God, I wish that man would use Listerine! He cornered Hennessey after he asked the question and gave him what for," said Dave.

"That bastard," snapped Kenny, more mouthing the whispered words for the others. He was aware Caroline was in the room. "He doesn't want a serious probe. Things wouldn't go well for his home state."

"Yeah, there might be a *serious* backlash. People all over the country won't be wearing cowboy hats for years to come," said Dave.

"They failed one by one and were no longer useful,
And hung from his sides like Bavarian streusel.
Unable to move he collapsed by a tree,
And leaned toward the trunk with no memory."

"But what will he do?" mused Kenny. "He can't stuff it back into a Texas court. It's gotten too big."

"I think he does the next best," inserted Bobby, "stuff it into a national committee." Bobby had been pondering this for a while. "He could get together a panel, a sort of blue ribbon commission. The same thing he was trying for before, but on a national level."

"I can see just about zero volunteers for that," said Dave.

"But let's say Lyndon gets a panel in line, mollifies the press that something is being done, gets Hoover to put the weight of the FBI behind it, then runs it for a year or so. You think Jack would go for that?" protested Kenny. He was assuming, as they all were, that Jack was going to rebound.

"Why wouldn't he?" asked Jackie. She wasn't usually a part of the political discussions, but here in the same room she felt entitled to chip in.

"All depends on the makeup of the panel," said Bobby, standing up and looking out the window toward the assembled crowds that could be seen obliquely through an opening between the buildings to the north. "I don't think he'd want Hoover as the sole source of investigative information, not with all the bad blood there."

"But the roots from the cedar reached into his being,
Like blood from the ground, the sap lifted his feelings.
The spark of his love for the oak, pine and fir,
Was kindled again by the sweet conifer."
"Mommy, what's a *conifer*?" asked Caroline.

"It's a name for evergreen trees, a tree that stays green all year long, like the Christmas trees we get every year," said Jackie.

"I heard he's trying to get Chief Justice Warren. Been giving him the treatment for a day or so, but old Earl's not going for it," said Dave.

"Yeah, Russell too," added Kenny, referring to Senator Richard Russell, the powerful head of the conservative coalition that had dominated Congress for so long. Then he added quietly, "Heard Dulles is volunteering."

"Not a fucking chance!" challenged Bobby, swinging around from his window view, quietly but intensely mouthing the curse. Dulles had been the head of the CIA when JFK assumed the Presidency. "Jack fired Dulles's ass over the Bay of Pigs for being a totally untrustworthy CIA screwup. There's no way Jack would let him within a mile of any investigation. There's no telling how it would be manipulated with him on the panel—and Hoover doing the investigation. Talk about fixing a committee—that would take the cake!"

"So now he lived happily ensconced in a tree,
Maybe not the best place for you or for me.
But his near dying allowed him to love his new home,
And Victor was happy, in the forest, alone.
...Oh, hi Daddy."

"Well, it's all going to depend on Jack," advised Kenny. "Lyndon can go through the motions, but everyone is just holding their water, seeing what happens with him. That's why Russell and Warren are holding back.

Lyndon can do whatever he pleases at the moment, but when Jack comes back, it's a whole new ball game."

"Mommy, Daddy's awake."

"Oh my God! Jack!" cried Jackie, springing up off the couch to hover near Caroline by the side of the bed.

Jack's eyes were open. He was looking at Caroline without expression, just gazing silently, blinking occasionally. Bobby, Kenny, and Dave had scrambled over to the bedside as well. Jackie picked up her husband's hand while Caroline bounced up and down in her chair, her book still open, saying, "Hi, Daddy!"

His gaze slowly shifted to Jackie, then back to Caroline. Then his eyelids closed without his having made a sound.

Chapter 14

Perhaps, after all, America never has been discovered.
I myself would say that it had merely been detected.
—*Oscar Wilde*

In times of change, learners inherit the Earth, while the learned find themselves
beautifully equipped to deal with a world that no longer exists.
—*Eric Hoffer*

Monday-Tuesday, September 30-October 1, 1968
Washington, D.C.

Jenna lived in a small Georgetown apartment just northwest of the Capital with her cat, Mickey. He was a sleek black shorthair with white paws and face, and wide, deep green eyes that bored into her when he jumped up on the arm of the couch to get a good look at his mistress. Jenna had chosen him from a litter a few years back because of his quirkiness—that, and the fact that he stopped playing and came right over to watch her as she entered the vet's office. He didn't drop his gaze even while other kittens playfully pounced on him from behind. She had wanted to get a little creature to keep her company, and, after a few visits to shelters and offers from neighbors, her interest was piqued for the first time. She asked the secretary about the little guy, and was told he was referred to as "crash test dummy" by the office staff. It seemed the other kittens used him as a pouncing bag. He didn't appear to mind, and seemed unusually serious for a kitten, having perhaps gone straight from the womb to contemplation of kitty astrophysics, with nothing in between. She pondered naming him Einstein because of his intense demeanor, until she brought him home and saw him sleep for the first time. He dozed, lolling on his back, paws in the air, and instead of snoring, squeaked like a mouse in the throes of some kitty dream adventure. This would often startle him awake, and he would look quickly around, feet still in the air, to see where the intruder might be. Relieved to find the source of the plaintive cry gone, he would relax and resume his paw-twitching slumber.

She just couldn't imagine the real Einstein making that sort of undignified chirp, so, reluctantly, Mickey—as in Mouse—it was. She was a bit disappointed that such a frivolous disposition had emerged, as she wanted her cat to reflect her own nature—serious and astute. But his irrepressible youthfulness would escape when he wasn't keeping it all buttoned up, and that just didn't seem right at all. Regardless, she became very fond of the little fellow.

Except for Mickey, she lived alone and had for almost six months now. Her relationship with Andrew had ended slowly over the last year, and in her hopes for a new start, she had slipped away from her girlfriends and gotten an apartment all her own. She didn't want to share it with anyone, and shouldered the expense, barely, on her salary as a librarian.

Jenna wasn't sure if she really liked living alone. It had a hollow quality to it after her three long years with Andrew. And yet it had been her choice to leave. She was turning twenty-seven, and things weren't going as planned. She had wanted to love Andrew, he really was a sweetheart, but try as she might, her heart wasn't in it. Things kept petering out between them. Moving in together had not helped, just made the discontent more evident. And on a brilliant day in early spring, when the bloom of love should have been in the air, she felt the bud of departure come to flower. They parted amicably, even seeing each other now and again for a dinner or a walk, but she always went home alone.

But now there was this Patrick Hennessey fellow ineptly stalking her at the Library of Congress. Too harsh, really, to define it as stalking; it seemed more of an instant obsession. Okay, more of an instant attraction. She had caught him staring at her more than a few times when he was supposed to be doing his research at his Reading Room desk. She had checked up on him. Since he was a regular, she asked her predecessor, Barry, for a few pointers. Seems Patrick *was* a reporter at the *Washington Post*. A very good one, with a lot of connections in DC, and the author of a book. She had pulled the book, with its Robert Frost title, and, keeping it hidden at her desk, read through it over the last week. In the past, she had even read some of his articles in the *Post* without at the time making an association to the oddball man who had invaded her life. He just didn't seem like a reporter. He wasn't brash and insulting. And he had a sense of humor, or at least *he* thought so! Jenna was familiar with the normal pick-up routines at the library, and had cultivated a barricade of sharp-tongued unapproachability. But Mr. Hennessey didn't seem to mind throwing himself up against that wall again and again, to his own consternation. She wondered if she might have been too harsh the last few times in deflecting his advances. He had made a claim of doing presidential research. But wasn't that what almost everyone was doing at the Library of Congress these days, thanks to the renaissance in politics with those Kennedy brothers in office? But his claim was possibly true. And those well-wrapped bundles he occasionally got from the conveyance—what about those? She had asked Mrs. Oberlin about them, as she was in charge of Archive Access and Distribution, but had been told in no uncertain terms that they were not something she need be concerned about. Jenna had worked at the Library for five years now, and it was the first time she had run across such mysterious activity. Her interest had been reluctantly aroused by this Mr. Hennessey. *Maybe I could go just a wee bit easier on the gentleman in the future,* she thought.

* * *

Patrick, in his traditional, possibly superstitious, manner, always picked a quote from one of the bas-relief texts as he walked through the arched entry to the Library of Congress.

Man is one World, and hath another to attend him.

It was Monday and, wanting to get a good start on the week, he arrived early at the Reading Room to go over the material he had been working on after his weekend with the president—golfing at Glen Ora and then talking at Camp David. Kennedy's comments about the practical steps he'd taken to avoid war in Southeast Asia had moved him, and he wanted to get his thoughts down in narrative form while they were still fresh. He needed to compare Kennedy's information to some of the literature he'd recently read, especially Halberstam's *Stepping Past the Quagmire* and Lacouture's *Vietnam: A Final Truce*, both excellent treatises on the roadmap to war and its avoidance in Vietnam. The Reading Room was his essential venue for writing, but today he was hoping to see that exasperating librarian as well. He had a plan.

But she wasn't there.

A burly male counterpart manned the central desk this morning, with no sign of Jenna, other than her small name plaque off to the side by a pencil cup. He pondered asking the large fellow where she was, but the man was very busy and Patrick didn't want to broach the subject of Jenna with someone else. He wanted her all to himself. He placed his orders with the call numbers from the reference catalogs and sat down across the room from the central desk, well away from where its usual occupant would have her distracting effect on him. He knew he needed to get going with his writing, some of which he had worked on late in the evening yesterday, but he'd brought a recent Marvin Weeks article with him and wanted to read it before he started on his main task. It was a guilty, time-wasting pleasure, he knew, but he felt it would warm him up to the task at hand.

* * *

Thank God for James Jesus Angleton!
-by Marvin Weeks

Washington, D.C. Over the first six months of the USCPASIC trials, there appeared to be a stalemate developing. The FBI, the CIA and Military Intelligence all presented witness after witness who gave bland assessments of their non-involvement in the events precipitating the shooting of the president. Kennedy administration prosecutors worried that they may have misjudged the involvement of the clandestine services in the attempted killing, or more likely, misjudged their ability to penetrate the agencies' veil of secrecy. In a surprising gamble that they denied was a late and desperate move, the Justice Department, under Robert Kennedy, permitted David Atlee Phillips and James Jesus Angleton to take the witness stand. "Permitted," because they had both volunteered, publicly and vocally, to take the stand in defense of their employer, the Central Intelligence Agency.

Mr. Phillips was first up. A CIA officer stationed in Mexico City at the time of the president's shooting, he had a long history with the Agency. Phillips was a World War II nose gunner who escaped across Europe from a POW camp after being shot down over Germany. A newspaperman and former actor, he found his home in the clandestine services after the war. He'd been instrumental in the CIA's disinformation campaign that overthrew Guatemala's democratically elected Jacobo Árbenz Guzmán in 1954, to be replaced by a military junta. Phillips was deeply involved in the failed Bay of Pigs operation against Cuba in 1961. His imprint was on many Agency activities throughout Central and South America. A jaunty, country-club elitist of the first order, imbued, along with Angleton, with a sense of supreme self-confidence and entitlement, he was accustomed to influencing government agencies and investigators. But after taking the stand and being questioned relentlessly by one of Robert Kennedy's lawyers, his prickly WASPish arrogance slowly crumbled; he was caught again and again in a series of lies relating to the tapes and pictures the CIA had taken at the Soviet and Cuban embassies in Mexico City. The lawyers had numerous eyewit-ness reports regarding the contents of the tapes and pictures, reports taken during and after the interrogation of Mr. Oswald. Phillips denied their existence.

But it was not Mr. Phillip's arrival for questioning in front of the committee that so sealed the fate of the investigation—it was his departure. One hour into his on-stand examination, which was observed by a rapt international TV audience, Mr. Phillips, having overestimated his own prowess and with his confident facade in shambles, stubbed out, in the ashtray by his chair, the last of a series of cigarettes, straightened his tie, stood up and walked off the stand! It so surprised the investigator that Phil-lips was out the door of the Hearing Room before a bailiff could be called to return him to his chair. It took another six weeks of legal maneuvering before he could be pried loose from the CIA's grasp to retake the stand, but by that time his cause was lost.

Next up was Mr. Angleton.

James Jesus Angleton, aka the Kingfisher, aka the Lock-smith, was the legendary Chief of the CIA's Counter Intelligence Section. A spectral figure under any circumstances, on national black-and-white television he was, for want of a better phrase, exceedingly creepy. He startled the nation more by his ap-pearance and bearing than by anything he might or might not have said. Tall and stooped, wearing a long black overcoat and matching black homburg, the thickly-bespectacled spy present-ed a cadaverous vision straight from a Grimm fairy tale. The na-tion was transfixed by his testimony, including the prickly banter between him and the soft-spoken Justice Department lawyer, Walter Sheridan. But mostly they were captivated by the man himself. Highly educated at Yale and Harvard, steeped in World War II spycraft, a fly fisherman and poet, an orchid breeder and spy catcher, he epitomized the caricature of a near-clinically par-anoid, patriotic zealot who had lost everything human save his laser-like analytical mind. And in the end, that's what undid him. Robert Kennedy instructed his lawyers to simply keep him on the stand for as long as possible. It was this dangerous strategy that eventually paid off as Angleton, who at first appeared to be a brilliant bureaucrat who could give a believably rational ac-count of almost any bizarre event the Agency had been involved in, slowly revealed himself as a brilliant sociopath concealed be-hind a veneer of Ivy League gentility.

Most damning was Angleton's explanation of Lee Harvey

Oswald. He stated in every conceivable fashion that Oswald was suspected of being a KGB agent who persisted on U.S. soil because the FBI had not been sufficiently convinced of his culpability to arrest and detain him. It wasn't until Angleton had presented this point of view repeatedly over the course of two days' testimony, promoting Oswald as a sharpshooter and Soviet spy, that Angleton's debriefing of Yuri Nosenko was introduced.

Yuri Nosenko was a Soviet defector who had been supplying the CIA with counter-intelligence information for over two years. Angleton had him spirited away to a CIA prison and held in isolation after the assassination attempt. But before this occurred, Nosenko had given verifiable wide-ranging proof that Oswald not only was *not* a KGB agent, but that the KGB was convinced he was a CIA agent. And for that reason the KGB held him at arm's length during his "defection" to Russia in 1959. Mr. Nosenko, intimately familiar with Oswald's Soviet stay, noted that when hunting with friends and party officials, Oswald consistently embarrassed himself as a worthless shot who needed to rely on the largess of his compatriots to supply him with game afterwards, thus contradicting claims that he was a marksman.

Having flayed the credibility of both Phillips and Angleton, the work of the committee took on new energy, breaching barriers at the CIA and FBI that had resisted penetration for many months, if not their entire bureaucratic lifetimes. And thus began the exposure of a plethora of unwholesome activities in the clandestine services.

"And as regards the splintering of the CIA, we'd have to thank James Jesus Angleton for that," stated Attorney General Robert Kennedy afterwards. "His performance in front of the panel was stunningly macabre. We couldn't have asked for a more fitting representative of the twisted criminality that ran through portions of that organization."

* * *

Plop! A stack of books and pamphlets smacked lightly on the table opposite Patrick as Jenna sat down across from him. She said nothing, just looked at him, tapping her finger lightly on the top of the pile she had just delivered.

Patrick looked up, startled not only by the delivery of his order, but also by the arrival of the woman across from him. His thoughts were still wrapped around Mr. Angleton. "I think my order has arrived," was all he could think to say.

"Hand delivered," she replied.

They looked at each other for a moment. He had the sense she was sizing him up for dinner, like a tigress wondering if she is hungry enough to eat now or should wait until her previous meal has settled.

"You have another packet from the secret gremlins in the tunnels," she said, flicking the twine wrapping the large manila envelope on the top of the pile with her finger. *She even has attractive fingernails,* thought Patrick.

"Must be more of the special committee docs that I—"

"Must be," she interrupted before he finished his lame excuse. Why hadn't he devised another plan with the president regarding their private dispatches?

"I thought today might be your day off," he said. She let him change the subject.

"I work downstairs for a few hours on Monday and Thursday mornings before I take over the desk. I spend those times tracking down patrons embezzling rare documents and such," she said.

"Oh. Caught any bad people?" asked Patrick. "I could swear that staff writer for the *Congressional Weekly*, what's his name, Frankel, had a rather swollen briefcase when he left on Friday. You might want to have him checked." He could banter like this for an eternity with her.

"He's clean. Security passed on him. It's you we're concerned about," she said.

"Me?" he swallowed.

"Suspicious behavior. Strange packages. Shifty glances. Claims of interacting with the president of the United States," she said. "By the way, how is he?"

"The president?"

"Yes. You know—Mr. Kennedy. Lives in that big house down the street."

"Well, he was in great form this weekend," said Patrick. He just couldn't help himself.

"Oh, really? Did you have dinner together at...uhm, The Monocle?" she didn't believe a word of it.

"No, we played a round of golf. Then popped up to Camp David," said Patrick, looking at her squarely.

She wasn't sure what to say to such rubbish.

"I shot a forty-nine," he added.

She furrowed her brow a bit. It seemed either she understood golf scor-
ing and realized it didn't fit into any of the standard ranges for decent play,
or wondered if he was a little too far gone for her attentions. He decided
he actually liked her glasses, clunky though they were, as a counterpoint to
her attractive features. Maybe she picked them on purpose?

"The president shot a forty-seven. He gets a bit of help, though. If it
weren't for the U.S. Marshals' detail spotting his balls, I would've beaten
him for sure." Patrick leaned just a little toward her in mock confidence.
"He kinda cheats that way," he whispered solemnly, nodding his head.

"So, was this the back nine somewhere?" *How does one shoot a forty-
nine, or forty-seven for that matter?* she wondered. "Not very good for nine
holes." She said it like an experienced duffer. She had regained her poise
and was back to probing.

"It was five holes," said Patrick. "They were very difficult."

"So it would seem," she laughed. This man couldn't even get a good
made-up story straight. Five holes?

"He has a course at Glen Ora, their estate outside Middleburg. A kind
of hidden course," Patrick trailed off, seeing she was losing what slight
flicker of belief he had kindled to life.

"One that only you and the president could see? Like a magical golf
course?" she said as she fluttered her fingers.

"No, really, the British ambassador and Senator Fulbright were there,
too. Even they can see it," he said. "It's a kind of macho guerrilla course
that winds its way through the forest. I felt like Robin Hood only without
the tights or giving anything to the poor. In fact, we all owed money to the
president, so it was sort of the opposite of giving to the poor, as he was the
richest guy on the course...." His analogy was in tatters and her interest
was dissolving. She was getting up.

"I lost three dollars to him," he added.

She stood, looking down at the envelope on the top of the stack she had
delivered. "We have our eyes on you, Mr. Hennessey," she said with mis-
chievous seriousness. "And remember—here, in the Reading Room," she
leaned in a little conspiratorially from the opposite side of the table, "we
can *see* you." She nodded her head a few times to accentuate the statement,
then walked off to her station. Patrick watched her as she departed.

Now that went well, he thought.

He got right to work, with a smile on his face, putting to paper what had transpired with JFK over the weekend. He would be getting the transcripts later from Evelyn Lincoln, but he liked to use his own words, then intersperse them with direct quotes from the president. It was most interesting to read Halberstam and Lacouture, knowing what he knew now about the background events of the Paris negotiations, especially the non-bombing campaign and how it affected the timing of the agreements. Reading Halberstam, he had the feeling that the man knew more than he let on about the whole affair. And as did JFK, he kept the secret so as not to endanger the fragile peace. Patrick had already read both books when they were originally published. He enjoyed the perceptive analysis of the conditions in Vietnam from the French perspective of Lacouture, who had been there during the many years of French occupation—and then Halberstam's analysis of America's growing involvement there as we took over the war from the French. It was a joy to read writers at the top of their craft. They described the complexity of big history, conveying the messy meshing of civilizations, grinding cultures and belief systems at their points of intersection.

The packets the president included this time were State Department documents from one of Kennedy's appointees, showing some of the negotiations highlights in Paris. Also, a few copies of Joint Chiefs of Staff documents from '61-'63 showed the suppression of information regarding the real conditions in South Vietnam and the Chiefs' efforts to prevent in-country analysts from getting around their restricted access to the president. And finally, there was one copy of a letter from Ho Chi Minh, or more accurately its translation from the French by Jackie Kennedy in her own handwriting, talking about the possibilities of peace in Vietnam, if all could find a way to work together.

The writing flowed from Patrick effortlessly. He was very much in tune with what the president was trying to convey for his memoir, and it showed in his quick development of the text. It should always be so easy. He was surprised when over two hours had passed. He packed up his belongings and made his way to the front desk. Jenna was there alone. He had looked up at her a number of times while working and was sure at least once that he caught her in the act of checking on him. He handed her his packages. He had rewrapped the packet from the president and it was bundled with the rest.

"Uhm, I have been assured that the golf course that I played on this weekend is still very much in the visible spectrum," said Patrick as she accepted his bundle and placed it on the conveyor.

"By whom?" she said, "Your imaginary diplomatic friends?"

He smiled. "Well...yes, them too. But I could actually show it to you." He let that sit there. She wasn't sure how to respond. "Do you have a car?"

"Yeesss," she said slowly and suspiciously.

"Well, I left mine at Glen Ora. Long story really, but the president seems to have forgotten to fly me back to pick it up, and I need a ride to go get it." *Before they tow it away*, thought Patrick.

"Is it an imaginary car?" asked Jenna.

"No. It's a Fairlane," said Patrick, as if that explained anything. "If you'd be so kind as to drive me out there, say tonight after work, I'd be most happy to treat you to dinner along the way." This had been Patrick's plan, and he felt a bit nervous now that it was out on the table. She was looking at him with an oddly worried expression.

"I can't tonight. I have other plans."

"Oh." He inhaled heavily. He had overplayed his hand.

"But I can go tomorrow morning. Tuesdays are my half-days. I have to be back here by one."

"That would be great," said Patrick. "I'll be at the *Post* early. Maybe you could just pick me up there?"

"Okay," she said.

Patrick gave her directions and his phone number and said he would be ready by nine.

"Oh, and be sure to bring some ID. For the guards at the gate," said Patrick. He wasn't sure how the U.S. Marshals detail would respond to his being dropped off by a female driver. Heck, he wasn't sure if his car was even still there.

"ID? You think they'll be able to see me?" she asked jokingly, still obviously unsure of what she was letting herself in for.

"Oh, yeah. You'd be very hard to miss," said Patrick.

* * *

Patrick took the bus in to the *Post*, getting an early start. His duties were curtailed since he had taken up working with the president. Everyone assumed his absence was due to finishing his upcoming book. But he still had contacts he liked to mine for his weekly column and would periodically arrive at his desk to spend a few hours writing and making calls. He didn't attract much attention. He was out on the curb before nine. Jenna showed up promptly in a little red Volkswagen.

"Good morning," greeted Patrick as he slipped his briefcase behind the seat and climbed in. He rubbed his hands together, ready for this adventure. It was a moment, though, before he realized Jenna, dressed in a heavy maroon sweater with her hair tied up in a bun, still had the stick shift in neutral and was looking over at him.

"What?" he said cautiously, unsure of what faux pas he had committed.

"So, we're going out to Middleburg?"

"Right," he said, rubbing his hands again. "Follow 66 out to Morgantown, then north."

"To pick up your car?"

"Right," he said again. "My Fairlane," he added just to be sure she remembered. Details can always be helpful.

"You're sure you don't want to change your story before it gets too embarrassing to maintain?" Jenna had thought about it the evening before and concluded that she would give him a chance to save himself.

Patrick smiled. "Really, I shot a forty-nine."

"I know. Without your tights," she said. "But I was thinking you might want to change other portions of your story so that when we drive up to your car, parked on the side of the road somewhere, say with a flat tire, you won't have to make up a whole other set of excuses."

"Have you ever had a boyfriend?" asked Patrick.

"Excuse me?"

"Well, I was just wondering if you give all your male friends such a hard time."

"Actually, you've gotten off easy so far," she said as she turned back to face the road and clutched her gearshift into first. "Mostly I just call the police on them."

"So you like me then," said Patrick, self-satisfied.

"I can always stop at a pay phone," she responded as they pulled into traffic. "There's still time."

She navigated through traffic with the skill of a taxi driver, rarely missing a chance to pass or to squeeze into spaces that Patrick cringingly assumed were too small for her car. He noticed she seemed to enjoy his startled unease at a few such junctures, so he willed himself not to respond even when they were nearly squished between a delivery truck and a. large black limo with diplomatic plates.

"So what makes you think the Soviets will give the Czechs a break? Why wouldn't they just roll right in with their tanks and quash the uprising?" she asked after they had gone a dozen blocks and were approaching the on-ramp for Highway 66.

"Ah, you've been checking up on me," said Patrick. "Probably a few years ago they would have done just that, but things have changed. The Cold War has thawed a bit, and I just don't think Khrushchev wants to aggravate the international situation with such heavy-handed action. Not since the United States and NATO countries have been working more closely with the Soviets on tariff reductions and grain sales. It would put a big damper on the recent progress if he were to drive a few tank divisions in and crush them. At least that's my opinion."

Last week he had written a piece for the *Post* about the reduced likelihood of an invasion of Czechoslovakia precipitated by political liberalization when Alexander Dubček came to power in January. Patrick suggested in his article that Soviet forces under Khrushchev were beginning to relax their stranglehold on satellite countries. The new détente developing between the United States and the Soviet Union was creating a thaw in relationships, substantially due to Khrushchev and Kennedy's emerging personal connection. Patrick suggested the Czechs would come to an accommodation with Moscow. After all, Dubček was the communist party chairman. It wasn't as if he were suggesting they join NATO. The Soviets had a very large military contingent poised on the borders of the country, but so far had not used it to extinguish the nascent breath of political fresh air. And Kennedy, through his connection with Khrushchev, was trying to broker a deal to allow the Prague government to be an experiment in Soviet leniency. If the Czechs were to agree to remain in the Warsaw Pact, but were allowed an expanded set of political freedoms, it appeared together they might avert a crushing invasion such as one that occurred in Hungary in 1956. The outcome was still uncertain, but so far the peace was holding. The Prague Spring had turned into the Prague Summer, then Fall, and maybe with a bit of luck, would turn into the Prague Year.

"It was a good article," said Jenna. "Well written. Except you used *affect* incorrectly in the third paragraph. It should have been *effect*. Don't they have editors at the *Post*?" She wasn't sure why, but she so enjoyed torturing the poor man.

"We do have editors, but I believe they're all Canadian, so they're not too proficient in English. It's a second language for them, I believe, so they just make the best of it," replied Patrick. "It's when they confuse countenance with continence that problems arise."

"Or continents," added Jenna smiling, adding, "His countenance reflected severe incontinence."

"Living on continents with severe incontinence *effected* her countenance," countered Patrick laughing. "It's really not fair. I saw you reading that book on etymology the first day. You know, the four-hundred pound behemoth crushing the desk it was sitting on. Anyone who reads that for fun should be prohibited from normal social activities, like crossword puzzles and conversations including big words. It makes the rest of us feel so inadequate."

"Actually, I just put it there to frighten people. Seems it worked," said Jenna looking smugly over at Patrick. "And it's *affected*."

They drove in silence for a few minutes. Somehow arguing with Jenna seemed like foreplay. The more they sparred, the more intimate he felt with her. And he was certain at this point she felt the same. He sparred because he felt she liked it. But for her it seemed different. She sparred, he thought, to determine whether he was up to her intensity.

Her Volkswagen was clean and tidy, but had only an AM radio. In his Fairlane, Patrick had mounted an under-dash 8-track cassette player—a life-altering experience. He would love to share it with Jenna. He had already purchased his second *Sgt. Pepper's Lonely Hearts Club Band* 8-track tape by the Beatles, as he'd completely worn through the first. He felt it to be the most miraculous piece of music ever produced, and often imagined lugging around a sixty-pound car battery hooked to his 8-track to be able to listen as he walked down the street.

Patrick noticed a small St. Christopher medal hanging from the rearview mirror.

"Catholic, are we?" he asked.

"We are...sort of," she said. "Sometimes I think I'm only covering the bases. Just in case the nuns were right. Or more likely, it's just a nod to my childhood infatuation with the saints."

"I was an altar boy," said Patrick. "Until I tripped over my cassock in the middle of Mass and fell down the stairs from the pulpit. It was a short and inglorious chapter of my storied career."

"Hopefully things are improving for you," she laughed.

"Very much so. I fall over in public far less often," he said. "So, what did you like about the saints?"

"Oh, I was a very difficult student..."

"Not you!"

She struggled to give him a hard look.

He couldn't help but drink in the sight of her. Her warm brown eyes seemed to take in every bit of him, and watching her lips when they parted to smile was like watching the sun rise. And such an elegant neck. And that lovely little ear peeking out below her hair. He just wanted to lean over and nibble on it for a while. *Man overboard!* thought Patrick.

"I went to parochial schools," she continued, "and would always pester the nuns. Catechism was just so absurd, I couldn't help myself. I mean *someone* had to ask why babies who died without being baptized would go to Limbo. And where were all these folks hanging about who got stuck in Limbo? Did they need to be fed and taken care of? And go to the bathroom? There must be quite a few of them in there, considering all the people who lived in China. And missing Sunday Mass or eating meat on Friday sent you straight to hell for all of eternity! Now that was a bit harsh," she laughed. "Oh, I was positively a brat."

"But then why your attraction to the saints?" asked Patrick, touching the little medallion hanging in front of him.

She paused for a moment, slipping into a more serious vein, as far as Patrick could tell. "I admired their extreme behavior, I think. They were always after something very basic that the Church and its hierarchy didn't have. Or had maybe forgotten. Some of them would probably be considered crazy today...back then, too. They were like spiritual astronauts, going out to the fringe of things and reporting back. They went full-bore ahead to find the truth and were pretty much indifferent to social norms. I'm so much tamer in comparison. I live such a circumscribed life."

"I hadn't noticed that," said Patrick.

"I'm a *librarian*," she said. "How much more staid can one be? '*Mar-i-on, Madam Librar-i-an*,'" she sing-songed from *The Music Man*.

"But at the Library of Congress. It's the most prestigious library in America...maybe the world," said Patrick. "That's not too shabby." *The sadder but wiser girl for me*, thought Patrick.

"Oh, I'm not complaining. I *love* my job," she said. "Being in the Main Reading Room is especially wonderful. It's almost the best of both worlds. It's mystical, like being in a cathedral, and yet it's so cerebral and enlightening. Sometimes I feel like I should make the sign of the cross when I enter each morning." She looked over at Patrick. "But then I see some of the patrons, and that brings me back to earth rather quickly."

"Oh, ouch!" said Patrick, knowing she was kidding. She *was* kidding, wasn't she? "Maybe you should try some of those psychedelics that are all around. That should keep you well above terra firma."

"No, not my style," she said. "And you?" she glanced over at him with a worried expression. "You aren't a hippie, are you?"

"Well, I am growing out my sideburns," he said, edging his face just a tiny bit toward her so she could see them. He was actually quite proud of his hair length. It had crept well over his ears, a demarcation line that had not been passed since childhood. "I did smoke some marijuana recently. It was fun, but mostly I just got hungry."

"Where did you get it?"

"Seems like it's everywhere. In the press pool, you'd be surprised how many people are playing around with it. It's not hard to get at all."

"So how did you get connected with Kennedy? Was it from some reporting you were doing?"

"So you believe me? I didn't hear any qualifiers in that question."

"I thought they were just understood to be there by now," she said.

"Heh. Well...," started Patrick. He knew he was skirting the edge here, and that he had set himself up to be deceptive, something he did not want to be with this woman. His desire to impress her was overriding his normal caution. Kennedy had sternly warned him not to talk of their memoir-writing project. He should have known probing questions regarding his connection with Kennedy would come up sooner rather than later with Jenna, especially driving up to Glen Ora. But for now he could not reveal his real connection with the president. "...he called me. Out of the blue. He wanted to talk about my upcoming book," he said haltingly, lying a bit by omission. "One thing led to another and he invited me up to talk. We ended up golfing, for the most part."

"Uh-huh," she said. They had been talking freely, and she could sense the incompleteness of his response in comparison. She realized he was hiding a secret, but felt she couldn't push too far to unearth it. She'd let things ride and just give him a hard time in general until the time was right. "So, what is your book about?" she asked. "I heard it was a recap of the '64 election, with a significant section having to do with the Vietnam conflict."

"How did you know that?" It seems everyone knew what his book was about, and it had yet to be published.

"I work at the Library of Congress," she said. "'The most prestigious repository of books in America...maybe the world,'" she parroted Patrick's earlier comment. "You think we can't find out what the major publishing houses are putting out? It just takes talking to the right person in Acquisitions, and presto, all is revealed."

"Well, yup, that's what it's about. I don't want to say too much, though. I'd give away the ending," said Patrick, to avoid talking politics about his upcoming book.

"Let me guess: Kennedy beats Goldwater and stays at the White House for four more years."

"Well, now, I'm very impressed," he said.

"My girlfriend works at the White House. She's a secretary in the West Wing. She knows all about this stuff," said Jenna. "By the way, she says there used to be a lot of hanky-panky going on there."

"Probably some truth to it," said Patrick. He had heard about it for years. The press pool was alive with rumors about JFK's free ways with the ladies, but there was an understanding that private and political lives were separate, so it was never discussed on the record. But the grapevine was charged with it. Things appeared to have changed though, because after Dallas, the talk dried up. Patrick had seen no hint of anything during the times he had spent with the president, but then his contacts were very limited. "Does your friend say it's still going on?"

"She doesn't know. It was mostly stories from long-termers saying he used to play offsides," said Jenna. "I wonder if he was playing it a bit too far over the line there for a while."

"Could be," said Patrick. He had personally given at least some credence to the rumors. "But getting shot and almost dying probably provokes some fundamental shifts in a person."

"Did he have a bunch of ladies out on the golf course with him?" she asked, half in jest.

"Unfortunately, no," said Patrick, "it was an all-male undertaking. Even the caddies were male."

"So sad for you," said Jenna.

"Actually, golfing with the president, talking with a senator and ambassador—it was, uh...groovy," said Patrick.

"Groovy? Did you just say groovy?" she asked.

"Well, yeah, I might have," said Patrick nonchalantly.

"And you're a writer?"

"It's a nod to current vernacular. I might be trying it out for later use in one of my articles," he said.

Jenna took a deep breath as she stared straight ahead. "And thus ended the illustrious career of Patrick Hennessey, reporter for the *Washington Post*, nineteen-something-or-other to nineteen-sixty-eight. It was sadly noted he used *groovy* in one of his articles and was summarily dismissed. All his previous books and articles were burned, banned, and fully expunged from the archives at the *Post*."

"Well, aren't we having fun," said Patrick. He was enjoying his time with Jenna. It was so different from their exchanges at the Library. "Morgantown," he said pointing to the exit off 66. "That's ours."

She turned off the main highway and went north on a road quickly engulfed in a canopy of fiery foliage. Fall was in full swing, and the quick conversion to a more rural setting was stunningly beautiful. They drove along quietly for a while.

"So, should I be looking for a car on the side of the road with a flat?" asked Jenna, not looking over. Patrick could see she was not so sure of herself now. They had gone pretty far with the game and their teasing, but now it was time to show his hand. Oddly, he didn't feel like pressing his advantage and was even feeling a bit guilty that she might be put off by firm proof of his boasts.

"Actually, we're looking for a gravel road to the left with white split-rail fences on each side. It's coming up here around this next bend, I think," said Patrick. It came on quickly, and Jenna turned onto the road. It had a large "Private Property" sign on one side. Jenna glanced over at Patrick, but proceeded slowly down the long gravel road. It opened out from a dense tree-lined drive to a wide expanse of pasture bounded with white fencing on each side. Just ahead, and far from the house, was a turnaround with a kiosk and a few cars. It was at this point that Patrick felt a little odd, driving up to the president's country estate in Jenna's little red VW. Maybe he should have just taken a taxi out here and not involved Jenna at all.

As they approached the kiosk, a marshal stepped out to the side, waiting for them to pull up. Two others were back to the right, near a second car. Patrick was sure, from his last visit, there were others about who were not so readily visible. A golf cart was parked near the kiosk as well. Jenna pulled to a stop as the marshal leaned in.

"I'm sorry Miss, but this is private property. I'll need to ask you to turn around."

Patrick ducked his head to be able to see the marshal to clarify their intent.

"Oh, it's you, Mr. Hennessey. Didn't recognize you there. Come for your car?" he asked, leaning down on the windowsill to get a direct view of Patrick.

"Yes, sir," said Patrick. "I was afraid you'd be towing it away by now." He was the same marshal Patrick had spoken with over the weekend when he arrived.

"No, no. In fact we'll miss it sorely. I do believe it sets off the natural browns of the barn with its—well, *interesting* color." Jenna bit her lip as she looked ahead to see the car sitting all alone about fifty yards away near the rustic barn. She flashed a nervous smile.

"Why don't you just pull on in, Mr. Hennessey? I'll first need to see your ID though, Miss," he said, then reached back for a clipboard off the wall from inside the kiosk.

Jenna pulled her purse from the back seat and handed the marshal her driver's license and Library of Congress card.

"Jennifer Brighton," he said. "Thank you." It was the first time Patrick had heard her full name. "You can pull up over there, and when you're ready, come on back out the same way." They thanked the marshal and drove in. Jenna parked the red Volkswagen next to Patrick's powder blue Fairlane. They both got out.

Jenna looked around the estate. It was a picturesque location with two pastures, the larger of which was on the other side of the drive, surrounded by sturdy white split-rail fencing. Two horses grazed on the far side. The main house was up to the right about a hundred yards.

"I don't see a golf course," said Jenna as they stood near the trunk of his car. She knew her suspicions were relieved. Having a U.S. Marshal detail guarding the front driveway was not an everyday occurrence, but she needed something to say in her shock at standing on what was probably the front yard of the president of the United States.

"It's hidden off in that area," said Patrick, pointing beyond the main house to the far side of the pasture. He had arrived at the end of his journey with Jenna too quickly; he didn't want to get in his car and just drive off. She lingered, too. He should ask if she wanted to stop for breakfast on the way back. "Maybe I should see if this thing still works," he said as he moseyed over to the driver's door. Looking up, he saw a golf cart approaching. One of the marshals was coming their way. He pulled up behind Patrick's car and the putt-putt engine died off.

"You've been noticed," said the marshal.

"What?" said Patrick.

"Mrs. Kennedy noticed your vagrancy, it would seem. She called down to the kiosk and sent me over to invite you up to the house for morning tea."

Jenna and Patrick looked up at the main house simultaneously, but saw no one, then at each other.

"We'd love to," said Patrick.

"That's the right response," said the marshal, as he slid to his edge of the seat. "Squeeze in here and I'll drive you up."

They climbed in, with Jenna between Patrick and the marshal. He enjoyed being so closely pressed against her. It was the first time they'd really touched except for the earlier aborted handshake at the Library of Congress. Patrick found the jostling ride toward the main house very pleasant. Halfway there, he leaned in closer to Jenna and whispered into her pretty ear, the ear he'd found so enticing earlier, "Pretty groovy, huh?"

An elbow to the ribs was her reply. A gesture he found most endearing.

Chapter 15

The self is a boat, filled with water, floating upon the sea.
—*Xavier Moraine*

Men go abroad to wonder at the heights of mountains, at the huge waves of the sea, at the long courses of the rivers, at the vast compass of the ocean, at the circular motions of the stars, and they pass by themselves without wondering.
—*St. Augustine*

Friday-Sunday, November 29-December 1, 1963
Dallas, Texas

The president had first awakened on Thanksgiving Day, in response to his daughter Caroline's reading of her favorite bedtime story. He would open his eyes numerous times to look about him, only to shut them after a few moments' contemplation of his surroundings. For the rest of the day, it was unclear whether he had regained consciousness, even though he looked at Caroline steadily that evening as she again read him a story while sitting propped up on a chair beside his bed. He seemed to be an occasional visitor to the waking world. News of his improvement spread to the outside world like rumors of rain in a drought. But the question for those closest to him was, "Is he really back?"

He showed no apparent interest in his condition or what had happened to him, and he seemed generally detached from his surroundings. He would look about for longer and longer periods, but said almost nothing. The way he quietly observed everything and everyone around him, it was as if he were watching a television show. As this persisted into the next day, Bobby and Jackie began to worry.

Finally, Friday evening, more than twenty-four hours after he first awoke, he spoke. Only Bobby and Jackie were in the room at the time. Caroline had returned to the house outside Dallas where she and John-John were staying. Dave Powers was sleeping in one of the adjacent rooms, having been up for many hours. It was about nine in the evening, after the day's activities had wound down. Jack's eyes were closed while Jackie sat next to him rubbing his hand, and Bobby sat on the couch flipping through some papers he'd received from DC regarding Justice Department developments.

"...some water?" he said in a hoarse whisper looking at Jackie.

Bobby looked up as Jackie reached over quickly to the bedside for a glass with a straw. She held it to his lips as he sipped from it.

"...been here...a while...haven't I?" The president's words came slowly.

"Almost seven days," said Jackie, wondering after she spoke whether it would have been better to slowly ease him into the knowledge of the recent events. He nodded his head, taking it in and asked for more water.

"Do you remember anything?" asked Jackie after he had another sip.

He took a long time in answering. "I remember...so much," he said with a crusty voice, breaking slightly from disuse. Bobby looked at Jackie, trying to figure out what he meant by the last statement, but she didn't want to press Jack. He seemed in such a delicate condition, and yet calm. And he was talking. She was encouraged that he was talking.

"...just...so...unexpected," he said, quietly drifting off again. Bobby and Jackie exchanged questioning glances. The president slept through almost the entire evening, only looking about the few times when he woke, and then silently dropping off again.

* * *

Saturday morning, Jack was more alert. He woke early and asked again for water. Jackie was asleep in the next room and Dave Powers was off on errands. Bobby had gotten up early, had already made a few calls to DC, and had stopped by the president's room to sit with him for a while. Jack's eyes were open as he watched Bobby enter, then, after quietly scanning the room, he looked toward the window. He did not show any need to engage in conversation. Evey had been in to adjust his bedding and replace a couple of IV bottles, and then had left.

"I've been having some second thoughts about the '64 primary. My staff thinks I should jump in now," said Bobby, hoping to engage his brother. After feelings of utter joy and relief at JFK's revival, reverting to gallows humor was the safest way to express his affection without being maudlin. Kennedys weren't maudlin. There was a running joke among Bobby, Jack, and their staffs that involved RFK running against JFK in the 1964 election. They joshed about it, creating oddball scenarios as to who would get their father's financial support, how they could save money on campaign signs and literature by just printing "Kennedy for President," and which districts' votes they would each have to buy.

"They were thinking I should press my advantage. You lounging in bed, me out campaigning. Makes a lot of sense," said Bobby.

"The same staff...that approved the Bay of Pigs?" responded Jack slowly. "That went so well."

"Well, they said the perks alone were worth the trouble. Not so sure now, seeing the downside and all. Not sure I want it anymore," said Bobby. "Damn, and I was *shuah* to get the nomination."

"Maybe you'd settle for VP?" said Jack, gazing toward the window. "Half vacated by Lyndon...position's open, I assume." He was only partly engaged in the conversation. Even though Jack spoke very slowly and deliberately, Bobby was glad to have him respond at all.

"I asked Father Connor to come down," said Bobby after a long silence. Father Connor Adairs was a Catholic priest Jack had been close to over the years. Father Adairs had become a personal confidant to Jack, both having been stationed in the Pacific during the war. Over the last week, Father Adairs had left messages saying he was available at any time to visit with his friend if the family deemed it appropriate.

"Spellman not available?" asked Jack hoarsely. It relieved Bobby to see his brother hadn't lost his sense of humor. Cardinal Francis Spellman was a sore spot for all of them, especially the president. The Catholic Cardinal of New York had not even been invited to the inauguration three years ago. He was a vitriolic expounder of rigidly conservative social and political views. A friend of J. Edgar Hoover, he was the embodiment of a politicized religious figure who reflected the worst qualities of the church hierarchy. On the other hand the Kennedys had a strong family relationship with Cardinal Richard Cushing. He had given the opening address at Jack's inauguration and was much loved about Boston, and a friend to the president. He espoused less stringent views regarding the singularity of the Catholic path to salvation.

"Think I need a priest?" asked Jack more seriously. But then he thought about it for a moment. "Hmm, he available?" Jack spoke slowly, but with lessening difficulty.

"Yeah. I called him yesterday afternoon and he's getting a flight. He was eager to see you. Said your sad-sack soul needed saving and he was just the man for the job." Bobby smiled. He knew his brother didn't go in for that line of thinking. "His words precisely, I do believe," added Bobby.

Bobby wondered about his brother's condition. He had been shot and severely wounded, hovering an inch from death for almost a week. He was diminished physically, paler and thinner, with listless hair and a very subdued demeanor. But the odd thing was, Jack seemed oddly serene. It seemed unnatural to Bobby that his brother would be in such a good state emotionally, and he wondered whether Jack had fully returned or was lingering in a euphoric bubble of contentment. He didn't seem grounded in his current predicament. And what with the odd comments he had made the night before, Bobby was glad he had had the idea to call in Father Adairs.

Jack was not overtly religious. He certainly didn't wear his beliefs on his sleeve, and Bobby couldn't remember his ever talking about his spiritual concerns. He was regular about church attendance, even when there was no one there to observe it. His was a privately held faith, but he did have a relationship with Father Adairs, and to be honest, Bobby wasn't privy to it and wasn't sure what they found in common. But if it would help Jack regain his bearings, it was worth a try. Father Adairs was scheduled to arrive tomorrow, early Sunday evening.

"I'll give him a run for it this time." Jack looked about the room and then toward the window again. "Did I get Extreme Unction?"

"You scared the shit out of us, Jack," answered Bobby softly. "Yeah, we had a local priest come in two nights ago."

"Well, that makes it number four, I guess," said Jack thoughtfully. "Dad's certainly getting his money's worth." Over the years, the ambassador had been a generous contributor to Catholic charities.

* * *

When John Kennedy was elected in 1960, some people thought of him as the Papist, the "Catholic President." The whole world wondered what his religion would mean regarding his actions in office. Would he, as required by a strict interpretation of his religion, believe the Pope in Rome was the foremost and final word on all matters spiritual, and possibly even temporal? Would Kennedy be a pawn of the Vatican as some feared? Would he use the presidency to impose a Catholic imprint upon policy decisions or spiritual practices in the United States? During the election many were afraid of having a religious ideologue in the office for the damage it could do to the separation of church and state.

Sam Rayburn, the Speaker of the House, said to Lyndon Johnson just before the 1960 Democratic National Convention, "Lyndon, you better run, otherwise we're going to have a Catholic in the White House." And then to Adlai Stevenson, he said, "If we have to have a Catholic, I hope we

286 The Memoirs of John F. Kennedy

don't have to take that little pissant Kennedy."

It is questionable whether Kennedy as a politician would have given anything but a carefully considered answer to the question of papal authority. On the one hand, he couldn't come right out and say his practice of Catholicism was divergent from the canons espoused by Rome, and that he really wasn't much in favor of some of the positions of the Church. Even though this was the actual perspective of many of his constituents at the time, this would show him to be insincere or two-faced in his beliefs. And he, of course, couldn't take the hard line that church doctrine was his doctrine. That would have immediately torpedoed his run for the presidency, as he would be unable to take the Oath of Office during the swearing-in ceremony. Allegiance to the Constitution of the United States is required above all other competing concerns.

But Catholicism is not a monolithic belief structure, at least not as practiced. A religious upbringing can have a profound effect on a personality—sometimes without a person being aware of it. Who, under dire life-or-death circumstances, has not pleaded for divine intercession? Does this plea prove the existence of a divine heavenly figure who can intercede on our behalf? Does it indicate a submerged but strongly imbedded belief system, erupting to the fore during an hour of duress? Or is it something else entirely?

* * *

Between Jack's long, restful sleeping periods on Saturday and Sunday, Bobby met with him to bring him up to speed on what had been going on while he was unconscious. The president was improving and was more responsive, partially sitting up in the adjustable bed, but he tired easily. Jackie and Kenny O'Donnell were present for parts of the conversations. They told Jack about the events of the shooting and the capture and killing of Oswald. Kenny told him of events in DC with Lyndon as acting president. Bobby saved some of the information for times when they were alone. He talked to Jack about the deal he had struck with Johnson and Hoover regarding the suppression of the investigation. Jack took it all in quietly. He asked a few questions, but mostly listened.

Father Adairs arrived early Sunday evening. Jack had awakened from another nap a little earlier and was more consistently alert. He watched as Bobby ushered his friend into the room, and after greetings, left them alone.

"*Cahnnie*," said Jack, as Adairs approached the chair next to the bed,

"This reminds me of our first meeting in Manila. Me in bed, green with malaria and weak adrenals, taking Atabrine. You trying unsuccessfully to wrest my soul from wickedness."

"Well, a lot of good that did. I hear you received the sacrament again," said Father Adairs, referring to Extreme Unction. "Pressing your luck a bit, don't you think?" He smiled warmly. "How are you, my friend?" he asked, gently clasping Jack's free hand. "This job you have is more dangerous than racing around in those claptrap PT boats, it would seem."

Father Adairs was in the Pacific during World War II. A naval chaplain at the time, he came upon Jack while the future president lay in a hospital bed recovering from wounds. His PT boat had been shorn in two by a Japanese destroyer, and he had spent a few weeks hopping Pacific islands, working his way back to friendly territory. Adairs acquired the habit, while making rounds, of getting into philosophical and political discussions with Jack. They became fast friends, and maintained their friendship after the war. Adairs percolated through the hierarchical strata and now found himself a sort of roaming mid-level prelate in the New York diocese, the diocese governed by Cardinal Spellman. He helped Jack keep abreast of the inner machinations of the church. But he was a relaxed ecclesiastic, a near-opposite of Spellman, and Jack had always wondered what sort of religious political intrigues allowed Connor to remain in the same diocese as Spellman since, from all outward appearances, they worked at cross purposes.

"You look like hell, Jack!" said Connor, never one to mince his words. It was a quality the president found utterly refreshing from a member of the priesthood. Connor could not help but notice the weakened condition of the president. Maybe it was not so obvious to the family, as they had seen him in gradual reduction. But his appearance was shocking. His pallid skin had lost its usual tanned glow. His lips were dry. His entire body seemed shrunken in size from its usual robust vitality as it lay still, covered with bed linen. He had always radiated a sense of sophisticated dash whenever they met in the past, even during his recuperation in Manila. But now even his hair, that naturally flamboyant eruption of Kennedy flair, was matted against his scalp. After talking with him for only a moment, though, he realized Jack still had a spark of presence about him undeniable even in these circumstances. In fact, it seemed the ordinariness of the room offset his natural charms and intellectual magnetism.

"And how is our Cardinal Spellman?" said Jack, as his friend settled in.

"Ah, that sanctimonious Holy Joe. He's raising all sorts of problems for us true believers. That's just between me and you, of course. The Pope doesn't need to hear any of this."

Father Adairs was a rare model of priestly appearance. He had close-cropped blond hair that was going grey-white in what little remained visible at his temples. He was compact in frame and efficient in movement, with a trim athletic build and a warm, engaging smile radiating from a mouth that seemed a little too large and expressive for such a quiet face. His wire-rimmed glasses created an accountant-like appearance, a clever disguise for his insouciant wit and the slightly heretical mindset that gave a sheepish nod to his Irish ancestry. He had entered Parkland without his priestly collar, since Bobby thought it would have raised unnecessary questions with the press. But in his well-dressed manner, he looked, God forbid, like an Episcopalian! "My favorite Anglican," Jack used to call him, to his chagrin. So tidy and neat, with every hair in place. Nothing like the old image of the careworn, big-hearted Irish bumpkin—too stylishly neat by an Anglican order of magnitude to be mistaken for an Irish priest.

Father Adairs and Jack talked a little about the past, catching up on some of the friends they had in common, circling for a moment the issues at hand.

"So what did my brother tell you, to get you down here?" asked Jack.

"He thinks you're bent," replied Connor with matter-of-fact humor. "Thinks you might be wallowing about in some sort of traumatic wasteland, thinking about staying put down here in this lovely hospital room to avoid that fracas in Washington. Wants me to get you off the dole, I'd be thinking." A moment's discourse and the Irish brogue got a bit thicker and the resemblance to Episcopalian tidiness a bit more remote. Connor wondered if his friend had shell shock, a condition common during the war. Robert had mentioned earlier on the phone that if he did, he was not showing any of the nervous ticks and fidgeting that usually accompany the condition. He seemed preternaturally calm rather than nervously disturbed.

"Well, I wasn't exactly planning on setting up residence here."

"That will be a load off his shoulders, to be sure."

"And your thoughts on the matter?"

"Now how the ruckus would I know? I just got here."

Jack smiled at the exchange. Their banter had always been affectionate and ever so slightly caustic. Connie was the one priest he actually enjoyed speaking to. And under his irreverence, Jack knew, beat a warm and caring heart. But in this instance, Jack was unsure how to proceed. They gazed at each other for an extended moment while Jack tried to find the words.

"Something happened...," said Jack, considering his words carefully, "something, well, very surprising. Even more unexpected than being shot," he added soberly.

"Yes, I saw that man Oswald killed. A shocking murder. And while the whole nation watched on TV. Must have been some real hanky-panky going on there," offered Connor, thinking this might be what the president was referring to.

"No, no. Nothing about that. Nothing to do with the shooting, mine or Oswald's. This is personal. And Connie, this needs to stay between the two of us, all right?" The president delivered the injunction seriously.

"Sure, absolutely," responded Father Adairs, even more intrigued now.

"I don't know how to describe it really," continued the president. "Maybe, being a priest, you've had people share this with you." Unusual for Jack, he was struggling for words. "I've been having an...experience. An inner sort of...event."

"In what way?" asked Connor. "Like a vision, or something?"

"No, I don't think so. It was more like *being* something. This is damn hard to explain, Connie."

"Sometimes people have odd dreams where they think they've visited other places when they've been unconscious. Like childhood places or...."

"No, it wasn't a dream." Jack was trying to express what he had experienced. Maybe he was limited by his usual impersonal detachment, or his general reluctance to share private feelings. But there was also the extraordinariness of the event that left him grasping for words. The urgency of the remembering was getting the better of him though, as he tried to describe to Conner what had happened, was happening.

"I can't describe when it really began. I just seemed to become aware of being in it. Of opening up into it. It has a very expansive quality to it. But it wasn't empty; it was intolerably impersonal and overwhelmingly powerful, yet drenched in feeling. Vastly empty, amazingly full. Utterly contradictory." He went on to describe something so alien to his normal experience of being, yet somehow deeply familiar. "It was me, yet more than me. I was aware there was a John Kennedy, but he was off to the side, like discarded clothes. As if my personality, everything I knew about myself, was over here," he gestured with one hand, "and another, larger part, still me, was observing it all. The personality side had all the things I know about myself—you know, my likes and dislikes and all the sort of, well, petty things that I am. But he was just a tiny little part of what I was experiencing. There were no trappings of *presidentiality* or wealth, nor for that matter a physical body...just immeasurable space...and power. It was a stretching of my self. Yet it felt so much more...complete. Words just don't describe...." Jack trailed off for a moment. "It doesn't fit any notion I've had of what might be possible. It was exhilarating."

Right in the middle of Jack's fervent explanation, his nurse Evey walked in. She caught a moment of the conversation and, realizing she was intruding, turned and left, shutting the door quietly behind her. It hardly registered on the two men deep in their conversation. Father Adairs was concentrating intently, listening to every word. The surprise turn of subject had him flummoxed. He had never seen his friend so animated, expressing himself so freely. The Jack Kennedy he knew was always mischievously confident, in charge and guardedly detached when sharing his feelings.

"The curious thing, Connie, it was not religious. No angels, no Jesus, no God," continued the president in a reverie of his own. "Well, unless God is an experience of vast and amazing *feeling*. Connie, it was unbelievable!

"I don't know if I've been in this experience for moments or days. I was just engulfed so naturally, and yet fully electrified by it. And that's what it was like," said Jack looking at Connie. "Like putting your finger in a wall socket and, well, just leaving it there.

"And now I'm back. Not completely. I seem to be passing in and out of it. For the last couple of days, I remember waking up and looking around, seeing everyone in the room, sensing everything around me, the hopes and fears of everyone present. Seeing right through them in a most peculiar but natural-seeming way. Then whoosh, off I'd go again."

Father Adairs sat quietly, listening.

"There was also this feeling of, well, expectation," continued Jack, speaking enthusiastically, loosened from his inhibitions. "That's the best word I can come up with: expectation of something else even grander. And it seemed like I could go on or come back. I didn't anguish over it, or really think on it at all. It was just, well, a decision being made. My God, it was the freest and most wonderful feeling I've ever had!" said Jack emotionally.

"But it would seem I've come back. Back to this damn mess of a body," said Jack ruefully after a few moments of quiet. Back to his lifelong ail ments and newly damaged physical form. He stopped his expansive description as he glanced at Connor.

Father Adairs was listening intently, but as he saw the expression on his friend's face, Jack realized his explanation was not having the infectious effect he had assumed. His was not a reflection of shared joy in the wonderment Jack had glimpsed. Instead he was frowning slightly with concentration, trying to grasp what Jack was describing. Trying to hold back judgment. But Jack could sense he was also trying to find the best way to reel in his injured president—delicately, without deflation.

"Not exactly what they promised us in catechism, heh?" added Jack, to lighten the load on his friend.

"Ah, that's quite a tale you're telling, Mr. President." Connor had a way of saying "Mr. President" that simultaneously conveyed both respect and indifference for the title. But he couldn't seem to grasp what Jack had described to him. "I honestly don't know what to say. I can see something real has happened to you. I've never seen you this way. But it's nothing that I've ever had described to me before. Now if you were to tell this to any other priest I know, he'd give you a stern talking-to about the delicious distractions of the devil. But you know I don't cotton to that kind of talk. There are many states of mind that resemble reality, but are imaginary. Do you think this could be an hallucination of some sort?"

"I don't really know how hallucinations feel, but this thing is as real as you and me sitting here. In fact, more so. Coming back to this—my body and this room—there's a sense of unreality about it all. A sort of fabricated or make-believe quality in comparison." Sadly, Jack began to realize he had had a glimpse of something that Connie, though he'd spent a life in service to the Church, was not aware existed, an impersonal world of great awareness and power that was literally indescribable but, as Jack was coming to understand, experiential in only a very private way. To his friend, though, it might just as well be imaginary.

"There was nothing evil about it, Connie." Jack found himself trying to ease Father Adairs's confusion. "There wasn't any Jesus in there, but it was wonderful—so much so, it was almost painful. Excruciatingly wonderful." He was counseling the priest rather than the other way around. He didn't want Connie to feel he had slipped over the edge, and he could tell his friend was trying to figure if that was the case.

"You're a priest, what about the more mystical orders—the Benedictines, Dominicans, the Jesuits? Well, maybe the Jesuits are a little too heady for this sort of thing. But there must be some precedent for this. I hear the canons of the church take all sorts of hidden and mystical meanderings. What about them?"

"I've read many a description of transcendent experiences. A lot of the earlier mystic traditions of the church speak of it, but the descriptions were different than yours, more religious, you might say. More concerned with the nature of the Beloved, an entrancing love for the Lord, that kind of thing. Like a love affair, not a galactic romp."

"Maybe it's just because they were more religious. More devotional. Maybe they colored it by what they believed in."

"You're a Catholic, though. What about your beliefs?" asked Adairs rhetorically.

"Devotional?" smiled Jack at his friend. "You've never heard anyone accuse me of that, now have you?"

"Nope, never crossed any lips that have flapped in my direction," said Adairs, sharing a laugh.

Jack closed his eyes and realized he should let this lie for a while. It was not something he could easily share. A president seeing visions, having out-of-body experiences of some sort—in his mind he could see the faces that would mirror Connie's, worried and dismissive looks for someone who had lost his mind. *A marble deficiency*, as Dave Powers would say. He needed to let his friend off the hook.

"I don't know, but the ball's in your court now. I'll wait for a report on just what it all means," said Jack with presidential dignity.

"Is it happening now?" smiled Father Adairs. As if he would submit a report for Jack, president or not.

"No," responded Jack, "but it's not far away. It lingers. Outside my peripheral vision, so to speak. When it's very quiet, I can feel it close by. It has a quality to it, a presence about it, but I haven't been in it since last night. It's a little frightening, like jumping off a high dive might be. I don't know whether I visited it, or it visited me, but it seems to be lessening."

While lying in bed, pondering his near-death experience and return to waking life, he was struck by the habitual quality of being "Jack Kennedy." It wasn't as if he *planned* to return as Jack Kennedy, he just did. A part of him took over and re-entered the world. The activity of thinking did not have the same aspect of consciousness he had just been experiencing. He didn't just decide to turn it on at one point—start the thinking motor again. It just came as naturally as a wolf would know to lope along through the moonlit night. He began loping through the landscape of intellectual thought as naturally as putting on a fresh shirt and with just as little applied intention. He did it instinctively. So what part of him knew to do that?

"Maybe it will pass," suggested Father Adairs.

"Maybe," said Jack thoughtfully. *But what if I don't want it to pass?*

* * *

Father Adairs said his farewells to Jack and left with much to think on. He had traveled to Dallas to comfort his president and help him regain his footing, but he was departing with far more questions than when he'd arrived.

Evey watched the man, who she was sure was a priest, stroll past her station. His exchange with the president seemed to leave him perplexed, judging from the pensive expression on his face. She figured it was okay to return to the room now to check on her patient's IV levels and adjust his bedding. The doctors would be in to observe the cleaning and dressing of his wound, if it looked necessary.

In a moment she would be alone with the president. Earlier, his brother had been in with him for quite a while, but for some reason none of the others was attending at the moment. She had never been alone with him. She wasn't sure if it was more unnerving to be with his intense brother, his wife, and that Mr. Powers who had spent every minute with the president while he was teetering near death—or to be alone with him while he was awake. The last few times she had been in, he had been aware of her presence and followed her movements with his eyes. He even seemed to assist her when she needed help to move his arm or adjust his pillow. He hadn't seemed confused or despondent. In fact, it seemed he was concentrating intently. But he hadn't spoken. It made her self-conscious, a feeling she'd not had in this circumstance since her early training years ago. Being up close with so many patients over her long career, she had learned to steel herself against feelings of unease when intruding into their very personal spaces. They were usually completely helpless while under her care. She had learned to respect their privacy while briskly doing her job. If she was completely confident during her intrusions, the patients usually responded similarly.

But there was a quality to the same activities with the president of the

United States that just wasn't like the others. Maybe the Secret Service scrutinizing every move she made, or maybe the first family's glamour and fame unnerved her. She didn't really think the latter was the issue, as she was more than able to hold her own among the administrators of the hospital. She never had a problem dealing with people in powerful positions. This was probably because she had so often seen them, or people like them, under her care, in distressed, defenseless, naked, and exposed conditions. Having a body was a great equalizer, as all eventually sicken and, of course, die.

She thought her uneasiness might be because she cared.

She exercised a healthy sense of detachment with most of her patients. However, even though she had no previous personal contact with John Kennedy, she was aware that she cared deeply about the well-being of this man, right from the start. It was a curious realization, as she was not very political and didn't follow much of the goings-on in the press about national politics. But the few times she had seen the president giving a speech on TV, she had stopped to listen, something she had rarely done in the past. She couldn't remember a word Eisenhower had ever said. What had shifted her perspective was a televised press conference where the president bantered with reporters in some big hall in Washington. He was being quizzed on numerous topics, going on and on about economics and international trade in mind-numbing detail. In the middle of this, a blunt reporter asked him about a resolution adopted by the Republican National Committee that said Mr. Kennedy and his administration "were pretty much of a failure." He quipped immediately, "I'm sure it was passed unanimously!" to great delight and laughter from the audience. In watching this interaction, she found his performance fascinating. He was obviously very clever and articulate and seemed to enjoy rising to the test of leadership. But what struck her most was his humor. He had such a fine stage presence and joyful quality of communication that she was immediately disarmed by his self-deprecating style. He laughed *with* the reporters. He genuinely seemed to like them. The affection was returned in their mirth at many of his responses.

Upon entering the room, she was immediately greeted with eye contact by the president. He was fully awake.

"Good morning, sir. How are you today?" she asked, a little startled that she might actually need to converse with the man.

"Well, I have been better. There certainly are a lot of flowers around *heah*," he added as he gazed about the room.

"Not just here, they're everywhere. Mrs. Kennedy had them dispersed all over the hospital. I think most of the flowers grown in the whole United States this year are right here in Parkland Hospital."

"Jackie does have the touch," he said. "So, how's my body doing?"

"Ah, pretty well. I...I should let the doctors talk to you about that. They'll be in soon. You're going to need a re-dressing," she said, noticing the hint of stains on his bandages. She had moved to the side of the bed to take a look.

"But I want *your* opinion. They can talk to me later." Jack had watched her over the last few days while she tended to him, although he had never spoken to her. "Presidential *ordah*," he added softly. She noticed he said "order" like his brother.

"Uhm...okay." She thought he was joking, even as he kept a straight face. She paused for a moment, then looked toward the door, just in case. "Your stats are good. You've bounced back faster than I would have thought, although I didn't for a moment think you would, well...you know. Anyway, your injuries from now on are going to heal just fine, in my opinion. It was the infection issue that was the nut for you, and you seem to have licked it. So I think you'll be fine." She finished up, "I could tell you in more medical language, but I figure you want the meat of it."

"No, that will do fine. I don't have much feeling in my arm," he said, glancing toward his right-side bandages.

"Partly painkillers, but probably some damage from the injury. The bullet went through some nerve tissue in your right shoulder. A little tingly?" she asked.

"Yes, very."

"A lot of that will heal slowly, but it may not disappear completely." The president didn't seem too perturbed by the information she had given him. "I was thinking you might like to have the bed moved to the window now that you're awake, but the Secret Service nixed that idea. 'Too exposed,' they said. They shuffled Governor Connally all over the hospital, to different rooms each of the first few nights for protection. Kept him away from the windows, too." She was talking too much.

"But didn't move me?"

"No, doctors voted that one down right away. You were too ill."

"How's your governor? I've been told he was pretty well shot up," said the president.

"He was in a bad way when they brought him in. But he's come around. He'll be fine."

"What did you think of the conversation I was having with my priest?"

"Ah...well, I didn't really hear much." He had sure shifted gears with that question. She'd almost blurted out her opinion of the clergy.

"Come now, I saw the look on your face when you came in and heard us talking. Just tell me. I'd hate to waste another presidential order on you. You don't seem to take them all that seriously."

She smiled cautiously. She had heard a bit of their conversation. "I'm sorry, sir. It's really not my business. I shouldn't have been listening," admitted Evey contritely, trying to deflect the conversation.

"That's all right. You were doing your job and walked in on our conversation. Unavoidable. Now let's hear it."

"But sir, really, I shouldn't. Religion is just so very sticky and I don't want to be bringing up my opinions and having you be angry at me."

"What do you think about death?" he asked directly. He was asking quietly, looking directly at her. He wasn't going to let this drop.

Evey had been standing by the bed, smiling and deflecting his questions as she looked over his bandages, checked his IV tubes, and puttered about. But at this she stood up and put her hands in the pockets of her white smock. She realized he wanted a serious discussion, even though he had come toward it in a joking manner. She might be the wrong one to ask, though.

"You come in every day at least a few times and clean and dress me. For which, I might add, I am very grateful and embarrassed," continued Jack. "People die here, lots of them. Being so close to it all the time, I would bet it sharpens your feeling. Are you religious?"

"Well, no, not really."

"Not at all?"

"Well, I don't understand God, so I don't like a lot of people in black clothes telling me what He says I should be doing." She blurted this out a bit harshly, but took a breath to collect herself and continued. "I'm not sure they know any more than I do. See, I don't believe in a religion as such, although I was raised sort of Presbyterian. We didn't go to church, really. Hardly ever. I don't ever think of myself as a member. But I'm sure there is a God, just not the way people think. Not with all the rules and all. I have feelings in that area, strong ones, just not religious ones." She was talking too much again, she thought.

"Most people don't like to talk about this. I'm usually one of them. I'm sorry to put you on the spot," said Jack.

She paused thoughtfully for a moment. "Something happened, didn't it?" He didn't respond but was looking at her steadily. "I overheard a bit of you and that priest talking." She paused again. "You had a little peek."

"A little peek?"

"That's what I call it." She leaned back against the wall near the bed. She needed all her concentration for this, a talk about religion with the president of the United States, and standing unsupported seemed a little too taxing.

"I've been a nurse for over twenty years, a lot of it in the emergency room: trauma and shocking injuries. No one plans on getting hurt, it's usually a big surprise. Hit by a car, gored by a steer, falling out of a tree, bein' shot. In Texas, a lotta people go and get themselves shot. Lotta guns here. People respond to it in different ways. Some get a peek." The way he was looking at her seemed to draw this from deep within her. This was definitely not her normal subject of conversation.

"I only see the way they are after, as I don't know them before," she continued, "but occasionally someone has a funny thing happen. It shakes them and they respond to it in different ways. It gives hope to some, despair to others. Some talk about it, but most only mention it once or twice, sometimes when they're coming out of sedation, and then never again. I think some people forget after. Then maybe some remember, but keep quiet."

"And how would you know that it's a peek?'"

"Well, I may not be a churchgoer, but I think about this all the time. I've had some funny experiences in my life. Hard to describe, but affecting to me. I don't really talk about them, as they seem to lose something when I come right out and say it. Like they're meant for a finer world and don't translate too well with just words. But they've moved me even if I can't describe them. Just beautiful in the deepest sense." She stated this very seriously, but quietly, remembering something obviously close to her heart. "It was like getting a teeny little glimpse of something so glorious that it actually hurt when it was gone. Oh, I hate to use that word—glorious, I mean. I've never forgotten them, and I'm so grateful, too. But it just doesn't fit into a religion unless you twist it around and squish it into a box too small."

"You have no doubt they are real?"

"I have no doubt. But there is no way to prove a thing. It's just my experience. Like, I know I'm here talking to you. But then my son, Sean, won't probably believe a word of that either, as he can't see this going on. He thinks I'm fooling him when I say I'm working with the president of the United States."

"You think of this 'peek' as a gift?"

"Yes, I do. But a gift with an invoice attached. It puts me at odds with what most people talk about and believe. The whole world seems to believe in a lot of religious ideas that only have a passing similarity to how I see it working. I read this quote one time by a poet. He said we aren't human beings having a spiritual experience, we're spiritual beings and we're having a human experience. I remembered it because it turned everything on its head, and yet it seemed so right. Most people seem to have it ass backwards, and it really affects the way they deal with their lives." She seemed to be getting a bit uncomfortable about the questions the president was asking.

"Just one more question. You see death.... Are you afraid of it?" asked Jack, after he had thought for a moment about what she had just said.

"I fear dying, but not death. I'm afraid of the pain and blood and disappointment, the loss of it all. I see it all the time from this angle, and it can be hard to watch. But down deep, I think it's a wonderful thing. Like finally getting off scot-free," she chuckled, "And I don't think, like your priest was probably saying, that God sits around and judges us. It's different than that somehow. More full of grace and beauty. And kindness," she paused. "But you'd sure never think that from looking at it from this end of the stick. It can look pretty grim from here."

Just then Robert came through the door and paused, seeing the concentration between his brother and the nurse leaning against the wall. He glanced back and forth once, between Evey and his brother.

"Is everything okay?" asked Robert.

"It would certainly seem so," said Jack, looking squarely at his nurse. "Thank you, Evey."

*   *   *

Late Sunday evening, Bobby was again at the podium in the auditorium being used as the press-briefing center. Just as at his previous press conference, the smoke-filled room was stifling, the lights were hot, the jostling crowd of reporters was demanding and the intense pack of humanity engulfed the senses. But, unlike the previous meeting, the mood was buoyant, almost joyous. The press was aware that Jack Kennedy was awake, and they were hoping his crisis had passed. They wanted confirmation, and Bobby was here to feed their needs. He had come nearly unannounced, slipping in again through the back door with only half an hour's notice that he was going to read a statement and answer questions. But the question foremost in the minds of all present and the millions watching around the globe was answered before he even opened his mouth to speak. In contrast to his previous appearance, with his deathly gray countenance and emotionally exhausted delivery, Bobby was buoyant today. He was composed and effusive as, caught by the cameras walking to the podium, flashing a smile and laugh of greeting to an aide, he mounted the stage.

Brushing the hair off his forehead in a typical Kennedy gesture, he again pulled a paper from his breast pocket to read a prepared statement. Someone behind him made a comment, and he turned and smiled, saying something in acknowledgment that was not picked up by the microphones. Returning to his notes, he paused for a moment as if preparing to speak, then looked up as he folded the paper in half.

"Questions?" he asked in his thick Boston accent, smiling into the den of reporters. There was a moment of quiet, like the undertow receding, before the wave of verbal interrogation engulfed the podium.

"Is the president recovering?" yelled a roomful of different voices, framing the general question in various arrangements.

"The president is awake. His condition improved noticeably with the new regimen of antibiotics that was administered by his doctors a few days ago. He awoke for the first time Thursday midday while members of his family were gathered around him in his room," said Bobby, clearly and forcefully. "It was a good Thanksgiving—"

"Has he said anything? Anything important?" yelled someone from the back before Bobby had quite finished his opening comment.

"Well, he was speechless, if you can believe that of my brother," he said jokingly. The room erupted in laughter. The gleeful exuberance in those present was a dramatic contrast to the generally decorous nature of previous press conferences. So much tension was finding its release. "Actually, he has spoken very little. We have had no international monetary policy discussions as yet," he said, smiling again. Bobby paused to allow the seriousness of the situation to sink in. "He has spoken a little with Jackie. He is gravely wounded and still sleeps most of the time. But he is awake, taking fluids, and resting normally. We, and the doctors, are very encouraged by his improvement."

"When will he make a statement?" asked someone from the left side.

"Not today, I don't think," he said, grinning. "Knowing my brother, he will certainly make a statement at some point. It will be long and lugubrious, sprinkled with obscure passages from ancient literature, as you would expect." Again laughter erupted through the room. Bobby smiled from the podium. "But I would not expect it to be anytime soon. He is awake, but he will need a long period of recuperation. How long, I couldn't say, but he is a vital man and I am sure will rebound quickly. His was a substantial injury and the body takes time to recover its strength."

"When will he resume his duties as president?" asked the AP reporter in the third row.

"We have not discussed any of that yet. It's simply too early to tell. The doctors want to wait and allow him to improve, and I am sure when he is ready, he will make an announcement publicly. Vice President Johnson is ably equipped to handle things in the interim, as he has already shown, and will work closely with Jack, with the president, as his health improves."

"There have been some reports that the president woke and read a story to Caroline," stated a reporter off to the side, near the front. "Is that true?"

Bobby paused a minute and smiled. "Actually, it was the other way around. The president awoke to the sound of his daughter Caroline reading him her favorite bedtime story."

"How is Mrs. Kennedy?" asked the sonorous, accented voice of a Dutch reporter from the second row center.

"Mrs. Kennedy is very well indeed. Medically she has recovered from her wounds and has spent the whole time since last Friday with the president in his room. And, as you can well imagine, she is just, well, so happy," said Bobby not quite able to find the right words. "She asked me to read a short statement." Bobby looked down at the paper he brought with him, unfolding it.

"Thank you" seems too insignificant a phrase to utter at a time like this. But it is with boundless gratitude that I wish to thank all those people who have prayed and yearned for the recovery of the president. Your president. My husband. Even though I have been a resident of the White House for almost three years, I never really understood the love and affection that was directed toward my husband until just these last few fateful days. I am overwhelmed

by the way America and the world have expressed so much and cared so deeply. So it is with the deepest part of myself that I wish to say "Thank you" to all who are listening and watching around the world.

"Will she be holding a press conference?" asked another reporter after a short pause.

"Not a press conference, but she will give some interviews in a more private setting. We have no schedule, as such, and it will probably be a week or more before these occur, but she will be available, probably next week. Pierre will talk to you about this later." Bobby paused, glancing over at Salinger for confirmation.

"I would like to add my comments to Jackie's—the first lady's," he said, correcting himself with a wan smile. Bobby slowed and spoke more somberly. The room quieted. "It was not until this last week that I realized how my own life is bound to Jack's. I have been deeply afraid this last week. I simply could not imagine a world without my brother in it. Then, when I looked into the faces of so many people, people whom I have never met, whom the president has never met, I think saw a similar fear. John Kennedy has infected us all with the sense that greater things are possible. And whether we acknowledge it or not, we are all bound in that expectation. And it was not just the fear of losing someone we loved that aroused such fear, but more that we would lose the connection with future possibilities, with a more grace-filled world, that struck at me, at us, so deeply. It will probably take a long time for the country to digest what has occurred— the shooting and near death of the president. But I am hoping we will find a renewed sense of justice and fairness from all this that will seep into all our national and international dealings."

The normally boisterous crowd of reporters was unnaturally, almost uncomfortably, quiet for a moment. So it was a relief when someone from the back spoke up clearly into the quieted room. "What was the story that Caroline read to the president that roused him?"

Bobby smiled bemusedly, "Ah, *Victor McGee's Trees*," he said.

That was clearly the end of Bobby's statement. But, as he turned to go, someone toward the back of the room began to clap. Slowly others followed until the room swelled with applause. It certainly wasn't for Victor's tree poem, nor even for Bobby's statement or Jackie's comments. In a simple shared understanding, the applause was sustained and all of the members of the press rose for the ovation. This was an outpouring of approval for the president, for his health, for the nation and his return, for the joy that they all felt at their collective release from an awful tragedy. Bobby had started to leave the lectern, stepping down off the podium, but turned. He started clapping, too. He wanted to be a part of it, not the object of it, and took part in the shared appreciation that the nation, and his brother, were so hopefully restored. He clapped along with the hundreds of reporters, aides, and technicians, many from countries around the globe, as they shared their emotion with the viewing audience around the world.

* * *

In walking back to the wing of the hospital where Jack was recuperating, Bobby couldn't help but be aware of the difference between his last passage over these grounds and what he was feeling now. He had been so deeply fearful of his brother's death while coming this way only a week earlier. In his despair and anger, he had nearly punched the mayor and another Dallas city official while passing through the same lobby. That would have been a great headline—*Attorney General Slugs Dallas Mayor!!*

He'd been so angry and tired that he could hardly contain his rage at the tragedy he saw unfolding. And yet now, all that seemed so distant. Jack was improving. It would obviously take a long time for him to fully recover, but he knew Jack and was sure he would bounce back in his own willfully determined way.

Bobby realized also that he would need to head back to Washington soon. Rose and the ambassador were coming down to visit and possibly stay with Jack for a while. And with Jackie here, he would be able to return to DC to pick up the pieces of the department's part in the investigation and commission being formed. He still had a queasy feeling around the issue of the commission that he knew he would have to deal with when he returned, but for the moment he was counting his blessings. They had sidestepped tragedy, just barely. Although Jack hadn't, everyone else knew they had dodged a bullet.

He had walked through the lobby and up the stairs to the second floor communications area when he saw Jiggs coming down the stairwell. Bobby was happy to see him. What a different feeling, again, from how he had greeted Jiggs when he had first arrived at Love Field nine days ago. He respected the dedication the man had shown to his mission and to Bobby personally. He had come to appreciate Jiggs' presence. Bobby had even missed him over the last day and a half when he had been replaced by his second, Martin, who was tailing him now as he walked back to the main hospital wing. Jiggs had needed a break, as they all did, and had taken some time to rest. Bobby treated him as a friend, which in his world meant rough humor and jocular ribbing.

"Up before noon. Must be an early day for you," deadpanned Bobby. But even before he had finished the comment, he realized something was wrong. Jiggs did not appear fresh and rested. Instead he had a hard and nervous appearance about him. His suit was wrinkled and looked as if he'd slept in it. He was edgy and had an air of cautious seriousness about him as he approached Bobby. There were a few people about, rushing in and out of the communications rooms, as Jiggs came closer.

"Sir, I have something for you," he said quietly. It was obvious that Jiggs did not want to let others in on the message he was relaying.

"What's going on, Jiggs?" asked Bobby. Not having seen a hint of uncertainty in Jiggs other than at their introduction the first day they had met, he found it disconcerting to see him obviously distressed now.

"Can we go in here?" asked Jiggs as he looked about him for a private room. "Martin, I'll take the detail now. Why don't you go up and spell Morgan," he said to his replacement. Martin nodded and walked off, a little uncertain at first, but having worked with Jiggs for a few years, he trusted his judgment.

Bobby and Jiggs went into one of the private rooms off to the side of the main communications area, only a few doors down from the office where Bobby had had his fateful telephone exchange with Hoover and Johnson a week earlier.

"What's this about?" asked Bobby. But Jiggs just handed him a manila envelope he pulled from his inside jacket pocket after he closed the door behind them. He said nothing as he waited for Bobby to open it.

Seeing he was going to get no further explanation, Bobby sat back on the edge of the desk and pulled a single page from the envelope and unfolded it. He had long experience with FBI and Justice department paperwork and recognized it immediately as an FBI cable. He took a moment to read it.

11/23/63
1:12 AM

To: Director, FBI (100-353496)
          EYES ONLY
From: SAC, Dallas (105-976)
Subject: Mexico City Embassy; tapes and photograph
Subject: Oswald

Re: Report of SAC GORDON SHANKLIN, Dallas 11/23/63

After communication through this office with SAC Mexico City, tapes and photo Subject LEE HARVEY OSWALD received this office via immediate flight LOVE
FIELD, DALLAS.

Subject LEE HARVEY OSWALD under Dallas Police Dept. interrogation numerous times in last 12 hours. As per my request SA HARLAN GISSELL and SA JAMES
BOOKHOUT attended interrogations. Held in the office CAPTAIN WILL FRITZ at the
Dallas Police Station spanning three line-ups required Subject's attendance. Interrogations lasted a total of approx. 6-7 hours.

After careful analysis by the attending agents, voice from subject LEE HARVEY
OSWALD reveals NO MATCH with delivered audio tapes regarding Subject discussion Soviet Embassy Sept. 27, Sept. 28, and Oct. 1 this year. All tapes appear to have
same speaker, but voice, tone, phrasing, erudition etc. are NO MATCH with Subject
in possession Dallas.

Attached photographs also show NO MATCH. There is a passing similarity to
subject from the photo images. But weight, hair and bearing are distinctly dissimilar to subject.

This information tightly held Dallas SAC office. No dissemination to Dallas Police Dept. Tapes and package delivered this office being immediately forwarded
flight L-319 to Washington. Please advise further action.

1- Bureau (100-353496) (RM)
1- Dallas (105-976)

ABSOLUTELY NO DUPLICATES OR PHOTOCOPIES TO
BE MADE FROM THIS DOCUMENT.

Bobby sat back after reading the memo the first time and then read it
again. He felt the bottom dropping out of his recently restored tranquil-
ity.

"How did you get this?" he asked Jiggs, without looking up. Jiggs could
see it was making the impact he had assumed it would.

"I have a *contact* at the Bureau," said Jiggs, accentuating the word cautiously. "This contact is aware I am on the attorney general's detail. He in-

formed me he had a very important document for the attorney general."

"And this *contact*," said Bobby, pausing on the word, "do you have faith in his information?"

"I do. As you probably know, I was FBI. I have a history with the Bureau," said Jiggs. "I still have some friends there."

Bobby realized he didn't know Jiggs. He had been so preoccupied with other more pressing concerns that he had no real knowledge of the agent assigned to protect him. He had come to appreciate his presence, but there were more complex undercurrents to this man than he had supposed.

Bobby was trying to organize his thoughts. This was explosive information. The cable was dated Nov 23 at 1:12 am, the early morning hours after the night of the assassination attempt. A direct cable to the Director of the FBI from his field office chief in Dallas. Hoover therefore knew there was no validity to the supposed tapes of Lee Oswald, the all-but-convicted and now dead "lone nut" who was accused of shooting his brother. All the conversations that Bobby had had with Hoover and Johnson regarding the potential plot and the assassination attempt possibly being Soviet- or Cuban-sponsored, which had occurred almost twelve hours after Hoover had received this cable, were lies. And Hoover had known it the whole time.

"That fucking bastard," uttered Bobby under his breath.

He had been duped. He was oddly aware he was in a calm moment before anger engulfed him. He sat there, baffled, trying to understand the implications of what he was reading before emotion overtook him.

If Hoover knew on the night of the shooting that the supposed conversation between Oswald and the Soviet Embassy's attaché, who was so dreaded in the West as an assassination expert, did *not* involve Oswald, why would he persist in supporting such a lie? How could it possibly help him? And Vice President Johnson, did he know this as well? Was he in on the fabricated story, or was he also conned by Hoover? Hoover and Johnson were such fast buddies that Bobby could not imagine they did not share the subterfuge. They had both used the information that Oswald was a Soviet agent to divert a thorough investigation of the events around the shooting to a special, handpicked commission. It was tacitly understood that this commission, which was still being assembled, would fashion the investigation around the results necessary to convict Oswald in the nation's eyes as the shooter, the *only* shooter, of the president. Bobby even heard that Johnson browbeat Chief Justice Earl Warren and Senator

Richard Russell into chairing the committee by invoking the potential of a nuclear exchange with the Soviets, just as he had with Bobby.

But the need for all of this collapsed if the audiotapes from Mexico City did not match Oswald's voice. And the reason for the subterfuge fell apart if there was no direct Soviet or Cuban connection with the shooting of the president. Bobby was trying to remember, in his conversations with Hoover, what he had said specifically about the tapes' acquisition and authenticity. As he remembered it, Hoover had sidestepped that point, and Bobby had not pressed it fully.

Yet he had sensed real fear in Hoover and Johnson regarding the information he was given about the Mexico connection implicating the Soviets as sponsors of Oswald's plotting. Were they faking that? That seemed hardly possible. Bobby had had many dealings with Hoover and had never noticed a twinge of concern or fear for humanity in him. And yet he was sure he had sensed it during his last telephone exchange. It was more reasonable to assume that the fear was real, but the reason for it deliberately misdirected.

"You know the implications of this, don't you?" asked Bobby, eyes boring into Jiggs. "You overheard my conversations the morning after the shooting while I was talking with Hoover and Johnson." It was a statement that required a response.

"I didn't mean to, sir." Jiggs was sincerely apologetic, but not contrite. "This hospital is not made for security. When I realized that I was overhearing your second conversation through the door, I moved down the hall a ways. But even two doors down, I could still make out parts of the conversation, most of it really. I considered going around the corner, but that would have eliminated line of sight with your location. So then I just settled into being sure no one else came out of the Comm room who might hear what was being said."

Bobby thought about that for a moment. "And what did you think of what you heard?" Since he knew about it, Bobby was grudgingly curious at Jiggs's take on it.

"It was a Faustian bargain, for sure. I know this cable shows that Hoover pulled a fast one. Hoover's sharp. A black hole right at the top of the Bureau. But I can't say I understand the particulars of it all."

Bobby looked intently at the cable. "Well, that makes two of us, Jiggs."

They stood silently facing each other in the small side office for a moment. "Does anyone else know about this?" asked Bobby. He sat back on the edge of the desk as he tried to maneuver his thoughts through the labyrinthine corridors of Hoover's deceits.

"No one outside the Bureau but you," answered Jiggs, "and me."

"How did your contact get this?" asked Bobby, holding the paper up slightly.

"I, uh, can't tell you," said Jiggs almost apologetically, shaking his head, "but I trust him. The one condition for receiving this was that its source not be revealed. I have to keep my word on that."

Bobby nodded somberly. He could tell this was not a question he would get the answer to anytime soon. "You know that the release of this information is a punishable offense. And I am not talking just loss of position. A person would do serious time for this."

"I am sure this party is very aware of the jeopardy they have placed themselves in," responded Jiggs. "*Very* aware."

Bobby sat on the desk edge, rubbing his face and forehead. "Shit, shit, shit!" he exploded, pounding the desk with his fist as he stood up facing away from Jiggs. "And I *believed* that *bastard*! I'll never make that mistake again," he said fiercely.

Chapter 16

For the great enemy of the truth is very often not the lie—deliberate, contrived,
and dishonest—but the myth—persistent, persuasive, and unrealistic.
Too often we hold fast to the clichés of our forebears. We subject all facts to a prefabri-
cated set of interpretations. We enjoy the comfort of opinion without the discomfort of
thought. Mythology distracts us everywhere—in government as in business,
in politics as in economics, in foreign affairs as in domestic affairs.
—*John F. Kennedy, 1962*

Half the truth is often a great lie.
—*Benjamin Franklin*

Friday, October 11, 1968
Hyannisport, MA

Patrick sat in his car in the parking area for military flight personnel at
Andrews Air Force Base, just outside of Washington, D.C. He was a few
minutes early. Listening to the ticking of the engine as it cooled after the
drive over, he wondered how it would look when the early morning light
exposed his powder blue Fairlane nestled among all the staid dark blue
and olive drab vehicles—an oddly exposed orphan among more serious
Detroit automotive machinery.

Evelyn Lincoln had called late last night and told him the president
was spending the weekend at his Hyannisport, Massachusetts, home, and
Mr. Hennessey's presence was requested. A military passenger transport
regularly shuttled between Andrews and Otis Air Force Base, located on
Cape Cod. A seat was reserved for him. "It will depart at 8:00 p.m. sharp,
so please, *do* be on time," Mrs. Lincoln said in her usual precise manner.
There was no denying a request like that.

There was still a ten-minute wait before he signed in for his flight.
Patrick spent the moments thinking about Jenna. He had been looking
forward to seeing her tonight, as they planned to go to the movies to see
2001: A Space Odyssey. It would be the second time for both of them.
After the recent Apollo mission, the film surged back into theaters to full-
house attendance. Everyone's heads were in space from the recent successful lunar orbit. Besides, he would have gone to see *Planet of the Apes* again
if she had wanted to. Spending time with her was all he desired. But he
called her this morning and broke it off, telling her of his weekend sum-

mons to the president's home on Cape Cod.

"Oh, that excuse. I get that from all my boyfriends," she said. "To play more golf, I suppose?"

"I don't think so. More book discussions, I assume," said Patrick. It was the first time she had called him her boyfriend, and it sent a little shiver up his spine.

"You sure you're not seeing another librarian on the side?" asked Jenna.

"I can hardly handle the one I'm seeing now," he blurted, at which she laughed approvingly.

He could tell she was disappointed, but Jenna knew about the nature of his and JFK's activities. It was all revealed during their morning tea with Mrs. Kennedy when they had driven up to Glen Ora to pick up Patrick's car. During that visit, Mrs. Kennedy mentioned "how pleased Jack was with Patrick's progress on his memoirs." Jenna's eyes had enlarged twofold. She put down the tea cup from which she was drinking and simply stared at Patrick for the longest time. The surprise was not lost on the first lady, who put her hand to her mouth and said, "Oh, I do believe I was not supposed to mention that." She seemed to find the whole exchange rather humorous, though, as she giggled about how Jack would never trust her with national secrets in the future. *As if this was in the realm of a national secret*, thought Patrick. He had the feeling she enjoyed revealing his role and playing innocent to Jenna's surprise.

Mrs. Kennedy was engaged for much of the time with little Joseph, their fourth child. Neither Caroline nor John Jr. made an appearance, as they were in school. Joseph, almost one year old, was quiet for most of their tea time, just wanting to be held, and only waking later to be fed as they were leaving. Even Patrick was given a chance to hold the sleeping tyke and spent about ten minutes walking him around the room cooing and bouncing him, to the approval of both women. When they were walking back to their cars parked by the barn, though, Jenna punched him hard in the arm. "That's for being so good at keeping secrets from me," she said, half angry, the other half obviously impressed. Patrick, now sitting in his car musing on the events of over a week ago, thought he still had a bruise from the assault.

So instead of going to the movies, they had squeezed in a quick meal at Marley's Grill before he drove out to Andrews. They talked of the upcoming elections, the recent Apollo mission to the moon, and whether the

Beatles or the Stones were the defining band of the decade. "Of course it was the Beatles," said Patrick. Jenna chose the Stones, probably just to be contrary. "Boys and their ballgames," she commented dismissively when Patrick mentioned that the Washington Redskins didn't look good for Super Bowl III. Jenna also made fun of his car, his musical tastes, and his proximity to the president giving him a swelled head. "Now don't let him try to get you to run for office somewhere, like North Dakota," she said. He took her quirky needling as an expression of nascent affection. At least he hoped so.

Just the night before, Patrick had gotten a call from his Uncle Duncan. He was motoring down to DC early next week and wondered about corralling Patrick for one of their driveabouts. Patrick responded enthusiastically and mentioned bringing along a new friend, Jenna. "I want you to meet her." His old Irish uncle paused a moment. Their roamings had included only the two of them, even when he was involved with Katherine.

"It's tha' serious, nuw?" Duncan responded thoughtfully in his native brogue.

"Fraid so, Dunc" said Patrick. Ever since meeting Jenna, he had day-dreamed about the three of them sharing a long evening drive.

"I'll be bringin' an extra sandwich then," replied his Uncle.

* * *

Having dallied long enough, Patrick pulled his bags from the back seat and entered the small air terminal. After showing ID and signing in for the flight, he was directed to a DC-6 sitting on the tarmac about fifty yards away.

"You can board right now, sir," stated the crew-cut sergeant. "The flight will be departing at twenty hundred hours."

The Douglas DC-6 was a prop-driven workhorse used as a shuttle between Andrews and Otis. Due to Kennedy's family home being only a twelve-mile drive from Otis, there was a steady stream of traffic, both civilian and military, that traveled the route. It was a balmy, wet evening in DC, and even though he was overly warm, Patrick pulled up his collar against the moisture as he walked to the waiting plane and up its retractable stair. On entering, he became aware of the sharp difference between this flight and previous ones he had taken on Air Force One. This aircraft had a carrying capacity of about seventy-five when fully loaded. There was no need to think about pilfering souvenirs as he had done on Air Force One, because there weren't any. He settled in as the half-full plane taxied out to the runway for a quick takeoff.

Patrick got to work on finishing up an article he was writing for the *Post*. He had spent part of the day tracking down sources on a recent Spiro Agnew comment. Less than a month from the election, the campaigns were ramping up to their November climax, and the Nixon/Agnew ticket was in trouble. It was unclear to Patrick whether Agnew was reaching for inflammatory comments in desperation or, as he supposed was more probable, just couldn't help himself from inciting the media. Just yesterday evening he responded to vice presidential candidate Robert Kennedy's reference to the extended calm in Southeast Asia and the sprinkling of protests over civil rights occurring in a number of cities. Agnew stated that "Ultra-liberalism today translates into a whimpering isolationism in foreign policy, a mulish obstructionism in domestic policy, and a pusillanimous pussyfooting on the critical issue of law and order." He then went on to denigrate the press with "Some newspapers are fit only to line the bottom of bird cages." Patrick, like many a reporter, had cried "fowl," and with avian allusions stretched to their breaking point, took up the challenge. "Parroting" his bird cage analogy, national reporters suggested a number of better uses to which Agnew's speech sheets could be put.

The *Daily News* put a special pair of reporters on Agnew's "tail" to "bird dog this queer duck" all the way to the election. A few reporters suggested Agnew was prime "jailbird" material due to some questionable financial practices in his past, and could line his cell with *Avian Weekly* when the time came.

Patrick had an hour and a half to while away. Between finishing up his article, daydreaming about Jenna, and reading the last part of the series by Marvin Weeks, he had more than enough to fill the trip. Since he knew it would be sobering, he saved the Weeks article for last.

Betrayal in Dealey Plaza
- by Marvin Weeks

Washington, D.C. By now everyone is familiar with Dealey Plaza, the small Dallas park surrounded by a number of municipal and commercial buildings, which formed the borders of the motorcade's path through which President Kennedy's entourage traveled on November 22, 1963, almost five years ago. The USCPASIC hearings—which involved testimony from FBI and CIA operatives, ballistics and military experts, eyewitnesses and four separate groups of investigative teams—led to capital charges against numerous individuals, as well as felony and misdemeanor convictions of many participants. A number of those charged never made it to court, due either to untimely death or disappearance. Others were convicted and are now serving sentences. A few have been recently pardoned or had sentences reduced, due to intercession by President Kennedy.

For our readers, I have deleted extraneous information and rarefied scientific discourse involving ballistic and medical evidence in order to more clearly summarize the events of that day and those that followed.

Marvin Weeks: Observing The Trials as closely as I have over the years, I've found no better source of information than Mr. Michael Blassdoe, a ballistics expert formerly with the FBI for eight years, currently lead investigator with the New York City Police Department for over twelve years and an investigative attaché to the hearings. Thank you, Michael, for discussing these serious issues with me. Let's get right to it.

Okay, one thing that is difficult to understand was the involvement of so many individuals in the shooting of the president. I think a lot of people get confused about that.

Michael Blassdoe: Thank you for that introduction, Marvin. Well, to simplify, there were three shooters, each with a spotter, a lookout, so to speak. They worked in pairs—a pair at the grassy incline in front of the motorcade's route, a pair in the Book Depository at the sixth floor and a pair on the roof of the Dallas County Records building. It was a well-thought-out plan executed by professionals. These men had military training and used a classic technique of triangulation, that is, trapping the target in a crossfire, so there is little chance of failure.

Weeks: But why so many? Why didn't the team in the Book Depository just take the shot?

Blassdoe: Well, they needed to be able to implicate Mr. Oswald in the shooting, and that required a more complex operation. The use of a weapon that was owned and registered to him, used in the shooting and left on site, meant Mr. Oswald could be forensically linked to the attempted assassination. But they also needed to be sure they used a weapon capable of hitting its intended target. And that was a problem with the Mannlicher-Carcano rifle Oswald had purchased. His ownership of such a poor weapon created some serious difficulties.

Weeks: And why is that?

Blassdoe: Because it was a World War II piece of mass-manufactured junk. The Italians should have been given a humanitarian award for creating a weapon that incurred so few casualties. It was hard to load, had a propensity to jam, often misfired and was poorly constructed, which made it inaccurate. Not the weapon of choice for a marksman, but cheap, which may have been why Oswald mail-ordered it. And Oswald's was a carbine version of the rifle; having a 9-inch shorter barrel made it even less accurate.

The FBI's initially released documents, purporting to show how Oswald fired three shots that accounted for all the wounds inflicted on both President Kennedy and Governor Connally, were very problematic.

See, the first shot supposedly taken by Oswald, this experienced marksman, the shot he had all the time in the world to line up—well, it missed by a mile. It was a shot from behind, which passed over the receding limo and landed 122 yards beyond the target. It never got within twelve feet of the president! Now how does someone who was initially presented by the FBI as such a practiced sharpshooter, using a telescopic sight, miss the first and best opportunity he has by such a huge margin? Then the second shot precisely hits the president and magically goes through him into Governor Connally? And then the third just barely misses JFK's head as it grazes the first lady in the neck?

The second and third shots were much harder. They were taken only a few seconds apart and required rebolting the rifle to load another round into the chamber, resighting the target slowly moving away from him, and then shooting. The targeting solution for a downward trajectory—remember the sniper's nest was six floors above street grade—with the target moving away from the shooter, requires a significant understanding of ballistics. It's a highly skilled ability requiring the best of equipment finely tuned from persistent practice. It would be hard to imagine such accuracy from a poorly manufactured military-surplus weapon that, upon analysis, had a misaligned, loosely mounted scope with defective optics.

These were all very difficult shots to make in such a compressed time frame. It confounded the Congressional Commission how Oswald could miss one shot, any shot, by such a wide margin, but hit the other two so precisely.

Weeks: You have mentioned earlier to me that these factors suggested to congressional investigators the possibility that the sniper's nest shots were just a decoy. How so?

Blassdoe: Yes. It was finally concluded that the carbine, shooting from the Book Depository, was just for show. It was hanging out the window for all to see, making a loud supersonic crack with no silencer above a crowd of people. At first it was thought that Oswald was just a clumsy simpleton who wouldn't have known better and didn't care if he got caught. After further investigation though, they realized it had been planned that way, to draw attention and implicate Oswald.

The three shots from that window were deliberately fired into the ground in grassy Dealey Plaza, beyond the range of the limousine in which Kennedy was riding. The first shot, and the next two, were intended to miss the limo. They wanted the sound and fury, but didn't want any of the slugs to end up in the vehicle as evidence. But they did need the freshly fired cartridges on the floor by the window of the Depository, and the recently fired gun to be found as evidence. So they planned to direct their shots into the dirt and figured no one would be the wiser. Ironically though, in trying to miss entirely, they hit a concrete curb beyond the motorcade, and the first bullet broke off sections of the curb that ricocheted into a bystander, Mr. Tague, who was standing beside a policeman. That shot was back in play as evidence. They couldn't have been happy about that.

Weeks: Did they even know?

Blassdoe: Probably not till later, when the whole thing started to unravel.

Weeks: So where did the bullets come from that actually hit the president?

Blassdoe: Well, that was the cunning part of this plan. He was targeted in two ways. The shooter who was to leave the ballistic evidence in the car was on the roof of the Dallas County Records Building, that six-story building southeast of the Book Depository. Now coming from a location on that roof, a fired round would present a ballistic solution very similar to a shot fired from the 6th floor of the Book Depository Building. They had a nearly identical line of sight. So this was well planned to again focus the attention on the suspect in the Book Depository. It was a partially silenced sabot round.

Weeks: A what?

Blassdoe: A sabot round. It's a method in which a bullet can be reused. It's first fired from a selected rifle into a big drum of water. You could shoot it into a swimming pool if you like. It leaves all the barrel markings from this rifle on the bullet as a kind of fingerprint, unique to every rifle. It's from these barrel imprints on the recovered bullets that the FBI matches a slug to the gun from which it was fired. But a person can gather up these undamaged, pre-fired bullets, reload them into cartridges with a thin protective liner around them that comes off when re-fired, and then use them in a second rifle. The slugs will then appear to have come from the original rifle. The sabot bushing keeps the bullets away from the new barrel during firing, leaving the original incriminating markings intact.

Oswald's Mannlicher-Carcano rifle, even though a poor excuse for a weapon, gave a distinctive rifling pattern to its bullets. The conspirators took the rifle from him, possibly without his knowledge—or maybe with it, we'll never know—and shot and recovered a few dozen rounds. They loaded them into new cartridges that could be fired from a high-powered, well-sighted rifle. The already existing rifling marks would give the impression they came from Oswald's gun. It's not too difficult for someone familiar with commercial or military ordnance. So while the most visible shooter was firing wide from the Book Depository, the real shooter was quietly and accurately plugging away from above and behind him, leaving implicating rounds in the limo, using a much better weapon.

Weeks: How did the Commission discover this? I mean, didn't these assassins cover their tracks?

Blassdoe: Well, for a long time they didn't. I mean the Commission didn't. They suspected as much for a while. Sabot rounds are tricky and lack some of the gyroscopic stabilization that occurs from barrel-to-bullet contact during firing. This can create a bullet that wobbles or even falls end over end while in flight. Judging from the elongated entry wounds to the president and the governor, the bullets appeared to have been unstable before impact.

The investigators repeatedly scoured the rooftops of the Dal-Tex and Dallas Records buildings for evidence to place a shooter up there, but they couldn't find a thing. Either it was a false assumption or the shooter, being very professional, made no marks and left no evidence. But the heat wave of '64 did them in.

Weeks: In what way?

Blassdoe: Well, if it weren't for that really hot summer, the evidence might never have been found. But the air handler on the roof of the Dallas Records Building failed.

Weeks: What's an air handler?

Blassdoe: One of those big air conditioning units they con-struct on the flat rooftops of office buildings downtown. It looks like a big metal box parked up there with a lot of fans on the outside. Well, the one near the west parapet wall started to leak. So they disassembled it to make repairs. And when they did, one of the sharp-eyed workers saw a little brass cartridge sitting under the tarpaper curbing, just as patient as you please. It had probably rolled under, well out of reach or even sight. Either the shooter and his spotter hadn't realized it, or couldn't do a thing about it. It was concealed there for about eight months.

Weeks: Why assume it was involved with the Kennedy shooting? Maybe it was from another rifle?

Blassdoe: You mean like someone up there hunting deer or squirrel? (laughing) Okay, sorry. What they found, attached to the business end of the cartridge casing, was the partial remains of a telltale grommet-like fitting. It was just what you'd expect from sabot round construction. The cartridge also had a 1953 sourc-ing mark from Twin Cities Arsenal, a military munitions supplier. They don't make sport munitions. It was an unusual and exciting discovery for the Congressional Commission. It went a long way toward verifying their assumptions about how the assassination attempt had been carried out.

I can just imagine what the spotter felt like when he saw the cartridge eject and roll under the lip of that air handler. Oh, god-damn! And...well, they almost got away with it.

Weeks: Okay, so there is a rifleman up on the roof of the Dallas Records Building behind the motorcade, and there is a decoy shooter in the Book Depository. Then why did they need a man on the grassy incline in the front?

Blassdoe: Insurance and accuracy. The Dallas Records rooftop shooter was to incur injury, but above all, to leave evi-dence. But the grassy incline shooter was what they'd call the money shot. He had the best, closest and most direct line on the president. The motorcade was moving toward him at low speed and only thirty yards away. With a sharpshooter in that position, it would be very hard to miss.

Weeks: Did he use those sabot bullets too?

Blassdoe: He probably could have, but then there would have been more bullets in the limo than shots heard fired. He instead used frangible bullets, disintegrating bullets. They explode on impact, cause a tremendous amount of damage to an intended target and are not identifiable afterwards. He had a spotter with him dressed and credentialed as a Secret Service agent. He used a rifle with a subsonic muzzle velocity and silencer. Right after this man fired his two shots, he passed the gun to the spotter and walked away. His accomplice disassembled the gun in about five seconds, then diverted attention away from the area by flashing his credentials. It gave them both enough time to melt into the crowd and escape.

Weeks: Okay, but if he was such a 'money shot' as you say, how did he miss?

Blassdoe: (at this point Mr. Blassdoe remained quiet for a moment) It would seem that Mr. Kennedy was saved by his injured back. Weird, huh? A lifetime of infirmity from degenerating lower vertebrae caused him endless pain. Some of the difficulties with his back came out in the hearings. In the end, it's what saved his life. It seems the painkillers he was on at the time were dissipating. He had a muscle spasm that hurt so much he twisted to his left, toward the first lady. He had the spasm just when the shots rang out. Because of that, shots that surely would have been fatal went wide, causing injury rather than death. And the force of the shots that did hit him pushed him over and into the lap of Mrs. Kennedy. The shooters tried to follow him down and get another hit, but they missed. It's assumed that the shot that hit Mrs. Kennedy in the neck was really aimed at the falling Mr. Kennedy. She was not an intended target. It was just incredibly beneficial timing on the president's part. If you're a religious man, well…

Weeks: That makes a lot of sense, but it seems so complicated.

Blassdoe: To me and you maybe, but not to a group of pros. Some were American military trained—the best in the world, and expert at what they did—which, incidentally, was killing people. There's a whole covert world of espionage and warcraft that the American citizen is not privy to, and its horrific nature is seen only when it erupts into public view.

Weeks: Michael, judging from the complexity of the plan and the possible pitfalls, how did they ever think it would succeed?

Blassdoe: Well, they took a massive gamble, that's for certain. It's hard to imagine now how they could possibly have pulled it off. But when the mechanics of the plot were exposed during the investigations, it became somewhat more plausible. They were quite certain that the scenario they created from planted evidence that indicated Cuban and Soviet involvement would immediately inflame an impassioned public bent on revenge. This furious groundswell would obscure all else. Remember, these people deal in misinformation and propaganda as their lifeblood. They had overthrown Asian and South American governments with these same techniques in the past. Their boldness was in trying the same formula at home, on American soil. But the conspirators failed to achieve two main objectives.

First, they assumed they would be successful in killing the president of the United States. And second, they assumed they would spirit Mr. Oswald, their designated scapegoat, out of the country and dispose of him. They were unsuccessful at gaining either objective.

Weeks: We've talked at length about this, Michael, but for our readers, would you outline the plotters' motivation and strategy?

Blassdoe: Well, the crucible of insurrection against the president was nurtured by a nucleus of CIA agents, with the involvement of organized crime and anti-Castro Cubans. They also gained support from various members of the military. Their main objective was to rid Cuba of Castro and reinstall a United States-friendly government on that small island, as well as to rid the government of a president who was thwarting their intentions on so many levels. It was not a CIA-wide conspiracy by any means, although it eventually engulfed a significant segment of the upper echelon of that organization due to the later cover-up.

Kennedy refused to allow American military assistance during the '61 invasion of Cuba at the Bay of Pigs. The blame for that CIA instigated debacle was laid at Kennedy's doorstep. When the president avoided an invasion of Cuba during the Missile Crisis of '62, opposition became even more vociferous. And when word of a possible rapprochement with Castro began to surface, their hatred toward Kennedy and their desire for a solution took on intense urgency.

You must remember also that the Justice Department was decimating the ranks of the Mafia under Robert Kennedy's direction, creating an added dimension to the pressure. The Mob, whose flourishing empire in Cuba was eliminated by Castro, needed release from RFK's assault on their embattled ranks. Added to this stew, a coterie of well financed right-wing enthusiasts sympathized with the Cubans and were diametrically opposed to JFK and what they perceived as his soft-on-communism policies. They provided the funding to circumvent the monetary restrictions such an operation would present if it were run through the agency or the military. These people were already funding small military operations against Cuba outside the purview of the U.S. government. This financial support gave the plotters a lot more freedom. And Texas, central to this financial cabal, was ironically the location in which this scheme finally played out. This was not the optimum original scenario, though, having the killing field be in their own front yard. Two earlier attempts, in Chicago and Tampa, never fully developed.

I'd like to quote Denzel Thurmond, the Chief Counsel for USCPASIC. In his summary he stated, "Trying to decide whether it was the Mafia, the Cuban anti-Castro extremists, the shadow military or the moneyed oil interests who were most responsible for the planning and execution of the plot to exterminate the president was like trying to separate bath water into distinct portions, all the while not understanding that the CIA was the bathtub."

With the killing of the American president by a pro-communist, pro-Cuban assassin, or at least one who appeared as such, there was a very strong probability that America would strike back. Castro would be the main target, Cuba would finally be invaded, and, it was hoped by some, that military action would then be expanded toward the Soviets. There was a very strong undercurrent of belief in areas of the military and the government that time was running out to strike a decisive blow against communism.

Oswald was the perfect patsy. He was a CIA-trained defector to Russia who was then repatriated to the United States. He was active as a flamboyant FBI troublemaker, drawing out pro-Castro Cubans in the United States to be tagged and investigated by the FBI. He had a public trail a mile wide showing communist sympathies with no one outside the clandestine services knowing he was an undercover provocateur whose whole life had been circumscribed by the agencies. He was doing their bidding. His past activities could be perfectly molded to appear to be those of a communist assassin intent on carrying out the designs of a foreign power. The CIA and FBI needed only to disavow any connection with him, leaving him dangling in the wind, to cement his appearance as a politically motivated killer.

Weeks: It was a scheme to make Oswald out to be precisely what he appeared to be.

Blassdoe: That's exactly right. A small cell of CIA operatives in Mexico City, six weeks before the shooting, faked voice tapes and pictures of an "Oswald" who was communicating with an assassination expert at the Soviet embassy. Later, when a scan of the name Oswald was initiated at the CIA, it was understood that these tapes and pictures would surface, giving him great credence as a communist operative who was violently motivated. They also had an Oswald look-alike creating memorable and incriminating scenes at numerous Dallas locations weeks before the shooting.

Weeks: Okay, here it is. I want to talk a little more about this. This was referred to as the "Twinning of Oswald" during the Trials. Could you go into that a bit?

Blassdoe: This portion of the whole endeavor gets a little surreal. It shows the twisted depths of the CIA in its "wilderness of mirrors" mentality, so to speak. There were effectively two Oswalds.

During the first stages of the investigation by the Congressional Committee, there appeared to be a number of anomalies. Oswald sightings had occurred in different locations at the same time. He was clearly identified by a car salesman, a local firing range member, coffee house employees and numerous others. During these sightings, he was full of swagger, boldly making attention-grabbing comments that were indelibly marked in the memories of the observers. During a more notable encounter two weeks before the assassination attempt, he gave his name to the salesman at the Dallas Lincoln Mercury dealership and took a fast drive in a new car, all the while talking about the big sum of money he was about to acquire. The real Oswald didn't drive, never had a driver's license, didn't own a car and always took public transportation. And during this incident, as well as all the others, the real Oswald was time-stamped at work at the Book Depository.

Immediately after the shooting, Oswald was seen walking out the front of the Book Depository, walking seven blocks east along Elm Street, catching a bus back toward the Book Depository, then switching to a cab when the bus was held up in traffic. At the same time, five witnesses, including a policeman, saw Oswald run out the side of the Book Depository, jump into a Nash Rambler on Elm Street driven by a heavy-set Latin man, and race away west.

At first it was assumed witnesses had simply been mistaken about either really seeing Mr. Oswald, or mistaken in their timing. But these observations accumulated to an alarming degree. Then the researchers looking into Lee Harvey Oswald's early life found similar anomalies. While Oswald was in Russia during his defection, he was also noted making numerous appearances in the United States. FBI Director Hoover even went so far as to memo field offices in 1960, three years before the events in Dallas, that an impostor might be using Lee Oswald's identification, since Oswald's name was flagged for observation by the Bureau as a defector.

The committee was shocked to realize that there had been two Oswalds, sharing the same name and a similar life trajectory for years, possibly working together, or at least aware of the existence of the other.

Weeks: So how did the FBI reconcile all these contradictory sightings of Oswald?

Blassdoe: Very easily. They simply discarded the ones that didn't fit their scenario. All contradictory information was culled from the FBI Summary Report of the shooting of the president as if it never existed. That little bit of deception dropped them in a lot of hot water later on.

But for this overall assassination plan to work, a living Oswald had to stay out of the reach of any real investigation. It was never intended that Oswald would be apprehended and interrogated. The strategy was for him to depart on a small plane from Redbird Airport, eight miles outside Dallas, and be on his way toward Cuba by the time his name popped up on police radar—a flight, incidentally, that he would most probably not have lived to see the end of.

This scenario was disrupted in two ways. First, Oswald deviated from his assignment. We think he slowly came to realize he was being set up. He'd been directed to go on a mission for which he would be met at the Houston Viaduct and transported to Redbird Airport for a short flight. Remember, he didn't drive, and public transportation didn't go there directly.

But he'd witnessed the president being shot. If this was the plan, it was far more than a diversion. We believe he decided, while walking the streets, to abort his mission. He would "go to ground" at the Texas Theatre near his rooming house and meet his contact for further instructions. When he arrives, he shifts from patron to patron seated in the 900-seat main floor auditorium. There were only a few customers scattered about in the middle of the day, and he was hoping one was his contact. Probably gets worried. He has worked with the services for years and knows of their cold-hearted tactics. Why did the police focus on his place of employment, even making a beeline to the floor he had been working on? The sounds of sirens run up and down the street outside the theatre. To his mind, something is very wrong.

The second disruption was caused by a Dallas Police patrolman, J. D. Tippit. He had been directed to transport Oswald to Redbird Airport. This might seem unusual, but it was not uncommon in the loosey-goosey Dallas force for officers to have activities unrelated to police work, even while on duty. He lived near the airport and worked three jobs to support his family. He needed the money. He knew Oswald by sight, as they had both spent time in Oak Cliff. So picking him up at the bus stop and dropping him at Redbird seemed simple enough.

But while Oswald was losing his religion in the back of the Texas Theatre, something similar was happening to Patrolman Tippit. Following instructions, Tippit waited at the Gloco gas station for the bus from downtown Dallas. The bus arrives, but without Oswald . While listening to frantic APBs on his radio describing the shooting of the president of the United States, Tippit probably realizes he is the only cop who hasn't converged on the Plaza. Plagued by concern that he might be way out of his depth regarding this little side job he's got, he spends the next few minutes racing around Oak Cliff looking for his passenger, who he thinks might have arrived another way.

Meanwhile, the Oswald-twin is well aware that things are coming undone. He had been staying at Jack Ruby's apartment in Oak Cliff, a clearinghouse for the conspiracy. He needed to deal with Oswald. He knows he will go to the Theatre, as they are aware of each other and have been working in a coordinated fashion for years. He goes to meet him, walking the half dozen blocks. On the way, Officer Tippit sees him from his patrol car and mistakes him for the real Oswald. Tippit stops. They talk. We don't know what was said, but something either didn't add up for Officer Tippit, or the twin realized Tippit had passed a threshold just by suspecting his separate identity. Tippit gets out of the car to talk with the man. But the twin, three moves ahead of him, shoots and kills Tippit as he rounds the front of the vehicle. The twin had a wallet full of ID showing himself to be Oswald. He drops it on the ground right next to the dead officer. He had planned on leaving it wedged into the seat of the officer's police car at the airport, where he had originally planned on killing him, finalizing the case against their fall guy. But leaving it beside the dead officer was probably the best he could do under the changed circumstances.

The twin then runs off to the Theatre, hiding in the balcony as the police follow and close in. Oswald is cornered, but instead of being shot down when he tries to fight his way out, he is arrested and brought to the station.

Weeks: Do you think Tippit had any part in the plot against the president?

Blassdoe: No, I think he was tangled up in something way above his pay grade. He probably had no comprehension of what he was mixed up with. He was just getting an easy hundred bucks to drive a guy seven miles to the airport on city time. Easy-sneezy. In a curious twist, he foiled their plot.

Weeks: So with both the president's and Oswald's unintended survival, this upended their strategy.

Blassdoe: Yes, significantly. Oswald had to be eliminated to salvage anything of the original plan. It was partially discredited a little later when the recordings and pictures from Mexico City arrived in Dallas during Oswald's interrogation, and proved to be similar but no match to Oswald. This put into serious question the original possibility of its being a foreign-led assassination attempt, as the supposed proof fell apart upon comparison to the living Oswald. The plotters' exposure was assured if Mr. Oswald was processed in the American justice system. The plan was coming apart at the seams. So the services of the local Mob were tapped to enlist one of their own, Jack Rubenstein, already deeply involved with the operation of the assassination. He was to kill Mr. Oswald. It was a choice made in haste and was imposed upon a reluctant Mr. Rubenstein—and the job was done right inside the Dallas Police station.

Weeks: So with all this information, what was Oswald's part in the plot?

Blassdoe: Now that has been a point of contention with investigators for a long time. With the self-inflicted death of George de Mohrenschildt, Oswald's suspected CIA handler during Oswald's time in Dallas, we may never really know under what assumptions he was operating. Oswald is dead, so there is no information there. His twin's trail ended in New Mexico, but he has never been found or named. Most think he was disposed of rather quickly. Some have contended that Oswald was an innocent, used by clandestine services for years on end and caught in the crossfire of their competing agendas. A few have even suggested he be treated as a patriot for following orders he was given, thinking himself to be a part of a larger plan to support America's strategy in the Caribbean. Remember, he wasn't just a deranged loner who was thrown to the wolves. He was a lifelong member of the clandestine community who was dangled before the public as an expendable scapegoat to take the brunt of the guilt.

But most believe he had some inkling of the larger plan involving the president. Whether he had full knowledge it was to kill Mr. Kennedy, or whether he was led to believe it was a sort of diversionary activity to test the Secret Service's presidential protection as some had speculated, may never be known. The real truth of his involvement probably died with him and has thus created a convoluted nest of competing theories.

I might quote the Dallas Police Chief Jesse Curry, though, when he stated, "We don't have any proof that Oswald fired the rifle, and never did. Nobody's yet been able to put him in that building with a gun in his hand."

Weeks: Considering all the potential pitfalls around such an exploit, it seems preposterous they could succeed with such a plan.

Blassdoe: You would think. But do you remember the original plan for investigation that was being floated just a week or so after the shooting—putting it all under the umbrella of a hand-picked commission, shunting it into a closed investigation? By that time, the FBI, CIA and Military Intelligence had concocted the "Mythology of Lee Harvey Oswald," as I like to call it. They certainly wove a convincing tale. But all that changed the day Bobby Kennedy turned the tables at that press conference at Parkland Medical.

Weeks: Yes. I was watching on TV at the time, I could feel the ripples of fear and excitement running through everyone who was watching.

Blassdoe: An extremely significant event, that's for sure. The fires of incinerating documents burned late that night as the branches busily covered up their cover-up.

Weeks: It is an amazing tale, all right, jumping right off the pages of a crime novel.

Blassdoe: Yes, it is. And with additional information coming from the archives of the now reconstructed CIA and FBI, we will probably find that it is not the only one.

Weeks: Thank you, Mr. Blassdoe, for your time and revealing information.

Blassdoe: You're very welcome, Marvin. Glad to be of assistance.

Patrick had just finished the report as the uniformed attendant announced the incoming approach to Otis. It had been a few years since he had followed all the revelations of the Trials. To read an overview of the issues reminded him just how close the country had come to a coup. A few inches one way or the other of a sniper's bullet would have changed the entire course of history. Would Lyndon Johnson have steered the nation on a peaceful course similar to Kennedy's? Would social unrest be roiling the country from unresolved Civil Rights issues? Would we be at war in Vietnam or with the Soviets? So many unanswerable questions. But Patrick knew one thing for sure, he wouldn't be sitting on this plane flying into an Air Force base on Cape Cod to talk with the president of the United States.

* * *

Patrick was met by a uniformed military attaché at Otis Air Force base, waiting for him in the small colorless departure and arrival building just off the taxi area of the runway. He was a crisply dressed younger man, all efficiency and "sirs" while meeting, greeting, loading, and then transporting Patrick to the president's compound. Patrick sat in the back of the military taxi and stared out the windows at what he could see of the passing scenery in the evening darkness.

"Was the flight comfortable, sir?" asked the sergeant—at least that was what Patrick assumed his rank to be from the stripes on his shoulder.

"An easy flight," said Patrick, "almost empty."

"The earlier afternoon arrival was full, sir," he said. "The Friday flee from DC, sir," he added, glancing knowingly toward his backseat passenger in the rear-view mirror. He probably transported a lot of Washington's elite along the same route they were now traveling. "I've been instructed to drop you off at the compound, sir. Will you be needing anything else, sir?"

"Sure, that's fine," Patrick had been told there would be lodging available for him when he arrived and that he should bring an overnight bag as he would probably be leaving the next evening on the six-o'clock—make that the eighteen-hundred hours—flight.

"I'm not sure I had your name right, sir. I only heard it over the phone." It seemed from the questioning that some independent probing was occurring, maybe to discuss Patrick's reasons for being here. Unusual for a sergeant to be pumping a VIP for info as to his reason for attending the president. *And what might you be here for, sir?* seemed more what the man was asking. Maybe he was adding Patrick's name to his personal roster of dignitaries and celebrities whom he normally ferried around the area.

"It's Patrick Hennessey. With the *Post*," he added.

"Oh, uh-huh," nodded the driver. But to Patrick it was obvious that it was a nod of incomprehension.

"Reporter. With the *Washington Post*," he added again with a little emphasis.

"Excellent, sir," came the response from the front seat, this time not even warranting a glance in the mirror.

Jenna has no need to worry about my swelled head, he thought as he returned to staring out the window at the darkened landscape. His status did not even register on the VIP scale.

The Cape Cod coastal area had been home to the Kennedy clan since Joseph Kennedy, Sr., purchased a Hyannisport estate in 1929. A prime slice of waterfront property on Nantucket Sound, it was an enclave for the wealthy that was bordered by Martha's Vineyard to the southwest and Nantucket Island to the southeast, providing a body of water protected from the harsh North Atlantic winters. Joseph Sr. greatly enlarged the existing home to accommodate his growing brood of children. John Kennedy, who had lived there since age twelve, had bought an adjacent waterfront home in 1956 to the east of his father's property. Soon thereafter Robert Kennedy purchased a home just to the north of John's, rounding out the properties' borders to a lot somewhat triangular in shape, with waterfront along the longest portion. Numerous improvements and additions were made over the years, including tennis courts, pools, and separate guest quarters.

The location served as a retreat from the business and political activities of the father and, later, his politically-minded sons. But for the last eight years, during JFK's presidency even more than during his senate and congressional career, the estate was under siege. To the consternation of other area residents, there were roadblocks at all the streets leading toward the compound, with guarded checkpoints. The coastline was patrolled twenty-four hours a day by Coast Guard and unmarked vessels. After the shooting in Dallas, all of these measures were intensified, with the duties taken over by the U.S. Marshals Service. During the summer months, when the weather was more tolerable, scores of tourists and newspaper reporters often milled about, hoping for a sighting or a scoop. Even now, at ten o'clock in the evening, at least twenty people who did not appear to be official loitered at the outer ring. Patrick needed to go through two identification checks where the car and its contents were probed, and his name was matched against a master roster for admission into the inner sanctum of the president's compound. A marshal climbed in the front seat and drove with them until he reached his quarters. The closer in, the quieter and less inhabited it became.

The press of curious humanity had become so distracting that Joseph Kennedy often rented the house of the famed Irish Nightingale, Morton Downey, on Squaw Island in order to get away from the gawking crowds that clustered around the Hyannisport compound. The Squaw Island home was a three-quarter-mile drive along an exposed but remote causeway dividing the brackish tidal flats that backed up to the Hyannisport Golf Club on the north and the Atlantic's Nantucket Bay on the south. It was a quick and private connection to a more secluded home compared to what had become the more exposed Hyannisport compound. Often JFK would be flown in to one or the other estate from Otis Air Force Base by a three-helicopter formation that would swing wide over the Atlantic before coming down either on the three pads to the south of the father's house in the family compound, or onto the expansive side lawn of the Downey estate. The first two choppers would land with a contingent of U.S. Marshals and aides getting off to form a greeting line for the president, then his chopper would arrive with either him or the family aboard. It was a regal entry.

But the evening of Patrick's arrival, he saw none of this. He did not even know if the president was present or where he might be staying. They took the drive off Irving Avenue into the small group of guest cottages that Patrick guessed would include his lodgings for this stay. The guest accommodations were separated from JFK's home by a tennis court, a lawn area with hedges, and a sweeping circular drive leading to the grand entry on the landward side of the president's mansion. Patrick was ushered into his new digs, a small, nicely appointed one-room guest apartment on the ground floor. When he got out of the car, Patrick was engulfed by the smell of the ocean. The unfamiliar location, the proximity to the president at the seat of American power, and the balmy weather all had a decidedly disconcerting effect.

"Mr. Hennessey, your home during your visit," said the marshal politely. "The kitchen and bar are well stocked, but if there is anything you need, just dial 22 on the phone and we'll be glad to assist. If you want an outside line, just pick up, and the switchboard operator will connect you. Is there anything else you need?"

"Well, I'm not sure if you have restrictions around it, but I was wondering about a walk on the beach." he said. "It's been a long trip and it's a fine night."

"That's no problem. I'll notify security, but be sure to bring your access tag and show it to any agents you pass." Patrick had been given an ID pass when he went through the last of the checkpoints on the ride in. On a little map of the property, the marshal showed him the preferred route to take to the beach.

"There is a message for you from the president requesting your attendance at the residence at ten tomorrow morning," said the marshal, and then departed. Patrick was unsure if he was supposed to tip, but the marshal left very matter-of-factly, solving that question. It was all very efficient and he quickly found himself alone, with an urge to wander.

He left his unopened bags in place and walked out the door. He could see a group of a half-dozen cars and limousines parked around the entry to the president's home. He turned and walked west through a gated hedge to the small service drive on the west border of the compound, and then south along a path on the side of the father's house toward the sea. Joseph Kennedy Sr. was still in residence but bedridden from his stroke seven years ago. He was rarely seen. Along the way, Patrick passed a couple of U.S. Marshals walking around the perimeter of the compound who asked to see his ID. He crossed over the circular drive with the raised flagpole and the expansive section of grassy field that was the famed front yard of the Kennedys where so much touch football took place, sometimes under the shuttered eyes of the press. This time of night it was dark and empty, with only the gentle lapping of the ocean heard from beyond the dunes. He was able to wind his way to the beach, and then walked west toward

Squaw Island after he was informed by a marshal that he would need to check back with him when he returned from his walk. But he was free for the moment from the security around the president's estate. The tide appeared to be halfway out, giving a wide berth for walking, and the illumination of a nearly full moon rendered the grassy dunes and nearby homes easily visible as his eyes adjusted.

He walked the sand along the ocean's edge, with the lapping waves to his left. Over the last few days, he hadn't been able to look up at the sky without seeing it in a much different light. It no longer consisted of pinpricks of stars against a dark, two-dimensional background, like a movie screen for earth's viewing. Instead, it had bloomed into three-dimensionality. Just last week, the Apollo 8 mission to the moon made the first human expedition outside the confines of Planet Earth. A little paper-thin tin can of a spacecraft successfully orbited another heavenly body and then returned in one piece. It seemed to Patrick like sailing across the North Atlantic in a boat made of folded newspapers. The three astronauts orbited the moon ten times in twenty hours. They recited passages from the book of Genesis. It was estimated that one out of four people on Earth had listened in on the broadcast as they joked with the president over the radio-phone about the quality of the food.

Patrick felt that such an amazing feat expanded not only our physical boundaries but also the limits of our imagination. Space, as harsh and pristine an environment as man could imagine, was accessible. Looking up at the moon now, he found himself squinting hard, trying to see if there might be any remaining orbital vehicle parts left behind, circling forever that far-off body. He wondered if there were other intelligent life forms about the universe, and what they would think if they came upon our discards. Would they view them amusedly as we would an old Model A jalopy, far surpassed by more current models? Patrick found the most deeply moving impression of the adventure to be the "Earthrise" photographed by William Anders as the satellite emerged from the dark side of the moon. It struck to the hearts of Patrick and the watching world, how mysteriously improbable was this brilliant blue-green jewel of a planet suspended in the infinite blackness of space—and how improbable was the life that inhabited its surface.

Patrick believed the confining boundaries in thought and belief by Earth's inhabitants were similarly expanding. Governments were peeking out from the half-opened doors of their bunkers and eyeing their mortal enemies with a little less contempt, a little more curiosity. The Cold War was thawing. The Soviets and Americans were actively participating in cooperative ventures—even working toward a joint moon landing three years from now. Weapons production, which gobbled up vast financial and physical resources, were being curtailed. An agreement on the table, being talked about as a real possibility, would restrict the manufacture and stockpiling of nuclear weapons as well as the sale of conventional armaments to smaller nations. Competition was replacing confrontation. Even as bilateral engagements (Soviets vs. Americans) were changing to a trilateral theater (Soviets vs. Americans vs. Chinese), there were breaks in which communication filled the openings rather than belligerent intractability. The world was getting very interesting. *This world and those beyond*, thought Patrick as he stared at the night sky.

Patrick re-entered the estate and, after an examination of his identification by the marshals guarding this side of the compound, made his way back toward the cottage. As he rounded the hedge and walked through the gate toward his front door, he noticed some activity at the main entry of JFK's home. The other cars were gone, but a woman was walking down the main steps toward the open back door of a waiting limo—an attractive, well-dressed woman whom he vaguely recognized from somewhere—a picture in the papers, or maybe film? She slipped into the back seat, the door closed and the black limo silently eased around the circular drive and drove slowly past, just a few yards from where Patrick was standing. The windows were darkly tinted, and in the evening light he could only make out the vague shape of the driver and his lone passenger. After it had passed and Patrick had entered his cottage for the night, he remembered the discussion he had had with Jenna earlier in the week on their drive to Glen Ora about the president's extramarital proclivities. Was he an unintended witness to one? Or was he just giving free rein to his imagination?

Patrick settled in as midnight approached and, looking forward to his meeting with the president the next morning, slept soundly.

Chapter 17

Cowardice asks the question—is it safe? Expediency asks the question—is it politic? Vanity asks the question—is it popular? But conscience asks the question—is it right? And there comes a time when one must take a position that is neither safe, nor politic, nor popular; but one must take it because it is right.
—*Martin Luther King, Sermon at National Cathedral, 1968*

We are not afraid to entrust the American people with unpleasant facts, foreign ideas, alien philosophies, and competitive values. For a nation that is afraid to let its people judge the truth and falsehood in an open market is a nation that is afraid of its people.
—*John F. Kennedy*

Sunday-Monday, December 1-2, 1963
Dallas, Texas

Bobby could barely contain himself through the long evening hours during which his brother slept, slowly regaining his strength. Even though Bobby was bursting with the newly acquired information Jiggs had given him in the FBI cable, he knew his brother's health was paramount. The intrigues of Hoover and potentially other forces arrayed against the administration would have to wait. Bobby had called Washington, D.C., numerous times to get an assessment of the current conditions regarding the formation of what was now being dubbed the Warren Commission. Its meetings were to be closed and its members would work in conjunction with the FBI to "get to the bottom" of his brother's shooting. But Bobby already knew what that bottom was going to be. His pact with Hoover and Johnson was to limit the investigation in order to direct the guilt to a lone individual, Lee Harvey Oswald.

Bobby had spent a frustrated evening in the president's room with Jackie, while Jack slept. The president had awakened once, but only for a few minutes, and had been too groggy for discussion. Jackie, irritated with Bobby's pacing, finally kicked him out for the night so she could sleep on the couch.

It wasn't until almost 9 a.m. on Sunday morning that Bobby was able to talk with his brother, and that was after a short private Mass was held for the president by the local Monsignor, assisted by Father Adairs.

"Lyndon's been in on it from the start," said Bobby heatedly. "When there's a power vacuum, he has the scruples of a dog in heat. He's just a mean son of a bitch!" Bobby and Kenny were finally alone with the president in his room.

Days earlier, Bobby had disclosed to Jack his discussion with Hoover and Johnson regarding the involvement of the Soviets and Cubans—information gained through intercepted calls between the Soviet and Cuban embassies in Mexico City. He had told Jack, with a sense of betrayal still grinding in his gut, of the agreement he had endorsed, to quash the investigation of the assassination attempt in order to avoid implicating the Soviet and Cuban governments. He had thought he was avoiding a nuclear war.

The moment Bobby walked into the room, he handed the FBI cable to the president saying, "You're not going to believe this!"

Jack read it over slowly. "That goddamn *bahstahd*," he said softly. Jack's response had a resigned quality, almost as if he saw this as an expected turn of events.

"I think you should hold a press conference in a day or so and announce Lyndon's resignation," said Bobby soberly. "That would surely get his attention. Hell, I'll announce it today if you want."

"That's a press conference I want to be at," said Kenny.

"No, not today. We need to think this through." Jack was the cool and detached one when under duress. Even lying on his back recovering from a near fatal injury, he was the calming influence. He also understood his brother's need to vent before getting down to business. "I want to go through everything we know about the shooting. I'm not clear on a number of things."

"Well, you know about Oswald and how he was picked up after the shooting and then shot by Ruby two days later," started Bobby. There had been a television set up in the president's room two days previously so he could gauge some of the information coming out in the press. "But I haven't told you about Dr. Marshall's findings."

"No, I've talked to him already, and the Bethesda specialists. They were in yesterday for an hour or so," said Jack.

"There's more," said Bobby, with a sidelong glance at Kenny as he pulled a chair up to Jack's bedside. "Did Dr. Marshall tell you about his theory?"

"What theory?" asked Jack. Kenny was also listening intently.

Bobby sat back in his chair. "I talked to Dr. Marshall quite a few times after I got here. But after the third time, he sought me out in private. He was distressed. At first, since the injuries were so substantial, it was not possible to really get a good recreation of the trail of the bullet. He originally thought it entered from the back and, since it had hit a bit flat from wobbling, the bullet caused more damage than would be expected. The exit wound was so substantial that there was no way to get a good picture of what had happened. Besides, at the time, and luckily for you since he's a first class surgeon, he was just trying to put you back together. But later he got to thinking about it. He said he got curious after he saw a picture of the bullet and fragments that the FBI had recovered from the limo. He thought that there was just too much remaining bullet mass to account for the fragments that were left in the wound. Something didn't add up. So he did a detailed tracking of the bullet fragments from the X-rays and concluded it revealed a second bullet."

"Damn!" whispered Kenny.

"On his own," continued Bobby, "he used the side-shot X-rays to reconstruct the pattern of the fragments that showed up on the film. He called it a lead snowstorm. By tracing the angular paths of the ones that were visible, he found that they radiated from the front rather than the back. They expanded outward from the front rather than vice versa."

"But I have a back entry wound." said Jack. "I can show you if you want," he added darkly.

"No, that's okay," said Bobby soberly. "Marshall says he can prove it was two bullets—one from the front and one from the back. He thinks they hit you at almost the same time. The back first and then the front, almost simultaneously. And this is curious," said Bobby. "The front impact was from a fragmentation bullet."

"He's sure about this?" asked Jack.

"He went over it with me in detail. He was very convincing," said Bobby.

"Why didn't he mention anything earlier?" asked Jack.

"Probably afraid to. He sees the FBI making statements about Oswald being the only shooter, and then Ruby kills him. They don't question him or any of the other surgeons who were involved in the operation, yet they come out with definitive conclusions. No, Marshall is keeping very quiet about this, as are probably a lot of other people who saw things differently than what the FBI is presenting. Hoover's made a point of leaking daily updates supporting the theory that Oswald shot you, on his own, all alone. The media is overloading the airwaves with Hoover's conclusions.

Anybody with a brain would probably think real hard about contradicting him publicly. Especially after seeing Oswald killed on live TV."

"You think there are others that would contradict the official account?" asked Jack.

"Hell, yes!" said Kenny. "I saw more than a dozen people run over to that fence up in front of the car. Even the cops went up there. A lot of people said later that it was where they heard a rifle shot. That's where I heard it come from while I was riding two cars behind you."

"But nothing about that from the FBI?" asked Jack.

"Nothing. When they were asked, they said everyone was mistaken. Just echoes," said Kenny. "But the thing is, agents are taking statements from everyone, but just using the ones from people who saw the Book Depository shooter. They're culling the reports to pick what they want and burying the rest."

"Probably smart for Dr. Marshall to keep quiet," said Jack.

"Yeah, I think so, too. He said he's only shared it with me," said Bobby.

"So getting back to Hoover, all this would make sense if the Mexico City tapes showing Oswald in cahoots with the Soviets was true, wouldn't it? I mean Hoover's doing what you agreed upon over the phone, right?" asked Jack, to Bobby's nod. "But now, with this cable showing that it was all a ruse to start with, a really different intention emerges. But this is where I get lost. Why would Hoover cover it up? I mean, what's in it for him?"

"I don't know that either. But knowing that bastard, he is hiding something big. He wouldn't put this on the line if it was just to cover for some other shooter."

"Unless the other shooter is in the Bureau," offered Kenny.

Bobby and Jack looked at each other. "No, that's just not him. He's a devious, bureaucratic son-of-a-bitch," said Jack, "but he's not up for that. He's knows he's getting canned when his time is up next year. But killing the president of the United States just to preserve his job for a few more years? It doesn't make sense." *Besides, he has other weapons at his disposal,* thought Jack.

"Maybe he's covering for someone else," suggested Kenny.

"Well, he has to be," said Jack, "but who?"

"I keep coming back to the tapes of Oswald in Mexico City at the Soviet Embassy," said Bobby. "If this wasn't Oswald, then who was it? And if it wasn't Oswald, then who was setting the man up six weeks ahead of time, *knowing* that the real Oswald would be somehow involved in taking a shot at you?"

"Maybe it wasn't Oswald who took the shot. Maybe when he claimed to be a patsy, he really was," said Jack. "Oswald made a comment in the Dallas Police station hallway. I saw it on TV yesterday. They ran it a few times on the news channel. He said something like, 'I'm just a patsy.' Well, I wondered at the time who would make a statement like that? 'I'm just a patsy.' I mean, wouldn't you say something like, 'I'm innocent' or 'I didn't do anything.' But he says, 'I'm just a patsy.' I get the sense he jumped to a pretty quick conclusion, a couple of steps ahead of the game. Like he was guilty, but maybe not of what we suspected him of doing. I don't know. It just didn't seem to fit."

"What about Lyndon?" asked Bobby.

"You think he had something to do with this? Knew the Oswald info was fake? Set you up with those phone calls?" said Jack. "Shades of *Macbeth*?"

"It has certainly crossed my mind," said Bobby. "I mean, they both worked me over pretty good on the phone that day. I swallowed it whole. I really was afraid that if this went public, there'd be no holding the Joint Chiefs back. It would be a scenario right out of *Seven Days in May*, followed by a nuclear free-for-all. You know Lyndon, he's such a damn good liar, you never know when he's telling the truth."

"Excellent skills for his line of work," said Jack ruefully.

"Yeah, well...." said Bobby.

Seven Days in May was a popular book, made into film, ready to be released with JFK's blessing. It detailed a scenario in which a group of ultra-patriotic members of the Joint Chiefs of Staff nearly wrest control from the president to take over the U.S. government in a coup. He promoted the movie, even allowing filming inside the West Wing and a riot scene staged outside the White House gates while he was away for the weekend in Hyannisport. Kennedy encouraged its release to the general public as a warning regarding the forces currently at play in the United States, but it hadn't yet been shown.

"Kenny, what do you think about Lyndon?" asked Jack.

"I think he's a big, crude, nasty piece of Texas dirt," said Kenny. "But I just can't see him doing something like this."

"Like what?"

"Like shooting a president and then getting it covered up. He's more the smarmy back-room wheeler-dealer. He'll tell you different," said Kenny, "but I don't think he has the balls."

"He's got balls. Why, even he'll tell you that," said Jack. "But I don't think so either. Not to come straight at you, not like this. But how about covering it up after the fact? Maybe getting pulled in on some twisted Hoover intrigue? They go way back, you know."

"Now, that's the big question, and I just don't know," said Kenny.

"Why would they shoot Jackie?" wondered the president. This was something that had been deeply troubling him. When Jackie had been in with him this morning, she had showed him her neck wound. "It's really nothing," she said. "It just stings a bit." But a jolt of anger welled within Jack at the sight. She had come to Dallas to support him in his political campaigning at his request, and was nearly killed by a sniper's bullet.

"I don't think they did," said Bobby, "not on purpose, I mean. You fell over toward her after you were shot. I think they were trying to finish you off and just couldn't get a clean shot as you slipped below the seat near Jackie's lap."

Jack didn't respond.

"Did you know they have a complete film of all of this?" asked Bobby a moment later.

"What?" responded Jack.

"Yeah," said Kenny. "A shopkeeper, a guy named Zapruder, shot the whole thing with his home movie camera in Dealey Plaza as you drove by. They say it shows it all. *Life Magazine* bought it up in about ten minutes and released some stills from it in their current issue."

"You've seen it?" asked Jack.

"Yeah, it's out. We got a few copies downstairs," said Bobby.

"No. I mean the film, not the magazine," said Jack.

"No. They were showing it to some of the Secret Service guys at an office downtown, but I haven't seen it yet," said Bobby.

"Why not?" asked Jack.

Bobby didn't respond. He just shrugged his shoulders. *I just wasn't ready to see a film of my brother being murdered*, he thought.

"What are we going to do about this?" asked Bobby shortly, changing the subject as he nodded to the copy of the FBI cable that Jack was still holding in his hand.

Jack was thoughtful for a few moments. "I want to meet with Lyndon.

Alone. Kenny, give him a call. Ask him to come right down—not as an order, just tell him I want a face to face with him. If he tries to put it off, tell him how good the PR will be of him briefing his president, that sort of thing. Just get him on a plane right away and don't give away any of this," he said, flicking the cable paper.

"I want to be here with you when you give him that," said Bobby.

"I think it would be better if I did this alone. I know you'd like to see him twist, Bobby, but if you were here, his defenses would be up the moment he walked through the door. I need it to be one on one."

Bobby started to protest, but Jack was ready for him. "I want you to give a press conference just as I finish up with Lyndon, and that's what we need to go over now. Kenny, why don't you get on the line to him now and get him down here tomorrow morning."

"Right," said Kenny as he got up. He paused for a moment, turning back as he walked toward the door. He wanted to say something about how happy he was to have Jack back, giving orders and running the show. He wanted to say that he had been devastated by nearly losing him. He wanted just for a moment to be free of the Kennedy tough love stoicism and let a little of his feelings out. But he opened his mouth to do so and said, "Right" again, a little more emphatically, as he headed out of the room.

Bobby remained. He and Jack went over plans for the press conference as well as some correspondence that needed to be sent to their Cuban and Soviet counterparts over the next few days. The president wanted to assure Khrushchev that he had no intention of taking any provocative military action. He'd have Evelyn Lincoln in later in the day to take dictation, but for now he wanted to go over the general outlines.

As they were finishing up the business at hand, Bobby was sifting through some papers. Jack was engrossed in his thoughts, staring off toward the window and the little peek of blue sky coming through blinds. Bobby, knowing the morning's activities had taxed his brother's energy, was about ready to leave, but he still had one question, one that he had been pondering the last few days.

"So, what were you thinking about?"

"Oh, just trying to put myself in Castro's place with all this going on…"

"No, no. I mean before, when you were out, when you were waking up. For a few days, you seemed only half back…you looked at me like you were seeing right through me."

Jack looked at Bobby for a while. "This is hard to describe...and I'd like it to stay between us. I don't want anyone thinking the president has come back damaged—bent, you know." Jack was thoughtful and seemed to be grappling for words. "When I woke up, I was aware of having been in another kind of environment. It wasn't physical, really and it's very difficult to explain. It was kind of like a dream, at least it seems that way now, but it was also as real as what we are experiencing this very moment, I'm very sure of that. It felt...*spacious* is probably the word, but that doesn't begin to convey how it really *was*."

"Were there others there? Like in a dream, where there are other people in it?" asked Bobby, trying to understand what his normally impersonal brother was trying to convey.

"No, it wasn't like that." Jack pondered for a moment, then took another tack. "You know, with all this discussion of landing on the moon in a decade and the Apollo programs that we've put in place, I had time to talk with John Glenn and ask what his experiences were in that capsule, all alone up there. He told me that looking down on the Earth, the blues and greens, the clouds moving over the oceans and continents, all crystal clear, and—well just the *life* of it, with the blackness of space all around. He said it was so beautiful, it pained his spirit. He couldn't expand enough to embrace it. I often thought about that and imagined what it would feel like being off in space, if you were in a space suit and just lost your tether and floated off into its vast empty reaches, seeing planets and stars all around. It would be a fascinating experience," said Jack. Then, smiling, "You'd also be dead in an hour or so, I suppose."

"Probably." Bobby wondered where this was headed.

"Well, I felt I had been out in that space, untethered in this vast emptiness. But what was so affecting was that—well, it *wasn't* empty. It was full...packed full. It wasn't a blank empty expanse, it was teeming. Overwhelmingly dense with thoughts and feelings and vitality and, well, *power*, for lack of a better word for it. And I was a part of it—of every little bit of it all at once. It was the *most* wonderful feeling." Jack, his gaze facing toward the window, was looking somewhere else.

Bobby looked at him with an intent expression, trying to understand.

"You know, if that was like dying, well, I think we have a hell of a ride to look forward to," said Jack. "Now, before you call in the shrink to talk to your older brother, I think we should finish up this draft to Khrushchev."

* * *

Later, in the early evening, Robert, Dave Powers, and Jackie gathered in the hospital room with JFK. Jack had awakened from a lengthy period of rest, and was looking through some papers Bobby had left for him earlier. Bobby was sitting in a chair near the bed while Jackie, on the sofa, was reading letters of encouragement and condolence that had been delivered via diplomatic pouch. Bobby was scribbling a letter to one of his sons on a notepad, something he did often. He wrote notes frequently to his family about all sorts of things. He had written one to his son days earlier, when JFK was first shot and Bobby had felt so alone and devastated. As Bobby wrote, JFK sat up in his bed and looked over at what his brother was doing.

"Who are you writing to?" asked Jack.

"Robert, Jr.," said Bobby pensively.

"That's very sweet of you, Bobby, to write to your son."

"Thank you."

"It would probably be even sweeter if it were legible. Do they ever write back about its contents?" The inscrutable nature of Bobby's chicken-scratch was well known to anyone who had been around him long enough to receive a written note.

"I can assure you that they are fully understood," said Bobby, showing no reaction to the insult. It was common jibing between them.

"Dave," said JFK, looking over at Powers, "take a look at that and see if you can read it."

Bobby reluctantly released the letter as Dave reached over to take it. Dave very thoughtfully settled back in his chair to look quietly at the paper, not saying anything for a long moment. Then the perplexed look on his face changed to comprehension as he slowly turned the page over, upside down. "I think I'm getting it now," he said.

Bobby grabbed the pad back from him as JFK chuckled.

"Sorry, Bobby," said Dave, "not familiar with that particular Mandarin dialect."

"That's why Bobby's staff likes everything to be verbally transmitted or typed up by Angie," said Jack. "I've heard they spend hours poring over his written instructions, looking for translation clues."

Bobby had gotten up during this last exchange as he folded the note and put it in an envelope. "Gentlemen, I'm going out to mail this. While I'm out in the hall," he said to Jack, "I'll see if the doctor can cut back on your pain meds." He started toward the door.

"Jack," said Jackie from the sofa, "have you ever actually met Mr. Minh?" Jackie was holding a small note with a frown on her face.

"Who?"

"Mr. Minh? The North Vietnamese president?"

"Ho Chi Minh," said Jack. "No, never. Why do you ask?"

"Well, I think you have a letter from him," she said as she got up and brought it over to Jack in his bed. Bobby had stopped by the door and came back to look over the president's shoulder. The letter was written on textured paper with an embossed administrative seal. Official but also personal, with a tight, well-organized handwritten text. It had an almost calligraphic appearance.

"It's in French. Where'd this come from?" asked Jack.

"It was in one of the diplomatic pouches. The same one that had the letter from de Gaulle I read to you this morning. There were about thirty letters in that pouch." She went back and looked at the envelope in which it arrived. "It's from a Mme. Lorraine Arnaud," she said as she handed the envelope to Jack. "A Paris address."

"Can you translate?" he asked as he handed the letter back to Jackie. Jackie was fluent in four foreign languages, French being foremost.

"*Dear Mr. President,*" she began. "*We have never had the occasion to speak together. In 1954 you presented a speech to your Congress about our country and what you call Indochina. Would you be surprised to know that I have read this many times? There is great misunderstanding regarding our two peoples, but it does not need to lead to war. You are the leader of a very powerful country with weapons that we cannot match. And we are a poor country of peasants and farmers. Yet we have a great desire to heal our broken land. Is there no way for our peoples to avoid fighting and dying? The tiger and elephant are bitter enemies, and as such they do not lie down with each other. But we are men and can we not act differently if we so choose? I cannot claim to understand the workings of your government, but I can understand the nature of men killing men. And for that I offer my condolences that you have been stricken.*"

Jackie stopped.

"Is that it?" asked Jack.

"*With deep regards, Ho Chi Minh,*" finished Jackie, "That's it."

"Read it again," said Jack. Jackie did so, twice.

"One thing is a little peculiar about this letter, Jack," said Jackie. She had the room's attention. "He uses a few French personal rather than impersonal pronouns. French is not like English. Pronouns can indicate warmth or affection. Most diplomatic correspondence uses formal grammar, yet this is more private, intimate. He creates a more personal touch. You would have to speak French to get the feeling of it. But this is a private letter."

Jack looked at the letter again. There was an official-looking stamp on it. "What does this say?"

"I don't know. That's in Vietnamese, I assume. A presidential stamp?" said Jackie.

"Have we ever had any direct exchange with Ho?" asked Bobby.

"No, all through the State Department," said Jack. "I do remember a short interview that was broadcast recently, though," he recalled after a pause. "It was translated from French TV. He was asked whether General de Gaulle could act as a referee between our two countries. 'Referee?' said Ho. 'We're not football teams!' That's the most recent time I've seen him. He's a little wisp of a guy. There were rumors that he'd been removed from power in the North. He'd not been seen for a while. But when I saw him on TV, I was surprised at his apparent control of the situation. He didn't appear to have been sidelined."

"Do you think this is a legitimate letter?" asked Bobby. "I mean, this is not through regular diplomatic channels."

"What would be regular channels for North Vietnam? We've got no ambassador there," said Jack. "Most of what we get is through State, and half of that is back-channel stuff. But I'm wondering that, too. I'm not sure how we could check it out, or if we even want to. I mean, are we talking to a representative of the head of the Vietnamese government, or a figurehead without any power?"

"A sidelined Uncle Ho?" said Bobby.

"Exactly," said Jack. "Starting up a dialogue with a leader gone to pasture would be pointless. Besides, we've had a practice of avoiding any communication with the North Vietnamese. It would be seen as undercutting our government in the South."

"But if this is real...." said Jackie. "If it is real, it seems like...like an olive branch or something. As if he's trying to make contact and convey concern, in a reserved but personal sort of way, at least from the style in which he wrote this."

Bobby and Jack looked at each other.

"Bobby, check with State about Ho's position over there, but don't mention this note. We want to keep this very private for now," said Jack. "I'll check with de Gaulle, too. If this is real, it might be worth pursuing. Maybe it's time for some different tactics. But we'd need to know first if he's still the head of government over there, and second, if this can be verified as being really from the man. I have an idea for the second, but I'm not too sure of the first."

Bobby and Jackie looked at Jack, wondering how he was planning to verify the legitimacy of the letter they had received.

"We'll send him a reply via this Paris address," said Jack, "and see if old Uncle Ho is a poet."

* * *

In 1941, Lyndon Baines Johnson, at the time a congressman from Texas, fought an uphill battle for a vacated Senate seat in his home state. Dubbed the "Screwball Election in Texas," the winner-take-all contest drew twenty-six aspirants. With his exhaustive work ethic of sixteen- to eighteen-hour days, Johnson emerged from a deep deficit of public recognition to a neck-and-neck race with then Governor "Pappy" O'Daniel. Pappy was a vacuous and unscrupulous Texas celebrity who had gained office more by his traveling song-and-dance show than by any leadership ability. With the near-final vote tallies recorded, Lyndon squeaked out a victory over the more popular O'Daniel with a mere 5,100 vote margin. After a jubilant party with his supporters, he retired for the evening. But in the vagaries of Texas vote-rigging, and reflecting the great desire of the local Texas power elite to rid themselves of the current inept Prohibition-supporting governor by moving him to DC, Johnson awoke to find that tardy overnight ballots had materialized to give his Senate-destined opponent a 1,100-vote lead before the election was declared final. Defeat had shocked and eventually educated young Mr. Johnson as to just how politics worked in his home state. He had tasted the office he had coveted, only to have it pulled from his grasp a day later.

And now it was about to happen again.

Lyndon tried to put on a congenial countenance, but it was easy to see a landscape of conflicting emotions in his face, and joy in the president's rebounding health was not one of them. Fifty-five years of harsh Texas weather and rough-and-tumble political skullduggery have a way of aging a person, and the Texas-size crags around his eyes and mouth became more evident as the years progressed; these were only more defined when the tantalizing taste of a long-desired power was gifted, and then quickly rescinded.

Standing in for the injured president had been a watershed event for Lyndon. During the previous three years, he had been shoved to the wings as a disrespected and marginalized vice president, wasting away to a shadow of his past glories. He had been a major power broker in Washington during the years he occupied the position of Senate Majority Leader. He wielded authority with an instinctive understanding of the strengths and weaknesses, desires and fears of the Senate members whom he herded expertly to gain passage of a record number of bills. To call him ambitious and talented was an understatement. But in the shadow of the cultivated Kennedys' popularity, and the near powerless position of the vice presidency, he had become a spectral vestige of his former self.

Over the last ten days, though, he had been reborn. The one thing he cherished most in life was the attainment of the supreme pinnacle of power. And that goal was within his grasp. For the last ten days, he had been the president, if not in name, then at least in position. He felt the surge of leadership in his veins. He saw the shifting deference as those attuned to the currents of political power viewed him with a burgeoning respect. He was finally at the table of power—only to have the meal left unserved. Jack Kennedy, the man he would replace, was recovering. Johnson could see debilitating, humiliating uselessness beckoning him back to his gilded cage, the vice presidency. LBJ might have been the most dejected man on the planet as he walked into JFK's hospital room. He knew his future was past.

"Mr. President," he said as he entered. It was probably an optical illusion from Jack's low vantage point, but it appeared Lyndon Johnson needed to duck to pass his six-foot-four frame through the door of the president's hospital room. "I cannot tell you how happy I am to be seein' and meetin' with you today. How are you?" Standing by the foot of the bed for a moment, Johnson's greeting was warm and effusive turning on the charms that oozed so readily on command. He quickly came around to the side of the bed to engulf Jack's uninjured left hand. A physical connection was a requirement for the vice president.

"Lyndon," responded Jack, lightly gripping the extended hand, "I'm glad you could come down here. I know you must be busy."

"I'm at your disposal, you know that," he said. "I flew down here right away when Kenny called me. He said you wanted a little powwow, and I think that's a great idea." Behind the veil of awkward enthusiasm, both men harbored conflicting agendas. "I haven't seen so many flowers in one place since I rode on that Rose Bowl float a coupla years back," said Lyndon as he looked around the room. "They're even in the hallway."

"That's Jackie's doing," said Jack. "Makes it almost tolerable here."

"And how is she?" asked Lyndon with a sincere look of concern.

"She's okay," said Jack more seriously. But Lyndon could see that Jack was not okay about it. "Have a seat," said Jack, beckoning to the open chair by the bed. "Treating you okay in the Capital while I'm vacationing in your home state?" Was there an accusatory edge to that?

"Yeah, some vacation. Well, every jack one of 'em is just leanin' back on their heels. Like the weather, everyone is just waitin' and watchin' to see if there's a storm comin'," said Lyndon.

"We've got a few issues to talk about," said Jack. "Bobby may be in later. He'll be giving a press conference again before he heads back to DC, but I wanted to talk to you first." Lyndon eased his lanky frame into the chair, which now seemed a little smaller than it had a moment before. He seemed to swallow a little harder when Jack mentioned his brother.

"What's on your mind, Mr. President?" asked Johnson.

Jack had been propped up in the bed so that he could gaze evenly at Johnson. He was looking better, and had washed and freshened himself. It had had a bracing effect, allowing him to feel a bit more like his normal self.

"You've probably had more contact with the FBI, with Hoover, regarding the developments in the Oswald case, but I wanted to hear from you what you thought of it all."

"Has Bobby talked to you?" asked Lyndon, a little warily. He would hate to try to explain the reason that he had redirected the investigation without first having the way paved by the president's brother. How to tell a man, especially the president of the United States, that his presumed assailant was being vilified individually at the expense of doing a true investigation of the crime?

"Yes, Lyndon, he has. He told me of the agreement he made with you and Hoover as a result of the situation at the embassies in Mexico City. I've also been reading the press reports that have been saved for me by the staff. It would appear that Mr. Hoover is getting right on this situation with his accusal of Mr. Oswald and the limited investigation of Mr. Rubenstein. I think he must be in leak overdrive there at the Bureau, with all the stories coming out regarding Oswald's guilt."

"What would you like me to add to that, sir?" asked Johnson, a little uncertain as to the line of inquiry. Lyndon wondered why he had been called down to Dallas when he and Jack could have jawed about this over the phone. For chrissakes, that's what they were invented for. Maybe he wanted the press to get wind of the high level meeting, bringing the VP into the circle. He could go along with that.

"It's the damnedest thing, Lyndon. These are very strange times. I'm now going to be in charge of deciding whether my attempted assassination will be investigated thoroughly—or not." He emphasized his words. "I mean, that's what it's coming down to, isn't it?

"Now, it may come as a surprise to you," continued the president, "but I have had more than one hundred pieces of correspondence with Khrushchev. We've exchanged personal letters and cables every couple of weeks, more often sometimes. I think I have some insight into the man by now." Unbeknownst to anyone but a few members of the staff and the diplomatic courier community, JFK had been corresponding with Khrushchev for years. It was oftentimes professional, but also surprisingly personal. "And I don't believe the man has it in for me. Maybe in the past, but certainly not at the present."

Lyndon had pulled back a little in his chair with a look of mild astonishment on his face. He was shocked to learn of this, and it showed. *The president had a back-channel relationship with Khrushchev? Why the hell didn't I know about this?*

"Similarly, and this is not to be repeated for the moment, Lyndon," continued the president, "Castro has been approaching our contacts through his UN emissary and other private avenues, regarding reconciliation. He feels cut adrift by the Soviets and is taking our temperature about an easing of tensions. *He* initiated the fishing expedition, not us. It caught us quite by surprise, as you can imagine. But we have been having back-channel talks for a few months that have a whiff of hope about them. Now, somehow I just don't see Fidel, as crazy as he can be, conspiring to have me assassinated. I may be wrong in this, but the pieces just don't fit. Hell, McNamara tells me they weren't even on alert or in any sort of heightened military posture at the time this occurred—the Soviets or the Cubans. They seemed as caught off-guard by this as we were.

"So what I need to ask you is this, Lyndon. How certain are you that this was a deliberate act of aggression by the Soviets? And the Cubans, for that matter?" It was obvious that the tenor of the conversation had changed. They had moved away from the genial greetings that had masked an underlying tension. "Of course, I was not available when this decision was made. I trust Bobby's judgment on this matter, but I wanted to hear from you."

"It is my understanding that the Soviets, probably with the help of the Cubans, conspired to have you killed," started Lyndon, sobered by the turn in the conversation. "I have been working my darnedest to get together a commission to look into the actions by that Oswald fella." Lyndon did not bother to mention that since the president had recovered, his carefully orchestrated arm-twisting of Chief Justice Earl Warren, Senator Richard Russell, and others to chair the commission was unraveling. "Now, the information I have is that he was in cahoots with another fella in the Soviet Embassy in Mexico about six weeks before. A professional assassin named Kostikov who is part of the Russkies' killing team. They met down there and talked a blue streak about six weeks before all this here happened in Dallas and—"

"How do you know that?" asked Jack very calmly. Too calmly. Lyndon was becoming aware that this was not a chitchat. He was being interrogated. It wasn't like the Jack he knew to treat him this way. Even when so many others in the administration had sidelined him with deliberate insults and indifference, Jack had done his best to treat him with respect and find projects for him to discharge with dignity. But something had shifted, and he knew he had to find a way back into the president's confidence.

"I have been talking at length with Hoover. Now I know that you and he don't see eye to eye about a lot of things, but I've known the man for twenty-five years or more. Christ, he lived across the street from me for almost twenty. Found my dog a few times when he got lost." Lyndon was beginning to wonder why he hadn't looked more closely at the Mexico City connection. "J. Edgar assured me that over at the Bureau they have tapes and pictures of this Oswald fella comin' and goin'." Lyndon had abandoned his genial veneer. He knew something was wrong and was beginning to sense he was about to be blindsided. "Now, I don't know about this Soviet guy, but I asked over at the CIA, and they assured me that he is one serious operator."

"So you're sure Hoover is positive about the communication between the two men? Previous to what happened here in Dallas ten days ago?

Previous by six weeks?" asked the president.

"Absolutely! We've talked about it numerous times," said Lyndon. He felt fear blossom in the pit of his stomach as Jack, after quietly digesting his last response, reached over to the bedside table. He grimaced a little as he stretched to pick up an envelope that had been sitting there the whole time, leaning against a glass of water, just now noticed by Lyndon. Why was it that a premonition of doom flooded his senses? Looking at Lyndon with an odd expression of intensity, not saying a word, Jack held the envelope out to the vice president. Did Lyndon see some sorrow in his expression? The envelope seemed to float there in space for an interminable moment before his hand, seemingly on its own, reached out to accept it.

He slowly lifted the flap and pulled out the page. Only one. Could this be so bad? He read the FBI inter-office cable while sitting alone with the president of the United States in a silent, drab hospital room. Two men at the apex of world power, contemplating a short note that would probably end the career of one of them.

Director...EYES ONLY...Mexico City tapes...interrogation LEE HARVEY OSWALD...voice tapes, NO MATCH with subject...photograph, NO MATCH with subject... distinctly dissimilar to subject...

He read it over twice, then looked at the date at the top of the page. *November 23, 1:12 am.*

Late the evening after the shooting, before Johnson had even talked to him, Hoover knew it was all false. Before they had even spoken!

Jack could almost see Johnson's body recoil from what he was reading. Watching his vice president scan the cable and then read it again slowly, he could swear the man was shrinking right before his eyes. His huge head tilted forward and his shoulders sagged. His suit, which had been inflated with energy and vitality only a few moments before, seemed a couple of sizes too big.

"Try and be kind to Texas Crude," Jackie had said earlier, using her nickname for Lyndon. She knew from the way Bobby and Jack had been talking that there was murder in the air. "I know that you have to see him and it isn't about just government business. He's been like a trapped animal as the vice president. I know you need to do what you're going to do, but behind all the crudity, he has some heart." Jackie was not a political animal, but she was very sharp. She could size people up in a minute. She had overheard all the chatter about Oswald, Johnson, Hoover, and Ruby, and was not immune to the reality that there were a great many questions unanswered around the shooting of her husband.

Johnson's big hands, an envelope in one, a sheet of paper in the other, rested in his lap. He just sat there with his eyes closed. Contrary to his *awe-shucks* vernacular, the vice president was an astute political tactician. He did not need a road map to explain what was transpiring here. During the long silence, Jack observed the vice president.

"Where did you get this?" asked the vice president.

"I can't tell you that, Lyndon," replied Jack.

"I assume you'll be wanting my resignation," stated Johnson. It wasn't really a question. His eyes were red, and he seemed in a state of shock. But his emotional state did not diminish his awareness of what this cable meant. He was done. "Hell, I haven't done nothin' but die a slow spit-turnin' death as VP, anyway," he said bitterly.

"Lyndon," Jack pressed quietly, "what do you know about this?"

Johnson was a powerful man, and in his prime, a time he had been so recently reminded of over the last ten days of near-presidential ascension, he had accomplished near-greatness. Many hailed him as the best Senate Majority Leader ever. And that is saying a lot. He was brilliant, hard working, crude, and overbearing, with an outsized ego matching the size of the state he hailed from. He could run a half dozen other men into the ground with his whirlwind of unrelenting activity. He lived for politics with a fixation that excluded all else. And even though he was cut from the cloth of exploitative political conflict, he had used much of his ability for the public good, enriching himself in the process as he figured any self-respecting politician would. He had sat on his hands for the last three years, ironically incapacitated by being the second-in-command of the most powerful nation on Earth. He hungered to achieve greatness. And for just a few moments over these last few days, he had tasted the flickering possibility of such a destiny. But his revival, ultimately, could only be gained at the expense of another—the death of the injured man lying in front of him.

"I am a lot of things, Jack, but I am not a goddamn traitor!" he started out slowly, dispensing with the honorifics. "I would, and have for that matter, cheated and lied to get where I am. Hell, we all have. There ain't a goddamn one of us that wouldn't shit our pants were all our double-dealin' shenanigans to come to light. Even you. And you know what I mean. Hell, I'd gladly screw another man's wife if I could use it to my political advantage." The hitch in his voice suggested the flood of emotion behind his statement. He realized that in this shit-hole of a Texas hospital it was all coming down on him. He was a tough operator, but his hands were shaking along with his voice. "You probably don't believe it, but this is beyond me."

"No," said Jack.

"I swear to you, Jack, I was not party to this," he said, shaking the page in front of him. "I will step down, in any manner that you see fit, but—"

"No, I mean I don't accept your resignation, Lyndon." Jack was quiet for a moment while he looked at the perplexed and shattered man sitting in front of him. Jack had already made his decision regarding the vice president. He knew he might never be absolutely certain of his innocence in this matter, but he wanted Johnson on the inside in the coming months and felt no reserve in his decision.

"What *do* you want?" asked Lyndon, baffled. "With this," he said flicking the paper in his lap, "I can understand why you'd think I was a back-stabbin' son of a bitch. But I believed J. Edgar when he told me 'bout this Mexico City thing." Lyndon paused for a moment. "Maybe I just wanted to believe it," said Lyndon almost to himself. "You've talked to him?"

"No, I wanted to talk to you first," said Jack, still not quite sure how much to reveal to his vice president. "I don't believe you knew about this, and I don't want you to resign."

Lyndon was speechless.

"Lyndon, if I were to let you go, you hailing from Texas, it would be a further indictment of the state and its part in the shooting of the president. I mean, how would it look if I were seen to be cutting away all association with the South? Mind you, though, if I thought you were a part of this, I'd do it in a second. But that would splinter an already fragile country, and we're going to need some unity with what's coming up," said Jack. "Lyndon, I need your assistance with something."

"My help? What the hell can I do now?" the vice president said plaintively.

"You know I've been working for the last three years to get a host of bills through Congress. Especially the Civil Rights Act, but also my poverty and tax cut initiatives, and hell, about ninety other initiatives that those bastards on the Hill are sitting on their butts about."

"Ninety-two," said Lyndon, always finely tuned to the conditions on the Hill.

"Yeah, well, I'm sick to death of being stymied by the Southern block that has them all bottled up!" The conversation was taking another radical turn that Johnson could hardly follow. "Now, you'll only hear me say this once. But I should have let you loose earlier. Call it personal, blame it on Bobby—but not too much mind you—or just on my stubborn resistance. But sitting right in the office across the street has been the key to all of this. And that's you, Lyndon. I want you to take a forward position on the Civil Rights Bill and the poverty programs. Liaise with Congress. I have a big agenda for striking while the time is right, and I think that is now. And I think you're the one to accomplish this."

"You mean from the vice presidency?" Lyndon was astonished.

"Well, I don't mean from a goddamn pickup truck!" blurted Jack.

Lyndon understood the implications. Politically, he would need to align himself with the pro-civil rights block and in turn divest himself of much of the support he had gained in the South. Up until now, he had been able to sit on the fence regarding many of these issues, playing both sides—as a Southerner, dragging his feet against the needed change to keep his Southern support, and as a Northerner, seeing the inevitable historical shifts that were coming to play. But this would require him to commit. And without needing to reflect, he was already sure that he could do so.

"But what about Bobby? He's deep into the civil rights issue. You know how it is between the two of us. We can hardly breathe air from the same room," said Lyndon, still in shock.

"Well, you are just going to have to figure out a way to use those charms of yours on my brother, because I need you two working together on this. At least parts of it. Besides, Bobby is going to have his hands full," finished Jack cryptically.

Lyndon put both hands up to his face and rubbed and rubbed as if to get his thoughts and senses to begin working properly. Jack reflected on the oddity of the man sitting before him, with the huge hands massaging a face that nearly had wings for ears. He was still teary-eyed, but his body was uncoiling in relief. Hell, Lyndon probably didn't know what he was feeling, but deliverance might aptly describe the bulk of it.

"I've always wanted nothing more than to be of use," affirmed an exhausted Johnson.

"Well, Lyndon, you may want to save that thought for next year's campaign," sighed Jack, well aware that Lyndon craved far more than that. "There is one other thing I do want your help with," added Jack.

"What's that?"

Jack held the vice president's eyes with his.

"I want *Hoovah*."

* * *

Bobby was at the press podium again. An aide had handed him the phone. It was a short call. All Jack said was, "Go ahead, like we planned."

"Okay," said Bobby. Lyndon was probably still in the room with the president.

The press had been assembled in the hall for the last half hour. They were aware that Vice President Johnson had arrived earlier in the day and was meeting with the president, but Pierre Salinger, the president's press secretary, had been tight-lipped about the meeting's content. They were a little surprised to see the president's brother step from behind the curtain, since they had expected the standard briefing from Pierre that had been the twice-daily norm. This was the third time Bobby Kennedy had taken the position of spokesman, and the press was getting more comfortable with his presence. A sense of happy release still permeated the room at the healthy turn of events over the last few days.

"I have a short announcement," he said in his crisp Boston accent as the room quickly quieted. "As you may be aware, the vice president has arrived this morning for a meeting with the president. They have been talking for the last hour or so in his room, making plans for the next couple of months." Bobby paused a moment. "The president's condition has been steadily improving, and with this in mind, he will be leaving for his home in Palm Beach, Florida, for a period of recuperation just as soon as his doctors release him for travel. We are assuming this will occur within the next few days. He has asked me this morning to thank the medical staff and all the doctors and surgeons of the Parkland Memorial Hospital facility for the exceptional care and attention he has received. He also wishes to thank the good people of Dallas for the overwhelming outpouring of support and prayers that he has benefited from over these last ten days. He will express this in person at a later date, but for now he wanted me to be sure that the staff at Parkland and the people of Dallas know how much he appreciates their kindness and attention." Bobby surveyed the room full of eager television and print reporters. Most had been here since the beginning, almost two weeks ago.

"I'll take questions now," said Bobby.

"Is Mrs. Kennedy fully healed, and will she be going, too?" asked a reporter in the front row.

"Yes, absolutely. The first lady has been with the president almost all day of every day he has been here. As you know, the children are here in Dallas as well, so she has been sharing her time with them since the president is now feeling so much better." said Bobby.

"How long will they be in Palm Beach?" asked another.

"It is assumed that they will be there for a couple of months. It will all depend upon the president's physical condition—and, of course, how long the doctors can convince him to remain inactive. The president is normally a vigorous man, and it will take a great deal of our family's efforts to ensure that he operates under the restrictions that the doctors will impose upon him. There will probably be a vote within the family, something akin to the selection of the Pope, and the loser, who will hopefully be Teddy, will be assigned this arduous and thankless task." Bobby's deadpan delivery of the last brought a great deal of laughter as he pointed to a reporter off to the side.

"There's been significant confusion right now about who is running the government. Did or does Vice President Lyndon Johnson have presidential authority? Could you clarify who is actually in charge at this time?" asked a regular White House reporter.

"Thank you for that question, Mike. During the president's period of unconsciousness, Lyndon Johnson had the full authority of the president of the United States as acting president. With the president's recovery, this situation was discussed at length within the Justice Department and then with the president over the last few days. The president's physical condition requires that he take a great deal of rest and, as you know, being the president is not a position that allows for much in the way of leisure.

"I want to expand upon this a bit," said the attorney general. "There is no clear path described in the Constitution of the United States regarding the conditions we are currently experiencing for presidential disability. Ever since the 'accidental presidency' of John Tyler, our tenth president, who rose to the presidency due to the death of William Henry Harrison immediately after election, there has been confusion about this issue. The Presidential Succession Act of 1947 is currently the operative route for a presidential transfer of power. This Succession Act addresses the line of succession, but does not address the current situation of temporary disability. Recently, there has been a Senate Joint draft resolution laying out a pathway for just such a situation as has occurred over these last difficult weeks. But this resolution is still in preliminary form without a final resolution or implementation schedule. It is not yet the law. The president is aware of this resolution, and even though it has not yet been fully implemented as an amendment to the Constitution, he wishes to invoke the spirit of its passage for the upcoming interim.

"The president is healing well, is mentally in excellent condition, but is unable as yet to resume his position. There is little in the Constitution regarding the situation as it now stands, with President Kennedy recovering but not yet able to resume the mantle of the presidency full-time. It is with this in mind that he asked Lyndon Johnson to meet with him in person and wishes to confer upon Mr. Johnson the position of *acting president* until such time as the president can fully resume his responsibilities. This will be a formal shift of authority so that Vice President Johnson will retain the powers that he has been acting under over the last two weeks, but with the understanding that John Kennedy will step back into that role when he feels he is well enough to resume a full schedule. The president and the vice president have a close relationship," a comment, thought Bobby, that would be believable to everyone except those who knew them, "and there will be no disruption in the president's programs."

"Will the president give a news conference soon? Will he be announcing this to the nation?" asked a woman in the row.

"It will probably be about six weeks to two months before he will be physically able to give one of his standard press conferences. You are probably not aware how difficult one of those is," said Bobby as an aside, to general laughter. "But there has been talk of having a short interview with Mr. Cronkite from CBS, to be broadcast over all the networks, within the next few days. We'll have more announcements about that as things progress. There are no definite timetables at this point, as everything depends on the president's health, and we will not be allowing him to go beyond what would be safe for his recovery." Bobby pointed to another reporter.

"There have been rumors the vice president is forming a closed blue-ribbon commission to investigate unanswered questions swirling about the shooting of the president as well as the shooting of his accused assailant. What are the president's comments about this?" asked a reporter who sounded French by the nature of his accented English.

Ahh! There it was. The whole reason for Bobby's presence here this morning. Both he and Jack knew that someone would raise this topic, and if they didn't, Bobby would hint around it until someone did.

"There has been considerable deliberation about the commission being set up by the vice president. The vice president relayed his concerns to the president just this morning regarding the development of this commission and its makeup. The question has always been, right from the start, how do we conduct an investigation that is thorough and complete without compromising the decorum that should be observed in such a serious matter? There are many questions about the shooting of the president, and history will judge the government on how well the information is presented to the public. The issue is trust. Can a closed investigation be seen, over the stretch of time and in the light of history, as appropriate to the magnitude of these events? The public has every right to receive a full explanation of conditions surrounding this crisis. With this in mind, the president and vice president have decided to initiate a thorough and fully transparent congressional investigation."

A murmur went throughout the hall.

"The vice president has been instructed, in accordance with the president's wishes, to oversee the creation of a pair of bipartisan committees within the House of Representatives and the Senate to conduct a full, shared, and impartial investigation into the events of the shooting. The president believes that running it as a congressional matter, with full subpoena powers and open hearings, would be the best approach. We have had great success in doing so with the investigations of Organized Crime and Senator McCarthy. We as a nation are dealing with grave issues that go to the heart of a democracy, and we believe that the more open, immediate, and thorough the investigation, the better it will be for the governmental health and well-being of this country.

"Over the next couple of weeks, after consulting with ranking members of Congress, the outlines of this investigatory framework will be released. The president feels that the American people deserve this and that the original plans for a closed commission to conduct this investigation in secrecy, although providing a more controlled situation, would not give the American people the confidence that there has been a full examination of all information regarding these events.

"This administration also believes it is the duty of a free press to actively and responsibly assist in this enterprise, while being fully aware of the complexity and seriousness of the situation from a national and international perspective. This near tragedy can be used as an example to other nations, showing that America is a country that operates under the rule of law, and that threats against the government are handled in a manner that

will be a blueprint for the thorough and equitable exercise of a government ferreting out the truth and dispensing justice in as fair a manner as
possible."

This came as a shock to members of the press. The commission was
already well along in its formation, with names of potential members—
Chief Justice Earl Warren, Senate leader Richard Russell, House Minority
Leader Gerald Ford, former CIA Director Allen Dulles, and others well
known to the press.

"As attorney general, would you chair such a hearing?"

"No. I would have to recuse myself from a direct leadership role in
this," responded Bobby.

"You'll have no part in it at all?" asked another.

"I am the attorney general. I feel it is my responsibility to be sure that
this investigation is properly organized. I will direct its early creation as
necessary to open lines of liaison with the FBI through the Justice Department, and will be on hand at all times to make sure that the lines of
communication are kept open and that bureaucratic red tape is kept to
a minimum. But I am the president's brother, and I think the nation deserves impartial leadership in this investigation. I will therefore adopt a
limited role and stay a reasonable distance from direct duties regarding
these hearings." Bobby said the last without really believing it himself. He
knew he would not allow the investigation to swerve from anything but a
complete examination of the issues, and even though he had stated his re-
cusal, he knew he would work behind the scenes to ferret out his brother's
assassins.

"How about the conclusions already reached by the FBI? Reports have
been released for days giving detailed information about Oswald as the
lone shooter," pursued the same reporter.

"The president and the vice president have full confidence in the findings of the FBI, especially under the hands-on direction of Mr. Hoover.
He has been a stalwart defender of the American system of justice, and
it is with great confidence that we believe he will open to the public the
appropriate findings of his great organization. It will be the crowning
achievement of his career to show the nation once again that, under his
leadership, there has been a clear and concise investigatory path that has
led to his conclusions."

Saying the last was the hardest part of the entire press conference. But
Jack had been adamant about the strategy for dealing with Mr. Hoover—

he was to be damned with fulsome praise. With the information revealed in the FBI cable, it seemed obvious that the conclusions reached by Mr. Hoover implicating Mr. Oswald as the lone assassin were false. Neither Jack nor Bobby was aware of the larger circle of involvement in these events, but had come to the conclusion that a full disclosure was necessary for two reasons. First, if the real perpetrators were not apprehended, they might simply bide their time until they could try again. Second, they were both aware that the forces arrayed against them controlled certain parts of the military and clandestine forces of the United States. By opening this investigation, they would be able to clear away significant resources from those that held these positions. Jack felt it was a risk worth taking.

"But you know that Hoover has files on you," Bobby had said. "If they're released, they could ruin you—ruin us." Bobby did not have to mention to his brother how his extramarital affairs were now coming back to endanger his presidency. They had talked of this before, and Jack, unable or unwilling to end these liaisons, had felt they would never come to light. Hoover's blackmailing had crushed or hobbled the careers of innumerable political aspirants over his long tenure as director of the most powerful information gathering organization in America. He certainly had documented reports and unauthorized tape recordings of at least some of JFK's philandering. He had made this very clear a few times in the past with oblique references that he "had the goods" on Jack. And it was the exposure of this information that was the main and only sticking point in the whole plan. Jack was fully aware it could cost him the presidency.

But the president had been adamant. "Open it up," he had said to Bobby as they talked in his hospital room just a few hours ago. "We'll take our chances."

"Thank you very much," said the attorney general, concluding his conversation with the press.

Chapter 18

I am certain that after the dust of centuries has passed...we, too, will
be remembered not for our victories or defeats in battles or
politics, but for our contribution to the human spirit.
—*John F. Kennedy*

It is our duty as men and women to proceed as
though the limits of our abilities do not exist.
—*Pierre Teilhard de Chardin*

Saturday-Sunday, October 12-13, 1968
Hyannisport, MA

Patrick woke with a start. Someone was pounding on the door of his cottage. He looked over at the bedside clock: 6:30 a.m. and still mostly dark. Barely awake, he got up and stumbled through the living room, putting on his trousers before opening the front door. He feared the worst for some reason, a feeling of dread heavy on him. A U.S. Marshal stood on his stoop with a serious expression on his face. But as he saw Patrick waken from a deep sleep, still buckling his belt, a glint of a smile broke through.

"You up for a little golf, Mr. Hennessey?" he asked.

"Uh, golf?"

Unperturbed by the sleepy reply, the agent launched into his message. "The president mentioned last night that if the warm weather held, with no rain in the forecast, he would like to put in a round this morning. *You* have been invited." The last was said with an inscrutable air of humor as if the marshal could not understand why the president would invite this unimpressive specimen for a run around the links. He stood there quietly for a moment.

"Huh. Well sure. I'd love to," said Patrick, realizing a response was required.

"Be out on the drive for an 8:00 a.m. lift," instructed the marshal, pointing behind himself toward the front of the president's home as he started to depart.

"Wait, I don't have clubs," said Patrick.

"They'll be provided," he said.

"...or cleats."

"Those, too," added the marshal over his shoulder as he walked away.

Patrick closed the door, tottered back to the bedroom in the unfamiliar apartment, and flopped down on the bed. He had an hour and a half before the day really began and needed a few moments to gather himself. He had awakened abruptly, thick with dreams, and felt like he was still carrying their remnants. Under more normal conditions, when he woke gradually, he could often remember intriguing dream scenarios. It sometimes seemed that he lived a second life in a private world populated by a second self. He lay down on the bed, quietly trying to trace his way back as images came slowly to mind.

...he was sitting at a library desk, leafing through a large picture book whose photographs appeared to be more cinematic than static. Turning the pages, the images came alive with ever-changing scenes of men and machines charging over huge, ravaged landscapes fraught with smoldering earth and charred dead. There was a constant barrage of weaponry, with fallen participants ground down by the machinery of war and the passage of time. He was mesmerized by the violent carnage, as well as the conveyed understanding of choices made, events created. Courage, cowardice, hope, and despair overlapped from scene to scene, one dissolving into another with contradictory emotions overlaying the urgency and violence. An agonizing dance of strangely willing participants with defeats and triumphs always mixed with the seeds and complexities of their opposites. There was an impersonality to it all, a recounting without judgment.

The images played through Patrick's mind as he digested the feelings around them. An archetypal dream such as this seemed to reach in and rearrange his cellular structure. No wonder he'd awakened with a sense of dread. But as he lay there staring at the filtered light playing on the ceiling, thinking of the arc of civilization and its warring ways, Patrick slowly drew himself back to more encouraging thoughts. He reached over to the phone on the nightstand and picked up the receiver. A woman answered.

"The number you wish to call?"

"It's in DC, MD7-2658." He had already memorized it.

"Thank you." There was a moment's pause, then the rhythmic buzz of a telephone.

"Hello," said a sleepy voice on the other end. He probably should have waited longer. It was only 7:00 a.m.

"Jenna, this is Patrick. I'm sorry if I woke you." There was no response for a moment.

"Hmm, Patrick. Do I know a Patrick? Oh yeah, deserted me for some sort of presidential conference. That Patrick?" He could hear the levity in her thick morning voice. "No, I was awake. I'm lying in bed looking at my cat. He usually gets me up around now. Are you back?"

"No, still here in Hyannisport. The president wants to play a round of golf this morning. Guess he didn't learn his lesson from the drubbing I gave him last time."

"Well, presidents are slow learners. They lead insular lives, you know."

"So true." There was a pause. "Are you busy Tuesday night? I mean really late on Tuesday night? Unreasonably late, actually?"

"Why? Are you planning on calling to wake me up then, too?"

"No, I wanted to invite you on a drive."

"Don't those usually happen during the day?"

"For normal people, but not my Uncle Duncan. I think I told you about him."

There was pause. "The impish Irish automobilist?" she said slowly. "That one?"

"Automobilist? Is that a word?" Her vocabulary was daunting even at seven in the morning.

"And you call yourself a writer."

"I don't claim the title myself. Others burden me with it."

"You poor dear." He could hear her soft breathing and the rustle of bedding. "It would be more fun if you were here."

"You mean so you can embarrass me in person when you pummel me with large words."

"Yes, that's exactly what I mean," she laughed. "When do you get back?"

"Probably on tonight's flight from Otis to Andrews."

"Why don't you drive that silly blue car of yours over here when you get in."

"It might be late."

"I'm okay with late. We can have a late dinner."

"Your cat would approve?"

"He'll adjust." Patrick couldn't come up with another wisecrack. He was imagining her lying there, snuggled into a warm blanket, the scent and shape of her. He wanted to be there.

"Well you'd better get along if you're going to whip the president of the United States into shape on the golf course," she interjected during the lapse in conversation. "And I think I can stay up late on Tuesday to meet your uncle. We'll have a lot to talk about. He can fill me in on your dreadful childhood."

"The two of you will get along famously. I'm sure of it."

"We will," was all she said. "See you tonight."

* * *

They gathered at the turn-around in front of the president's home, the same spot where he had observed the mystery woman's departure the night before. Three limos were parked in a line. Patrick was directed toward one whose trunk was open. Inside was a jumble of golf cleats.

"Take your pick, Mr. Hennessey," said the marshal.

Patrick tried on a few of the shoes as he looked around at his group, who were mostly U.S. Marshals. He noticed red-haired "Red" Fay, his previous golf companion at Glen Ora, standing up by the front door talking to someone. Red looked over and gave a smile and nod when their eyes met, and then came down the steps.

"Guess you made the cut," he said, shaking Patrick's hand in a friendly greeting. "The president's feeling a bit superior today, so you'll want to knock him down a few pegs when we're on the course," he added with a wink.

"I don't think that would be wise," chuckled Patrick, remembering Senator Fulbright's comment at the end of the previous game on Patrick's wisdom in not winning when competing with the president. "I'd be happy to take a dive."

"No, give him a workout," encouraged Fay earnestly. "He needs it."

"Okay," shrugged Patrick, although he didn't really intend to take the advice seriously. He sensed his position as a pawn in Red's and the president's games of one-upmanship. Then the man Red had been talking to walked up beside Patrick. Turning, he was surprised to see Pierre Salinger. The surprise was mutual.

"Hennessey. From the *Post*, right?" said Salinger, sticking out his hand in greeting. "What the hell are you doing here?"

"I...uh, well, just a bit of golf—" started Patrick. But before he could fully answer, JFK came out the door and the group came alive. The marshals corralled everyone into the cars. Grabbing his shoes, Patrick was shown around to the passenger side of the middle limo and climbed into the backward-facing jump seat. Red got in opposite, with Salinger getting in from the other side to the adjacent jump seat. They watched the president come down the steps. He wore a thick-knit sweater with a windbreaker over it. He turned to talk to someone, and Patrick could see the presidential seal on his back. He wondered if he'd enjoy wearing clothes with the symbol of the *Washington Post* all over them. Patrick watched the president and noticed how gingerly he walked down the steps, as well as how carefully he climbed into the backseat beside Red Fay before his door was closed.

"Pierre," he said in acknowledgment of the man now facing him across the interior.

He looked over at Patrick. "Good morning, Hennessey."

"Good morning, sir," responded Patrick. He wondered, from the cautious entry, how much will was required to "enjoy" a game of golf. He remembered his first personal contact with the president at the White House when he was delivered into the room in a wheelchair. The man must be taking some kind of painkiller to allow such mobility, considering his infirmity.

"Just to note my intentions—I regularly crush Mr. Fay here on our golf outings," he said as he looked over at Fay with a deprecating glance. "This has become rather repetitive, so I am going to put all my attention on kicking your butt from one end of the course to the other this morning, Hennessey. I just wanted to warn you ahead of time so there won't be any whining about it later." The president looked over at Patrick to give him a wide and almost compassionate smile. It was a smile he had seen often on the face almost anyone on the planet could recognize.

"Yes, sir," said Patrick. "I'll try to make my crushing defeat at least a slight bit challenging for you." He looked over at Red Fay, who shrugged imperceptibly while rolling his eyes.

"That would be the least you could do," said Kennedy. Patrick looked questioningly at Salinger sitting by his side. Kennedy followed his gaze.

"Don't give a thought to Pierre, he can't play worth a damn," said Kennedy in mock disgust. "That's why I sent him to France. So I wouldn't have to watch him hack apart good real estate. But now he's back, so we'll just have to put up with him for now."

"Your powers of observation are still strong, Mr. President, even at your advanced age," said Salinger, enjoying being taunted. In fact, they all were.

Salinger had been Kennedy's press secretary during his first term. But toward the beginning of his second term, as the shock of the Trials and the infirmity of the president faded, he was appointed as Ambassador to France, a position he'd long desired. He was Kennedy's link to Charles de Gaulle and his France-first shenanigans over the ensuing years, for which he probably absorbed the brunt of the president's frustrations. But as Lyndon Johnson's campaign approached, Pierre returned to the States to work with Bobby Kennedy. In fact, a number of Kennedy stalwarts had migrated toward Bobby's campaign, including Kenny O'Donnell, Larry O'Brien, and others. JFK made noises about the shifting allegiances and desertion by old friends, but privately he had encouraged them to go, in order to have as many New Frontiersmen on the Johnson ticket as possible. It would inoculate the new administration from straying too far from long-established Kennedy initiatives.

The procession started moving, but it was over almost before it began. They exited the enclave, went a block on Irving Avenue, then a few blocks up Scudder, turned again, went across a tiny bridge, and then through a gated fence. It took all of three minutes. A group of utility sheds, with two side buildings and a small tractor, stood adjacent to what looked like groundskeepers' quarters. They had come through the back door of the Hyannisport Golf Club, which Patrick would never have seen without a presidential escort. It was a private course with high membership fees and generation-spanning waiting lists designed to keep out the unanointed, like Patrick. The clubhouse and front nine were avoided by coming through the rear entrance. Patrick had heard about this before. JFK would often slip onto the back nine of public or private courses to get in a partial round of golf far from the prying eyes of the public, often without ever being seen from the clubhouse. With a quick call from the presidential switchboard, the normal flow of foursomes would be frozen to allow the president to slide in without too much fuss. Here at the Hyannisport course, it was probably a common event, considering its proximity to the president's home and its stature as one of the best courses in the state.

Everyone piled out of the cars to waiting golf carts, which had already been assembled for the president's arrival. U.S. Marshals were all about, and Patrick even saw a few wandering the fringes of the property outside the chain-link fence line.

Red Fay handed Patrick a scorecard showing the layout of the course.

"We play it a little differently," said Red, tracing his finger over the card. "We start on fifteen, then play three through twelve. It keeps us away from the clubhouse, which is on the other side of the channel." Patrick could see that a creek running through the center divided the front and back of the course. It appeared to be a part of the tidal flats that extended toward the sea. "We also get to play the ocean side for a bit. And with eleven holes total, it's almost a regular round." Patrick could have added what they were both thinking, *It's also not so taxing to the president physically.*

The presidential fanfare was surprisingly short. "How about two dollars a hole, gentlemen?" asked Kennedy. "Ties carry over to the next hole. I think you can all afford to lose that much."

"Okay with me," agreed Patrick, while Red and Salinger nodded. He had been prepared to listen very closely to an overwrought description of a complicated betting structure and was instead puzzled at its simplicity.

"Should I just make my contribution now?" asked Salinger, acknowledging his dismal lack of skill.

"No, we can wait until the end when everyone else is paying up," responded Kennedy. "Besides, I'll want your payment in cigars, Pierre."

Patrick looked over at the nearby cart. Strapped on the back was a full set of McGregor clubs in a plump beaut of a black leather bag with red piping. No doubt about whose that was. It had *John F. Kennedy, Washington, D.C.* embossed on it, with a presidential seal. Next to it was a thinner but still elegant brown leather bag, just as luxurious, but with no insignia.

"Those are your clubs," said the president, noticing Patrick's glance. "They're actually Bobby's, but the future vice president's game is utterly useless, so they've hardly seen a fairway. And I doubt that will change in the future. My brother has never really understood the political necessity of a good golf game."

They took off in two carts with their bags in the back, Patrick in the front cart with JFK, and Salinger following with Red. In front and behind were small contingents of marshals, some walking and some in carts, staying well away from the group. The morning weather was still balmy, with hardly a breeze coming in off the sea. A vaporous sea-scented fog floated around the course, wafting over the fairways and greens, drifting between the trees as it crept stealthily from the sea toward land. An otherworldly quiet kept conversation subdued and lent a mystical aura to the outing. It was a beautiful course—rolling fairways, with a clubhouse barely visible in the distance that looked a little like a Cape Cod, gray shingle-clad version of the White House. A large American flag hung on a mast at the front turnaround.

Entering the course was like coming into another world, one that was ordered, precise, and picturesque with hazy, tree-lined fairways that faded in the foggy sea air, perfectly manicured tee boxes and greens, clear demarcation lines between the fairways and the rough. Maybe that was the attraction in sports, and golf in particular—a well-defined set of rules to navigate a beautiful natural setting. Here, sand traps were sand traps. They could be seen easily and hopefully avoided. Sand did not simply appear under one's feet unannounced, as tended to happen during the course of real life with its ethical traps and moral deceits—often difficult to see until one was fully upon them. If only real life had such clearly accepted rules of the game determining ball drops, score, and out-of-bounds.

Unlike their previous outing at Glen Ora, on that creative, rough-and-tumble mongrel of a homemade estate course, Hyannisport was laid out like a thoroughbred. And Kennedy played it as such. With the morning quiet thickly enshrouding them, there was little fanfare as they teed off at the first box. And even with his obvious infirmity, Kennedy had a beautiful swing with a powerful drive off the tee. Patrick had heard he made a film of his golf swing a few years back, which he sent to Arnold Palmer for advice. The request prompted many a game between the two over the ensuing years. Patrick was envious of the personal lessons at that level of the game, and wondered at the conversations they might have had.

But conversation today was sparse. Maybe it was the muting quality of the misty surroundings that lent a hush to their activities. JFK was all efficiency in moving the ball around the course. He was familiar with the layout of the holes and showed his mastery of the game with minimal effort. Patrick couldn't quite keep up this morning, although just being asked made him aware that JFK respected his game enough to enjoy his company. But the president was wrapped in his own thoughts for the first few holes as they wound around the southern side of the stunning tidal flats. There was little comment other than "Nice shot" when things went well or silence when they didn't. The president parred the first three holes.

But on their fourth hole, the par-three number five, Red shanked his strike off the tee, almost hitting one of the marshals, who danced around the ball at the last minute in a comical pirouette. The president couldn't hold his laughter.

"You may be Undersecretary of the Navy, Redhead, but that doesn't mean you can take out one of my security detail," joked the president. "I may need that guy in the future."

"How about I get you a sandwich, sir?" said Red, dejected from his errant shot. The president gave him a withering look, then shook his head, grinning.

"Did you know that you can die from eating a ham sandwich?" said the president, turning to Patrick. "No, not necessarily you, Hennessey," said Kennedy when Patrick responded with raised eyebrows pointing at himself. "The *you* meant *me* in this case."

"I'm not sure I follow," said Patrick as he prepared for his drive off the tee. Was this more of the presidential distraction parade to which he had been exposed on their previous game?

"When I was down in Dallas—and in a complicated and ironic way this shows there is a silver lining to even the most heinous of events—my doctors discovered I'm allergic to wheat. Always have been, and it's been poisoning me most of my life. Eating away at my bones, destroying my digestion, probably the cause of all my earlier years of distress when I was in and out of hospitals." The president had Patrick's full attention. "I'm Irish and have a thing called celiac syndrome. My body thinks wheat is poison. Happens a lot to people of Irish descent."

"How did they find out about that?" asked Patrick.

"There's a clinic in Dallas, of all places, and the doctors there kept pestering my doctors to test for the condition. They figured it out after some of my medical history came out. Adding my Irish ancestry to the mix, they got suspicious. Makes you wonder. Maybe I got shot in Dallas so they could figure out I was allergic to toast," deadpanned the president.

"What about the shooting?" asked Patrick a few moments later, after he had made his shot off the box. "Are you ever going to go public about that?" The subject had never been fully tackled by the president, either in his press conferences or between the two of them. Patrick was sure it needed to come up at some point, and wondered if he could nudge the information loose now.

"You're up, Pierre," was all the president said as they waited for Salinger's feeble drive. He lofted a shot that landed just on the edge of the green, to everyone's surprise. They drove to the next tee without discussion.

The remainder of the morning they talked of the upcoming election, laughing freely about the Agnew-Bobby exchanges in the media. The president obviously felt good about the expected outcome. They also marveled at the recent Apollo flight to the moon, discussed with frustration the ongoing deliberations with Cuba, with satisfaction the developments

in South America, and with confusion what to do regarding the chaotic
social conditions gripping the country.

"I hear you played a round with John Lennon out here in '66," said
Salinger as they were putting on their tenth hole, the par-four number
eleven. "I didn't know he golfed." Salinger had been in France at the
time, but news of the Beatles' meeting with JFK had traveled around the
world.

"He doesn't," replied Kennedy, smiling. "I cleaned him out for about
thirty bucks, if I remember. We had marshals replacing divots all afternoon. I was afraid the course would charge me for damages. It's good the
man has a music career to fall back on because his golfing abilities are below even Bobby's, if that's possible." Patrick remembered the pandemonium over the Beatles' U.S. visit a couple of years before. It had saturated
the news media and even came up during one of JFK's news conferences.
A UPI reporter had asked about the president's upcoming meeting with
the pop group and whether he considered himself a fan of their music and
whether he felt they were a good role model for the youth of the day.

He had answered very diplomatically to a lot of laughter. It went something like, "Well, I will need to answer that question very carefully, as my
daughter Caroline may be listening. She, if you don't know, is the popular
music critic in our family and has been rather candid in her remarks as to
my tastes leaving something to be desired. (laughter) Yes, I do believe the
Beatles will be coming to the White House next week for a short meeting. And I do believe they represent a positive role model. Youth is always
dynamic and will often go off in directions with which we, as an older
generation, may not be comfortable. But sometimes that discomfort may
broaden our horizons." He then added, "If the press has any serious or in-
depth inquiries about the Beatles, they should talk to an authority, namely Caroline. I do hope I answered that adequately, or else I'll be hearing
about it at dinner tonight." That clip had been played over and over again
on television and Patrick had seen it a dozen times.

When they got around to teeing off on their last hole, the par-four
number twelve, conversation turned to the economy and the bite the
British took out of the incomes of the wealthy, such as members of their
world-conquering rock groups. Kennedy had made modest tax cuts during his second term, but not nearly to the extent that many in industry and
banking had called for.

"Tax cuts," started Kennedy, "would create greater discretionary spending with an increase in consumer purchasing. But is that really the best course forward? I wanted to balance that with another approach, the reinvestment of tax revenue into broad public improvements such as education, health care, infrastructure, upcoming pollution control mandates, and the like. Investments that secure the foundations of the public good rather than just profiteering."

"There is a lot of talk about tax cuts improving the overall economy," said Red. "A rising tide lifting all boats, and all that."

"That's a great metaphor," said Kennedy. "Especially from my Undersecretary of the Navy. But the poor don't have boats."

"You took a lot of flak for your position," said Salinger. "You still do."

"But from what quarter?" responded Kennedy. "You see, public resource reinvestment is extremely important for those of moderate means, the lower and middle portions of society—the great majority of the population. It affects them in a more substantial manner. Those resources aren't as essential for the rich, such as myself, who can purchase those services with their wealth. And since the rich pay more in taxes and have far greater means to vocalize their dissent, they are always preaching about the need for tax cuts. It was Roosevelt who said, 'It is an unfortunate human failing that a full pocketbook often groans more loudly than an empty stomach.'"

"So you're a Galbraith proponent?" asked Patrick.

"Well, the man has a point," said Kennedy, "and he's doing a bang-up job as Ambassador to Russia."

"I think economics is like religion: Everybody talks about it, approaching it from their own position, but it's still one of mankind's deeper mysteries," said Red.

"And speaking of economics, and judging from the scorecard," said the president, "I believe there is a balance of payments issue to resolve."

They finished putting out their last hole, which brought them back to where they had begun, near the grounds-keepers' utility sheds. The cars were waiting. They quickly piled in and took off, back to the house for lunch.

"Hennessey, meet me after lunch over at my dad's house. We can have a session on the sun porch. Make it two hours from now," said Kennedy as an aside after everyone had gotten out of the car. For all the record-keeping and chatter about winnings, the president never bothered to actually collect when the match was done, always putting it off until later, which never seemed to arrive.

* * *

"The irony of this whole affair is that the conspirators plotting to kill America's president had great trust in the American system. They were patriots, although in a perverted sense of the word," said Kennedy. JFK was sitting back on a comfortable old leather couch, legs crossed and one arm lying easily on the armrest, looking out over the aquamarine waters of Nantucket Sound. A Dictaphone was on a side table. Patrick realized the president was answering his earlier question on the golf course about the assassination attempt. "These people, even though they circumvented the will of the populace, trusted in the basic functioning of the American governmental system. They understood it to be self-healing: remove the leader at the top, and the gap, from a bureaucratic point of view, would be automatically filled. They saw no need for military force or a general insurrection. No need to impose a selected leader, as one was already waiting in the wings who would suffice. They had great belief in the mechanics of the process, but none in the people's right to choose. The decision to kill the president came about because they were confident the American government would continue, but with different leaders at the top and thus different and more palatable national policies. It would have been the first American coup d'état, had it succeeded. And it might have remained hidden had I been killed."

They were sitting in the enclosed sun porch of Joseph Kennedy, Sr.'s house. Patrick had walked over from the president's home after lunch and was ushered up to the room by one of the servants. When walking through the house, he was surprised at how ordinary the furnishings were. He had expected a rich interior similar to that of the White House, whose renovations Jackie had orchestrated, but instead found aging interior surfaces and sofas and chairs well-worn from generations of family use. At the president's house, the interior had been newer and more tasteful, but still not of the lustrous quality Patrick had expected from a scion of American wealth who was also the leader of the United States.

The weather was still balmy, but it appeared to be turning as the wind picked up, sending ripples skidding across the sea. As was usual in these sessions, the president had launched into his topic immediately. A tape machine lay on the small table between them. It appeared the president did a lot of his private reading and writing here, attested to by numerous books, official looking pamphlets and papers stacked on the desk that faced obliquely toward the water view. Patrick sat down in a cushioned chair, worn by years of use, between the sofa the president was occupying and his desk.

"Three presidents have been killed by assassination: Lincoln, Garfield, and McKinley—the last over sixty years ago. There were also numerous close calls, including both Teddy and Franklin Roosevelt, and then more recently Harry Truman right on the front steps of his temporary residence at Blair House. In each instance the plots were exposed, and the guilty were tried and convicted, or killed in the process. This situation, my shooting," he said as he looked over at Patrick, "was more frightening—at least to those who put their hope in the democratic system—as it was hatched from within and then almost concealed by those very groups that we rely upon for honest investigation. Assassination is a dark enough subject, but when it springs from corruption within, it is even more foul.

"You know," said the president, "I've always thought that if we could divorce ourselves from the political need to vilify our opponents, we might be able to see that their positions often have at least an element of truth. Otherwise they wouldn't hold such power. But it's the way those truthful elements are interwoven into an argument that determines the ultimate attraction of those positions. Within some segments of the government, there had been a great push for war—in Vietnam, in Cuba, and against the Soviets—to effect a complete supremacy of American power on the international stage. The plotters, and those aligned with them, believed there was an open window of opportunity available to create American dominance with military action. It has been very difficult for me to give any credence to this argument—that is, that my concrete steps toward peace were subverting the course of American history." Kennedy paused and lit a cigar, taking a draw and looking toward the sea. "Sometimes the other side is simply wrong."

"What did you feel about the original findings put forth by the FBI?" asked Patrick. He felt he needed to get these questions in early, since Kennedy had been reluctant to speak of this until now, and he did not know how long this openness would last.

"Well, the idea that one lone nut, Mr. Rubenstein, killed another lone nut, Mr. Oswald, was pretty hard to swallow," he said with a bit of sarcasm, "especially since these two disaffected miscreants acted within days of each other, right under the noses of the authorities, nearly silencing the entire investigation. It would take more than a few Alka-Seltzers to digest that. But had events transpired differently, they might have gotten away with it. Such a little thing, a back cramp, altered the course of history. But then, isn't that always the case? If one were to look back at the small things that ripple into larger events, there is always that special moment when just a slight adjustment in action might have created an entirely different outcome. Why one outcome and not the other? Not for me to know," he mused.

"But a real investigation was necessary. Early on, Bobby and I discussed the framework. I wanted to avoid the 'establishment effect.' A real investigation would never be considered authentic if it was sequestered behind closed doors, as was suggested with the Warren Commission, nor if its makeup was totally governmental. A certain insular deviation occurs once a person enters the gravitational orbit of Washington, D.C. Vision distorts, and partisan and political considerations rise to the top of the decision-making process. Not that anyone would actually admit to that," he laughed. "But that tendency needed to be counteracted by drawing members from academic and economic segments of society into the committees—scholars and businessmen unfamiliar with normal congressional participation. Involvement of the media was also required, which would not be the case with a closed investigation. Their presence, intrusive though they might be, was essential. And I think they proved themselves, for the most part, with a level of participation equal to the gravity of the situation."

"Why did you promote a fully open investigation in the first place?" asked Patrick.

"A good question. It was out of character in many ways to allow the examination of the inner workings of the government to be displayed for the world to see. But the American system was at a pivotal moment in history. Military and anti-communist stridency was out of control. It created an unrealistic view of the world that needed to be rectified. Its forces within our society were strong, so strong that they resulted in the attempted purge of an elected president. For a healthy nation-state to emerge, a fundamental realignment was necessary. I was willing to gamble that America was mature enough and wise enough to take a hard look at itself as it entered the second half of the twentieth century and to make the necessary corrections.

"Public realization that the nation was just as at-risk from internal forces as from those without would be difficult to absorb. That's why I spent so much time, after I healed, giving reassuring talks around the country in '64 regarding the inherent strength of the American government. I felt that keeping the United States on a steady course would allow us to re-set our priorities. The sixties has been a time of great change—chaotic, impetuous, and transformative. That self-examination was not easy, but was essential in order to redirect the energies of our nation along a path of peace.

"And then there was the basic trust of the American people. In their gut, they knew something of a Shakespearean tragedy was being played out. They wanted to believe that the government had the best intentions, but intuitively suspected far less. The investigation had to be transparent, or the seed of mistrust it planted would have festered over the years, cre-ating an embittered people and an embedded suspicion of a system that allowed the murder of its leader and then declined to investigate or bring the guilty parties to justice.

"Many deceits lie at the soul of a government. In the final analysis, it is only made of ordinary men and women. But a deceit so substantial and so antithetical to the idea of democracy—the seditious elimination of its principal leader—would lay waste to the public's trust. And I am not just referring to a casualty of American trust, but to international trust as well. Because want it or not, internationalist or isolationist, I believe the world depends on America to succeed. I do not think it is overreaching to say that the world's citizens lean the weight of their hopes on the vitality and articulation of America's dream of democracy. It is an enterprise recog-nized around the globe by ordinary people who have greater dreams than living in a repressive society or under a corrupt regime. And if the heart of the American dream is shrouded in a lie, the international community senses it, and their future interactions and aspirations will be deflated ac-cordingly, to the detriment of us all."

Kennedy paused, and then looked over as if to say, 'You satisfied now?' To which Patrick could only nod.

"But that danger has passed," continued the president. "There has been a transformative pruning of the American government. And I think we are cautiously rebounding as a humbler, healthier, and more robust force for peace. Look at the world stage. Vietnam, once a flashpoint for a potential conflict on the order of the Korean War, is emerging as a whole country. There has been no influx of Soviet or Chinese communist forces control-ling the region. It is still communist and still in turmoil, as any such reorganization on the scale of re-cementing two portions of a divided country would be. But there is real hope that the region will emerge from this period as a partner for peace rather than for division. And having a partner in the Indochina region with which America can interact diplomatically has made a great difference in the balance of power there, vis-à-vis China and the Soviets.

"In South America, the Alliance for Progress has opened up a continent of goodwill for Americans. We are seeing that differences in political and economic structures do not need to be destructively divisive. They have embraced a socialist economic model as opposed to our capitalist one. Some would say these systems are not compatible, but I think the opposite is being shown to be true.

"In Cuba, we are still having problems with the Castro regime, but there have been significant strides. The Caribbean Accords, signed in '67, laid out a blueprint for rapprochement with that regime that removed them from the sphere of Soviet-backed satellites. It stipulated significant disarmament, compensation for appropriated lands, businesses, and displaced nationals over a twelve-year timeframe, administered by the UN, the release of political prisoners, a freer press, eventual popular elections, cessation of the export of revolution to neighboring countries—and a host of other points.

We in turn lifted our embargo in a staggered time frame as benchmarks were met, unlocked Cuban assets in the United States, enacted diplomatic recognition of Cuba, and submitted a formal UN international agreement to cease all hostilities directed toward the island. We will respect their sovereignty. The larger scope of these advances was made possible, in an ironic twist of fate, by virtue of the participation of anti-Castro Cubans in the assassination plot. Due to that finding, domestic political support for the Cuban community in Florida collapsed.

We are seeing Cuba's adequate, though not stellar, respect for the Caribbean Accords. But what has been most interesting is the regional reaction to the accords. Latin and South American countries are now judging Castro's regime on its economic and human rights conditions, without seeing the United States as a bullying overseer. Castro can no longer play the martyr. No longer can reversals in Cuba's progress be blamed on U.S. restrictions. Castro has had to make it on his own, and the middling results so far are not burnishing his reputation. I feel that in the years to come, when Castro is eventually eased from power by his own people, there will be room for greater U.S. accommodation and interaction with the country.

"It appears that Mr. Khrushchev will soon be out of power. He survived a purge in '64, mainly, I believe, on the strength of the progress toward peace that we were making jointly. Remember, he had hardliners in his government of the same caliber and fervency that we had in ours. I do not know what will come of our relationship in the future, but our time in office will end on a far better note than it began. I can still painfully remember the first summit we had in Vienna where he ran roughshod over me. The fear of war was upon us all. How things have changed!

"The Peace Corps has been a huge success, and with its expansion, and the creation of the Home Corps, a generation of Americans are making real commitments both internationally and domestically to help their fellow man.

"International politics has shifted dramatically, and it seems to be mirrored at home as well," said Patrick.

"Yes. Domestically, civil rights has been a difficult issue. But the Reverend Martin Luther King's moral leadership has been extremely effective. I personally believe it will take generations to rid our culture of racially charged beliefs, but we have come so far. And with Dr. King's levelheaded influence on what could have been an explosive issue, we are making real strides toward desegregation. A great deal of credit goes to Lyndon, who, during his interim presidency, shepherded the passage of the Civil Rights and Voting Rights Acts through a very reluctant Congress."

"The sixties have seen an impressive amount of change come to our little planet," said Patrick.

"But with all our movement forward, there are a number of issues that America will need to give its full attention to in the future," responded the president. "The first regards nuclear weapons. They represent the negative side of the advancement of technology and present a host of problems. If they are used in any sort of wholesale exchange with the Soviet Union, it will be a catastrophe from which the human race will not recover. The annihilation of our cities would be only the first stage of the damage. After that would come global radioactive contamination, creating sickness and death on a scale we can hardly imagine. The complete destruction of the human race is quite possible.

"I also fear that we have created a nuclear Maginot Line. You're familiar with the concept?" asked JFK.

"With the French Maginot Line, constructed after World War One, but not its nuclear counterpart," responded Patrick.

"After the First World War, France built a line of powerful stationary artillery casemates along its German and Italian borders," continued the president, "assuming that any assault would be either easily repulsed or at least give them ample time to mount a defense. It created a false sense of security. The Germans simply went around it, rendering it futile. I fear that nuclear weapons give the same sort of perverse assurance of safety—thus, a nuclear 'Maginot Line.' As the superpowers confront each other and stave off each other's advances with the threat of nuclear annihilation, the underbelly of that sort of posturing is exposed. Population pressures and local insurgencies have the capability of undermining any sort of protection that nuclear weapons could afford, because nuclear weapons will never be used by a sane government. It would be suicidal.

"Look at Vietnam, as an example. The United States has unlimited firepower and could bomb the entire North into a pile of smoldering ash over the course of a few days. But will we? Not if we have any shred of humanity, we won't. And it will never happen on my watch. But without resorting to that type of firepower, I don't feel we could possibly win a war in that region. We have neither the manpower nor the willpower to do so. Look at the French and their decades-long attempt to subdue that country under colonial rule. They were soundly defeated. We can create huge stockpiles of nuclear weapons whose only benefit toward keeping the peace is if they are never used—a rather perverse human endeavor.

"The modern world, inhabited by so many different cultures, must be managed differently. We need to wean ourselves from the idea that superior military force will provide security on an international scale. It may not even provide security for countries that already possess that power, as internal dissolution can cause collapse. America needs to re-evaluate its assumption that a big stick will endear us to the international community, or protect us from the same. And that means we need to direct our diplomatic and national treasure toward peaceful cooperation rather than arms build-up and sales of weapons to arm every country on the planet. The pursuit of peace is not as dramatic as the pursuit of war, but is the most essential pursuit that rational men can undertake.

"And that is where the Untied Nations comes into play. 'One World government' is a term used derisively by the extreme right in American politics. It denotes an Orwellian organization that would usurp American political autonomy. The fear is that we would be folded into a governmental system dominated by some faceless bureaucracy from a foreign land. Nothing is further from the truth, and no single belief system is more debilitating to the eventual cooperation of the peoples of this planet than that exclusivist viewpoint. For an analogy, when our country was first founded, it consisted of thirteen individual states making up the eastern portion of what eventually became the United States of America. There was a great deal of animosity and mistrust between those states, their legislative bodies, and their respective inhabitants. But it was through the eventual union of these disparate entities that the United States was born. In fact, its name is its very definition. We created a much stronger entity by its union than in its separation.

"The world is shrinking, and the nation-states that make up its inhabitants are bumping up against each other in a greater number of ways: economically, environmentally, culturally, politically, and in our individual methods of self-defense. The United Nations, for all its current problems and ineffectuality, is the initial blueprint for eventual cooperation. Just as our country is a nation of states, and stronger and more peaceful for it, the Earth will be a planet of nations, and far more secure and harmonious because of it.

"Mankind still has a great deal to accomplish. I believe we are only just getting started. But to surge ahead into greater arenas of development, we need to make significant and sustainable inroads toward international cooperation. We can do this. I am sure we can do this. Without it, I believe we have a harsh future."

Kennedy had been talking very intently while Patrick listened and took some notes. But Patrick had stopped as the president's delivery became more forceful and impassioned. When he came to the last comments, it was evident to both of them that he was finished. Neither got up to leave. The president sat in reflection for a while, relighting his cigar, which had gone out from inattention, gazing out the wide windows at the beautiful maritime vista of Nantucket Sound stretching over the horizon.

In the pause, Patrick was aware of feeling self-conscious, to be sitting silently after such a rich and illuminated discourse by the president. His gaze wandered, at first out to the oceanscape in front of him, then around the room. He looked over at the desk beside him, his eyes running over the stacks of books cluttering its surface. Peeking out from amid the unruly bundles of pamphlets, briefing papers, and White House folders was a dog-eared copy of Joseph Campbell's *The Masks of God*—an incongruous title amid the clutter of national policy briefs, economic studies, and the cornucopia of topics a president needed to be conversant with in order to run a government. Patrick looked closer, and another seemed misplaced among the official documents. He tilted his head a little to get a view of the title: *First and Last Freedom* by Jiddu Krishnamurti. Kennedy was renowned for his voracious and eclectic reading habits, but these were surprising explorations even for an intellectually inquisitive president. Patrick knew of Krishnamurti from passing references by friends. An influx of spiritual teachers from the East, gurus and such, had fallen on America like a steady rain. Krishnamurti was one—a spiritual teacher who had declined his own deification. *An odd choice of reading material,* thought Patrick.

He suddenly became aware that JFK was quietly watching him, and he felt a bit awkward. He had been intruding into private space. He turned toward the president. But in looking back, he realized Kennedy was not bothered; it was more that he was pondering what he might say.

"The sea can have so many faces," he said, looking out at the water. "Calm and embracing, invigorating, frighteningly brutal and impersonal. It stretches to infinity, disappearing over an endless horizon. Yet, no matter what it is one day, it's usually something else the next. It's good to remember that, both for sailors and for anyone relating it to human endeavors. It changes and stays the same. There is immense freedom out there, with no real boundaries. One could spend a lifetime exploring its depths." He looked at Patrick now, and his glance flicked across to the books Patrick had noticed. "But it would seem, Patrick, that for all we've done, when it comes to understanding our place in all of this," said the president with a slight wave of his hand toward the cluttered desk and the window, "we're still swimming in the shallow end of the pool."

Unusually philosophical, at least in Patrick's experience, Mr. Kennedy took a draw on his cigar to shift the mood. He exhaled slowly, savoring it as he took a last look at the ocean view from the sun porch.

Patrick realized it was the first and only time the president had addressed him as Patrick. But the moment was short-lived.

"Next week, Hennessey," he said sharply as he stubbed out the cigar in the ashtray on the side table, his usual directness returning, "I want to explore Keynesian economic theory and how it holds up regarding the emerging monetary models in Latin America. Now *that* should be fascinating."

Oh, great! I can't wait, thought Patrick. Economics, the dismal science, and one of the least comprehensible topics that might invade his consciousness.

"So, at the White House, Thursday morning, usual tour entrance. Mrs. Lincoln will call you about timing. And, Hennessey," he said, smiling as he gingerly rose to leave, and surely aware of Patrick's scant enthusiasm, "I'm *really* looking forward to it."

"Yes, sir," responded Patrick. "Also one of *my* favorite subjects."

Epilogue

But words are things, and a small drop of ink,
falling like dew upon a thought, produces
that which makes thousands, perhaps millions, think.
—*Lord Byron*

How many legs does a dog have if you call a tail a leg?
Four. Calling a tail a leg does not make it a leg.
—*Abraham Lincoln*

The Memoirs of John F. Kennedy is a novel and, as such, a work of fiction. Then again, about three-quarters of the American public view the *Warren Commission Report*, which chronicles the assassination of John Kennedy, in the same light. The *Warren Commission Report* was intended to be received as fact. Yet, even at the time of its release, fully half of the public doubted its findings. That number has grown steadily during the ensuing years.

It is a dubious distinction, in a democracy such as our own, that the responsibility for ferreting out the true events surrounding the killing of a popular president has been left to private citizens—a dubious distinction, and a difficult task. Yet vast public interest and a dogged demand for an honest accounting, even in the face of bureaucratic stonewalling, has paid off. It has exposed the true dimensions of a national crime that was never properly investigated, and now, due to the passage of time, probably never will be. A great debt of thanks goes to all the men and women over the last half-century who have tirelessly pried loose from a reluctant U.S. government page after heavily redacted page of documentation. Over the years, this mountain of data has shown the *Warren Commission Report* to be riddled with inconsistencies and blatant misinformation.

It would be difficult to recount here even a fraction of the findings that point toward a deliberately flawed investigation. Hundreds of books have done so, concentrating on different portions of the crime. These include the ballistic and medical forensics, the re-interrogation of witnesses, the discovery of new witnesses or those deliberately shunted aside at the time of the initial investigation, the examination of the Warren Commission's operation, the investigation into the lives of Lee Harvey Oswald and Jack Ruby showing far more complexity than was originally revealed, and many other facets that show a tangled but hidden agenda.

Many find unbearable the idea that a domestic intrigue claimed the life of a sitting president. The mainstream media has consistently taken a dim view of "conspiracy theorists." But as history rolls on, there is little doubt to anyone who cares to look, that our government trades actively in the marketplace of deception—and sometimes on a grand scale. America's entry into the Vietnam and Iraq wars are just two recent examples.

There will always be major unanswered questions regarding the killing of JFK, and legitimate disputes about the complex nature of the crime. But the tidily constructed fiction of Lee Harvey Oswald as the lone and crazed assassin of a popular American president will hopefully always elicit a disbelieving response from informed members of the American public.

As the author of this book, I have given a personal and subjective suggestion of events. Familiar historical figures were inserted into historical domains they did not really occupy and into actions and life-paths they did not really follow. Yet, given a more fortunate turn of events, and after a careful consideration of their previous stances, these are actions they *might* have taken and lives they *might* have lived.

Many readers have asked just where the boundary between fact and fiction is drawn in this story. That is a hard border to define precisely, as after the shooting, fact and fiction are interwoven throughout. But even so, the reader may be surprised to find that this story leans heavily upon fact. The following explanations and short reading lists might be helpful to give perspective on these issues.

The Warren Commission Investigation

The *Warren Commission Report* has been a source of controversy since the moment of its release, ten months after the shooting of President Kennedy. The FBI, under the domination of Director J. Edgar Hoover, was the only investigative source of information provided to the Warren Commission. There were no independent investigators, and early attempts during the creation of the commission to employ independent investigators were stymied by Hoover.

The "magic bullet theory" was ardently promoted by Arlen Spector, legal counsel to the Commission, to solve the dilemma posed to the commission by the minor injury of Mr. James Tague, a bystander struck by a bullet fragment. Up until that point, six to seven months into the investigation, the Warren Commission members agreed that two separate shots had struck the president and one had struck Governor Connally sitting in a more forward seat. But if Mr. Tague was also hit, this created the conundrum of a fourth shot and a second shooter—thus a conspiracy. To salvage this unacceptable supposition, the tortured Single Bullet Theory was created to account for both the president's and the governor's wounds. It was not embraced by the FBI, which, under Hoover, still thought it an erroneous and unnecessary contrivance to fit the facts around a grand lone-nut theory. Hoover never acknowledged that a fourth shot hit bystander Jim Tague under the nearby bypass, even though many witnessed it, including a policeman standing near Mr. Tague.

The Warren Commission was comprised of nine national figures chosen by Lyndon Baines Johnson. Most were reluctant participants in this exercise, did not attend meetings regularly, and were only marginally involved with day-to-day proceedings. The main thrust of the investigation was left to Allen Dulles, the previous CIA chief and a long-time antagonist of JFK who was dismissed from his position by the president after the Bay of Pigs fiasco, and to legal counsel that steered the commission's investigation away from anything that would supply information or witnesses disagreeing with the one-shooter conclusion the commission was supporting.

Commission member Senator Richard Russell (as well as members Senator John Cooper and Congressman Hale Boggs) disagreed with the commission's findings. Russell stated, "I'll never sign that report if this commission says categorically that the second shot passed through both of them." Transcripts of his disagreements, consisting of a proposed "minority report," were not included in the final version, even though he had assumed they were and signed off on the findings with publication of his disagreements assured. He was later shocked to discover they were missing from the final printing and even expunged from transcripts held in the National Archives.

The Zapruder film was spirited away from public viewing and only released by the FBI during the investigation in the form of still-frame shots that were rearranged out of order, showing ballistics results that supported the shot originating from behind at the Book Depository and not a shot from in front of the limousine. It was not until 1972 that the entire film was released to the public after a series of lawsuits demanding the public be allowed to view its disturbing and controversial images.

Breach of Trust: How the Warren Commission Failed the Nation and Why,
by Gerald D. McKnight

The House Subcommittee on Assassinations

The House Select Committee on Assassinations (HSCA), funded in
1975 to further investigate the killings after so much misinformation
was uncovered, was also emasculated. Its original Chief Counsel, Richard
Sprague, and Deputy Robert Tanenbaum intended to carry out a *homicide*
investigation and proceeded to do so (12,000 people volunteered to work
as researchers for this committee). When the implications of their prob-
ings into CIA actions in Mexico City and elsewhere became obvious, the
committee was defunded and its lead proponents removed. James Blakely,
Sprague's replacement, stated that the focus of his investigation would be
legislative in breadth, not criminal. He even went so far as to contact the
CIA and FBI to allow them to view the Commission's findings before
they were released, to be certain they were acceptable—similar to waiting
for approval from a criminal suspect before releasing a jury's conclusion.
But even after forging into such a headwind of bureaucratic resistance, the
HSCA still could not deny the facts, and stated:

> *"The committee believes, on the basis of the evidence available to it,
> that President John F. Kennedy was probably assassinated as a result of a
> conspiracy. The committee is unable to identify the other gunman or the
> extent of the conspiracy."*

These findings, based upon witness testimony excluded by the FBI
and Warren Commission counsel, contradicted the lone-gunman theory:
upon evidence that Jack Ruby had deep and persistent involvement with
organized crime, which was completely "overlooked" by the FBI during
the Warren Commission investigation; upon acoustical studies showing
that more than three shots were fired in Dealey Plaza; and upon evidence
of tenacious stonewalling by the CIA, FBI, and Military Intelligence in
releasing information at every phase of the inquiry.

After the inconvenient findings of a probable conspiracy, there was
no attempt to discover the members of this conspiracy. The House Select
Committee on Assassinations folded with its work only half completed.
Years later, Chief Counsel G. Robert Blakey lamented the continuing
cover-up by the CIA that blocked a full exposure of the events occurring

around that dark day. He had not realized until after the commission disbanded that he had been effectively diverted away from information vital to the probe.

"*The Agency (CIA) has never cooperated in the investigation of the president's death.... I do know now that everything I thought back in the seventies, I no longer think. I think the agency double-timed us.... So what do you conclude about the agency? You have to conclude that they don't tell the truth to the government for which they work, about the most important single thing that happened in the 1960's, President Kennedy's death.*"

Calling it a closed investigation does not make it so.

The Last Investigation, by Gaeton Fonzi
Corruption of Blood, by Robert Tanenbaum

Vietnam and JFK

JFK had great reservations about entering a ground war in Vietnam. Very early in his term, he resisted the pressures of the military to introduce significant ground troops, allowing only sixteen thousand "advisors" as a tactic to keep his generals mollified. That is a substantial number, but miniscule in comparison to their demands at the time for over 205,000 troops. It will always be an unprovable assertion that Kennedy would have avoided that conflict, as he often covered both sides of the argument publicly, giving conflicting comments regarding his future intentions.

But significant evidence supports the proposition that he would have opted out of the conflict, not the least of which were his past actions. He had avoided an easy entry into a war with Cuba during the Bay of Pigs invasion, allowing that early fiasco to envelop his administration, even to his political detriment. Two years later, he alone was the stalwart promoter of a peaceful solution to the Cuban missile crisis, against the strident advice of his military. He refused to escalate the conflict in Laos, again against the hawkish demands of his military and the CIA for ground troop intervention. Instead, he supported a path of neutrality and independence agreed upon with Khrushchev during numerous public and private exchanges. And he was following a similar strategy in Vietnam, stalling and probing for a means to allow a reduction in and eventual departure of troops from that country. As early as 1954, in a speech to Congress, he stated that the French were mistaken in their colonialization of Vietnam and that America should not follow in their footsteps. He maintained that intention even in the face of withering disapproval and deliberate subterfuge from his military leaders and the CIA.

He stated to Senator Mansfield, Bobby Kennedy, and a number of his close confidants that he planned to remove U.S. troops after the 1964 election. Since that was very unpopular with certain portions of the populace, he would need to win that election by a significant margin to claim a mandate. Only three weeks before his assassination, he signed a presidential order (NSAM 263) for the initial removal of one thousand in-country advisors. Only two days after JFK's murder, this order was rescinded by Lyndon Johnson, who later chose a full-on military intervention.

> *Choosing War: The Lost Chance for Peace and the Escalation of the Vietnam War*, by Fredrik Logevall
> *JFK and the Unspeakable: Why He Died and Why it Matters*, By James W. Douglass
> *JFK and Vietnam*, by John M. Newman
> *Perils of Dominance: Imbalance of Power and the Road to War in Vietnam*, by Gareth Porter

Cuban Tactical Nuclear Missiles

The Berlin Wall fell in 1989, and with it, over the next few years, the Soviet Union. Afterwards, in a period of glasnost (openness), significant records from the former Soviet Union were shared. These included detailed information regarding the Soviet side of the Cuban missile crisis, information that underscored the precarious nature of the confrontation. Not only were there intermediate-range ballistic missiles (SS-4s and SS-5s) of which the Kennedy administration had become aware from U-2 photographs, but also operational tactical nuclear weapons. Unknown to the US military, about 100 of them were arrayed against the United States to repel an island invasion. Orders from Moscow to Soviet field commander General Pliyev fluctuated during the crisis—at one point giving him permission to use them at his own discretion if attacked, and then later rescinding that order and telling him to wait for further instructions from Moscow.

When the crisis passed and the SS-4s and SS-5s were removed, there was still Soviet confusion regarding the tactical missiles already in place. Castro wanted them to remain under either his or Soviet control, while the Soviet military wanted them out. They were finally removed from the island over Christmas of 1962, almost two and a half months after the conclusion of the nuclear standoff—all of this without the knowledge of the United States.

During the 30-year anniversary of the Cuban Missile Crisis held in Havana in 1992, Castro revealed the details of this situation to visiting dignitaries from the United States. Former Kennedy administration luminaries, Robert McNamara and others, were shocked to learn of missile placement for the first time. It was also revealed that one of the Soviet submarines that was depth-charged to force it to surface during the island's quarantine had nuclear-tipped torpedoes that required the agreement of three onboard officers to allow their firing. In a fiercely argued undersea exchange, only two agreed.

The US had no inkling at the time of the crisis that the Soviet-Cuban forces were in such a state of readiness. Were it not for JFK's adamant resistance to an island invasion and insistence upon a peaceful resolution, there might well have been a tragic civilization-altering event that month, leaving Cuba and the southeastern United States uninhabitable for generations.

One Hell of a Gamble: The Secret History of the Cuban Missile Crisis,
    by Aleksandr Fursenko and Timothy Naftali
One Minute to Midnight: Kennedy, Khrushchev and Castro on the Brink of Nuclear War, by Michael Dobbs

Cuba and Rapprochement

William Attwood, Special Advisor for African Affairs at the UN, was, in his previous incarnation, an international journalist. Over the years, he developed extensive contacts and a good rapport with Fidel Castro. During the fall of '63, he became aware, through back-channel talks with Dr. Carlos Lechuga (Cuban Ambassador to the UN) and Major René Vallejo (Castro's personal aide), that Castro was interested in accommodation with the United States. This information was relayed outside the normal power structure in Cuba and without the knowledge or support of Che Guevara or the communist hierarchy in Cuba.

Contacts included Lisa Howard, an ABC-TV correspondent, who met with Castro a number of times, each time noting the Cuban leader's desire for talks that would dramatically change the course of relations with the United States.

The CIA was aware of these contacts and strongly discouraged them.

The agency was still actively trying to overthrow or eliminate Castro and found such accommodations repellent. It even attempted to prevent Lisa Howard's ABC interview with Castro from airing on U.S. television for fear it might sway Americans to his side.

On November 18, 1963, JFK gave a speech in Miami. Fully aware of Castro's shifting allegiance and the issues that separated Cuba and the United States, he publicly paved the way for rapprochement with the condition that Castro stop exporting revolution to neighboring Latin American countries. He stated, "This and this alone divides us. As long as this is true, nothing is possible. Without it, everything is possible.... Once Cuban sovereignty has been restored we will extend the hand of friendship and assistance to a Cuba whose political and economic institutions have been shaped by the will of the Cuban People." Three days later, Kennedy was murdered.

In mid-November '63, JFK sent a message to Castro via Jean Daniel, a French journalist who was on his way to Cuba for a meeting. While Daniel was speaking with Castro in Havana, news of JFK's assassination came over the radio. Both men were devastated. Castro stated, "This is an end to your message of peace. Everything is changed."

Lyndon Johnson never responded to repeated requests from Castro to continue negotiations, and the possibility of rapprochement withered.

Robert Kennedy and His Times, Arthur M. Schlesinger, Jr.
The Reds and the Blacks, by William Attwood
Brothers: the Hidden History of the Kennedy Years, by David Talbot

The Mexico City Impostor

The events in Mexico City involving an Oswald impostor, preceding the assassination in Dallas by seven weeks, are well documented. The knowledge of same by J. Edgar Hoover, and to a lesser degree Lyndon Baines Johnson, is also well documented. (Tapes of conversations between the two in the days following the assassination are available on the LBJ Library website.) These earlier events cannot be reconciled with the accusations that Oswald acted alone. It was not the real Oswald taking these actions in Mexico City. It therefore required the planning of at least a tight circle of individuals intimately familiar with the inner workings of the CIA, FBI, and military intelligence to have planted this information in a manner that would allow it to bloom into the wider clandestine sphere of "knowledge" once the real Oswald was charged with shooting the president. These Mexico City tapes would have directly implicated the Soviet Union and its surrogate, Cuba. If Oswald were eliminated, as may have been planned, there would have been no corroborating evidence to prove the impostor and Oswald were not one and the same.

The Assassinations: Probe Magazine on JFK, MLK, RFK and Malcolm X,
    Edited by James DiEugenio and Lisa Pease
Our Man in Mexico: Winston Scott and Hidden History of the CIA,
    by Jefferson Moreley

John Kennedy on the Links
JFK was an accomplished golfer who hid his prodigious abilities from the public so as not to be lumped into the same patrician category as Dwight Eisenhower, his presidential predecessor. Had he been able to play regularly, those who played with him thought that he would legitimately shoot in the mid 70s, even considering restrictions due to the condition of his back.

First Off the Tee, by Don Van Natta, Jr.

JFK by Oliver Stone
In 1991 Oliver Stone released his seminal motion picture, *JFK*, to a deluge of protest from establishment media. Popular with the general public, it was dissected by many members of the national press as having hijacked the legacy of John F. Kennedy for anti-government conspiracy theorizing.

However, there is a curious persistence to the legacy of John F. Kennedy. It insists on being revisited. It insists on being respected. And the truth of his demise insists, through the relentless persistence of history, on being exposed. Polling reveals that over seventy-five percent of the American populace believes the assassination of this respected American leader was more than the doing of one lone gunman and instead involved a conspiracy.

Calling it a killing by a lone assassin does not make it so.

Acknowledgements

First and foremost, I would like to thank the many hundreds of JFK researchers who have toiled in relative obscurity over the last half century toward the solution of one of the greatest crimes of American history. They are far too numerous to name here, but because of their diligent investigation in the face of an unforgiving system, this information has been kept front and center in America's consciousness.

I would like to extend heartfelt thanks to the early readers and editors who gave much of their valuable time and skill to assist in the creation of this book. They are Jef Westing, my French Connection, for initial editing and support; James Bacca, Jay Jerman and Betsy Westing for substantial input that helped shape the manuscript; my Orcas readers—Moriah and Daniel Armstrong, and Todd and Leota Shaner who also gave valuable feedback early on; and Charles Weisfenning M.D. for excellent advice on medical terminology and procedures. I want to give special thanks to 'Lucky Pierre' and Susan Helm for their thoughtful reading and commentary. I am most grateful to other readers who gave encouragement and helpful feedback along the way including Norm Stamper, Karna Sundby, Steve Keller, Robert Downing Richards, Bran Meade, Marc and Alex Tuchman, Joan Jerman, Wynne Blake, Alfred Pound, Ann Major Hubbs, Bruce Phares, Therese Frare, Greg Davis, Brett Clifton, Patricia Lewis, Elaine Hanowell, Kevin Purdie, Alice Acheson, Stephen Metcalf, Sarah Ford, Becky Nadesan, and Penny Bolton.

For their persistence and precision in the final editing I am indebted to Kathy Bradley, Patty Monaco and Deborah Johnson.

Most fondly, I thank my wife, Erica Helm Meade, a fellow writer whose unswerving faith and loving encouragement over the years have been invaluable. Her writing experience and patience with my JFK daydreaming gave me perspective on the entire process of creating a work of fiction and were the foundation for my adventures in writing.

And of course, I thank the silent muses who gently push to the fore the inspiration and ideas that seed and shape what we mere mortals attempt to accomplish, thinking all the while that we are toiling on our own.

Made in the USA
Lexington, KY
11 August 2012